I dedicate this book to my son Patrick,
who was killed many years ago at the age of nineteen,
and to the staff at Polygon for their support and kindness
throughout its publication.

Praise for Agnes Owens

'The bleak, startling, tell-it-as-it-is style of these luminous stories has a cinematic quality . . . very black, totally unsentimental and often very funny . . . The woman is a genius' DAILY MAIL on *Agnes Owens: The Complete Short Stories*

'Her stories carry the emotional clout of a knockout punch. Her prose is unique: unsentimental but not unsympathetic; calm and clear . . . undeniably funny' THE OBSERVER

'Characters in Agnes Owens's short stories are capable of anything . . . In Owens's world, family relationships are never straightforward . . . This is a terrific collection' THE TIMES on *Agnes Owens: The Complete Short Stories*

'*Bad Attitudes* is a mini-masterpiece – a delicious, wicked, beautifully observed little black comedy' INDEPENDENT ON SUNDAY

'George Orwell would have liked Agnes Owens . . . droll, sparse and clear' INDEPENDENT ON SUNDAY

'A simple parable of harsh hospitalities and home truths . . . *Jen's Party* is a beauty of a vignette: genuinely funny, light where *Bad Attitudes* was dark . . . Owens stuns her readers, as usual, with her good, blunt-weaponed clarity' ALI SMITH on *Bad Attitudes*

'Owens pulls no punches. Her understated prose finds acerbic humour in the lives of characters hovering between farce and tragedy . . . Owens is a gift to the Scots urban world' THE OBSERVER on *Bad Attitudes*

'Like all Owens' fiction, [*Bad Attitudes*] is as tense and grimly, iron-ically, comically deadpan as the best of Evelyn Waugh and Beryl Bainbridge' BOOKS OF THE YEAR, DAILY TELEGRAPH

'A remarkable book, funny and sinister' BERYL BAINBRIDGE on *A Working Mother*

'[Agnes Owens is] living evidence that the best writers are not necessarily the best known' HELEN SIMPSON

'Owens is a gift to the Scots urban world' SUNDAY TIMES

'Her black humour and piercing observation bear comparison with the work of Muriel Spark' THE GUARDIAN

'Has something in common with early Billy Connolly . . . in the sense that its observation and timing bring humour to a sad reality' NEW MUSICAL EXPRESS on *Like Birds in the Wilderness*

'A moving picture of a hard, surprising world which is forcing a young man to understand both it and himself' ALASDAIR GRAY on *Like Birds in the Wilderness*

'Agnes Owens has an appealingly wicked eye for familial love on the dole . . . reminiscent of Muriel Spark and Shena Mackay' SUNDAY HERALD on *Bad Attitudes*

'Agnes Owens is the most unfairly neglected of all living Scottish authors. I don't know why' ALASDAIR GRAY

'Owens has a voice no one could imitate, and humour to match . . . Scottish life as lived by those far from the comfort zone, depicted less with loathing than with love' ROSEMARY GORING

AGNES OWENS

THE COMPLETE NOVELLAS

Agnes Owens

This collection published in Great Britain in 2009 by Polygon,
an imprint of Birlinn Ltd

West Newington House
10 Newington Road
Edinburgh
EH9 1QS

9 8 7 6 5 4 3 2 1

www.birlinn.co.uk

ISBN 978 1 84697 137 2

British Library Cataloguing-in-Publication Data
A catalogue record for this book is available
on request from the British Library.

Typeset by Palimpsest Book Production Limited,
Grangemouth, Stirlingshire
Printed and bound by
CPI Cox & Wyman, Reading

Contents

LIKE BIRDS IN THE
WILDERNESS

I

All day I had tramped the streets of this strange city in a fruitless search for work, head bent against the wind and lugging my shabby holdall. Already my money was spent on scrappy meals and fags. The only thing I possessed to the good was an address for a lodging house obtained from the local Department of Health and Social Security, but since they were unwilling to advance me the rent I had slight hope of being accepted. All the same, I decided to try it. I was cold, tired and hungry. One night's kip was my present notion of paradise. I stopped a guy to ask the way. He told me to cut along Barrack Road, first on the left, until I reached Hawkers' Lane, second on my right, then to carry on until I reached the cenotaph. He was still mouthing directions when I left him. Eventually I reached my goal, one of a row of faded Georgian terraces.

A dour-faced youth answered the door. I explained that the broo had sent me.

'Broo?' he questioned.

'Labour exchange, then. They said ye took in ludgers.'

He jerked his head backwards to convey that I should follow him down a long lobby into a big kitchen that smelled of onions.

'Wait here till I fetch ma Da,' he said.

I sat at a big table covered with an oilcloth and faced a pot on the cooker. It was boiling over. I felt I should turn off the gas, or at the least turn it down, but I was afraid that I might appear forward. I became agitated with the problem and had decided to creep away from it all when the youth returned with a stockily built man who said straight away, 'It's sixteen pounds a week for yer digs. Danny here will show ye the layout and the rules. Take note that we don't put up wi' drinkin' in the rooms, women in the rooms, or ony other kind o' activity, apart frae sleepin'.'

'Sixteen pounds a week,' I said thoughtfully.

'We're wan o' the cheapest places aboot here, but if ye don't fancy it . . .'

Quickly I said, 'That's fine, but can ye wait until Friday for the money, since I've jist newly started work?'

There was no point in telling him otherwise. I sensed he wasn't the type to take chances with an unemployed brickie.

'So long as ye're workin', ye can pay a tenner a week extra until ye're clear.' He passed me over to Danny who gave me another jerk of the head. I followed him out of the kitchen. The pot was still boiling over.

Some time later I returned to the kitchen, dampened by the sight of the sleeping quarters, which I was to share with another two guys. This was a big square room, furnished with three narrow beds pressed against the walls and a huge dark wardrobe – reminiscent of the kind seen in old creepy silent films, wherein some mad creature lurks. The walls themselves were emulsioned a brownish yellow that may or may not have been the colour of the original paint. The floor was stained the same dark colour as the wardrobe, and the carpet in the centre of all this was threadbare. My brain was further dulled by Danny's tight-lipped references to the required code of conduct expected from boarders, which apart from no drinking and no women – as ordered by his Da – included no visitors of any kind, no eating, no pets and no music in the room. I wondered if he was all there in the head. An elderly man, possibly in his late fifties, sat at a table engrossed in a newspaper spread out in front of him. He said, 'Good evening,' and returned his attention to the paper. I asked him at what time the dinner was served.

'When everybody's in,' he said with a furtive look towards Danny who was stirring the same pot that had boiled over.

'When will that be?'

He leaned over and whispered, 'Ye canny tell exactly, but onyway,' he added winking, 'it helps if ye're hungry.'

He looked back at his newspaper and studied the sports page through a pair of thin gold-framed spectacles, similar to the type Woolworth's used to sell. I was reminded of a model house lodger who takes pains to look tidy against the odds.

Two guys entered and scraped back the chairs in a way that put my teeth on edge. They began to strum their fingers on the table, fixing their eyes in a direction opposite mine. They wore the building site gear. You could tell this from the clay marks.

'Whit's the poison?' one of them asked the old man. He was red-haired and maybe about my age, which is twenty-three.

'Stovies.'

Both guys howled simultaneously. 'Stovies!'

Danny looked up from the cooker. 'Don't gimmy ony lip,' he shouted as he shook a wooden spoon. The guys shrugged, and one began to strum again. The red-haired guy grabbed at the elderly guy's paper saying, 'Gie us a read at that paper, Dad,' and tearing it in the process.

'Just when I wis studyin' form,' said the old man.

'Ye likely stole it onyway,' said red-hair throwing the paper back to the elderly guy. He finally acknowledged my presence by saying, 'Keep an eye on auld Dad here. He's a con-man by trade and a tea leaf on the side.'

'I've nothin' tae steal.' I laughed and drew my chair close to the table, glad to be included in the company.

The seats filled up gradually. Ten men sat at the table, all dressed in the working gear, except Dad. I wore the working gear too, since it's all I had. Danny hurled over a trolley full of steaming plates. He skimmed each one round to us as though he was playing quoits. I looked close at my heap of brown mashed potatoes.

'Where's the meat?' I asked.

'In wi' the tatties. Have ye no' had stovies afore?'

I shovelled down the stodge quickly in order to calm my rumbling stomach.

'Is it always as good as this?' I asked Dad when I had scraped my plate clean.

'Not always,' he answered, searching my face perhaps for a trace of irony. He cut through his pile of potatoes as though he was dealing with steak. He appeared to be a delicate eater. I leaned back and tried to force out a belch as a mark of appreciation, but didn't quite make it. I asked if there was any pudding to follow. 'Only breid and cheese,' said one of the lodgers in a mournful way. I nodded as though I wasn't bothering. Afterwards we all drifted into another big room containing some tattered couches and chairs and, surprisingly, a colour television – all, that is, except Dad who had gone out the front door. Immediately the seats were occupied and I was left standing. 'Sit here,' said the red-haired guy, squeezing up to offer me some space beside him on the couch. I perched myself on the edge, forced to lean forward and face the television as if I was absorbed in it, though I couldn't hear a word for the hum of voices around me.

'Pipe doon everybody,' someone called, 'I want tae listen tae the telly and so does that new fella.'

'I'm no' botherin',' I said. Everyone was staring at me. I closed my eyes and pressed myself back against the couch.

'Well ye can see he's tired,' said the same guy. 'Gie him a bit o' peace and quiet.'

'How can he be tired?' someone else said. 'He's no' been here long enough to get tired.'

When an argument arose among them about whether I should be tired or not I stood up and turned off the television.

'Is that whit ye want?' I asked.

Everyone looked away and began to talk amongst themselves except the guy who had wanted to watch the television. He started to protest and was told to belt up once and for all. The red-haired guy handed me a fag. I squeezed back into my space and we began to talk. I explained that I had come up here to look for work.

'But that's great,' he said. 'We're needin' a brickie to make up the squad on oor site. Ye can start first thing in the mornin'.'

'Are ye sure?'

'Sure, I'm sure.' He added, 'By the way whit's yer name? Mine's Jimmy.'

'Mac,' I said as we shook hands.

I then suggested that he lend me a fiver so I could buy him a drink, saying I would pay it back plus two pounds extra for his trouble when I got a wage.

He pondered this for a minute, then said with a grin on his freckled face, 'I think that's a great idea.'

The pub, named The Potted Head, was heavy with smoke and loud with the high-pitched northern twang. We sat with our pints at a table for two, well back from the bar and facing the entrance. Jimmy did most of the talking. His subject was mainly women. His attention was continually distracted by their arrival into the pub. I suspected he had deliberately picked the table for the view.

'Whit aboot yersel'?' he said. 'Hiv ye got a bit o' stuff?'

'Naw – er – that is, no' at the moment. I mean, I'm jist newly up here.'

'We'll hiv tae see whit we can dae aboot that then, eh?'

Before I could reply he said, staring at two young females pushing their way up to the bar, 'Wull ye look at them – they're smashers. Dae ye no' think so? I fancy the wan in the green jumper. The ither's no' bad either.'

'I suppose so,' I said. He pushed back his chair and informed me that he was going to the bar for another pint, adding, 'Amongst ither things.'

'Get me wan while ye're at it,' I called.

'Sure,' he said, moving away with a rapt look.

I didn't mind being left alone. I was tired and didn't want the bother of chatting up birds, since I can only do that after I've had around five whiskies. I suspect I lack finesse even then, but at that stage I don't care.

A man sat down beside me and asked if the seat was taken. I shook my head. I didn't expect Jimmy back for a while. He set his pint tumbler on the table. It was almost empty. 'I'm glad to sit,' he said. 'I hate standing at bars.'

I replied, 'I know whit ye mean. I canny be bothered gaun up there for anither pint either.'

He looked at my tumbler, also almost empty. 'Don't worry,' he said, and called on a guy collecting the glasses. 'Get this lad a pint of beer, Alec, and one for myself at the same time.'

'Right, sir,' said Alec.

'I didny know ye could get served at the tables,' I said.

'You can't really,' said the guy, tilting the chair as he leaned back. He added with a superior smile, 'Only those and such as those can.'

I was prepared to sneer at his upper-class style, the handlebar moustache matching the colour of the grey locks combed fashionably onto the well-cut collar of his well-cut suit, but he looked so much at ease and friendly with it that I could only say, 'Thanks. I'll get the next round.'

'Don't bother, young man. I won't be stopping long.'

I grimaced. 'I know. This place is a dive.'

He raised his eyebrows and said, wagging his finger at me, 'But it's not really. I like this place. They serve a good pint.'

For some peculiar reason I was reminded of the guy with the moustache in the ancient poster who states that your country needs you. When the beer arrived he watched me closely as I took the first swallow. To please him I smacked my lips, wiped the froth from them, and told him it was a good pint.

'You're right, young man,' he said, as if I had passed a test.

'Do me a favour,' I said, retaining an amicable expression, 'Don't call me "young man". Where I come from it disny go doon well.'

'And where is that?'

'The west coast.'

'Ah, the west coast. A fascinating area with its rivers, lochs and mountains, and the people so friendly. I'm surprised you left it.'

'It's no' sae fascinatin' when ye're on the dole.'

'Ah, the dole.' He tapped his teeth and sighed. 'A dreadful situation.'

'At least I've a job here,' I said. 'So I'll be OK.'

'I would guess,' he said, searching me with his eyes, 'that you are an outdoor worker.'

I showed him the palms of my hands still calloused from my last period of work. 'That widny be hard tae guess. I'm a brickie.'

'And I'm a travelling salesman,' he said.

'That's a helluva thing tae be,' I said, feeling cheated that he had turned out to be a mere traveller. 'Thank Christ I'm a brickie.'

He finished his beer and said, 'You're right, young man. Travelling is a dreadful occupation. I'm thinking of giving it up.'

He brought out a card from his pocket and handed it to me saying, 'If you feel lonely or simply in the need of a chat with someone, such as myself, in a quiet pub, call in at this place after eight o'clock. My name is Colin Craig.'

With that he was gone. The card read: THE OPEN DOOR, 2 LANTERN LANE. OWNER MICHAEL MCLERIE, LICENSED TO SELL BEER AND SPIRITS.

Jimmy returned carrying two pints of beer. 'Who wis that?' he asked.

'Naebody in particular. Ye took yer time.'

He smirked and drew two curves in the air with his hands. 'You should have seen these birds.'

I stared ahead bleakly as we sipped our drinks. Jimmy was casting anxious glances towards the bar. I sensed I was spoiling his evening, but I had no inclination to chat up birds, particularly on the strength of three beers.

'I'm gaun away soon,' I said. 'It's been a tirin' day. If ye're wantin' tae get back tae the bar, don't let me haud ye.'

'Are ye sure? I could get ye fixed up easy wi' a bird.'

'Maybe anither time.'

'Aye, maybe,' he said, giving me a doubtful glance.

2

The building site was muddy and damp on the feet, particularly if your boots let in.

'Ye'll need wellies,' said Jimmy as I stood poised, searching for a dry patch to leap upon.

'I've nane.'

'See the ganger, then.'

He squelched off in his sturdy boots.

'Wellies!' said the ganger when I approached him about this.

'I wis telt ye supplied them.'

'It depends on how long ye've been on the job. We don't haun' them oot straight away.' He looked in the direction of my feet concealed by mud. 'Ye'd think ye've never worked on a site afore. Ye should ken whit gear ye need when ye start.'

'It wis hard frost when I left hame,' I explained. 'I didny think I'd need them.'

He stroked his moustache. His eyes brooded upon me as he said, 'Ye'll jist hiv tae buy a new pair, then.'

'I canny afford tae buy nothin' until I get ma wages.'

'That's typical!' he said. 'You folk come up here expectin' everythin' laid on. It's nae good enough.'

'I didny expect a' this abuse because I asked for a pair o' wellies.'

We faced each other. My eyes became strained with giving him the fixed stare.

He said, looking away, 'If ye don't like it ye know whit ye can dae.'

I replied, 'Only when it suits me.'

My feet embedded in the mud were freezing. I believe I would have walked off there and then if I could have easily extracted them. I can usually tell on my first day if I'm going to stick the site. Already the odds were stacked against this one.

'Is that so?' he said, his eyes bulging. 'If it suits me ye can collect yer books.'

'Hiv ye no' heard o' the Employment Protection Act?'

His eyes lost their bulge. He said with a trace of humour, 'Dae ye no' ken there's nae protection onywhere nooadays?' and walked away.

Jimmy left the cement mixer to ask what had happened.

'He said there's nae wellies.'

'Ask him next week. He's always moody wi' new starts.'

'I might no' be here next week.'

'Hing oan.'

A few minutes later Jimmy returned with a pair of wellingtons. 'They wir lyin' in the hut,' he said. 'They're no' new but they're better than nothin'.'

I began to lay the brick, slowly at first. The clay was rough on my fingers. My shoulders ached from lack of practice. Gradually I became more adept and was working at a fair speed when one of the labourers stopped to watch.

'Hopin' to make a big bonus?' he said.

My concentration faltered. I turned to him saying, 'Maybe.'

'Ye michny be popular wi' the rest o' the squad.'

'Bugger the rest o' the squad.' I turned my back and spread the mortar. I wished he would vanish, but he remained, gawping.

'Wan o' the new starts?' he asked.

I laid down my trowel and wiped my hands on a piece of rag. 'Seems an unpopular thing tae be.'

I faced him to see he was a wee thin man, neither young nor old nor disagreeable looking. He wore a loose jumper over a pair of baggy flannels.

'Och naw, laddie,' he replied. 'It's normal tae be a new start but don't tire yersel' oot straight away. It's a long day, ye ken.'

'Ye widny have a fag tae spare?' I asked.

'I'll gie ye a roll-up. I've nae use for these ither corktipped things.'

He brought a tobacco tin from his pocket and rolled me a smoke. As we puffed we studied a bit of wall I had built. 'Ye're daein' fine,' he said.

The day wore on and I felt a great need to eat the rolls and cheese Danny had wrapped up for me in a newspaper.

'Whit's the time?' I asked an apprentice working further along the wall.

He didn't hear me. I thought maybe he was deaf. Apprentices often are. I moved nearer to him and repeated the question.

'How should I ken?' he said.

I noticed his top layer of bricks was uneven. 'That's aboot as straight as the Rocky Mountains,' I pointed out.

'Mind yer ain business.'

'It is ma business. I don't want the bloody wa' hauled doon because you canny build straight.'

He turned to say something unpleasant no doubt and bumped against the structure. The bricks scattered. I pulled him clear and slid on the mud. A brick struck me on the temple.

'Are ye a' right?' he said, wide-eyed as he bent over me.

'Jist gie us a haun' up.'

My head throbbed and felt sticky when I touched it. Two workers arrived on the scene and escorted me to the hut, with the apprentice close at my heels still saying, 'Are ye a' right?'

Inside the hut I was told to sit down and have a fag. A mug of tea was shoved into my hand. The place filled up with workers, most of them stationed beside the electric kettle. The ganger entered and looked round the hut. 'Whit's a' this?'

'The apprentice built his bricks slack and they fell doon.'

'The new fella copped wan on the heid.'

The apprentice was shoved in front of the ganger, his face extremely pale. 'I didny mean it,' he said.

'Don't worry aboot it, I'm a' right,' I told him.

The ganger roared at him, 'Get oot ma sicht!' and the apprentice slunk out the door.

'Where's the first aid kit?' asked the ganger.

'I didny know there wis a first aid kit,' said someone.

'There wis wan here a month ago, and if it's no found somebody's gettin' hauled ower the coals.'

I thought their search would be useless. I've never seen a first aid kit in any site, unless you counted a bottle of aspirins left by a labourer I once knew who used to swallow them along with Barr's Irn-Bru as a substitute for booze. A tin of plaster was found under a bench. With a serious expression the ganger applied it to my cut and wiped it with a rag. When he stood back to survey his handiwork another cup of tea was placed in my hand. 'For shock,' said the donor. The ganger turned to stare at the group of men standing close to the electric kettle, drinking tea.

'Ya bloody skivers,' he roared. 'Ye're fifteen minutes aff the tea break. Are yez on strike or somethin'?'

The wee guy with the baggy flannels stepped forward and said, 'Here, take this tea, Geordie, and gie us a' a break.'

The ganger said nothing; his moustache twitched. Slowly he sipped from the mug of tea, as if he was judging a rare wine. We all watched him open-mouthed. Then he said, 'Ye've put too much bloody sugar in it.'

Everyone relaxed and took down their pieces from the shelf. Jimmy rushed in breathless as we sat chewing away. 'Whit's happened?' he asked.

'Nothin' much.'

He stared at my sticking plaster. 'I heard ye were hurt bad. I've phoned for an ambulance.'

'An ambulance!' spluttered the ganger.

'The apprentice telt me he wis hurt bad,' Jimmy was saying, when someone shouted in the hut door that there was an ambulance coming up the track.

'Run oot quick and tell him it wis a hoax,' said the ganger. 'Afore ye know it we'll be havin' the polis in. We don't need that, dae we?' he added, addressing me.

'Naw,' I said, doubtfully. 'It's no' as if I'm supposed tae make a claim, is it?'

'There wid be nae point in daein' that.'

He then informed me that he would try and get me a new pair of wellingtons for Friday, which was the earliest he could manage, since he had to order them. I said that was fair enough.

'Dae you know,' said Jimmy to the lodgers when we were back at the digs waiting for our dinner to be served, 'the apprentice would hae been a goner if it wisny for the lad here? Saved his life he did, and nearly copped it himsel'.'

I shook my head to dispute this statement, automatically touching the sticking plaster on my temple.

'Nae wonder ye look pale,' said Dad. 'Are ye feelin' a' right?'

'I'm fine.'

Actually I felt squeamish and unable to face any food.

'Mind and gie this guy a double helpin',' said Jimmy to Danny when he was hurling the trolley over. 'He needs it efter riskin' his life.'

'Is that so,' snapped Danny, slinging over my plate. 'Well I risk ma life every day staunin' ower bilin' pots and pans and naebody cares.'

I took one look at my helping of boiled cod and potatoes and headed for the bathroom.

'Ye're no' sleepin', are ye?' Jimmy's voice broke into a dream I was having where I floated above rooftops like a barrage balloon ready to burst.

'Whit time is it?' I asked, sitting up, dazed.

'Time ye were oot enjoyin' yersel'.'

'I don't feel sae good.'

He pulled at my wrist. 'Get up quick. I can hear Danny comin' up the stairs. Ye're no' supposed tae be in bed wi' yer boots on.'

By the time Danny walked into the room I was on my feet, stretching and yawning.

He said to Jimmy, 'Ye've nae right bein' in here. It's nae your room.'

'Whit's the big deal aboot that?' I asked.

'The big deal is that we don't want lodgers traipsin' aboot places they've nae right tae be in. It's the rules, ye ken?'

'I didny know aboot that rule,' I said to Jimmy. 'Did you?'

'Fine he knows,' said Danny. His gaze fell on the bed. 'Will ye look at that black mark —' he began, but we were out of the room and running down the stairs two at a time.

The streets were empty and warm for a change. We strolled along with hands in pockets, passing some pubs on the way. I had no cash so I had to keep passing them. Jimmy was strangely silent. At last I asked, 'Where are we gaun?'

'D'ye fancy meetin' a lassie?'

'It depends,' I said, after thinking about it.

'Well, I've got a date wi' wan o' the lassies in the pub yon night. She said she'd bring her pal along for you; a nice quiet lassie, seeminly, real class.'

'Ye mean the ither wan that wis in the pub?'

'Naw. This wan doesny like pubs, frae whit I hear.'

I explained that I preferred to get my own dates, plus the fact that I was gasping for a pint.

'But they're waitin' for us. I hope ye're no' gaun tae back oot.' As I started to lag he added, 'There they are staunin' by the picture hoose. Look, they're wavin' to us.'

He crossed the road. Reluctantly I followed. Only one of them had waved. The other was intently scanning the photographs of the film stars inside the glass frames on the wall. He introduced me to the one who had waved. She was a dumpy blonde with a pug nose named Jean. She giggled when I shook her hand.

'That's Nancy,' she said, pointing to her friend who looked round from the photographs and gave me a cool nod. I put my hand in my pocket, deciding that there was no future for me with this skinny dame, even if she was passable looking in a snooty way.

'Right then,' said Jimmy, assuming a grin as we stood around staring at each other awkwardly. 'Noo that we're acquainted where dae ye think we should go?'

When no one answered he said, 'Whit aboot the pictures?'

'We've seen them,' said Jean.

'So have I,' I said, and caught the eye of the tall dame called Nancy. She gave me an uncertain smile which I was obliged to return.

'We might as well take a dauner through the park,' said Jimmy with a defiant look all round.

'Might as well,' said Jean. She grabbed his arm and they walked away so quick they almost ran.

'Dae ye fancy a stroll?' I asked Nancy.

'I suppose so,' she said.

When we entered the park Jimmy and Jean had disappeared. I felt uncomfortable and noticed I was walking too fast. This dame could barely keep pace with me. I ventured to say, as I slowed down a bit, that it was a fine night.

'Yes,' she said.

To fill in the silence I began to whistle on one low note as dreary as the morse code. When I stopped I heard her sigh. I wondered if I should feign a sudden attack of migraine as an excuse for a quick departure. It would appear feeble, though, if not insulting. It might be better if I ran over the hill flapping my arms like a rooster about to take off. Then she would think I was a genuine nutcase and be glad of her narrow escape.

'You remind me of a boyfriend I once had,' she said, breaking through all this conjecture. 'He was a Canadian and always whistling, imitating birds. He said it reminded him of the backwoods of Canada.'

'I've never been tae Canada, let alane the backwoods.'

'It was nothing to do with Canada really,' she said. 'It was the whistling.'

I didn't know how to answer this. I could only say vaguely, 'Maybe you still miss him?'

'Why do you say that?'

'I don't know why. Maybe I look like him. How should I know?'

I was becoming annoyed with the subject and felt like telling her this when she said, 'Actually you're much better looking than him.'

Being heartened by this comment I asked her if she would like to take my arm, which she did; and we walked over the hill, still not saying much but feeling a lot happier. At least, I was, and I think she was. As we travelled I was pressed with an urge to kiss her; but how could I? I hardly knew her and couldn't think of any way to accomplish this intimacy. She suddenly stopped walking when we were near a tree.

'It's a fly,' she said. 'It's in my eye.' Right enough the place was thick with midgies.

'Let me see,' I said. She gave me her handkerchief, which was lucky for me since I never carry one or even possess one. With a bit of manoeuvering I managed to ease the mangled insect out, wiping the water from her eye in a most natural fashion, which made it easy for me to kiss her without any awkwardness.

'Yer hair smells like fresh cut grass,' I said afterwards, burying my face in her curls and blessing the midgie that gave its life in such a good cause.

'It's only Sunsoft shampoo,' she said.

'It's the nicest shampoo I've ever smelled. I could inhale it a' night. It's as good as chloroform.'

'Don't be stupid,' she said, pushing me away. 'You hardly know me.'

'Whit's that got tae dae wi it? I feel as if I've met ye some-where afore in a different time.'

'I don't believe in reincarnation,' she said, laughing.

I tried to kiss her again but she backed off and said that she preferred to walk. I didn't mind this because she still held on to me. For the sake of a subject I mentioned the Canadian guy, which was a mistake. She said that he was none of my business, then withdrew her arm.

'I'm sorry,' I said, stopping to light up a fag, 'but ye shouldny have spoke aboot him in the first place.'

She walked quickly on ahead. I became angry. I shouted, 'Seems tae me ye're still keen on him if ye're takin' it that bad.'

She flounced back and slapped my face. Her action was so unwarranted it made me laugh. 'Ye must be some kind o' screwball,' I said. She would have lashed out again if I hadn't caught her wrist. She struggled feebly when I told her that I might as well kiss her again whether she liked it or not, since she was going to be angry whatever I did or said.

'That's not true,' she declared, and let me kiss her without making any move to get out of it.

'Are you satisfied now?' She was smiling. I thought she had a very nice face, thin, with a turned-up nose and green eyes that sometimes looked yellow, depending on the light.

'No' really,' I said.

We carried on kissing and cuddling for a while. I would have liked to do more than that, but didn't want to risk angering her. I decided she wasn't really a screwball, but I sensed that she was unpredictable to say the least.

I told her a bit about myself, explaining why I'd left my home town to come here for work. She raised her eyebrows and said that it was a shame I had found this so difficult. For her part she'd never had any bother finding work. She had worked in the same office as a typist since leaving school.

'Dependin' on who they are,' I said, trying to keep my voice free of irony, 'some folk have no problem.'

'But I know it can be difficult nowadays,' she assured me.

The subject trailed off and I thought it just as well not to pursue it. By this time I liked her so much I wouldn't have cared if she was a top class model. Then she said, 'It's getting dark. The park gate will be closing soon.' So we hurried back and the gate was still open.

'I'll have to go anyway,' she said.

I didn't want to argue with her, but I asked if she would meet me tomorrow night outside the park gate.

'I don't know,' she said. 'Why not make it Saturday?'

'Let's make it the morra night.' I thought that by Saturday I could have faded from her memory.

She hesitated, then said, 'All right, tomorrow night.'

Before I could say any more she was running towards the bus stop across the street from the park, and had caught the bus as it was drawing away. With her free hand she waved back to me.

3

'Whit's happened tae Dad?' I asked. We were all sitting at the kitchen table. The space which he usually occupied had been empty for a few days.

'Dad comes and goes like the weather,' said the guy beside me. 'Ye never ken whit thon wan's up tae.'

Henry Bell, a big slow-speaking chap who was a street sweeper, said, 'I'm sure I saw him on a park bench lyin' under a bundle o' newspapers.'

'Is he a tramp then?'

Jimmy laughed. 'Aye, wan that can eat wance a week at the Station Hotel.'

'Whit does he dae for a livin'?'

'Onythin' and everythin'.'

Another guy said, 'I think he's a salesman. Mind that time he wis sellin' encyclopedias.'

'Ye mean he took the deposits,' said Jimmy. 'Naebody ever got wan.'

I asked, 'Did ye gie him a deposit?'

'Naw, but I've known them that has and are still waitin' for the encyclopedia.'

'Wance he wis takin' photies,' said Henry Bell. 'I gave him a deposit for wan he took o' me.'

'Did ye get the photie?'

'No' yet,' said Henry wistfully.

Someone else said, 'He's got nae sense o' heilan' pride.'

'Is that some kind o' breid,' said Henry Bell, grinning like mad. We all looked away from him.

★

Later, when I was studying my face in the bathroom mirror in an anxious way, someone kicked the door and shouted, 'Wull ye be long?' I ignored the thumps for a while. It's normal for guys to pound at the bathroom door and use any pretext to get you out.

Finally I unlocked it to face Jimmy, who said, 'Jean wis on the phone to say that Nancy canny make it. It seems she's got a cauld, but she'll see ye on Saturday, if she's better.'

'I couldny care less,' I said. 'She wisny ma type.'

'How are ye lookin' sae angry then?' said Jimmy, following me into my bedroom.

'I'm no' the least bit angry. By the way,' I added, 'ye're no' supposed tae be in this room. Ye know the rules.'

'Don't take it oot on me,' said Jimmy, 'jist because a bird gave ye a dizzy.'

He was leaving so I said, 'OK. I'll no' take it oot on you if ye lend me a fiver. That'll be twelve I owe ye, and I'll buy ye a drink intae the bargain.'

We walked through a dingy back street to what Jimmy described as a joint where I was bound to meet a bird to my taste. I did not fancy this idea. Inadvertantly I put my hand in my pocket and brought out the card given to me by the toff with the handlebar moustache. I showed it to Jimmy and said on the spur of the moment, 'I've jist remembered I wis to meet a guy at this place in connection wi' a business deal. Dae ye want tae come?'

'Whit kind o' business deal?'

'I'll let ye know when I get there,' I said, hurrying on while Jimmy studied the card. Now that I had some money I wasn't caring whether he came or not, but I was determined I wasn't going to be palmed off with another bird.

He ran after me saying, 'I think I've been there wance. It's a wee auld fashioned dive wi' nae lounge and nae juke box.'

'As far as I'm concerned that'll make a chinge.'

'I don't really fancy it,' said Jimmy but he kept pace with me all the same.

We travelled over cobbled pavements which scuffed the tips of our footwear. It didn't bother me since my boots were well scuffed already but Jimmy said, 'This is murder,' examining his black casuals. It was a long street of archaic three-storey tenements. Women hung over their window sills, surveying the packs of kids and dogs belting up and down the pavements. One black hound leapt on Jimmy, slavering with friendship. He aimed it a kick, a mile wide fortunately.

'Leave that dug alane,' a woman shouted from her window, 'ya cruel midden!' Then to the dog, 'Come awa' up here, Sheba.'

With a glance of regret at Jimmy it bounded up a close, followed by three canine admirers.

'We shouldny have came here,' said Jimmy. 'This place is a cowp.'

'I never forced ye tae come,' I said. 'Anyway, it's your toon, no' mine.'

We arrived at an area of wasteground, deserted apart from a cat sniffing into a pile of rusty cans. Ahead were the crumbling remains of a tenement.

'How much further?' I asked.

'See yon wee buildin' alang at the end?' said Jimmy, pointing.

'At whit end?'

'At the end o' this buildin'. It's a wee place a' by itsel'.'

'Oh aye,' I said, unable to see anything. However, we came to a wee hovel of a place with a sign above the entrance which read The Open Door.

'It is a right pit, innit?' I said.

'I warned ye,' said Jimmy.

Inside the place looked no better. It was distempered in a shade of brown like the colour of dried blood. A naked bulb hung from a low ceiling. Some drab male figures were pressed against the counter and the barman on the other side surveyed us suspiciously from deep-set eyes.

Jimmy whispered, 'Whit did I tell ye?'

'It's got atmosphere,' I said, and ordered some beer and whisky from the barman in a loud and cheerful voice to convey that I found nothing amiss with either him or the pub. If the guy called Colin Craig had found it quiet and friendly, who was I to doubt it?

'Is yer name McLerie?' I asked the barman, and to prove I had a sound reason to drink within these walls I added, after showing him the card, 'I'm only enquiring since a guy called Colin Craig gave me this and telt me to look him up in here. Dae ye know who I mean?'

He shook his head and returned the card. 'I've never heard o' him,' he said, and didn't mention whether he was the owner or not. He flashed me a warning look and disappeared through an opening behind the bar.

'Definitely friendly,' said Jimmy.

'So, he's never heard o' him. Whit does that prove?' I said, and began to study the four bottles of Red Hackle whisky on the shelf above the bar. I asked a guy standing on my other side if it was the only brand they sold.

'Who dae ye mean by they?'

'The owner for example. Is he no' the guy that's servin' called McLerie?'

'I never kent that wis his name.'

He stared at me owlishly through his specs, looking like the school dunce with his cloth cap resting on his ears. He explained that he hadn't a clue about anything that had happened recently, such as the names of new pub managers, because he had been in bed all winter with the gastric flu. I looked beyond him to the guy at his back, also wearing a cloth cap, though the fit was better.

'Dae ye know a guy called Colin Craig who drinks in here? Tall guy wi' a moustache and speaks posh,' I asked him, mainly to impress Jimmy who was sipping his beer with a martyred expression.

The second guy with a cap thought this over and asked if this Colin Craig wore a kilt.

'I don't know. He hudny one on when I saw him.'

The guy next to me said, 'It's big Eck who wears a kilt. Have nothin' tae dae wi' that yin for he's a violent man. Kicked a hen tae death while he wis waitin' for a bus.'

I was going to ask if the hen had been waiting for a bus as well, but the other guy interrupted to say he had heard big Eck had killed his own dog for watching him eat his dinner.

'I doubt it's the same guy,' I said, and informed Jimmy from the side of my mouth that we were in the presence of loonies. Immediately he stated loudly that we shouldn't have come here anyway, especially as there was no juke box.

'Never mind the juke box,' I said. 'If ye don't like it ye know whit ye can dae.'

Sullenly he threw a fiver on the counter to pay for the next round. The guy standing next to me informed me in a sincere manner he was sorry that he could not place this man called Craig, then stared hard at the fiver. I told Jimmy, again from the side of my mouth, to buy the loonies a drink. It was as well to have friends in the place. He complied with an even more sullen expression. After that I stood, leaning with one elbow on the bar, watching the barman pass up and down with his face as austere as a grand master of the Orange Lodge being introduced to the local priest.

Then Jimmy nudged me. 'Will ye look at that!'

I turned to see a man standing further along the counter. I thought at first he was wearing a mask, the pink and white plastic type used by guisers at Halloween, but on closer inspection I saw he was a burnt-out case, maybe caused by the war or a car crash. His face was definitely a remodelled job.

'That's a bloody shame,' said Jimmy. 'Dae ye think we should get him a drink?'

'The guy'll be used tae his condition. Ye don't want tae embarrass him.'

'How should that embarrass him? The wans beside ye wereny embarrassed.'

'Don't talk sae loud,' I whispered and gave the cloth-capped ones a nod and a smile to which they responded by a lift of their tumblers. In order to change the subject I said to them, 'It's no' a bad pint in here.'

'Oh, indeed, aye,' said the guy next to me, smacking his lips. He enquired if I was from these 'pairts'. I explained that I was from the west coast, naming the county. He informed me that he had a sister living in the same county by the name of Mary McPherson. He wondered if I knew her.

'I don't think so . . .' I began to say, when Jimmy thrust his face between us and stated, 'I know the McPhersons well. I went tae school wi' them. Whit did ye say her first name wis?'

The guy recoiled and mumbled, 'McPherson is her married name.'

'So, maybe I went tae school wi' her man. Whit's his name?'

I gave Jimmy a dig in the ribs and told him to forget it. I explained to the other two guys who were looking confused, 'The fact is, we're in here waitin' on this Craig guy. We know naebody at a' except for him, and ma mate here doesny even know him.'

'And I don't particularly want tae,' said Jimmy.

It was at this stage I put my hand in my pocket and brought out some loose change. 'I'm skint,' I declared.

'And I've only enough left for fags,' said Jimmy.

The man beside me in the cloth cap said, 'I wid buy yous a pint, but I'm a bit short too.'

'Especially wi' him bein' on the sick,' said his pal. He added, 'But I'm sure McLerie would gie you a pint on the slate.'

'I thought ye didny know the barman's name.'

'I knew his name. It wis ma freen' here that didny.'

McLerie, who must have been within earshot of all this, came over and said to the guy beside me, 'Did I hear you asking for tick?'

'Not at all,' said the guy, pointing towards me, 'it's him that's wantin' it.'

McLerie studied me from his suspicious deep-set eyes, then surprisingly asked me what I wanted.

'Two pints and two haufs o' whisky,' I said quickly. 'I'll pay ye first thing Friday when I get ma wages.'

'I'm sure you will,' he said, with a touch of sarcasm, but he poured out the drink hurriedly as if he had a lot on his mind, then vanished into the back premises. Jimmy and I wasted no time in emptying our glasses. We left the pub without any kind of farewell to the cloth-capped guys. They had lost interest after we had been served, as though they had done their duty.

I said to Jimmy when we were outside, 'A' the same it wis queer, him lettin' us drink on the slate. He didny look friendly and he didny even know us.'

'I think he wis jist wantin' rid o' us,' said Jimmy.

'I think you're right,' I said. 'And ye know whit – I think he wis wantin' rid o' us before Craig came in.'

'Could be,' said Jimmy. 'Maybe he thought we were plain-clothes detectives tailin' the guy.'

We both laughed at this idea. Jimmy stepped on to the waste-ground which was now covered two inches thick with mist, explaining that he was going to have a slash. I was about to do likewise when someone tapped me on the shoulder. I turned to face the burnt-out case. His face shone waxen in the moonlight.

'Jesus Christ,' I said, reeling back with fright. 'Whit the hell dae ye want?'

'I wis gaun tae ask,' he said in a quavery voice, 'if I could walk alang wi' ye a bit. It's a quiet road and I get nervous by masel'.'

'Nae problem,' said Jimmy. 'We'll see ye're a' right.'

The burnt-out guy then placed himself between us holding on to each of our arms for support.

'Is yer eyesight bad as well?' I asked.

'It's no' that bad, but ma feet are.' He continued plaintively, 'I hope I'm no' ony bother.'

We both assured him that he wasn't any bother, but I wasn't happy with the situation. He seemed to be leaning all his weight against me, and was heavier than if he had been drunk and incapable. I tripped over his feet. 'Help ma God,' he shouted, hopping on one foot with great agility. 'That wis bloody sore.'

'Sorry,' I said. 'I'm no' used tae walkin' sae slow.'

Jimmy addressed me. 'You should watch whit ye're daein'.' Then he broke off to exclaim, 'Christ almighty!' which wasn't surprising. The burnt-out guy appeared to be peeling the skin from his face.

'Ye mad bastard,' I shouted. 'Whit's the game?'

I calmed down when I looked into the mild grinning face of Dad, dangling a rubber mask.

'Ye very near gied me a heart attack,' said Jimmy. 'Ye were worse lookin' than the phantom o' the opera. Whit's the big idea?'

'It's like this,' said Dad, after giving one or two quiet chuckles. 'I'm testin' masks for a theatrical company. I thought I would try this one oot in the pub to see if it looked real. I think it worked well enough.'

We assured him that it had worked very well. Then I asked him if he had left his digs.

'No' exactly. I owe three weeks' money, but I'm no' botherin' aboot it meanwhile.'

He broke off to say that he heard we were skint and if we wouldn't be offended he was prepared to give us a fiver. 'Ye can consider it a wee loan,' he said.

Jimmy said he would sure appreciate it. I asked him how he knew we were skint. Did McLerie tell him?

'As a matter o' fact he did,' said Dad, handing me a fiver. 'We sometime get on the talk now and then.'

'At that rate,' I said, surprised that McLerie talked to anyone, 'maybe you'll know a guy called Colin Craig?' and I gave him a description.

After a pause Dad said, 'I believe I have seen such a person, though I never knew his name.' He went on, 'Wis it somethin' urgent ye wanted him for?'

'How should it be urgent?' I asked. I had the feeling Dad knew Craig a lot better than he made out, but I wasn't concerned. The important thing was that we had enough for another couple of drinks.

'No reason at all,' said Dad. 'Except that I wis gaun back tae McLerie's later since I can get a doss on the floor for nothin'. If I had seen the guy ye were referrin' tae I could have passed on a message.'

'There's nae message,' I said, as we waved him goodbye.

After Dad had vanished into the dark I said, 'That's the queerest thing I've ever come across.'

'Whit's that?' asked Jimmy.

'A guy testin' masks for a theatrical company. Who'd be sae daft as tae dae that?'

'I know whit ye mean, but Dad's no' sae daft, though he's got a' these queer occupations. I widny be surprised if he's workin' for the polis and the mask is tae disguise himsel' in places where he's known.'

'At that rate I'll be giving him a wide berth,' I said.

'On the ither haund,' said Jimmy, 'maybe no'. Maybe he's just eccentric.'

'Aye, maybe.' I thought that Dad was one very devious guy, but I was pleased with his fiver.

4

S omewhere in the city we heard an explosion which shook the top layer of our bricks. We wiped the sweat from our brows and stepped back to survey the wall. It was hot and for once there was no wind to cool us.

'Whit the hell wis that?' I asked.

'Maybe a gas pipe burst.'

'Sounds like dynamite.'

'Maybe war wis declared and we never heard.'

'Or some o' them political bampots. It's no' the first time they've planted a bomb.'

We all lit up a fag. Benny, the wee thin guy with the baggy flannels, said, 'It wis in the paper a couple o' weeks back that fuse wire wis found in a plastic bag near an oil tank.'

'Imagine blawin' up an oil tank,' said the apprentice.

Benny said, 'Personally speakin', I think somebody wis jist stealin' fuse wire and drapped it.'

'There's terrorists everywhere nooadays,' said Jimmy. 'It's the new craze.'

'Plantin' bombs is no' new,' said Benny. 'Look at Guy Fawkes.'

'He wis whit ye call an anarchist,' said the apprentice.

We all stared at him deliberately wide-eyed. He added sheepishly, 'So I heard.'

'I bet you don't know whit an anarchist is,' said Jimmy.

'Is it no' somebody that's against the government?' asked the apprentice.

'At that rate we're a' anarchists,' said I.

'Look oot,' said Jimmy. 'Here comes Hitler.'

The ganger, who was actually called Butler, came up to us and said, 'Is there somethin' wrang wi' yous lot? Ye're staunin' aboot as useless as a crowd o' female geriatrics at a beauty competition.'

Jimmy explained, 'We're jist seein' that the wa's steady efter that explosion.'

'Whit explosion?'

'Did ye no' hear a big bang as loud as when the landmine drapped on Fermer Watson's field during the war?' said Benny.

'Naw, I didny,' said the ganger. 'I don't even mind o' Fermer Watson, never mind a landmine.' He ran his hand over the wall and stated, 'These bricks are gey slack.'

'We're tryin' to tell ye, there wis an explosion. That's how they're slack.'

'And I'm tryin' tae tell ye,' said the ganger, 'that if this job is no' up tae scratch you'll a' be aff this site quicker than craws aff a dyke durin' target practice.'

Benny hitched up his trousers aggressively and stepped in front of the ganger. 'Dae ye no' think ye're gaun ower the score talkin' like that. There's nothin' wrang wi' the wa'. Maybe ye want rid o' us so as ye can get in yer masonic pals.'

'So that's whit it's aboot,' said Jimmy ominously.

In a grim manner we all moved one step nearer the ganger, including the apprentice. The ganger, give him his due, did not budge an inch, apart from the bulge of his chest and eyes.

'Ya ignorant shits,' he said. 'It's nothin' tae dae wi' the masonic or ony ither faction. It's tae dae, first of a', wi' the new architect, who's been complainin' aboot everythin' tae the new manager, who's got his orders frae the authorities to cut back everywhere so they can save money for the big shots at the tap o' the tree, who appear to feel a draught blawin' through their wine cellars these days. That's whit it's aboot.'

There was silence for a moment. Then I said with a nervous laugh, 'I thought this wis a boom toon.'

'Maybe that wis the boom ye heard then,' said the ganger.

He added, addressing me personally, 'And anither thing, yer protection act ye mentioned is no' worth a damn noo. They've made anither act which states that the buildin' trade is tae be streamlined; in other words haufed in two doon the middle. Nane o' us is protected, includin' masel'.'

With those mighty words he ambled off like an elephant heading for its last resting place. Jimmy said, after a gloomy pause, 'I'm gled o' that.'

'Gled o' whit?'

'Gled that he'll cop it alang wi' us when the time comes.'

'I wouldny bank on it,' I said.

'He's only a worker like oorsels,' said Benny.

'Anither thing,' said the apprentice. 'They canny sack me because I'm supposed tae serve ma time nae matter whit happens.'

Jimmy gripped the apprentice by the neck of his tee-shirt. 'Jist you shut yer face and gie us wan o' yer reefers. I've seen you smokin' the hash through a hole in the bog door. We a' know ye're a junky.'

The apprentice wriggled free. 'It's nothin' tae whit I've seen you daein' through the bog door!'

He backed away while we all grabbed Jimmy to keep him off the apprentice.

'Tell us, son,' we asked, 'whit does he dae in the bog?'

'Nothin',' he shouted, and ran towards the site hut.

'Goes tae the bog and does nothin',' I said, amazed.

'Maybe it's constipation,' said Benny.

Jimmy said, after we released him, 'That apprentice is wan o' the cheekiest swines I've met.'

Later that afternoon the ganger handed out the pay packets.

'I suppose you'll a' be gettin' fu' tae the gills,' he said. We all nodded except the apprentice.

'Whit aboot yersel'?' I asked him pleasantly.

'I gied it up years ago. It's a mug's game.'

Benny said, 'Man canny live by breid alane. Ye need tae blot oot yer worries at least wance a week.'

'It's still a mug's game.'

I tore up my pay packet, counted the notes, stuffed them into my hip pocket and tossed the empty packet away.

'Pick that up,' said the ganger.

'Whit for? It's empty.'

He shook his head. 'Have they nae idea how to act where you come frae? Tossing litter doon like that.'

I turned my head away to hide the disdain in my eyes. The ganger tapped my arm and said, 'Try and screw the heid at the weekend, particularly wi' the booze.'

'It's nane o' your business whit I dae at the weekend.'

'Maybe so, but keep in mind that ony guy who's no' in sharp on a Monday is paid aff. Too bad if it's no' due tae a hangover for it's taken for granted that's the reason.'

By the time I got back to the digs after having a few pints with Jimmy and paying him the money I owed, as well as paying the landlord his dues, I felt tired and unwanted. Everyone was going out, except me.

After the meal of fish and chips – something of a treat to give Danny his due – I retired to the lounge and fell asleep in front of the television. When I woke up the room was empty. I stared at the television for some time, trying to work up enough energy to stand up, but I must have fallen asleep again. The next apparent thing was the sound of Danny switching off the set.

'Nae point in wastin' electricity,' he said.

'Whit time is it?'

'Time ye were in yer bed by the look o' ye.'

He was almost right. The clock on the mantelpiece said eleven. The lodgers should be staggering in any minute, with a carry-out I hoped. Then I remembered that the rules of the house cancelled this out. The night was truly dead. Perhaps it was just as well because Jimmy tiptoed into my bedroom later to inform me, with fumes of beer blowing over my face, that Nancy had told Jean to tell Jimmy that she would meet me at the park gate on Saturday.

'This is really a nice place, don't you think?' said Nancy, as we sat in The Cosy Nook licensed restaurant. 'It's so clean you could eat off the floor.'

I handed her back the menu card informing her that I wasn't hungry. After a week of Danny's stodgy dinners my stomach felt it was due a rest.

'I'll jist have a drink,' I said.

'But it looks funny if you don't order a meal,' said Nancy.

'I'll have some scrambled egg then.'

'It's not on the menu.'

I beckoned the waitress and asked if I could have a drink to be going on with since I couldn't make up my mind about the food.

'Have you any scrambled egg?' asked Nancy.

'We haven't,' said the waitress.

'So, I'll jist have a drink in the meantime,' I said again, and ordered a double whisky.

'Bring me a martini,' said Nancy.

When the waitress was gone I said, 'I thought you were havin' somethin' tae eat.'

'I'm not eating alone. It looks funny.'

I studied her across the table. Her hair was arranged to look like feathers and her lips shone like pink icing. I thought she looked great, even though her face was screwed up. When I complimented her on the spotted green blouse she wore, she said, 'It's an old one,' and shifted her gaze along the room to another young couple who sat clutching long amber glasses. They seemed depressed, perhaps on account of the Val Doonican record playing in the background. When the whisky arrived I swallowed half of the glass straight away, partly because I had waited a long time for it, partly to offset the weight settling on my brain. Nancy asked, after she had taken a sip of her martini, if I usually drank so fast.

'Aye,' I said, and tossed back the other half.

The waitress returned and asked if we'd made up our minds about what to order.

'The fact is,' said Nancy, 'my fiancé is on a diet and can only eat scrambled egg, so there's no point –'

'That's right,' I broke in. 'I'm under doctor's orders.'

'Don't worry about it,' said the waitress. 'But if you come in on a Wednesday we'll have scrambled eggs then.'

'Since we can't order food we might as well leave,' said Nancy, closing the menu card with a sigh.

'Do you know?' I said when we were outside, 'I hate scrambled egg.'

Nancy began to giggle. 'How you managed to say you were under the doctor's orders I'll never know.'

She continued to act in a light-hearted way and I ceased to be depressed.

'Have you always worked on a building site?' Nancy asked.

We were walking through the park. If we had been sharing a wee bottle of booze the situation would have been perfect. I knew that was out of the question, but I was happy enough.

'If ye mean since I left school, aye.'

'Is it hard work?'

'Hard and mucky.'

'Why don't you do something else then?'

'I don't want tae. Anyway, I'm lucky tae have a job.'

'I suppose so.' She added, 'I've never been out with anyone who worked on a building site.'

'How does it feel?'

She gave me a diffident smile. 'Uncomfortable sometimes.'

35

I was cast down again. It occurred to me she found me uncouth, which I knew I was. I began to brood on the Canadian, who had likely been a very suave guy.

'What's wrong?' she asked, after we had walked a good while and I had remained deliberately silent.

'If ye find me so uncomfortable why are ye here?'

'You take everything very seriously.'

'Not always. In that restaurant you were the serious one because I didny want tae eat.'

'I see,' she said quietly. 'You're now going to pick on trivialities. You shouldn't have had that double whisky.'

'You think I'm drunk because I had a double whisky?'

'I don't think you are drunk, but a double whisky can influence your judgement.'

'You don't say?' I said sarcastically.

At that point we came to a halt, not far from the tree where we had kissed before.

'If you're going to be like this I might as well go back home,' she said.

'You might as well since I make you feel uncomfortable.'

'I really detest you,' she said. Her face was red and angry. When she drew back with her fists clenched I grabbed them and said, 'Let's chuck it. Ye know I'm crazy aboot ye.'

She struggled for a bit, then finally calmed down. I pulled her under a tree and we kissed long and satisfactorily. We were very compatible when kissing.

Afterwards she said she thought she had a temperature and I asked her if that explained her bad moods. 'You are the most inconsistent dame I've ever known,' I told her.

'I bet you haven't known many.'

'That's true.'

'I'm not surprised,' she said, 'you've no manners.'

I wasn't bothered when she said this. I had no wish to be like the Canadian, who likely had plenty of manners.

'That wasn't the problem,' I said. 'My mother wanted me tae be a priest, but I couldny gie up the booze.'

'Liar,' she said. 'You're not even a Catholic.'

I tickled her under the arms. She laughed as if she was enjoying it. We were acting like kids, but I think we were never so happy as at that moment. Then she told me a bit about herself. For instance, how her parents were from her point of view old-fashioned – particularly her mother, who worried about appearances, and what the neighbours said, and keeping up with the Joneses. 'You know what I mean,' she finished.

'I know whit ye mean,' I said, thinking about my mother, who mainly worried about paying the rent and buying the grub, apart from worrying about me, which she said she did all the time. I spoiled everything by changing the subject and asking Nancy if she loved me better than the Canadian.

'It's none of your business,' she said, drawing back and assuming the untouchable look. I lit up a fag to conceal my chagrin. Then she said that she was cold and wanted to get home because she didn't feel well. We walked back through the park in silence. When we reached the gate where she caught the bus I asked her if she would see me the next afternoon at the same place. She sighed and said all right in a sullen manner. She allowed me to kiss her, but her lips were cold.

On Sunday afternoon I sat on a bench inside the park watching young lassies dance in a circle as they sang, 'Here we go like birds in the wilderness, birds in the wilderness, birds in the wilderness. Here we go like birds in the wilderness on a wet and windy morning.'

I was reminded of my first day at school when I had stood snivelling with humiliation in a similar circle. It was queer how the song had cropped up again after all these years, like a bad omen. I moved on, but not too far, so that I could keep my eye on the park gate for Nancy. A crowd had gathered in the valley below, some standing and some sitting, in front of a big wagon altered to make a stage, on which three guys wearing check shirts were strumming guitars in an experimental fashion. It was a busy scene and one I hadn't bargained on. A guy approached me holding a collection box. I shoved in some change and asked what it was all about.

'It's aboot peace,' he said.

'Peace?'

'Aye, the peace festival.'

I moved on down the hill and sat on the grass at a spot where I could be seen from the path above if Nancy showed up. I was beginning to have my doubts. She was fifteen minutes late judging by the town hall clock which struck every quarter of an hour. When another fifteen minutes had passed and the guitarists were playing in earnest, I gave up hope and lay back with my arms under my head wondering if the pubs were open on a Sunday afternoon, yet not really caring too much.

A voice from behind shouted in a gravelly tone, 'Hiv ye a match on ye?'

I looked round to see three mature guys sprawled on the grass, obviously sozzled. A fourth lay on his back snoring. The question was repeated by a man with a threatening look on his face, which could have been merely a slackening of the facial muscles caused by too much booze. I flung over my box and he asked if I wanted a 'swally' of the South African wine bottle he held up before me.

'We're a' freens here,' another one assured me, wiping the sweat from his brow. They must have been roasting in their dark greasy suits.

'I might as well,' I said.

I swallowed as much as I could before the bottle was taken from me, then I pointed to the snoring man. 'He could get sunstroke.'

'No' him', said the guy who had asked for the matches. 'He's immune frae a' the elements on account o' his brain cells bein' deid.' He attempted to light his shag roll-up which was bent in two different angles.

'Have a fag,' I said, and handed round my packet, hoping for another swig at the bottle when everyone had had their turn.

'Big crowd here the day,' I said conversationally. 'I'm telt it's a peace festival.'

'Peace!' said another guy. 'That's a bloody good yin.'

He winked at no one in particular and took a long pull at the bottle. He might have finished it if the man on the grass hadn't sat up and grabbed it off him.

'Ya bastards,' he said, 'there's hardly ony left.' Then he looked at me and asked, 'Who the fuck are you?'

I thought he was a man who looked better asleep. Awake he appeared mean-faced and cross-eyed. At first I wasn't sure if he was talking to me or the guy beside me. However, the guy beside me answered. 'He came ower and sat beside us, Wullie, and put the bottle tae his mooth afore we could dae a thing aboot it. That's how there's hardly ony left.'

'Is that so?' said Willie. He transferred the bottle to his right hand and held it by the neck in the manner of a weapon.

'Don't worry, I'll get anither one right away,' I said, rising to my feet. He advised me to hurry up and bring some shag while I was at it.

'Sure, Wullie.'

'Make it two bottles,' said the guy with my matches safely in his pocket.

'Sure, I'll make it three.'

With that and a careless wave of the hand I was off down the hill. The beer tent loomed up before me, which was handy. I was in the mood for a pint.

Inside two customers stood drinking beer at a table laden with heavy tumblers. One of them said, 'Help yersel' tae the beer. The guy in charge is away for a piss. I'm takin' in the money.'

The other one said in a clipped accent, 'Possibly he drank too much of his own beer,' and wiped his handlebar moustache lightly with the back of his hand. This guy was Colin Craig, the toff whom I had met in the pub; the man I had pretended to be looking for in The Open Door. Now I really was glad to see him. He looked friendly and I was lonely.

'How's it gaun?' I asked.

'Remarkably well,' he said. 'And you?'

'Smashin'.'

His companion, who had a face as sharp as a blade, informed me that he'd hardly sold anything from his stall so far and that it was a particularly mean crowd out there who would sooner put ten pence in a collection box than buy one of his lovely Honolulu tee-shirts. He went on, giving me a sharp look to match his face, 'Ye widny like wan? I've got a great selection, only three quid each.'

'No thanks,' I said.

'Or some jewellery for the wife or the girlfriend bein' selt for next tae nothin'?'

I lifted a pint tumbler of beer and looked at the thin-faced guy blankly when he held his hand out for the money. Craig shoved his hand down, saying sternly, 'This lad is a friend of mine who has come all the way from the west coast to find work.'

'Is that near the Gallowgate?' said the other one with a sniff.

'Only as the crow flies,' I said.

We all laughed and moved outside, carrying our tumblers. 'I thought you had to collect the beer money,' I said to the sharp-faced guy.

'I've got ma ain business tae attend tae,' he said, and pushed off through the crowd, who were swaying to the rhythm of the guitarists. At that moment I pined for Nancy.

'By the way,' I said to Craig, 'McLerie telt me that he'd never heard o' ye. I visited The Open Door, at your suggestion if ye mind, but ye never showed up.'

'Please accept my apologies. I usually round off my evenings in that pub but there's the odd time I don't. As for McLerie, I can't account for his attitude. He's a strange fellow, and very secretive. He may have thought your interest in me was suspicious. I'll have a word with him on this score.'

'Anither funny thing,' I said, 'is that Dad, wan o' the lodgers where I stay, knows ye as well. I met him in The Open Door.' Inconsequentially I added, 'Wearin' a false face, tae.'

'Of course, Dad!' said Craig after wrinkling his forehead for a second. 'A wonderful character. Yes, I know him very well.'

'Seems a strange coincidence,' I said, thinking for the first time how strange it really was.

'Not at all,' he said reprovingly. 'There is no such thing as a strange coincidence. There is only such a thing as a coincidence, but if it bothers you –' He broke off and shrugged, as if to imply he was prepared to end our association if I felt bad about it.

'It doesny bother me,' I said. 'I've made a few pals since I met ye last. McLerie and Dad's nothin' tae me and coincidences don't bother me either.'

Craig raised his eyebrows and said, pointing his head in the direction of the guitarists beating it out loud on the stage, 'Wonderful music,' but twisting his mouth as if he meant the opposite. I nodded and told him curtly I was away to look for my bird since she was the reason for me being here in the first place. I placed my empty tumbler on top of a post and left him, to make my way through the folk standing thick and stubborn like cattle. I collided with a guy coming in the opposite direction. He reeled back and fell into a wee space between the bodies. I helped him up before he was trampled into the ground.

'Ye'll no' get through there,' he said, 'it's the lottery wheel.'

I turned back and found Craig standing on the same spot. The last note of the guitarists' number was vibrating on the air.

'Did you not find your bird?' he asked cautiously.

'I couldny get through the crowd. I wis too late onyway.'

A voice spoke through the microphone, loud but indistinct. 'I'm not in the mood for this,' said Craig. 'Let's go somewhere.'

'The beer tent?' I suggested.

He shook his head and stared about restlessly. I asked him if he was looking for somebody.

He shrugged. 'Not exactly. Like yourself, I'm too late.'

'I'll tell ye whit,' I said, concluding that this man was as lonely as myself, 'how aboot gettin' somethin' tae eat?'

Craig took out his wallet as we waited beside the snack van. I told him that I would pay but he was already handing the money over to the guy serving the hamburger rolls. I noticed the initials on the wallet were A.R.B. It occurred to me he was a pickpocket, but it scarcely interested me. I decided I would ask him about it later, if it began to bother me.

'Let's eat at the top of the hill where it's quiet,' he said.

I agreed to this readily because there was the faintest of possibilities that Nancy would be waiting, desperately scanning the crowd for me, but of course when we got there she wasn't.

'It's a pity,' said Craig as we wiped the grease from our fingers, 'that your friend didn't arrive. I could tell you were upset about it.'

'I'm no' botherin',' I said, adding ruefully, 'It's only one o' these things that can alter yer life, I suppose.'

After a pause he said that my life was more likely to alter if I did something about it rather than wait passively for things to happen.

'How d'ye mean?' I asked.

He looked me straight in the eye and said, 'I can't make any promises or even say very much at present, but I have been making some plans to start my own business, and I will need to hire some good men.'

'If you're offerin' me work,' I said, 'I'm obliged tae tell ye that I only like bein' a brickie.'

'That's all right, young man,' he said, patting me on the shoulder. 'You are as well to do what you are happiest doing. Money isn't everything.'

'What kind o' work were you referrin' to?' I asked. 'I can always change my mind for a higher price, dependin' on whit it is.'

He laughed. 'Already I have said too much. In a few weeks' time I can be more explicit.'

'I canny be bothered wi' vague promises,' I said. 'I widny like tae think that ye're havin' me on.'

'Then don't think it, young man,' he stated, and said no more about it.

From the same bench I'd sat on when I'd arrived in the park, we looked down on the scene below. The crowd had thinned. Kids and dogs ran about unchecked. Folk were drinking openly from beer cans. Some were drunk and staggering. There was no sign of the sozzled guys I had spoken to, except for the empty wine bottle lying a few yards away. The same guy was speaking through the microphone.

I said, 'You'd wonder how anyone bothers tae speak through a microphone – it's obvious naebody's listenin'.'

'There's always someone who is.'

'But ye know the words aff by heart. No more war, love thy neighbour and ban the bomb. Naebody seems tae care.'

'Except the man on the speaker.'

'That's right,' I said. 'Except the man on the speaker.'

A wind sprang up and blew empty crisp bags and paper cups over the grass. Folks stood shivering, shouting on their kids and dogs, then cramming things into plastic bags. The guitarists were back on the stage belting it out with gusto, but the day was finished; the mood was gone. A church clock struck five.

Craig said, 'The hotels should be open soon.'

I fixed my thoughts on the promise of booze, though I couldn't help mentioning to Craig as we left the park that my bird's hair smelled of fresh cut grass. I asked him if he thought this was an unusual perfume. He said that it was one of his favourites.

6

'That wis some carry oan, last night,' said Jimmy.

We were eating our breakfast and I was pushing aside a plate of porridge.

'Whit's wrang wi' it?' Danny asked, pointing to my plate.

'Nothin', but it brings me oot in heat spots.'

'I'll take it,' said one of the lodgers. He worked in a sawmill and had two fingers missing from his left hand. They called him 'the gannet' or sometimes 'the hoover'.

'I hardly got a wink o' sleep,' said Jimmy.

'That wis terrible,' I said, shoving my plate towards the sawmill worker.

'So ye' mind o' kickin' open ma door and punchin' the wa', then sittin' on the edge o' ma bed for ages?'

'I don't mind anythin'.'

'Ye were in a bad state. I'm sure Nancy couldny have been pleased.'

'Do me a favour,' I said. 'Don't mention her name to me and if ye ever see her tell her to keep oot ma road.'

Unintentionally I had raised my voice and everyone was looking over at me. Danny shouted from the kitchen sink, 'Did ye get a dizzy, then?'

'You jist mind yer ain business and get a move on wi' the tea,' I shouted back.

'Did she no' show up?'

'That's of no consequence beside the sore head I've got at this moment,' I said coldly.

'I wonder why she never showed up,' said Jimmy, regarding me thoughtfully. I shut my eyes.

45

After drinking my tea and nibbling apathetically on a bit of toast, I told Jimmy to explain to the ganger that I had contracted a severe bout of diarrhoea and wouldn't be able to start work until dinner time. Then I went upstairs to my room, lay down on the bed, and immediately fell asleep.

I was awakened by Danny's aggrieved voice calling in my ear, 'Ye've nae right tae be in bed at this time in the morning.'

I sat up slowly and regarded him with loathing. 'At whit time can ye be in bed if ye're no' feelin' well?'

'It's nothin' tae dae wi' me if ye're no' well. It's ma job tae see everybody's oot the rooms afore I clean them.'

'How can ye no' dae the room later? I might feel better then.' Stupidly I threw back the cover to expose my boots to his shocked countenance.

'That's the maist disgustin' sicht I've seen. Ye'd better get oot this room afore I tell ma Da.'

'Wait a minute,' I said as he headed for the door. 'If ye let me lie for another hour I'll gie ye a pound and I'll take ma boots aff as well.'

He paused and turned. 'I canny,' he said. 'If they find oot they'll ask questions.'

'Who'll ask questions?'

'The polis.'

'The polis? You must be jokin'.'

'I've got ma orders tae report onythin' unusual that happens wi' the lodgers tae the polis. Lyin' in bed wi' yer boots on when ye should be at work is definitely unusual.'

'Ye're a crazy bastard,' I said. He stood studying me like a gigantic mole, with his eyes beady and his long nose twitching. I became angry and leapt out of bed. I stood close to his gangling body and said, 'Why should the polis be watchin' me?'

'Nae reason,' he said, backing away. 'I wis jist sayin' that to get ye up. There's nae need to go aff yer heid.'

'If I think onyone's spyin' on me,' I said, 'I'll render them incapable wi' ma haunds roon' their throat.'

Danny gulped and said, 'I'll tell ye whit, make it two pounds and ye can stay in bed for an hour if ye take yer boots aff.'

'Ye're no' sae crazy,' I said. 'Take this pound and beat it before I really lose ma temper.'

After he left I didn't take my boots off, or shut my eyes, or even yawn. I was so wide awake it was painful. I felt uneasy, guilty and ashamed for no good reason – a familiar state after I've drunk to excess, particularly if it is accompanied by loss of memory, and even more particularly when I've been dumped by a bird I am crazy about. I grabbed my jacket, walked out of the room, down the stairs and into the kitchen, where Danny was emptying rubbish into a bin.

'Fetch ma pieces,' I said as he regarded me open-mouthed. 'I'm gaun tae work.'

When I was collecting my tools out of the site hut, the ganger entered. I explained while he lit his pipe that I felt a lot better than I had done earlier, so I had decided to show my face. He continued to puff with his eyes on the floor as though his thoughts were far away. When I headed outwards he said, 'Haud on.'

I turned to him with raised eyebrows and he added, 'Ye canny start at ony time ye happen tae fancy, ye ken.'

I said in a reasonable manner, 'But there wis nae way I could have came earlier considerin' I had a dose of the skitters in the first place and you are aware of whit the toilet facilities are like here in the second place.'

'So it wis the booze?' he said.

'It definitely wisny the booze for I hardly touched it a' weekend.'

'That's no' whit I heard.'

We stared hard at each other for a minute, then I said less reasonably, 'I don't care whit ye heard.'

'Is that so,' he said, pointing the stem of his pipe towards me. 'Well, ye were telt that onyone no' in sharp on a Monday gets paid aff.'

'For Christ sake. I wisny well. Deduct the lost time aff ma wages if it'll make ye feel better.'

He didn't answer so I thought I'd change the subject. 'Did ye get me a new pair o' wellies?'

He shook his head. I became angry and told him I was going to report him to the foreman on a matter of victimisation, but he remained unperturbed, puffing and blowing his pungent smoke in my face. I walked out and banged the door hard enough to loosen its hinges. When I joined the rest of the squad I was deliberately silent.

'Whit's wrang wi' you?' the apprentice asked. 'Did somebody pinch yer lollipop?'

Jimmy said to the apprentice, 'Ye'd better no' talk tae him. He had a dizzy at the weekend and hell hath no fury like a man wi' a dizzy.'

At that moment I made up my mind I was going to pack in the job on Friday and return home. The folk up here were all hustlers. The place wasn't fit for a dog.

'Hey,' said the apprentice, 'don't lay these bricks sae fast. It's no' as if I canny keep up wi' ye, but I don't particularly feel like it.'

'Fuck the lot o' ye,' I replied in an explosive manner, startling the apprentice who dropped the bricks from his hod, which gave Jimmy the excuse to curse him strongly. He hadn't forgiven him for the hole in the bog door incident.

'Leave him alane,' I said. 'It wis ma fault.'

We all picked up the bricks and Benny asked me if I felt better now. I wasn't sure if he was referring to the state of my bowels or my bad mood, but I nodded anyway. Jimmy offered me a fag. I took it and said, 'You want to keep yer big mouth shut.'

'How's that?'

'Ye telt the ganger I wis on the bevvy last night.'

'Whit makes ye think that?'

'How else wid he know?'

'It stauns tae reason he wid say that if ye were in late. If yer leg wis hingin' aff he wid say it wis because o' the booze.'

I had to admit to the truth of this and pointed out to Jimmy that I wouldn't have been on the booze if Nancy had shown up.

He shrugged, 'So these things happen. It's no' the end o' the world. You'll likely see her afore the week's up.'

'No' me,' I said firmly.

When I returned to the digs, Danny handed me a white envelope. Inside was a typed message which read, 'I WILL SEE YOU OUTSIDE THE CINEMA AT SEVEN O'CLOCK AND WILL WAIT THERE FOR TEN MINUTES ONLY. YOURS SINCERELY, NANCY.'

I was overjoyed by this brief communication.

'Is yer nose botherin' ye?' I asked Danny, who was trying to read the words upside down, but there was no malice in my voice. I felt sorry for the lonely bastard. He hadn't even got a bird, never mind a bird like Nancy. When he was slinging the plates round the table I told him that his cheese pie looked great.

'Makes a chinge frae yer usual opinions,' he said stiffly.

Afterwards I studied my reflection in the bathroom mirror and thought that if I didn't purchase some new gear soon my clothes would fall apart. I could follow Jimmy's advice and put down a deposit with a city tailor for an outfit and if I left the area I needn't bother about the rest of the payments. According to him guys were always doing this. In the meantime I had only enough money for fags. It appeared I had blown most of it on Sunday's escapade. I didn't even remember having a good time and I suspected I hadn't. It was just as well Nancy wasn't a bird with expensive tastes. I was grateful to her on that score alone. I unfolded her crumpled message, which struck me now as being a bit too brief. She could at least have apologised for not keeping the date, or even explained why she hadn't. On reading between the lines of the neat typing I detected some indifference. Perhaps I shouldn't go. If I had any pride I wouldn't. On the other hand, when I thought it over, I knew there was no way I wouldn't go.

'Ye're a sicht for sore eyes,' said Jimmy when I bumped into him coming up the stairs.

'Whit dae ye mean?' I asked, aware of my threadbare condition.

'Am I supposed tae mean somethin'?' he said, wide-eyed and debonair in a bright yellow pullover.

'I don't like yer tone o' voice. It's insinuatin'.'

'Insinuatin'?' he repeated angrily. 'The trouble wi' you is ye've got wan big chip on yer shoulder. Ye want tae knock it off or ye'll have nae freens left.'

As I slowly descended the stairs I thought perhaps he was right, but I wasn't caring about friends just then. I only cared about Nancy, and felt dismally aware of how little I had to offer her.

'Have you been waiting long?' said Nancy. She had arrived breathless outside the cinema, as if she had been running, which I considered a good sign.

'Naw,' I said. Actually I'd been waiting for fifteen minutes.

'I bumped into someone I knew,' she said. 'I couldn't get away.'

'I see,' I said, feeling dampened. Curtly I asked what had happened to her on Sunday.

'Oh that,' she said. 'I had one of these terrible headaches when all you want to do is lie in a darkened room.'

'And did you?'

She drew me one of her looks. 'Of course. What do you think?'

I decided to pay her back. 'I wis late yesterday. I met a guy on the road tae the park and we had a couple o' jugs. I wisny sure whether you'd been and gone.'

'I'm glad your day wasn't wasted,' she said quietly.

I studied her from the side of my eye. She looked as sensational as a model from a clothing catalogue. She wore an olive-green dress that touched her slim figure in all the right places. Her arms and legs were bare and brown.

'You'll catch cold,' I said as an excuse to stroke her arm.

She laughed, 'Then you'll have to lend me your jacket.'

Apart from a few can rings and paper cups on the grass, the park was cleared of Sunday's litter. A faint imprint of tyres marked the place where the wagon turned into a stage had stood.

'That's where I was wishing you were here,' I said, pointing to the imprint.

'Probably drinking,' she said.

'Whit else could I dae?'

She became serious. 'I wish you didn't drink so much.'

'I wish I didny need tae.'

I confessed as I took her hand that I hadn't been late at all. In fact I had been too early and had waited for a long time for her before I had taken a drink and when I had it was only beer. I told her also that if I thought she felt as much for me as I did for her I wouldn't need to touch another drop of liquor again.

'How much do you feel?' she asked, smiling.

'Let's go somewhere quiet and I'll show ye.'

We lay on the grass in the shelter of some bushes. Her head rested on my shoulder. Slowly and imperceptibly we moved our positions until she lay under me. I asked her if I was too heavy. She said that I wasn't. Later I asked if I was hurting her and she shook her head. At least I thought she shook her head. By this time I was in such a state of exaltation that I was incapable of being sure of anything.

Afterwards I said I was sorry. I hadn't meant to hurt her or do anything like this. I had only intended to do some heavy kissing.

'You didn't hurt me,' she said, then sat up and began to comb her hair. It was incredible how composed she was, as if nothing had happened.

'Ye know I'm crazy aboot ye,' I said.

'Crazy?' she said, with a rueful smile.

'I love you then, if that's any better.'

'Just as well,' she said. 'I don't do this sort of thing with anyone.'

It was on the tip of my tongue to ask her if she had done it with the Canadian, but I only just refrained.

She began to shiver. 'I'm cold,' she said. 'Let's walk.'

'Can I get a smoke first?' I asked. 'It's a well-known fact ye always have a smoke afterwards.'

'But I don't smoke,' she said.

'Ye'll have to learn, because we might do it again.'

I was only joking, but her face became set. 'You can stop and have a smoke if you want, but I'm walking on.'

'What's wrong?' I asked, when I caught up with her after I had lit up. When she didn't answer I asked, 'Wis it yer first time?'

'No,' she said, looking at me, her eyes disturbed. 'Maybe that's the trouble.'

I didn't want to aggravate her with questions. I said, 'If it's any consolation it's no' ma first time either.' This was a lie.

7

The sun shone over the building site, drying the mud on our boots and forcing us to throw off our shirts as we wiped the sweat from our brows.

'They say it is to be like this a' weekend,' said the apprentice.

I nodded at him amiably and accepted one of the reefers which he now displayed openly. He confided that he was going to be the owner of a second-hand motorbike.

'I hope ye can drive it?'

'I'll be OK. I've had plenty shots o' ma cousin's.'

Benny said, 'And I hope ye're no' gaun tae become one o' them Hell's Angels.'

'I'll never be good enough for that,' said the apprentice.

'Ye don't have to be a' that good on a bike,' said Benny. 'So long as ye know the Hitler tunes, and better still if ye join the National Front.'

'I think I'll join them then,' said the apprentice.

Jimmy said, 'I've a nephew who ca's hissel' a Hell's Angel and he's a quiet fella.'

'So he will be,' said Benny, 'until he gets on his bike and aff wi' his pals tae beat up the Jews.'

'As far as I ken he only goes roon' the ring road and there's nae Jews there.'

'That's only as far as you ken. It doesny have to be Jews. It can be Italians, Pakkies, or the tinkers; in fact, ony bugger that walks across their path.'

'How the tinkers?' asked the apprentice.

'If ye wereny sae ignorant you'd ken that in Europe they're called Gypsies and Hitler got rid o' them alang wi' the Jews.'

'I hope,' said Jimmy, addressing Benny, 'ye're no' suggestin' that ma nephew's a Nazi.'

'There's nae difference between them and the National Front.'

'I wish tae Christ I hudny mentioned aboot the motorbike,' said the apprentice.

I said to Jimmy, 'I widny be surprised if Dad is one.'

'A Hell's Angel?'

'Naw, somethin' mair in the line o' a National Front member. Look how he walks oot the ludgings withoot sayin' a word to anybody, then shows up a few days later as if he'd never been away.'

'Whit does that prove?' said Jimmy. 'He's always been like that.'

'And that false face business. That wis weird if ye ask me.'

Benny said, 'I dinny ken the guy yous are talkin' aboot, but here's somebody comin' who's definitely weird.'

It was the ganger delivering the wages. We turned to our bricks while he pondered long upon us. After a time Benny looked round and said as if surprised, 'Why, it's yersel', Geordie, wi' the pay pokes, and a welcome sicht ye are.'

The wages were handed round in grim silence, which was normal for the ganger, so it came as a shock when he handed me mine and said, 'Ye're on a week's notice.'

I shoved the envelope in my pocket and turned back to the bricks, uncertain if it was his idea of a joke, though he wasn't in the habit of joking. He said, dispelling my uncertainty, 'They're cuttin' back the men. I warned ye a while back.'

'So ye did,' said Benny, 'but there's plenty work. We're a' needed, even the apprentice.'

'I've got ma orders.'

'Are ye sure ye've got yer orders?' I asked. 'Or wis it jist yersel' that wanted rid o' me?'

'If ye don't believe me, see the foreman.'

'When dae we ever see a foreman?'

By now he was heading back to the hut with his usual elephantine gait.

'That's rotten,' said the apprentice, breaking the two minutes' silence after he had gone.

'I'm helluva sorry,' said Benny.

'It's pure shit,' said Jimmy. 'I'll have tae dae the work o' two brickies.'

I handed him the brick I had lifted. 'Ye can start wi' that one then.'

'I heard the firm's changin' haunds. We'll a' likely go eventually,' said Benny.

'They'll no' get rid o' me, surely,' said the apprentice, after taking a deep draw of his reefer.

Benny said, 'Listen, son, they can dae whit they bloody well like.'

'It seems to me,' Jimmy said to Benny with a red angry face, 'that you ken a lot mair than I dae, and it seems to me as well that you and the ganger are gey pally at times. I wouldny be surprised if ye're baith tryin' to get rid o' me.'

'Aye, and me tae,' said the apprentice.

Benny shook his head. 'I wis never pally wi' Geordie in a' the twenty years I've kent him, and he kens that if you don't.'

I interrupted. 'Ye'd think it was yous that were gaun instead o' me.'

'I ken, son,' said Benny apologetically. 'This is whit happens when there's a pay aff. It causes a bad atmosphere wi' the ones that are left. Maybe you're the lucky one, bein' well oot o' it.'

'Sure,' I laughed. 'I'm the lucky one.'

'I'll tell yous something,' said the apprentice, startling us all by the extra loud way he spoke. 'I've been thinkin' how I've never had a kind word aff ony o' yous since the day I started. Wait and see, I'll be the next to go.' He then blew smoke in our faces.

Jimmy said, 'Ye want tae chuck that stuff. It makes ye imagine things.'

I asked the apprentice for a last draw of his reefer. He calmed down and handed it over, telling me to keep it if I wanted.

'We'll a' have a wee puff,' I said, and passed it round.

Benny coughed after he took his draw and said, 'Man, that stuff fair chokes yer lungs. I dinny ken how ye can smoke it.'

'There's a knack tae it,' said the apprentice mournfully.

We continued to take draws until the reefer was finished. Benny said that the hash made him tired. I said that I felt no different.

'That's because you don't inhale it deep enough,' said the apprentice.

He was probably right because the pupils of his eyes were like pinpoints, and he looked stupefied.

'Ye'd better pick up yer trowel afore ye drap aff tae sleep,' said Jimmy to the apprentice. 'Yer eyes are as squint as ma first piss.'

When they all lifted their trowels I told them I might as well get going since I was paid off anyway.

'But we'll see ye next week,' said the apprentice.

'That's right,' I said, but I knew I wouldn't. No one ever works a week's notice in the building trade.

Back at the lodgings I informed everyone in a loud and cheerful voice that I had been paid off and so I would be going back home. I smiled to convey how pleased I was by this turn of events.

'Whit dae ye want tae go hame for?' asked Henry Bell. 'I could get ye a start at sweepin' the roads.'

'When?'

'Efter the fair holidays.'

'I canny wait that long. I feel hamesick.'

'Don't forget to pay yer dig money,' said Danny, who had been listening to all this with his arms folded.

'I'm no' gaun away right this minute,' I said. I surveyed my plate of stovies. 'A' the same, it's an ill wind that blaws nae good.'

Dad, who had only recently returned to his place at the table, said, 'Maybe I could get ye a start wi' Sanderson's Soft Shoe Polish. They'll soon be needin' folk tae pass roon' the leaflets.'

'I'll think aboot it,' I said, with a sidelong glance at his mild, friendly face.

After swallowing some forkfuls of the stovies I passed my plate over to the sawmill worker, who accepted it with a grateful nod and said that he would be sorry to see me leave.

I asked Jimmy, 'How's aboot comin' alang tae the pub for a quick one? I'm chokin' for a drink.'

'I'm meetin' Jean in a wee while.'

'It's only for a quick one,' I said. 'Somethin' tae stiffen ma nerve when I tell Nancy that I'm fired.'

'I thought ye wereny botherin'.'

'Nancy will be botherin'. Ye know whit dames are like.'

'I'm sorry,' said Jimmy. 'I widny trust masel' to get one drink. I'd end up gettin' bevvied.'

'Never mind,' I said, and headed quickly for the outside door. I caught up with Dad, who had left the lodgings some minutes before me in his usual unobtrusive manner. 'Fancy a drink?' I asked.

'Actually I've an appointment tae keep.'

'No' at The Open Door, surely?' I said, adding with a sarcastic titter, 'wi yer false face on.'

He smiled politely. 'No' this time.'

'Anyway, I'll get ye alang the road a bit,' I said.

'If ye like.'

I sensed by the way his lips were clamped together he was dying to get rid of me. I felt angry at his sudden change of attitude, so for spite I mentioned that I'd heard someone say he was a member of the National Front. His only reaction was to raise his eyebrows and state mildly that folk were capable of saying anything at all to break the monotony. Then without warning he crossed the road and skuttled round the side of a building like a beetle heading for its den. I carried on, passing some pubs but reluctant to enter them in case their clients were partisan to certain causes I had no notion of. I thought it best to head for The Open Door. I had retained a good impression of the place. McLerie was a kindly man when he gave strangers credit. If I ran there and back I would be in time to meet Nancy at the park gate. There were minor considerations like not having washed or shaved and reeking of beer, but surely she would understand that a couple of drinks is the first thing a man needs when he's paid off.

There was a moment as I stood outside the pub, breathless, when I considered turning on my heels. Perhaps it was a premonition of something unpleasant in store for me, but that is not unusual and seldom deters me. Perhaps it was simply that I knew there was no time for drinking and I was blowing my chances with Nancy if I did, and me crazy about her too. Despite it all I walked straight in and ordered a double whisky and a pint. McLerie served me with a face of stone, so I said to him quickly, 'I believe I owe ye some money?'

His nod was barely discernible. After I paid him and he looked no happier, I asked if he thought Colin Craig would show up this time, adding with an edge to my voice, unless he still hadn't heard of him. He ignored this statement and informed me in a pointed way that he was closing early because he was auditing. My head spun with this information, plus the double whisky I had swallowed in one gulp.

'Ye're auditin'?' I repeated with disbelief.

'That's right. We're auditin'.' His sunken eyes bore into mine.

I became angry and called to a customer further along the counter, 'Did ye know that this pub is closin' early because they're auditin'?'

The guy shuffled his feet and told me it was all one to him as he was going shortly, and to prove it he threw back his beer and left. I could still catch Nancy yet, I thought, as I banged my glass on the counter to convey I wanted to be served. McLerie shot up from behind the counter like a jack-in-the-box.

'Anither whisky,' I said, 'and I'll be leavin' ye tae yer auditin'.'

'There's nae immediate hurry.'

Now he sounded more irritated than anything else. This encouraged me to order another whisky, and then another one, and another one. After that I became stoned. I stood with one foot on the brass rail running round the bottom of the counter, staring in stupefaction at the customers surrounding me, who appeared to have emerged from the walls. I think I was happy at that stage. McLerie approached me and accused me of being drunk.

'I'm no' surprised,' I said, laughing at the idea of being drunk and the sight of McLerie's angry face.

I don't remember much of what happened after that until the moment I awoke lying on the floor of the back room in the pub. The place was scarcely big enough to swing a cat. Most of the space was occupied by a wooden table, around which sat McLerie, Dad and Colin Craig. They were staring at an open ledger, and paid me no attention when I struggled up from the floor to sit on a chair beside them, feeling sober but ill and thinking if I could get just one short alcoholic drink I would feel better. Craig was running his finger down a page in the ledger.

'It's not bad, what we've got here, and in fact it should be enough for the first payment,' he said.

'So long as it looks good on paper,' said McLerie.

'Let's hope there's nae hitches wi' this Lifeline deal,' said Dad.

I sat as still as I could in order not to disturb them. They were an ill-assorted trio: Craig the toff, McLerie the sinister pub owner, and Dad the shabby lodger. I judged them to be villains of some kind, perhaps about to bump me off for intruding. I was wondering whether I should make a run for the door when Craig turned towards me and asked civilly if I felt any better. Immediately I apologised for any bother I might have caused and explained that usually I didn't pass out so easily.

'It was probably one of Michael's Mickey Finns,' said Craig with a mocking look in the direction of McLerie, who continued to look stern. I don't think the man was able to smile.

'Ye widny have a drink tae spare?' I asked. 'I'm parched.'

Dad pointed to an old jaw-box sink displaying one tap covered in verdigris. 'Help yersel'.'

'It's no' that kind o' parchedness.'

'Fetch a bottle of rum,' said Craig, giving me a wink, which reassured me further.

'I don't know why I should,' said McLerie, 'and I'm damned if I know how he's here listenin' tae everythin'.'

'Because I said so,' stated Craig and banged the ledger shut.

'There's nae harm in the lad,' said Dad. 'He's up here on his ain and he's lost his job.'

I decided that if they were villains, at least they were friendly ones, and being friendly is what counts.

'You've lost your job already?' Craig asked.

'When it comes tae a pay aff the foreigner's always the first tae go,' I pointed out.

'That's true,' said Craig. 'Don't worry. I'll get you fixed up some-where.'

His words, said so casually, gave me a great feeling of warmth and security, which wasn't diminished when McLerie said, as he placed four glasses and a bottle of rum on the table, 'Next thing ye'll be cuttin' him in.'

'Don't forget we can always do with a strong fellow,' said Craig.

'Can ye drive?' Dad asked me.

'Aye,' I said happily, wondering if they were smash and grab jewel thieves and I was to drive a getaway car.

'Whit dae we need a driver for?' asked McLerie.

'I dinny ken,' said Dad, 'but it's always handy tae know.'

'Well,' said Craig, holding up his glass, 'here's to a prosperous future.'

'You bet,' I said.

In no time at all, and without any revelations being made as to the manner in which I was to be fixed up, the bottle was finished and we were out on the pavement while McLerie was locking the door.

'Ye're no' a' gaun away,' I said with dismay.

'We've got an early start if some folk haveny,' said McLerie in his usual surly fashion. Drink had made no difference to his mood.

'True,' said Craig. 'I'm afraid we'll have to be on our way.'

'But whit aboot me?' I said, panicking. 'I thought ye were fixin' me up.'

'Don't worry,' said Craig, looking over his shoulder as he walked away, his face a blur in the twilight. 'I'll be in touch with you through Dad.'

They were all walking away and my legs were buckling under me. The fresh air on top of all that I had drunk was like a shot of chloroform.

'Aren't you coming?' Craig called.

'Walk on,' I groaned. 'I feel sick. I'll catch up wi' ye.'

I leaned against the pub door for support, automatically searching in my hip pocket for my wage packet, which is a reflex action on my part no matter how drunk I am. My last conscious thought, before I slid down on to the step, was that it had gone.

The copper came into the cell and thrust a mug of tea into my hand.

'Whit am I in for?' I asked.

'Are you no' the drunk and disorderly?'

'How should I know?'

'You must be. There wis only one admittance last night as far as I ken.'

I nodded in miserable acceptance and drank the tea, unable to remember anything that had happened the previous night after Craig and company had left me, apart from losing my wages.

'Ye didny find ma pay poke lyin' aboot?' I asked.

'Lyin' aboot where?'

I shrugged. 'I lost it, but it doesny matter.'

'We gathered last night ye'd lost it. By the noise ye were makin' it seemed tae matter then.'

'Is there nothin' tae eat?' I asked. 'I prefer tae eat when I'm drinkin' tea.'

'You've got a hope at this time in the mornin'. It's only five o'clock. Ye're lucky tae get tea.'

'When dae I get oot?'

'It's hard tae say. As far as I ken ye've been recommended for hospital treatment.'

'Hey, wait a minute,' I said, aghast, 'there's nothin' wrang wi' me, apart frae a hangover.'

'According to your record,' stated the copper, 'this is yer tenth time picked up drunk in the past six months.'

'Ye've got the wrang man,' I said. 'It's ma first time in this jail.

I've only been a few weeks in the district. Ye'd better check the other cells.'

He said, standing with his hands on his hips like a big sweetie wife, 'Surprisin' as it might seem tae you, ye're the only drunk and disorderly in here, so there's nae mistake.'

I stood up and pointed to my face, placing it close to his. 'Tell me,' I said, 'have ye seen this particular set o' features afore?'

'I believe I have.'

'Ye're a bloody liar,' I said, 'and furthermore I want a lawyer.'

'Wid that by ony chance be a criminal one?' he said, heaving with suppressed laughter.

'I'm tellin' ye,' I said desperately, 'ye've got the wrang man.'

'I shouldny be in here,' I told the guy in the bed next to me in the hospital ward. 'It's a case of mistaken identity.'

He looked at me blankly, then removed a set of earphones which had escaped my attention. I repeated the information.

'Where should ye be, then?' he asked.

'No' in here. I only had a few drinks.'

'They a' say that. On the ither haun', ye could be one o' the weirdos or one o' the cracked up shots. It's no' a' alcies in here.'

He put the headphones on again, and closed his eyes as he leaned back on the pillow. He looked peaceful and happy. A male nurse appeared at the side of my bed and handed me three different coloured pills. He ordered me to swallow them immediately.

'I shouldny be in here,' I informed him. 'Somebody's made a mistake.'

'Yer mother, nae doubt.'

He winked at me and moved over to the guy with the earphones. 'Wake up, Charlie, and take yer pills, pet.'

Charlie opened his eyes, groaned and removed the earphones. 'These pills make me constipated. I huvny shit for three days.'

'At that rate,' said the nurse, wagging his finger, 'we'll have to gie ye an enema, won't we?'

'Jist gie me the pills,' said Charlie.

Afterwards I swung my legs over the bed, surprised to see I was wearing green pyjama trousers to match the green pyjama top, which I had thought was a shirt.

'Ye're no' supposed tae get up on yer first day,' said Charlie.

I explained that I was leaving straight away, but before I could take a step the male nurse along with a taller, broader male nurse approached me hastily and threw me back on the bed, then thrust me under the blankets and tucked me in very determinedly.

'Be good,' said the tall, broad nurse, flexing his muscles a bit, 'or we'll need to gie ye a wee jag tae calm ye doon.'

In a quiet and sensible way I explained that my presence here was a blunder on the part of the law, which I was prepared to overlook if they fetched me my gear and released me. Otherwise it wasn't improbable that I would be awarded a fair amount of compensation for wrongful detention. 'It happens a lot nooadays,' I told them. They shook their heads and surveyed me with sympathy, especially the one who had given me the pills.

'We'll see aboot this, pet,' he said.

Smartly and in step they marched out of the ward and returned in a short time. The big broad nurse carried a hypodermic needle.

'I've been around and I'm tellin' ye, man, there's a lot worse places than this,' Charlie was saying on what I gathered was my second day in the ward. I had been doped up for so long it was hard to tell.

'Free meals and a good bed,' he added wryly. 'Whit mair dae ye want?'

He was a good-looking guy, probably in his thirties, despite his grey side-locks.

'There's a few things I could mention,' I said. 'Like fags and a bottle o' whisky.'

He threw me over a packet of Embassy Regal. 'Ye can smoke as much as ye can afford. As for drink, well, it can be smuggled in if ye've got contacts, but I'm tellin' ye, man, they gie ye a particular kind o' pill afore ye go tae sleep which has the same effect as a stiff drink o' liquor. It's really some buzz.'

'I can hardly wait for it,' I said.

'So,' he continued, 'ye might as well dae whit they tell ye and take these vitamin pills on yer locker. It pays in the long run.'

I stuck the pills in my mouth and swallowed them with a glass of tepid water.

'It's like swallowin' golf balls.'

'Think yersel' lucky ye're no' gettin' the shock treatment.'

I became indignant. 'Lucky!' I said. 'When I shouldny be in here.'

'The first time I came here I got it for kickin' up a rumpus,' said Charlie.

'Maybe ye deserved it.'

'It's no' whit ye deserve. It's whit they think ye deserve. I learned the hard way tae be docile. Ye get on fine in here if ye're docile, so take ma advice and –'

'I know,' I said, 'dae whit they tell ye.'

I rested my head back on the iron rails of the bed head and watched a wee guy shuffle along the ward, trailing the cord of his dressing gown behind him like a tail as he peered at the floor.

'Whit's he daein'?' I asked. 'Lookin' for fag ends?'

'Aye, it's force o' habit. He used tae search the railway station for fag ends and onythin' else he could find.'

'Is that whit he's in for? It doesny seem much.'

'Aye, it doesny,' said Charlie. 'At one time the porters didny bother wi' him, but that wis afore the station wis modernised. Efter that he didny fit in wi' the new image. When the passengers signed a petition to get him removed because he smelled bad, he wis shoved in here temporary, for observation, they said. Then he really went bonkers, so he stays here a' the time. He's better aff noo, if ye ask me.'

'I think you're bonkers as well if ye like this looney bin. First opportunity I'm off, with or withoot ma gear.'

'Watch it,' said Charlie. 'Here comes Maurice. Act cool.'

Maurice, who was the coquettish male nurse, asked me how I felt.

'Great,' I said. 'There's nothin' wrang wi' me. It's a shame to take up a bed when some poor bastard's likely needin' it.'

'Relax and enjoy yersel',' said Maurice as he lifted my wrist and pressed it with his thumb.

'Just as I thought,' he said. 'Yer pulse is too rapid. Ye've got an anxiety problem.'

In panic I backed away when he tried to shove a thermometer under my oxter. It fell on the floor. Breathing heavily, he picked it up and studied it with a frown.

'Is it broke?' Charlie asked anxiously.

'Luckily it's no',' said Maurice, and placed it in his top pocket.

He regarded me sternly, then asked Charlie if I had shown any previous signs of violence.

Charlie said, 'Usually he's as quiet as a budgie.'

I sank further down the pillow while Maurice continued to study me.

'We'll see,' he said ominously, and moved off to the next bed, occupied by an old guy who slept most of the time. He didn't leave me a single pill.

'Dae ye think I'll get the shock treatment?' I asked Charlie, now engrossed in a paperback called *Rustlers' Ransom*.

'I warned ye,' he said, keeping his eyes fixed on the page.

I stared up at the ceiling, thinking that Maurice could be right about my rapid pulse and anxiety problem. My heart was pounding and I felt anxious, but when he returned to the ward later he didn't even look in my direction. He simply clapped his hands and told us all to sit up and look cheerful. The visitors had arrived.

'That's us trapped in bed for a whole bloody hour,' said Charlie.

'Dae ye no' get ony visitors then?' I asked.

'Are you kiddin'?' he sounded as if the very idea of a visitor would make him sick.

'It would pass the time,' I said, but I was content to be in the same boat as Charlie.

At the last minute someone shouted from the other side 'Jackie's shit hissel',' whereupon Maurice and the tall, broad male nurse, arrayed with screens and a bedpan, charged down the ward in a ferocious manner. When the visitors entered the ward, dubious expressions on their faces, we were all holding our noses. Then Charlie picked up his paperback and I pulled the cover half over my face to suggest extreme debility to anyone looking in my direction. I closed my eyes and might have dozed off if someone hadn't scraped a chair near at hand. I opened my eyes a fraction to see Nancy sitting at my bedside regarding me sadly, her fresh cut grass perfume wafting up my nostrils. My first sensation was joy, then embarrassment.

'You shouldny have came,' I said stiffly.

She handed me a box of fruit jellies and said with resentment as she stared at me, 'I didn't know you were allowed to smoke.'

I sat up slowly and gave her a cautious glance, thinking that every time I saw her she always looked better than before. 'How did ye find me?' I asked.

'It's a long story.' She went on to say she had found out where I was through Jimmy, who had found out through the lodger called Dad, who said that he'd been delivering newspapers to the hospital and had seen me being escorted into the ward by the male nurses. The thought crossed my mind that this was no coincidence and that my movements were being noted, but since my head was as fuzzy as a ball of wool I couldn't hold on to the notion. It was much easier to concentrate on Nancy's green eyes with the yellow flecks, and the way the bridge of her nose was covered in freckles that I hadn't seen before.

'Gie's a kiss,' I said.

She leaned over and barely touched my lips.

'Why are you in here?' she asked.

'I'm no' sure. I must have taken a blackoot.'

'What caused it?'

'I'm no' sure.'

We both fell silent. I began to rummage among the fruit wellies. I offered her one. She took the box and handed it over to Charlie, still absorbed in his paperback. He looked startled and shook his head.

'He's on a diet,' I explained.

She placed the fruit jellies on top of the locker and we fell silent again. When she began fiddling with her watchstrap I asked her if she wanted to leave. She said of course not and asked me if I wanted her to leave. I said why did she have to twist everything. I could hear Charlie thrashing around in his bed like a fish on the rocks.

'I've been told you've lost your job,' she said.

'Don't worry. I'll get anither.'

At this point Charlie threw the paperback down on the cover, leapt from his bed and ran down the ward wearing only a pair of pants under the pyjama top. His legs were surprisingly thin.

'What's wrong with him?' asked Nancy.

'I think it's his gall bladder.'

'That's funny,' she said, looking at me suspiciously. 'I was told this was a psychiatric ward.'

'That, amongst other things,' I said vaguely, looking towards the exit and expecting to see Charlie being escorted back any minute with his feet scarcely touching the ground.

'They said you had drink-related problems.'

'Who said?'

'Is it true?'

I sat up straight and confronted her fierce expression. 'I have ither problems as well. Did they tell ye that?'

Then Maurice the male nurse came over and stared at Charlie's empty bed as though he couldn't believe his eyes. He looked at me and said, 'Are ye all right, pet?' without making any reference to Charlie.

'Sure,' I said, and added, 'I think Charlie's away for a –' I was going to say piss, but hesitated because Nancy hated the word.

'Not to worry,' said Maurice, hurrying off. I hoped that Charlie hadn't blotted his record of docility.

'I'm sorry,' said Nancy, as if chastened by the arrival of the male nurse. 'I can see you are not well.'

I said, 'I might feel better if you came and sat on the edge o' the bed so's I can get a whiff o' yer perfume.'

Shyly she sat on the edge of the bed. We held hands and were very friendly for the remainder of the visit.

Before she left she said, 'I almost forgot about this message I was to give you from Jimmy.' She fumbled in her bag saying, 'I've got it written down somewhere.'

She handed me a scrap of paper. The writing in pencil was not very clear, but I managed to make out the words 'Dad says be prepared for a fresh start. He will contact you at the lodgings.' Under this was the separate scribble of 'A' the best, Jimmy.'

What impressed me most about this note was that there was no mention of any money found, such as my lost wages.

Without any explanation I was discharged two days later. Before I departed Maurice took my blood pressure. 'Just a formality, pet,' he said as he tightened the band on my arm. 'Better to be safe than sorry.'

'Aren't you the lucky one,' said Charlie in a listless way. He was lying flat on his back without a pillow. There were purple rings round his eyes. He looked dazed. It was the first time I had seen him since Nancy's visit.

'Whit happened tae him?' I asked Maurice, who merely shook his head and put a finger to his lips. I shook Charlie's hand before I left and said to him in a jovial manner that I hoped to see him in Donavan's pub the following Friday. This was a pub which he had mentioned frequently in his discourses on the subject of drinking places.

'You bet,' he said in a slurred voice and closed his eyes.

Maurice slapped me playfully on the shoulder. 'Charlie's a good boy,' he said. 'No' like some I could mention.'

9

I was picking up my holdall in the bedroom of the lodging house when Danny crept up behind me. 'Whit are ye daein'?' he asked.

'Collectin' ma gear.'

He grabbed the handle. 'Ye don't collect nothin' until ye pay whit ye owe.'

I shoved his hand aside. 'I'll send the money when I can. I'm skint.'

He grabbed the handle again and I shoved him on to the bed, where he lay reclining on one elbow. When I left the room he shouted on his father, who was waiting at the bottom of the stairs with his arms folded across his chest like something from Stonehenge.

'Take his bag aff him,' shouted Danny from above. 'He owes us money.'

'Whit's in it,' said his father, 'gold?'

'Look,' I said, 'I'm startin' anither site on Monday. I'll send ye the money when I get a wage. I canny dae any better than that.'

'Confiscate his possessions,' said Danny, his breath now heavy on my neck.

'Possessions?' I laughed.

His father told Danny to be quiet and asked me what was in the holdall.

'Holey socks and semmits. Dae ye want a look?'

When I made to unzip it he gestured for me to leave it alone, saying, 'I don't want tae see yer dirty rags, so long as ye've nane o' ma sheets or towels.'

I assured him that I hadn't and asked him to let me past since I had to catch a bus.

'It so happens yer digs have been paid,' he growled.

'Naebody telt me that,' said Danny, shoving his face between me and his father.

As casually as I could I said, 'I suppose it would be auld Dad that paid it. He mentioned something to that effect when I saw him last and I would gie him the money later –'

'Who said it wis Dad?' Danny's father interrupted.

'Who wis it then?'

'There wis an envelope shoved under ma door wi' money in it for yer digs as indicated in the letter, but there wis nae signature.'

To quell his suspicious stare I said, 'I think I know who it wis.' Recalling Dad's cryptic message that I should be prepared for a fresh start, I asked, 'Wis there nothin' else mentioned in the letter?'

'Not a thing, but if ye don't believe me –' he began to say.

'Sure, I believe you,' I said quickly. I was actually more concerned about making a rapid exit from their company than wondering who the benefactor was. I was sure it was Colin Craig, but I had lost interest in his plans. Besides, Nancy was waiting outside.

'I should have been telt aboot this,' said Danny.

'You get through tae the kitchen and attend tae yer chores,' his father said, taking a step towards him. Danny moved quickly out of the lobby with his father following. I paused only long enough to hear the sound of Danny's raised voice, then the noise of something banging, like a pot falling on the floor.

I walked outside, blinking in the sunshine, to where Nancy was leaning against the railings surrounding the grass verge in front of the terraces. She linked her arm through mine in a proprietory manner, as though we were married. She had taken a day off from the office when she learned I had been released from the hospital.

'There was no trouble then?' she said, giving my shabby hold-all a critical glance.

'Why should there be?'

I told her I would have to pay a visit to the labour exchange.

'For another job?'

'For broo money, if I can get it.'

I explained brutally that there was no chance of me getting a job, and not much either of getting money. She might as well take note of the fact that I was a pauper.

'Don't worry,' she said gripping my arm, 'I'll get you a room with my aunt. She's very nice.'

'I canny dae that,' I said.

But she dismissed this with a laugh. 'Of course you can, and the good thing about it is that I can come to your room whenever I want.'

It sounded fine, especially the bit about her coming to the room, but the sudden release from the mental ward had left me depressed. I was crazy about this classy dame, who surprisingly hadn't complained too much about all the trouble I had given her, yet all I wanted at this moment was a pint of beer in a quiet bar where the ashtrays were still fresh from the morning's rub.

'Won't you like that?' she asked.

'Sure,' I said. 'It's the money situation that bothers me.'

'But you'll get some from the labour exchange, surely. No one starves nowadays.'

'I keep forgettin' that.' I gave her a sidelong glance and asked, 'Ye widny like tae buy me a pint o' beer? I've got a terrible thirst. The hospital makes ye awful dehydrated.'

She released my arm, saying, 'You'd better get it straight that from now on it's either me or the pub.'

'Whit kind o' choice is that?' I said meekly, and pulled her arm back through mine. 'Ye know I wis only jokin'.'

There were no jobs to be had in the broo, but I had the promise of a giro from the female clerk amounting to twenty-five pounds plus dig money, which was still to be assessed. I felt like shaking her hand when she informed me that I would get it through the post first thing in the morning.

'I suppose it's better than nothing,' said Nancy, her brow furrowed as though she had expected more.

'So,' I said, 'could ye lend me some money for the digs?'

'Any friend of my niece is a friend of mine,' said the aunt. She was a fat lady with plump smiling cheeks who explained that the room would be twelve pounds a week, including breakfast, and she did not require the money in advance. 'You have an honest face,' she said.

The room she showed us was cosily cluttered with pictures and ornaments and bits of furniture arranged round a high bed which looked as bouncy as a trampoline. There were silver framed photos jammed together on a table by the fireplace and the carpet was the heavy pile type that you sink into. I was afraid to move in case I marked it with my boots or knocked an ornament over with my elbows. I nodded to register approval, though inwardly feeling ill at ease under her fond gaze.

'I'll make you a bite to eat,' she said as I placed my bag gingerly on the bed. I fingered the tenner borrowed from Nancy which her aunt had not required in advance. 'We're jist gaun for a meal.'

Nancy raised her eyebrows in surprise.

'It's ma birthday,' I said.

'Why didn't you tell me?' said Nancy.

'I would have made you something special,' said the aunt.

'There's nae problem,' I said, backing towards the door.

On the way out the aunt followed us to the doorstep and expressed the hope that we would enjoy ourselves, adding wistfully, 'You're only young once.' I felt especially guilty about this, since I had been wondering how I was going to retrieve my bag from her room.

★

The licensed restaurant where we sat studying the menu wasn't my idea of a place to enjoy yourself, with its oak panelling and aspidistra plants, and most of all its steep prices.

'I thought we'd go somewhere special, since it's your birthday,' said Nancy.

'It's the prices –' I began.

'Don't worry,' she said, patting my knee under the table. 'It's my treat.'

Shamefaced, I admitted that it wasn't my birthday and that I had said this to get out of her aunt's house, because, though I thought her aunt was a very nice lady and the room comfortable, the fact was that the place gave me claustrophobia, something I was prone to in certain premises, the reasons for which were unaccountable.

'I see,' she said, looking downcast.

'Cheer up,' I said, returning the pat on the knee, 'we'll kid on it's ma birthday. I'm bound to have one some time.'

The chicken that we ordered was a problem. It slid off the plate when I stuck in the fork, marking the tablecloth. I picked it up with my fingers and told Nancy that this was how the upper crust ate their food, as far as I knew. 'The easiest way possible,' I said with a laugh.

Her eyes were fixed on her plate as she cut her own chicken delicately.

She said, 'There's a napkin on the table if you want to wipe your hands.'

'Thanks,' I said.

'And mouth,' she added.

The waitress returned to ask if we wished for a sweet.

'I didn't even wish for the chicken,' I said, attempting to joke.

'I know what you mean,' she said. 'Chicken can be dodgy at times. You've got to be in the mood for it. But I can definitely recommend the sweet.'

'Well –' I began, looking at Nancy.

'I don't think we'll bother.'

Before she could take out her purse I paid for the meal with the tenner in my pocket and told the waitress to keep the change. 'It's too much,' she said, but I waved this aside. It was fine to act rich for once.

'Last of the big spenders,' said Nancy when we were outside.

I shrugged as I smiled full into her face. 'I must say I enjoyed that chicken.'

'No you didn't,' she said. 'But since it's your birthday I'll buy a drink. I know you'll like that.'

'But it's no' ma birthday.'

'You're bound to have one some time.'

We walked along the street arm in arm and stopped outside a close tiled in the corporation style of white with blue borders, though the tiles were cracked. The place was very quiet.

'Do ye think I could get a wee smooch in here to be gaun on wi'?' I asked.

She nodded shyly and I led her by the hand up to the first landing. We made love in the corner of this landing in such a still and furtive way that it would have been hard to prove, apart from our painful and heavy breathing. But there's always someone who can see through a situation. A female voice called from above, 'If ye don't get away frae this decent close I'll get the polis.'

Giggling but embarrassed we scurried down the stairs. Outside, Nancy said, her face flushed, 'Where should we go for a drink? It's your choice.'

I couldn't think where to go that would be suitable. I knew hardly any pubs apart from The Open Door, which was about the worst place to take any dame. Then I thought, why not? It was my choice, but more important it was an opportunity to see McLerie and enquire about the fresh start, if there was such a thing. Anyway, there was no harm in trying.

'I know a place,' I said. 'It's no' very nice, but there's a guy goes there who's startin' up his ain business. There's maybe a post in it for me.'

'It's as good a reason as any,' said Nancy, linking my arm.

'This place is a ruin,' she said when we stood facing The Open Door.

'I'll admit it's a mess, but it's better inside.' I shoved the door but it refused to budge.

'It's definitely closed,' said Nancy.

'I think the hinges are stiff.'

I gave it some heavy kicks and it swung open with the lock dangling.

'You shouldn't have done that,' said Nancy. 'The place was locked.'

'Maybe,' I said vaguely and walked straight through into the poky drinking quarters. There was no one about and the air was chilled as if there had been no one about for some time. Most of the glasses were gone apart from a few extremely dulled ones on the shelves standing alongside the Red Hackle bottles, which turned out to be empty.

'This place is disgusting,' said Nancy.

'Ye're right, but we might as well look around while we're here.'

Whistling to convey that I wasn't daunted by all this, I entered the back room with Nancy close at my heels. The cupboard door swung open. The shelves inside were bare, apart from an old newspaper lying on the top one. I brought it out to have a look at the date. It might give me a clue as to when Craig and his pals were last here. Then something scuttled under the sink with the verdigris tap and Nancy gave a shriek.

'It's only a moose or a rat,' I said, throwing down the paper. She now moaned with fear. On my knees, I peered into the corner, but the rodent had vanished. All I found was a cloth stiff with age next to a bottle, which I took out and discovered to be half full of gin, according to the label.

'Look,' I said, holding it up as though I'd won a prize.

Nancy wrinkled her nose. 'What is it? Weedkiller?'

'I'll soon find oot.'

I fetched two tumblers from the bar and washed them under the verdigris tap. 'Will ye be wantin' some if it's gin?' I asked her.

'I might, if there's orange.'

I gave a mock sigh of despair and told her, after taking a deep sniff at the contents of the bottle, that it was gin, but she would have to take it with water as there was no orange.

She smiled. 'Whatever you say.'

'There's one thing aboot this pub,' I said, 'it's quiet enough.'

'And the drink's cheap, too.'

I spread out the newspaper to cover the dust on the table and poured the drink, adding a suitable amount of water. We sat facing each other sombrely as we sipped the gin. I decided I would be a fool not to take the room with Nancy's aunt. It looked as though the birds here had flown the coop. There was no point in trying to chase shadows.

'The only thing missing now,' said Nancy, as though she could read my mind, 'is the man with the job.'

'Ye canny have everythin'.'

I was about to kiss her and tell her that my claustrophobia might not be as bad as I thought and that I was going to take her aunt's room, when I spilled some gin on top of the newspaper. As I glanced at the mark a headline caught my eye. It read: LIFE AS NATURE INTENDED. But what really riveted me was the photograph of the guy underneath called Major A.R. Burns, who was the living spit of Colin Craig, even to the handlebar moustache. I hurriedly read the article. It stated that this Major Burns was the leader of a group called Lifeline, who intended to live in the northern wilderness as close to nature as they could. 'Free from the shackles of civilisation' was the quote. I pondered on this for a while and decided that the guy's resemblance to Craig was no coincidence; neither were the initials A.R.B. that I had noticed on Craig's wallet on the day of the peace festival. It was Craig. It all fitted: the business he was about to start, the abandoned pub, and now the group called Lifeline. I could have been part of it if I had waited on at the lodgings for Dad's message.

'What's the matter?' Nancy asked.

I showed her the paper, indicating the article and the photograph. 'That's the guy who wis gaun tae gie me a job,' I said.

'He looks nice, like someone I've seen somewhere.'

'I widny be surprised if he's part o' some spy ring.'

'You'd take a job with a spy ring?' she said, surprised.

'If the money's good enough.'

I was joking about the spy ring, but I suspected something shady was going on with Dad, McLerie and Craig. I'd have been a fool not to, considering all that had happened since I'd encountered Craig. For instance, getting arrested for only being drunk and tossed into a local institution, then released without explanation as if I was being held pending enquiries. Then Danny had let slip about the police watching the digs. Who were they watching, me or Dad, or just anyone? Yet at the same time I was interested. It was as though the article had been written solely for me. Hadn't Craig said that my life was more likely to alter if I did something about it, rather than waiting passively for something to happen? Here was the challenge.

'Actually,' I said to Nancy, 'this guy's a mate o' mine. He's a real gentleman. It's a great pity I didny catch him afore he left the district.'

'I'm surprised he chose to drink in here if he's such a gentleman,' said Nancy, looking around disdainfully.

'It wis jist a meetin' place. Folk like him don't need tae be seen in fancy places.'

I don't know why I was trying to convince Nancy how great the man was when the signs about this were doubtful.

There was a long pause before she said, 'Perhaps you should go to that place and see him, if it means so much.'

'Did I say it meant so much?'

She didn't answer. She merely took a sip of her gin, then stared at her glass.

'Anyway,' I said, 'dae ye think I'd want tae leave you?'

'And there's my aunt's room,' she pointed out.

'I know.'

We fell silent, then we both spoke at the same time. We began to laugh.

'Whit were ye gaun tae say?' I asked.

'I suppose you can't give up the chance so easily,' said Nancy.

'Whit chance?'

'I thought you said this man had work for you?'

'That's true,' I said. I wondered now if it was true. I tried to remember Craig's exact words about getting me fixed up. I said to Nancy, 'I could definitely get a job. So dae ye think I should go up tae that place –' I peered into the newspaper – 'Langholm Valley, that's whit it's called?'

'How would you get there?' asked Nancy, sadly.

'Hitch-hike, I suppose.'

I lapsed into silence again while I calculated how far I would get on the twenty-five pounds giro plus the dig money to be sent care of Nancy's aunt, less the ten pounds I owed Nancy.

'If you go,' said Nancy, 'I might never see you again.'

'Of course you will,' I said. 'Dae ye think I'd be gone forever?'

'And if there's no job . . . what if it's a wild goose chase?'

I smiled. 'A wild goose chase? I like the sound o' chasin' the wild geese.' I became serious. 'I honestly don't know whit I'd dae if there's nae job.'

'There you are,' she said. 'You don't know what would happen, so I'd likely not see you again.'

'Anyway, I've changed ma mind. I'm no' gaun.'

I poured out the last of the gin into each of our glasses and stared ahead morosely. What a fool I was to talk about going anywhere in the impoverished state I was in. Then she said, suddenly excited, 'Do you know, I've got a brilliant idea?'

'Whit's that?'

'I could take my holidays now from the office and come with you.' I stared at her open-mouthed as she continued. 'It could be a camping holiday, and at the same time we could travel up to that place you mentioned.'

'Langholm Valley.'

'That's right. I know where I could borrow a tent and sleeping bags as well as a stove and pots. We would be killing two birds with the one stone, and I've always wanted to go camping.'

'But,' I said, taken aback now that a definite decision was being made, 'ye know whit they say?'

'What?' she asked, slightly breathless.

'He travels fastest who travels alone.'

She shook her head impatiently and went on to tell me of the arrangements she would have to make with her boss in the office, her parents and her aunt, and some other relatives she'd never mentioned before. I felt vaguely uneasy, but glad in a way it was all being settled for me.

10

We stepped down from the train, Nancy and I, at the end of the line, at a place called Grinstone, along with another solitary passenger who shot through the barrier while we fumbled for our tickets. The air was damp and cold, like the look on the collector's face when he let us pass.

We dumped our rucksacks on a wooden bench and I muttered under my breath, 'Welcome to sunny Grinstone,' feeling depressed.

'I wonder where the ladies' room is,' said Nancy.

'Ask the collector.' When we looked round he had vanished.

'Don't tell me it's raining,' said Nancy, mystified and holding out her hand.

'It's wet whatever it is,' I said, studying my damp packet of fags.

Nancy said she was hungry and began to loosen the belt of her rucksack. I told her to leave it meanwhile, since the food was at the bottom. 'Yes, sir,' she said, with narrowed eyes.

I told her if she was going to be awkward there was no point in going on, even though we had just newly arrived.

Her lips quivered. 'Do you want me to go back?'

'I'm only askin' ye tae be reasonable.'

'I am being reasonable. I'm hungry. What's unreasonable about that?'

To placate her I said that we would buy pies and ginger when we reached the first shop.

We came to a church, a school, and a row of cottages.

'Where's the shop?'

I didn't answer. I was looking for a pub or a hotel.

'What's that?' said Nancy as we passed what seemed to be a cottage with a notice in the window, which on closer inspection read: 'Licensed to sell Beer and Spirits'. I dumped my baggage on the pavement and told Nancy to wait while I investigated. I tripped down three stairs into a dim room with low rafters, which appeared to be the style of the northern drinking dens. The barman, who was polishing the counter, looked up startled. Two old guys came out from the shadows.

'Is it OK to bring the girlfriend in here?' I asked.

'Why not,' said the barman. He was the broad and burly type, like the proverbial village blacksmith. The old guys nodded approvingly.

'Meanwhile, I'll have a pint,' I said.

I enquired if there was a bus that went anywhere near a place called Langholm Valley. He informed me that there was no bus that went near anywhere. One of the guys said, 'Farlane McFarlane might take you as far as the Auchenachen Inn, which is about halfway, but he'll be doing his milk round at present and will not be back for maybe two hours.'

'Halfway is better than nothin',' I said. 'Where can I reach him?'

'His house is the last one in the street with the milk-for-sale notice in the window.'

Nancy entered, looking agitated. The barman's face lit up and the old guys moved in closer. She informed me in a loud voice that she had decided to go back home on the next train.

'How's that?' I asked, aware of the old guys tutting and the barman leaning over his counter with arms folded.

'You left me alone in a strange place while you went drinking.'

'You knew I wisny far away.'

'I felt such a fool standing on the pavement with two rucksacks.'

'Where are the rucksacks?'

'On the pavement, where I left them.'

'For Christ's sake,' I said, 'they'll get stolen.'

'Don't worry,' said the barman who was looking to and fro from me to Nancy, 'there's no demand here for rucksacks.'

'And I'm absolutely starving,' said Nancy, catching her breath pathetically.

'Now, now,' said the barman in sympathy, 'I can let you have tea and sandwiches if it so pleases you.'

She clapped her hands in a childish way. 'That would be wonderful.'

The old guys smiled and nodded. I cleared my throat and asked if I could have some too.

We consumed thick beef sandwiches under the speculative gaze of the old guys and the barman, who had tossed his duster aside to concentrate his attention on Nancy. She munched her bread and drank her lager apparently unaware of the tension around her. A crumb stuck in my throat. I coughed and gasped for breath and thought I was going to die while they all watched. The panic subsided and I wiped the water from my eyes.

'Did you choke on something?' she asked.

I became unjustifiably angry. 'Hurry up,' I said, 'we're leavin'.'

The barman refused money for the meal. 'It was my pleasure,' he said, his eyes still on Nancy. She blushed and wiped her mouth, now looking embarrassed out of all proportion to his remark. I threw some silver down and brusquely told her to move. The old guys shrank back. One of them called, 'McFarlane should take you to the Auchenachen Inn with no bother. The owner is a fine figure of a woman and he always likes the excuse for a visit – that is, if he is not attending to his cows.'

McFarlane's house was easy to find, displaying the milk-for-sale notice in the window. His wife, a straw-haired woman as thin as a rake, told us that he wasn't home. She added, 'He's likely at the Auchenachen Inn visiting that black-haired besom Jessie

Broden, so he could be there all day,' and slammed the door in our faces.

'We'll wait anyway,' I said to Nancy.

Two hours later we were bumping along a rough track in Farlane McFarlane's milk van, skirting close to a steep cliff. I had told this sandy-haired guy that we wanted to reach Langholm Valley, and explained that according to the newspapers a group of folk were about to develop the land in this area. Casually I asked if he had heard about it. He shook his head and said, 'Ach, the newspapers.' I kept quiet after that, since I didn't want to distract his attention from the abyss of rock falling away before us at every bend. Besides, Nancy's grip on my arm was painful.

'It's a bit rough,' McFarlane shouted above the rattle of his van, 'but it's a short cut. I don't like to leave the wife too long on her own.'

When we came to a main road he slowed down as long as it takes to draw a breath, then he was off again like a rocket, but at least it was a less nerve-wracking journey. Soon we were drawing up outside the Auchenachen Inn. Against the backdrop of gloomy hills this solid white building with its latticed windows and patio surrounds looked like an optical illusion. The rusty motor lying adjacent to the pub was another incongruous touch. We had scarcely picked up our rucksacks from the back of McFarlane's milk van before he was away, the dust flying behind him. Maybe he had his cows to attend to.

The lounge inside was spacious, with pale plastic divans placed round glass-topped tables and scores of tumblers hanging from the roof. A dark-haired female was leaning over the bar reading a magazine – no doubt the dreaded Jessie Broden. She looked up startled when I coughed. She touched her throat.

'In the name o' God, where did you come from?'

I explained that Farlane McFarlane had dropped us off in his milk van.

'Isn't he the civil one?' she said.

'I was wonderin' –' I began, looking around doubtfully. The room was empty apart from the three of us.

'We're open,' she said, 'if that's what you are wondering.' She added with a throaty chuckle, 'Come to think of it, we're always open.'

Although she was too plump and old for me, I could understand what McFarlane saw in her. The look in her eye alone was distracting.

Nancy whispered in my ear, 'Ask her if we're far from Langholm Valley.'

'Gie us a chance,' I said under my breath.

'I would say,' said Jessie Broden, 'it's about four hours to Langholm Valley by car, and four days by foot.' She added sympathetically, 'I suppose you'll be hiking it.'

'We might as well stop for a bit then,' I said, and turned to Nancy. 'We could get a drink and something to eat.'

Nancy said angrily, 'We've had that already.'

As though she hadn't heard this Jessie Broden said, 'At the moment I've only got some soup left over from yesterday, but it's always better the second day anyway.'

'It's much too hot for soup,' Nancy retorted, but the woman was out of the bar and calling for two platefuls.

We supped this at one of the glass-topped tables with red faces, on account of the hot meal and the drawing of a naked woman in the depth of an ashtray lying between us which strongly resembled the hostess.

'I can't swallow any more of this,' said Nancy letting soup from her spoon trickle back to the plate.

'Right,' I said, and explained to Jessie Broden that we would have to leave if the journey was as far as she had indicated.

'You're not thinking of starting off already?' she said, and suggested that we should camp at the river nearby, adding, 'And you can come back later when the place is busy. Someone might give you a lift. Forbye that we'll be having a cheery sing-song.'

'I don't think so,' said Nancy, tossing her head as she walked out.

Jessie said consolingly, 'It's the heat. We're not used to it.'

'I didn't like the look of that woman,' said Nancy when we were erecting the tent. 'She looked as if she could eat you. I bet she's man mad.'

I ignored this statement and told her that she wasn't driving the pegs in hard enough.

'And she looks forty if she's a day,' Nancy went on.

I frowned at the sight of clothing spread over the grass. Already the place looked like a tinker's camp.

'Leave the pegs and get some water from that stream,' I said, pointing vaguely in its direction.

'Anything else?' she asked threateningly.

'Try and keep the place tidy.'

'I refuse to be ordered about like a servant,' she said. 'You've been bossing me about ever since we got off the train.'

'An' you've moaned every inch o' the way.'

'Another thing,' she said. 'You're always heading for pubs.'

'There's nothin' else tae head for. Besides, so far I've only had two pints of beer.'

'If you had your way it would be a lot more.'

I picked up the hammer she had flung on the ground and started to go over the loose pegs. She lifted up a pot and headed for the stream. After the pegs were fixed and all the articles were arranged neatly inside the tent, I sat cross-legged scanning the ridge of hills confronting me, where sheep moved slowly like lice on a shaved head. I wasn't exactly entranced, but I thought that in time I might get to like the view. At the moment it unnerved me. I wondered why Nancy was taking so long with the water. Possibly she was wandering about gathering wild flowers, which are only weeds. I've seen dames do this sometimes when I've been trying to sleep off the booze on a hillside in the warm weather.

If they see you they panic because they think you're either a flasher or a rapist. It's not possible for them to think you're only wanting to sleep. You can't blame them, though, for being like this because it happens now and again. On their own they've no chance against some kinky guy. I guess that's why they can never be equal. They're too weak. Even a kinky dame is no match for a kinky guy. I became worried. Where the hell was Nancy? She had been in a reckless mood when she left. I jumped up and ran through the tough grass shouting her name. It echoed back to me eerily. I was dragging my legs towards the stream, weighed down with anxiety, when she sprang out from a bush holding up a bunch of heather.

'I was trying to get lucky,' she said.

I grabbed her shoulders. 'You stupid dame. I thought you wir a goner.'

'You mean you hoped I was.'

'Throw that stuff away, and come back tae the tent and I'll gie ye somethin' that's luckier.'

Afterwards when we sat outside the tent watching, as if bemused, two eggs boil inside a pot on top of the primus stove, I chanced to suggest that we take a jaunt over to the inn to celebrate.

'Celebrate what?' Her voice was edgy.

'Our first day and that?'

'I'm tired.'

'Jist for a wee while. We'll come back early.'

'Why is it,' she said sadly, 'that you're always wanting to enter a pub? Isn't it much nicer to stay here and see all this?'

'Sure,' I said, 'I think it's great, but it can get monotonous, especially when the sun goes doon.'

Her face became set. 'I'm not going, especially to see that woman ogling.'

'Whit dae ye mean – ogling?'

'You know what I mean. I suppose that's why you're going.'

'Christ's sake, I wis gaun for the sing-song. As you say, that woman's forty if she's a day. Dae ye think I'd fancy a dame o' forty?'

She turned away and scooped the eggs from the pot with a spoon. White blobs had burst through the shell. She placed them on the grass. Her face was tragic. 'I hate sing-songs,' she said.

'I think ye are a snob,' I said. 'Ye don't like anythin' except maybe staring at the scenery. When we leave this place we might no' see anyone for days. Whit's wrang wi' a sing-song?'

In answer to this she stood up and tossed the eggs into the long grass, then crawled into the tent, pulling the flaps together behind her.

I stood at a corner of the bar swirling two inches of beer around my tumbler. The place was busy. On the way in I had passed a variety of vehicles, including Farlane McFarlane's milk van, but at this moment there was no sign of him. Hefty farmer types were holding up the counter. Their womenfolk sat at the glass-topped tables playing cards. They wore loose print dresses like the kind my mother buys from Oxfam, but their fingers glittered with diamonds.

A voice spoke in my ear, 'It's yourself, is it?' I turned to face Farlane McFarlane. He looked beyond me to where Jessie Broden was conversing with some guys. Their eyes were fixed on the neck of her low-cut dress.

'I was chust saying,' said McFarlane when she came over to serve him, 'that it's himself, the one I gave the lift to.'

'You mean,' she said, giving me a bold stare, 'the one who is camping with his wife.'

'She's no' ma wife,' I said.

She raised her eyebrows, 'Fancy.'

'I wouldn't mind a bit of camping myself,' said McFarlane, after he had ordered a pint for both of us, which I thought was decent of him, 'if I could find a nice wee woman to share the blankets with.'

'I'd have thought,' said Jessie, her elbow on the counter and her face close to his, 'that you'd be all played out milking your cows.'

McFarlane stated, 'Right enough. It's a terrible profession I have for putting thoughts into your head.' He stared at Jessie's chest over his tumbler.

She said, tapping my arm but addressing McFarlane, 'You'll be putting ideas into this lad's head.'

'He'll have all the ideas there already,' said McFarlane.

'No' me,' I said, feeling self-conscious.

Jessie shrugged and moved away to serve, her hips shaking like blancmange. Furtively McFarlane brought out a half bottle of whisky from his inside pocket. 'Be quick with your beer and I'll pour some of this in before she spots it.'

I thanked him sincerely and explained that I wouldn't be stopping long. 'It's the girlfriend,' I said, 'she's no' keen on the drink.'

'They never are,' he said. 'That's why we do so much of it. If my wife kept a bottle in the sideboard at home it would save me the bother of leaving.' As Jessie wobbled past our line of vision he added, 'On the other hand, there's something to be said for the company.'

Jessie turned back to us to say, 'If that's you drinking from your own bottle, McFarlane, you'll be out quicker than you can say your name.'

'You wouldn't be doing that to a man who's on the brink of a divorce,' he said quickly.

'Divorce – on what grounds?'

'On the grounds that my wife has gone off her head and soon will be entering an asylum.' He openly splashed more whisky into our tumblers. 'I'll be in sole charge of the milk round, which is doing very nicely.'

Jessie's eyes widened. 'You don't say.'

'Is that true?' I asked when she had moved off again. 'That your wife is gaun tae the looney bin?'

McFarlane sighed. 'Unfortunately no'. Actually, I'm a desperate man, with her being as hard and plain as a plank of wood and three of my cows dying with what might be the foot and mouth. But so long as Jessie thinks my prospects are good I'll be all right for the night, if you know what I mean.'

I was annoyed by his lascivious expression. I thought he had no right to have it at his age, when there were better fish in the sea, such as myself – not that I fancied Jessie, but in my opinion she deserved better than McFarlane, even in a temporary way.

I said, 'And bein' the owner here would be a great chance.'

'Indeed so.'

At this stage the whisky must have inflamed my brain. I considered asking Jessie for a job as a barman or anything else that was needed. Apart from the occasional drink on the side, it might lead to better things, like becoming her business partner. I even visualised Nancy installed as a waitress and my mother in the kitchen baking scones, which goes to show how drunk I was even if I didn't feel it. My mother has never baked a scone in her life as far as I know. When Jessie came back and reached out for the empty tumblers I grabbed her wrist and asked her for a kiss. With her free hand she slapped me and told me to get going. The farmer types and their womenfolk, who had been squawking like their hens, went quiet and stared over. McFarlane broke the silence by saying in a loud and pompous voice, 'I'd advise you to clear off this minute, since we're not the kind of people who allow our women to be molested by strangers.'

'Well spoken, McFarlane,' shouted a florid-faced guy. 'Dae ye need a haun' wi' the rascal?'

I held up my hands as though somebody had pulled a gun on me, but it was only in placation. 'OK,' I said, 'there'll be nae trouble. I'm leavin',' and walked out backwards. Outside I sat on the step of the rusty motor with my head in my hands, wondering how to reach the tent. The sky was pitch black.

★

I awoke to face a grey dawn shining through the canvas and Nancy standing over me holding out a mug of tea. 'I've got everything packed,' she said, 'except the tent.'

I sat up shivering, with nothing to cover me and only the cold touch of the groundsheet under me. 'I think I've got the flu.'

Nancy said, 'Hurry up and get up. I want to undo the pegs.'

Like a sick dog I crawled outside on my hands and knees a minute before the tent collapsed. I said that I felt terrible. 'Get out of my way,' she said. 'I'll need to fold up the tent.' I sat helpless while she did so.

As we walked past the Auchenachen Inn, with Nancy in the lead, I stopped to stare at Farlane McFarlane's milk van standing alongside the old rusty motor. My eyes travelled up to a latticed window where a light still shone.

Nancy looked back. 'Are you expecting a wave?' she asked sarcastically.

'No' really,' I said.

'Hurry up, then. I want to get away from that inn before it opens.'

I caught up with her and began to feel better. The nip from the early morning frost was clearing my head. 'I'm sorry aboot last night,' I said.

'We won't talk about it,' she said stiffly, but she let me kiss her on the cheek anyway.

'Things could be worse,' I said, thinking about Farlane McFarlane, with his wife as plain as a plank of wood and his fancy woman who was only crazy about his prospects, and him with his cows having what might be the foot and mouth.

Our progress was slow after we left Grinstone, mainly because we had wasted time trying to thumb lifts from drivers who passed on blindly.

Nancy said, 'You'd be the same yourself if you had a car.'

'I wouldny pass anyone hikin' through this wilderness. They're jist pure bastards.'

The sun had come out in full blast. We were just about ready to drop when we came to a farm track with a notice pinned to a tree reading: 'Eggs for Sale'.

'Should we get some?' asked Nancy.

'If you like.' A blue Cortina zoomed by as we threw down our rucksacks. 'We might have got a lift,' moaned Nancy, her face red and sweaty. I told her to sit beside me and rest against the rucksacks.

'People might see us,' she said. We sat so close to each other we were nearly welded together with the heat. I stopped her protests with a kiss and we hurriedly made love on the grass verge, whilst remaining alert for traffic.

'It was hardly worth it,' she said afterwards, lying on her back with her eyes screwed up at the sun.

'It's always worth it.'

'What about the eggs?'

'They would cook inside their shells. Jist leave them.'

We walked on for an hour too exhausted to speak. Finally Nancy said, 'Let's stop or I'll collapse.'

'It makes it worse if we stop a' the time.'

'I don't care. I can't go on.'

'Look,' I said, pointing to a circle of trees in the distance, 'we'll stop there.'

'But it's miles away, and all uphill.'

'After that it'll be downhill. We'll make some tea,' I promised.

We climbed up and down and through a field of thorns to reach the river. The good thing about this wilderness was there were plenty of rivers. Nancy picked her way through the nettles with furrowed brow. 'You always take the worst paths.'

We sat on the riverbank gazing serenely ahead, drinking tea from the flowered mugs provided by the aunt.

'The mountains are so peaceful,' she said.

'You mean hills.'

'Whatever they are, they're peaceful. I could stay here forever.'

She stretched out flat and put her arms behind her head. I hoped she wouldn't sleep. I wanted to reach a less desolate area. I moved over and peered into the side of the river.

'Come and see the shoals of young fish.'

'I can't be bothered.'

The words had scarcely left her lips when she jumped to her feet screaming, 'I've been bit. I've been bit. I'm being bit everywhere.'

I ran towards her and was immediately stung on the side of the neck.

'Clegs,' I yelled.

We ran through the thorns back up the hill, trailing our rucksacks behind us with the clegs hot on our trail. Strangely enough they faded away when we reached the road. A few tardy ones stuck to our arms, still gorging. 'Let them take their fill,' I said, 'otherwise they'll bite.'

'I've been bit everywhere as it is,' wailed Nancy. 'I think I'm going to die.'

Eventually we got rid of them and Nancy asked me what the symptoms of blood poisoning were.

'Don't worry,' I said, 'yer blood's too fresh to get poisoned.'

'Are you sure?' she asked, staring at me through puffy eyes. She had lumps all over her face.

'Sure I'm sure.' I felt her burning forehead. 'You'll be OK. The best thing to make sure is to start walking and get the blood circulating.'

'Just when we were so happy,' she said.

By the time we reached the ruins of an old cottage our wounds were less painful. Two youths, nattily dressed in white tee-shirts and khaki shorts, leaned against a broken piece of wall drinking Coke. The green nylon haversacks lying at their feet looked like a dream. They were both fair-haired, as if related, and one of them had a beard. He asked us if we had come far.

'Far enough.' I stared at his can hoping he would offer us some Coke, but he finished it off and threw it behind him. The other one asked us jokingly if we had caught the plague.

'We were attacked by clegs,' said Nancy. She held out her arms for inspection.

'That's a shame.'

'Absolutely rotten,' said the bearded one.

I wasn't impressed by their style and their polite accents, and I didn't miss their sly glances towards each other. I told them that we'd have to keep moving since we were in a hurry to reach a certain destination.

'Wait a minute,' said one of them. 'We've got ointment that's good for cleg bites.' He rummaged in his haversack and brought out a wee tube, which he handed over to Nancy.

'Thanks a million,' she said.

I noticed they watched her intently rubbing the stuff on her neck and arms.

'You're definitely good Samaritans,' she said.

The one with the beard nudged his pal and said, 'We always like to give a helping hand, don't we Frank?' The other one grinned and winked. I refused their ointment and told Nancy to get moving.

'Already?' she said, regarding me with annoyance. She had taken off her rucksack.

'Aye, already.'

'Don't go, darling,' said the one called Frank. 'Stay with us and have fun.' They both giggled unpleasantly. I was surprised at their gall and thought they must be having some kind of trip when they were so sure of themselves.

Nancy looked at them doubtfully, then said to me, 'We'll go then.'

When she lifted up her rucksack the bearded one took it off her saying, 'Don't go if you don't want to.' His eyes flickered towards me as he added, 'We'll take care of him, won't we Frank?'

They both took a step towards us. Frank raised his arm holding the Coke can. I got the impression it was still heavy with Coke and good for a hefty blow to the head. The only thing I could do was to make a run towards them, like a bull on the rampage, with my rucksack still on my back. Frank's Coke can went flying as I landed on top of him. The other one ran off. Nancy was shouting, 'Leave him alone!', to whom I wasn't sure, but she pulled the rucksack off my back. I rose to my feet taking Frank along with me, then I placed him against the broken wall and slapped the dust from his tee-shirt and shorts. They were not so natty any more. He was crying with rage. I beckoned on the bearded one standing some yards away to come and join us, but he shook his head.

'Whit did ye have tae dae that for?' I asked the Frank guy, who was now rubbing his eyes with his fist and making a right dirty mess of them.

'It was him,' he snivelled, pointing to his friend in the distance, 'he's always egging me on to do things.'

'That's a shame,' I said, as I emptied out the contents of their blissfully light haversacks lying against the wall. Inside there were only some lightweight groceries and a flimsy box, which could have been anything from dope to French letters. I didn't investigate. I jumped on them for a bit, then crushed the mess under my heel. 'Let this be a lesson,' I said as I departed.

'Filthy wee creeps,' said Nancy when I caught up with her.

'It's a' your fault.'

'My fault?'

'Ye should never throw yersel' intae a situation withoot thinkin'. Ye've always got tae be wary o' strangers in lonely places.'

'Why should I be when I've got you to protect me?' she said snappily.

'That's true, but I'm no' Superman. They might have been bigger and had weapons.'

For a while she was silent as we tramped on, then she said, 'Do you know what I think?'

'Whit?'

'I think you're an insufferable prig.'

It was late afternoon and we were standing on a cliff top. We gazed down into a span of water that stretched as far as the eye could see. We tossed off our rucksacks and lay flat on our stomachs in order to view it better. Big white waves were dashing against the rocks below us and everywhere there were seagulls – hundreds of them, rising and swooping and perching on ledges in the cliff. Their cries were sad and eerie.

'I wish there was a beach where we could sunbathe,' said Nancy.

'That would spoil everythin'. It's no' a holiday resort. It's a lonely, wild place. You could call it untamed. Look at these waves. They must be nearly ten feet high.'

'It gives me the shivers.'

I pointed to an area of shingle between the rocks. 'I bet there's a cave doon there and there's bound to be plenty o' seagulls' eggs.'

'I don't fancy seagulls' eggs.'

'That's because ye've never tasted them.'

'I don't want to taste seagulls' eggs. You'll slip and get killed. I'll be left here alone.'

'Don't be daft,' I said, and was over the cliff before she could protest. A few minutes later her voice drifted faintly on the air, then faded under the roar of the waves. Slowly I descended backwards, placing my feet into grooves in the rock. I was alarmed by the whish of seagulls' wings close to my head as they screamed at me, but for the sake of the challenge I forced myself downwards and reached the shingle, which was covered in ice-cold water. There is not much you can do when standing with wet feet on a patch of gravel with a circumference of about three yards facing an opening in the rock, other than enter it and advance a few steps. I found it difficult to continue since I appeared to have entered a black hole that smelled poisonous. I put out my hands to feel my way and touched something wet and scaly. Reason told me it was fungus or seaweed, but still I was shot through with a strong urge to retreat back to the shingle. I had remembered the tale of the legendary cannibal caveman Sonny Bean. I backed off in panic. Outside the seagulls perched on ledges followed me with their pebbly eyes. I scrambled past them expecting the thrust of their beaks any second, but they kept their heads better than I did. I could almost feel their scorn as I clumsily pulled myself upwards. I reached the top panting and breathless and threw myself down on the grass, exhausted.

'Where are the seagulls' eggs?' asked Nancy, the bottom of her jeans on a level with my face.

'Still in their nests. Actually there wis nothin' much tae see doon there.'

'Didn't you hear me shouting about that warning over there?'

I raised my head to follow the direction of her finger pointing to a notice which read: DANGER – EARTH LIABLE TO SUBSIDENCE.

'How come I never seen that?'

'Because you never took the time to see anything. I tried to warn you. Didn't I say that you'd get killed?'

'But I never,' I said defiantly, trying to erase the thought of being buried alive under a ton of rock.

Nancy said, 'Now who's throwing himself into situations?'

'I always know whit I'm daein',' I replied.

We were on a long stretch of road, flanked on one side by flat grassland and on the other by a monotonous line of hills. The clouds were gathering and there was no sign of shelter. My back ached under the weight of the rucksack. Nancy was humming under her breath, but then her rucksack was lighter than mine and she'd had a good rest during the time I had climbed down the rocks.

'Looks like rain,' I said.

'We'd better put up the tent before it starts.'

'It's too boggy here. We'll have to keep goin'.'

'This bit looks dry enough,' she said, stamping on a grassy mound.

'It's too near the road.'

'Are you expecting a camping site somewhere?' she asked heavily.

I said that I wasn't but I didn't believe in camping in a place without shelter where the tent would be flattened by a heavy downpour. She said that she was willing to take the risk since there appeared to be no end to the dismal view ahead, but if I wanted shelter there was something which looked like an old castle lying on the slope of the hill that she had been watching for the past ten minutes.

'Ye might have mentioned it sooner,' I said.

It was only the shell of a castle without a roof. Inside the circle of stone there was grass and sheep dung.

'At least it's shelter,' said Nancy.

I thought if the stone collapsed it would be oblivion, but it was pointless to worry about everything. Already spots of rain were falling.

'OK,' I said.

Soon we were huddled inside the tent. Sausages were sizzling in the frying pan on top of the primus. It was warm and cosy. The light from the lamp hanging on top of the tent pole shone on Nancy's face. It was unusually serene. I wanted to hug her, but I might have spoiled the effect.

Quietly I said, 'I wish we could stay here forever like this.'

'Like what?'

'You and me, snug as a bug frae the rain. Nothin' to worry aboot apart frae burnin' the sausages.'

'Don't be daft. I could think of nothing worse than to stay here forever,' she said, her face still serene.

12

We might have passed the place altogether if a lorry hadn't slid out from an entrance hidden by shrubbery. Being curious we wandered a few yards down a woodland path, where everything shimmered in the heat trapped within the trees. The birds were going crazy with their shrill songs. I thought I could feel some kind of magic here. I always feel this in woods or old estates. It's something to do with the smell of leaf mould.

'We could be trespassing,' said Nancy.

'We could be. I wish I had a knife so I could carve oor initials on a tree to mark that we were here.'

'What a funny notion.'

We moved along the path on tiptoe, though I don't know why. Our steps were soundless in the grass. We came to a big house, grimy with age but grand with its turreted roof and engraved doorway.

'It's definitely private property,' Nancy whispered.

'But it's empty.' I pointed to the blank windows, then to the sunken garden where flowers grew alongside weeds and tall grass, then to the rhododendron bushes.

'Let's go back,' she said.

Ignoring this, I went round to the rear of the house, which was cold in the shade and neglected looking. I peered through a window into what appeared to be a kitchen with a sink and cooking range. Two filled canvas bags rested against a wall. When Nancy asked me if there were signs of anybody about, I told her with a meaningful stare, 'No' for miles.'

'I hope not,' she said, smiling weakly.

We sank down in the long grass and made love slowly and expertly, as though we had been doing it for years.

Afterwards a thought occurred to me: 'Whit if ye get pregnant?'

'I'm on the pill,' she said.

I said, 'Thank goodness,' but my sentiment wasn't altogether genuine.

We walked to the other side of the building and came to what might have been a vegetable patch, though there were no vegetables that I could see, only rhubarb growing near a shed. I threw away my fag end and idly followed its direction with my eyes. It had landed near a boot protruding from the shed, scuffed, but with a modern plastic sole. I investigated to see if there was another one to match it and discovered a guy sitting on the floor of the shed with one leg stretched out and the other bent beneath him.

'I wis jist lookin' aboot,' I said. 'I thought the place was deserted.'

'That's a' richt.' He stood up and I saw he was roughly dressed, which meant that his gear was worse than mine. 'So long as ye're no' wan o' them snoopers,' he added.

I gave him a fag and explained that I was hiking around the country with my girlfriend. At this point Nancy peered in the hut and asked what I was doing. When she saw the guy she quickly withdrew. He stubbed out the fag after taking only one draw and placed it behind his ear, then started to tie up a canvas bag, similar to the ones I had seen in the kitchen, with a piece of string.

'Scrap,' he explained.

'Scrap?' I repeated. 'Is there much o' it aboot?'

He gave me a direct look. His eyes were the blue shade you associate with sailors and other guys who are continually exposed to the elements. I decided he was one of the travelling folk, in other words a tinker.

He said, 'Sometimes ma brither and me gets lucky. Sometimes no'.'

'Wis that yer brither in the lorry?'

'Very probable.'

'I wouldny mind bein' in that line masel',' I said wistfully.

He said, 'It so happens this hoose wis a bit o' luck, bein' oot the road, for we've got tae watch, ye ken. If we're caught loadin' the stuff it's the jile, or a heavy fine at the least.'

Impulsively I asked, 'Ye're no' needin' an extra pair o' haunds?'

'We've got a' the haunds we need for we're a big family.' He gave me a stealthy look. 'We're the travellin' folk.'

I told him that although I was hiking with the girlfriend I was looking for work at the same time.

'Whit kind o' work?'

'Buildin' work. I'm a brickie.'

He shook his head. 'There's nae buildin' up here. Naethin' but sheep and heather, as ye can see for yersel'.'

I told him that I'd heard there was a place near at hand where a new project was starting up, mentioning the word Lifeline and what I'd read about it.

He looked puzzled. 'Never heard o' it.'

'It's bein' run by a guy called Major Burns. It wis in the news-papers.'

'I never read the newspapers,' he said quickly.

'Maybe the word's no' got roon' yet.' I added with a grin, 'So I'll be the first to get ma claim in.'

I then asked him if it was far to Langholm Valley.

'Christ man, ye're staunin' in the very spot, and there's naethin' happenin' here except for a couple o' fellas diggin' a ditch two miles back.'

I shrugged. 'Ach well, somethin's bound to turn up, even if it's only ma toes.'

He regarded me with sympathy. 'If ye hing oan until ma brither comes back he micht gie ye a day's work.'

'Don't worry. We'll manage. Anyway the girlfriend's in a hurry to get movin'.'

'Aye,' he said, peering outside the shed, 'she looks gey fed up.'

From over his shoulder I saw Nancy staring sullenly down in our direction. When I bade him farewell he told me that if we were to keep going we would come to a wild and stoney region which would be sore on the feet, so maybe the best thing to do was to turn back. He doubted if there was any project starting up anywhere near here. I said that we would go on anyway since the weather was good. He waved me off looking concerned.

'This is a terrible place,' said Nancy. We were striding it out along a road running through hills of black rock, lumps of which lay close to the trail.

'There's hardly any grass,' she went on.

'Don't worry. We've still got grub left.'

'I mean, it's all so barren. It's like a huge quarry.'

'Probably been like this since the Stone Age.'

'Stone Age is right.'

A cloud spread itself over the sun and a wind sprang up. We both shivered simultaneously.

'Ye'd better put yer jacket on,' I said.

'I can't be bothered undoing the rucksack. The sun will be out again any minute.'

'I wouldn't bank on it,' I said, looking up at the rock above. It wasn't so much black as a mixture of brown and dark green, mixed with the purple, prickly heather which I had come to detest. It grew everywhere, camouflaging quagmires and rabbit holes and other traps.

'Wid ye fancy a picnic up there?' I said to Nancy, pointing at the rock with a facetious smile on my face. She drew me a look so hard it was like a slap. I hurried ahead of her, tight-lipped. We walked in grim silence for half an hour and the sun still did not come out, nor was there any break in the terrain. I began to whistle a doleful air. Inwardly I was worried.

'What's that you're whistling?' called Nancy from behind me.

'A tune,' I said, and stopped to turn round.

'I know it's a tune,' she said, then burst into tears.

'It's no' as bad as that, surely?' I said, walking back and putting my arms round her.

'I don't want to go any further,' she said, her face pressed on my shoulder, soaking my shirt.

'I don't like this place masel',' I said. 'We'll have a wee rest then we'll go back. Tae hell wi' it.'

We had scarcely put our rucksacks down when a car drew up and stopped. The woman at the wheel asked, 'Do you want a lift? I'm going as far as Lornack.'

'That would be fine.' We climbed into the back seat, pulling our rucksacks behind us.

After some minutes the woman said, with her eyes on the road, 'I hate this part of the journey. It's so ugly.'

'Ye're right there, missus.'

She looked round at me and repeated the word 'missus' with a twist to her mouth. With her heavily-powdered face and blue-rinsed hair I wondered what I was supposed to call her. Nancy said quickly, 'I don't know what we would have done if you hadn't come along.'

'It would have been a pity to have missed Lornack,' said the woman. 'It's a fine town.'

I asked her if there was any work in Lornack.

'If you mean employment,' she said, with her eyes still on the road and giving us a view only of the back of her head, 'I'm afraid not.' She added, 'But even so, there are far too many unemployed people who don't try for anything. When I was young it was no better. I was forced to leave the district to get a position as a housemaid in London. That's what I had to do, but what can you expect when they get their money for nothing nowadays?'

We both stared stonily ahead for the remainder of the journey with no inclination to speak. She must have sensed our disapproval, for she dropped us off at a hotel near the edge of a loch explaining that she was going no further, then after that she drove straight on over the highway.

'Anyway, I'm glad to get away frae her,' I told Nancy, who was walking quickly past the hotel. She needn't have worried. I had spied the notice in the window which read TEMPERANCE HOTEL.

Eventually we arrived in the main street of Lornack, with its shops and cafés and windows full of souvenirs.

'I wish I could buy something to take back,' said Nancy, looking in at some knick-knacks.

'I don't know aboot somethin' tae take back,' I said, 'but ye can buy somethin' such as two fish suppers.'

While we were waiting for the fish to fry I purchased two packets of cigarettes. 'In case I run oot o' them when we get back tae the lonesome trail,' I explained.

She frowned. 'It's a pity you smoke. It costs such a lot.'

'Ye knew I smoked when ye first met me.'

'I know, but it's still a pity.'

Outside the café I could hardly wait to throw away the brown wrapper and bite into the crisp batter round the fish. 'This is terrific,' I said, panting to cool down the hot food in my mouth.

'Do you have to be such a litter lout?' she said, picking the wrapper off the pavement and depositing it in a bin. I shrugged and continued to eat. I was finished long before her. She swallowed her food as if there was a lump in her throat. 'I'm not all that hungry,' she said when I looked at her enquiringly.

I asked a passer-by if there was a pub near at hand. 'The Locheil Bar is round the corner if you fancy a ceilidh,' he said.

'Let's go,' I said to Nancy, pretending not to notice her frown.

Inside the pub, which was noisy and overcrowded, we were asked to leave our rucksacks near the men's toilet and go into the lounge. Women weren't allowed to drink in the public bar.

'But that's discrimination,' said Nancy.

I shoved her through the door marked 'Lounge' saying, 'These are primitive parts. Don't argue.'

The clients, who were all fairly sunburnt, or maybe just red with the booze, squeezed up to make a place for us on the bench running along the length of the wall. Crushed against me was a stout woman who said that we were just in time for the McCann Brothers. 'They're smashin',' she stated. I asked Nancy if she preferred a vodka and orange.

'Prefer it to what?' she asked with dulled eyes.

The McCann Brothers, who were fiddlers, played lively tunes much appreciated by the clientele, who stamped their feet and clapped their hands to the beat. They all had drinks in front of them on the tables, which can doubtless make a difference to your capacity for appreciation.

'They're no' a bad group,' I said to Nancy. She nodded slightly, but remained withdrawn. I asked her what was wrong. She said that she had a headache. I was about to suggest leaving when the waiter arrived and took my order. It was no better after that because the music was loud and insistent on the eardrums and we were pressed as close as sardines in a tin, but more miserable, I suspected. The music stopped and the stout woman next to me left her seat. She charged over to the fiddlers with her hand outstretched.

'At least we can breathe noo,' I said to Nancy; but her eyes were strained towards the lounge door like a prisoner under guard who spies an escape route.

'We'll go then,' I said, 'if that's whit ye want,' but I didn't move because at that moment who should I catch sight of but Dad, standing in the doorway holding a pint of beer.

'Wait a minute,' I said to Nancy, 'this is one o' the guys that knows Craig – the one with the business. He canny be far away.'

She muttered something under her breath, but I wasn't listening. I was on my feet and beckoning on my old friend. He came over and squeezed in beside me, his smile as bland as ever. He took a long pull at his pint, then put his tumbler on the table with a sigh of satisfaction and wiped his mouth. I wished I had one to go with it.

'This bloody place,' I said, 'takes you all day to get served.'

'So I've noticed,' he said distantly.

'Anyway,' I said, deciding not to beat about the bush, 'I saw the article in the paper about this Lifeline business. So I decided to take a dauner up here to see whit was doin'.' I added with a deprecating laugh, 'And maybe to get a job, if there wis one gaun, that is.'

'Is that so?' said Dad, looking quizzical.

'Oh, by the way,' I gestured towards Nancy, 'this is the girlfriend who's came alang wi' me. We've been campin' on the way here, as an excuse for a bit of a holiday.'

Dad leaned forward to say 'Howdy do,' which fell on deaf ears. Nancy had turned her head away.

'She's no' feelin' well,' I informed Dad, and thankfully called on the waiter who had entered. I ordered two pints of beer and asked Nancy what she wanted to drink. She said she was leaving. 'I can't stand any more of this place,' she announced, and gave Dad a tight smile on the way out.

'A very attractive girl, if ye don't mind me sayin' so,' said Dad.

'Aye,' I said, longing to run after her and tell her to be reasonable and consider how lucky I was to meet Dad. But she had disappeared through the swinging door.

'At least you got the weather,' Dad was saying.

'How dae ye mean?'

'I mean for the campin'. You got good weather.'

Impatiently I said, 'It wisny bad, but the main thing is for you to tell me where Craig is, or Major Burns as he's named in the papers.'

Dad stared ahead, as if deaf. After the waiter had returned with the beer and I had paid him with the change in my pocket, which was just enough, I repeated my statement.

'Craig's gone,' Dad said.

'Gone? Whit dae ye mean, gone?'

'The last time I saw Craig wis ootside this pub when we were staunin' on the pavement discussing various matters. Then a car drew up and somebody called on him. I thought it wis tae ask him directions. Well, he got into the car. It drove away and I hivny seen him since.'

I stared hard into Dad's face. It struck me for the first time that without his bland smile his eyes appeared too close-set and his lips too thin for my liking.

I said, 'Ye must think I'm daft if ye expect me tae believe that.'

'I don't care whit ye believe,' he said, sounding insolent.

I drank some beer and informed him that if he didn't take me to Craig or whatever he was called, I might do something drastic, like kicking him very severely.

'Ye'll jist have tae dae that,' he replied, 'for I don't ken whaur he is.' In turn he drank his beer and banged his tumbler on the table in a righteous fashion. I thought maybe he was telling the truth.

'OK,' I said, 'but I still want tae know whit ye're a' up tae. You, McLerie and Craig, and in particular I want tae know how I wis bein' watched at the lodgin' hoose, and don't waste time in denyin' it.'

'All right,' said Dad, unperturbed. 'I'll no' deny that we had an interest in ye, up tae a point, but it never ran deep, ye ken. Ye jist happened tae arrive when we were lookin' for somebody tae stir things up.'

'How dae ye mean, stir things up?'

'Things like passin' roon pamphlets, speakin' on soap boxes, or daein' a bit o' hecklin' at political meetin's — stuff like that, ye ken?'

'I don't ken one bit,' I said.

Dad sighed. 'It's no' straightforward, right enough, but politics never are.'

'I think I know whit it's aboot,' I said. 'It's the National Front. Is that whit ye are?'

'No' really,' said Dad, looking more like his old affable self again. 'It's much mair important than the National Front.'

'Don't tell me it's the Secret Service?'

Dad hesitated, then said, 'I canny gie ye the whole story for I don't know it masel'. It stauns tae reason when ye're dealin' wi' somethin', say for example like the MI5, ye're only gaun tae know so much.'

'MI5?' I exclaimed.

'I'm no' sayin' it's MI5. I'm only gi'in' ye an example.'

I stared hard at Dad for a few moments, wondering if he was taking the mickey out of me, especially when I remembered the rubber mask. 'Tell me,' I said, feeling tired and out of my depth and worried about Nancy, 'why dae ye want trouble stirred up in the first place?'

'The fact is,' said Dad, 'though ye micht no' believe me, but even in a great wee country like oor ain, folk are aye plottin' things. Ye micht say that there's always an undercurrent o' unrest against the wans at the tap.'

I nodded and said, 'It's no' surprisin' when ye consider how the wans at the bottom are treated.'

'Well, there ye are. There's always some that want tae dae somethin', but usually they don't bother until somebody comes alang and stirs it up. Afore ye know it there are organised groups tryin' to create disorder. Dae ye see whit I mean?'

'That's a bloody good idea,' I said. 'I'd support that. Is that whit yous are − anarchists? Plantin' bombs and a' that?'

He chuckled. 'Oh naw, no' anarchists. We're no' in tae that kind o' thing. The opposite, fact.'

I said irritably, 'I wish ye'd come right oot and tell me exactly whit ye are in tae. I've come a long way tae see Colin Craig, or should I say Major Burns. He promised me a job and that's a' I'm interested in, so whit the hell is this Lifeline aboot anyway?'

He shook his head and sighed. 'Patience is no' a virtue o' the young, I ken, but if ye're that keen tae know I'll tell ye this much, for mind I only know so much masel'. Lifeline is the code name for wan o' the latest drives in stirrin' things up, and that's whit me and Craig are paid tae dae – forbye gettin' recruits tae help us, and that's where you'd have come in. It's a method whereby we can get a' the troublemakers to expose themselves right away. Ye see, we'd be infiltratin' wi' them and we'd know in advance whit their plans wir. At least, that wis the idea, but the plan has been scrapped for this area meanwhile, since the folk here are no' sae easily roused. Likely Craig's been sent doon south where there's mair unrest.'

It struck me Dad could be telling the truth, otherwise why should he make up such an unlikely story? But true or not, this encounter was a blow to any prospects of a job, and outside all this I was worrying about Nancy. She had been in a grim mood when she left.

'Well, it's a' one tae me whether it's been scrapped or no',' I said, 'I widny work for you or Craig if that's whit yer game is.'

'Whit game?' he asked slyly.

'Whit ye were explainin'. Gettin' folked stirred up, as you describe it. Onyway, I'm no' sure I get the point of it.'

'Well,' said Dad patiently, like a teacher dealing with a thick pupil, 'we tip the leaders aff tae the polis and they get done for sedition, which carries a heavy sentence. It's troubled times noo-adays, and it'll get worse. There are them that want tae bring doon the government, and oor job's tae spot the dangerous wans afore they can start their ploys.'

'So,' I said, 'we set traps for oor ain folk.'

'We set traps for them that are a potential danger tae the country. We're daein' decent folk a favour,' said Dad indignantly.

Depression swept over me as I sat with my head in my hands trying to sort things out. No matter how I looked at it there was nothing in Dad's account of Lifeline that I liked, nor was there anything now about Dad that I liked, or his accomplices and their peculiar business. From what he was saying I guessed they were nothing better than informers creating circumstances they could inform on. I felt like bashing him. I had decided to leave before

I did so when Dad said, 'Ye're lookin' kind o' seedy. Wid ye like somethin' a wee taste stronger than beer?'

It occurred to me that I might as well get some Dutch courage in order to face Nancy, who might not be easy to talk round. 'If ye like,' I said. 'As usual I'm skint.'

He ordered whisky for both of us, then said after we had been served, 'It's a damned shame that a fine big fella like yersel' has to be shoved on the scrap heap.'

I nodded absently and asked him what had happened to McLerie. Had he gone with Craig?

Dad chuckled and said, 'McLerie's in jile. He was a leader o' an organised group that played intae oor haunds. He wis an activist afore we met him.'

'I thought he wis Craig's man,' I said, surprised.

'So did he. He thought the sun shone oot Craig's arse. It wis laughable to see how much he trusted him, but he wis one o' these immigrants frae across the water. His pub wis a shelter for the assassins that are bred there. He actually thought Lifeline wis tae be a base for a' kinds o' terrorists, and he selt his pub tae come this length. But ye'll no' see him for a while, if ever.'

I smiled weakly at Dad and swallowed my whisky in one go, hoping it would settle the churning in my stomach. I told him all I had wanted was a straightforward job as a brickie. I doubted that I had the temperament for anything else. Dad watched me intently as I spoke. His eyes and lips were curiously moist.

'Ye're much too modest,' he said. 'I think ye'd be useful at a lot o' things. If ye stick wi' me for a wee while I'll be able to put ye on tae somethin' good wi' plenty money in it.' He then squeezed my hand, which I had innocently placed near his on top of the table. I swiped it off so violently that I hurt my knuckles. Dad flinched and groaned.

Roughly I asked him if he wasn't worried that I would repeat all he had told me to folk of consequence, who would possibly create a big stink about it.

He said, still looking pained, 'But who'd believe a hobo like yersel', and where's the proof, if ye could even catch us?'

I thought this over and decided that he was right. I even began to wonder if his tale was true. Dad was a very devious man, and maybe even a cracked-up shot; but whatever the truth of it was, it was certain to be as unpleasant as the touch of his hand. As for Craig, if he could stomach a guy like Dad, he was capable of anything. They were all bad medicine, including McLerie, even if he was in jail. The important thing now was to find Nancy.

'Excuse me,' I said to Dad, 'I'll have tae leave afore I puke all over ye. But let me warn ye, if I meet ye ootside I might be tempted tae stamp ye intae the ground like the black beetle ye resemble.'

His composure had returned. When I left he was smiling blandly towards the fiddlers, who had now begun to play again.

Later in the evening Nancy and I were standing inside a shop door not far from a bus stop. After I had left the pub it hadn't taken me long to find her. Lornack wasn't such a big place. She had been staring in at a shop window full of souvenirs.

'Buyin' something?' I had asked.

She shook her head and told me she didn't want anything to remind her of this place, or for that matter any part of the expedition. Besides, there wasn't much money left and she was going home.

'But ye canny.'

'But I can.' She gave me a look of pity, or maybe it was contempt, but I knew she wasn't joking.

'I'll be stayin',' I said, 'for there's nothin' to go back for.'

'I thought you might,' she said, and walked away.

I had followed her round the town giving her reasons why she shouldn't go. In my heart I knew they weren't good ones. Even as I spoke I was gasping for a couple of jugfuls to get the adrenalin started, which had expired from the time I left Dad.

Now I was asking her how she knew a bus would be leaving this one-eyed hole for anywhere.

'I enquired when you were in the pub.'

'Dae ye have to go?'

'Yes,' she said.

With her mouth set firm and her chin held high I had never seen her look so good. Perhaps it was the effect of the neon light from the shop window, but recently it had seemed to me she had looked better with every day that passed, and this was to be the last one.

Desperately I said, 'There'll be nae mair pubs from now on, if ye stay.'

She frowned and shook her head. In the dusk her eyes seemed smudged.

'It's no use. I'm going home.'

'I thought ye loved me.'

She must have thought hard about this because she took her time answering. Finally she said that perhaps she did, but she wasn't sure. She couldn't judge matters clearly at the moment. Then she burst out passionately, 'It's the way you act. You've no consideration. I can't stand it. I was brought up to believe that consideration is very important, and I think that's true.'

The expression 'brought up' defeated me. It conjured up the opposite situation of being 'dragged up' which I must have presented to her in the course of our relationship. I made another try. 'I promise I'm finished wi' the booze. Cross ma heart.' I made the sign.

'You're not even a Catholic,' she said.

'Ye don't have tae be,' I began to say when I heard the noise of the bus in the distance. 'Stay one mair day,' I pleaded. 'Everythin' will look different in the mornin', especially when the sun's shinin'. I can tell by the sky it's gaun tae be good.'

She fumbled in her purse and gave me a fiver, saying, 'Don't drink it all. You'll need it for fares.'

She picked up her rucksack and swung it on to her shoulder before I could help her. The headlights from the bus were upon us, blinding us. She stepped onto the platform and turned round to stare at me so miserably you would have thought I was forcing her to go. I waited at the halt until the bus was a speck in the distance, then I moved off. As I headed for the first pub – not the Locheil Bar, though, since I had no wish to see Dad again – I thought I could still smell the fresh cut grass perfume of her hair.

I cut through a cobbled lane for no other reason than to give me time to compose the expression on my face, which I suspected was one of severe pain. By the time I reached the end of the lane which led into a main street my face had stiffened.

I had spied two figures crossing the street beyond the lane. Even in the dark I knew it was Dad and Colin Craig. Partners in dubious dealings as they were, in every outward aspect they looked ill-matched. I headed for the street to confirm what I already knew and saw the short squat figure of Dad scuttling along the pavement hastily to keep up with the longer and steadier footsteps of Craig.

For a moment I hesitated. One part of my brain said forget them. In every way they were bad medicine. Another more urgent part of my brain wanted explanations and compensation, particularly from Craig. For the short time I had known him I had liked him, and admired his cool and upper-class style – so much that I had followed him on this wild goose chase, dragging Nancy with me, on the strength of a vague promise of work. And for my pains I had lost Nancy. What made it worse was that I had always professed to despise rich and successful types like Craig. Not that Craig struck me now as being rich and successful. If what Dad said was true he was no more than a villain – but worse than the average, being an agitator and informer. Whatever he was, the fact remained that I had been duped. I decided it was imperative to let them know that I wasn't quite the country boy they took me for.

I caught Craig by the shoulder as they turned round a corner where the pavement and the street began to slope downwards.

'Remember me?' I asked.

He studied me for a moment with one eyebrow raised but otherwise unsurprised. 'Certainly,' he said, adding pleasantly, 'How strange to find you in this Godforsaken place. You are on holiday, perhaps?'

'No' really,' I said.

'He's been trailin' efter us,' said Dad, giving me a mean look.

'Trailing after us,' said Craig, sounding amused.

Patiently I said, 'If ye remember, ye once promised me a job, and so naturally when I saw yer photo in the paper under the name of Major Burns askin' for folk tae join this Lifeline project, I decided to take the plunge and come up. So whit aboot it?'

Dad addressed Craig. 'See him. He's lookin' for trouble. I've telt him there's nae job.'

'Is that right, Craig?' I asked. 'There's nae job?'

Craig shrugged. 'Sorry, young man. Just one of those deals that didn't work out. Pity your journey was for nothing, and such a long way too.'

'It wis an experience,' I said airily. 'One that I'll keep in mind, especially efter whit Dad telt me.'

'And what did Dad tell you,' said Craig, with a swift glance at Dad.

'Spyin' on folk is whit ye're intae, and then informin' on them.'

'I never telt him that,' said Dad indignantly. 'He's makin' it up.'

'He telt me, as well, that McLerie's in jail and it wis you two that put him there. He telt me a lot of other things that were hard tae believe. I would be obliged if you could put me in the picture a wee bit better.'

There was a pause during which Craig regarded Dad steadily, then regarded me steadily. I noticed a pub across the street with fancy stained-glass windows. Somebody entered the swing doors and I heard a hum of male voices. It looked cheerful. I decided to head for it soon with my fiver.

Craig said in a colder voice than formerly, 'Lifeline was a perfectly legitimate venture which did not come to pass. If Dad told you otherwise, it is untrue; but then he always had a vivid imagination, because of his theatrical connections, no doubt. Some people might call him a liar.' Then he addressed Dad, 'Isn't that right?'

'It is,' said Dad.

'That's too bad,' I said, 'because it so happens I believed every word that Dad telt me; and it also so happens trailin' yous wisny ma only reason for comin' up here. I've got relatives in this toon who are a very close lot, very sectarian they are, in fact real trouble-makers. They would knife you as quick as look at you, and see that pub ower there, that's where they drink.'

When Craig automatically looked towards the pub I was pointing at, I caught him with a hard blow to the side of the face. He stumbled sideways and I caught him with another blow. I wasn't worrying what Dad would do. From the side of my eye I saw him scuttling down the sloping pavement. Give Craig his due, he attempted to come back at me, but he had lost the place. A few more blows and he was on the pavement saying, 'No more.' I must admit I administered another couple of kicks, which wasn't sporting, and probably done for the loss of Nancy, which if you look at it truthfully wasn't entirely his fault. Before I left him on the pavement, still conscious, I put my hand inside his well-tailored jacket and took out a wallet containing a cheque book, which was of no use to me, but the twenty-pound note inside it was. I returned the wallet to his jacket pocket while he was feebly attempting to rise. It was the same wallet he had had at the peace festival, the one with the initials A.R.B.

'For auld times' sake,' I said, and headed for the cheerful pub across the street.

13

I stayed in the pub long enough to drink two whiskies. I was aware of curious stares in my direction, perhaps because I exuded an air of violence, or perhaps because it was obvious from my rucksack that I was a camper – sometimes not a popular thing to be. I couldn't have stopped long in any case, being haunted by the thought of Nancy arriving back in Lornack in order to give me one more chance. This didn't prevent me from ordering a bottle of whisky as a bulwark against the pain of disappointment on that score.

The barman avoided my eye as he served me, staring at my bruised knuckles instead.

'Jist had an accident,' I explained, and left quickly before he could say anything.

I wandered the shaded streets, stopping every so often to drink from the bottle, thinking it had been absurd to consider she would return, but caring less about it the more I drank. A policeman approached me and asked where I was going, at the same time frowning at the bottle.

'Lookin' for ma mate,' I replied. 'We're daein' a bit of hikin' and I've lost him somewhere on the road.'

Now, looking at my rucksack, he said, 'You'd better be warned that there is no camping allowed either here or within the vicinity, so get as far away as you can or I'll be taking you in.'

'In whit direction?'

He pointed up the road, saying, 'Just go.'

I walked a few yards then shouted back to him, 'I didny like this place onyway.'

Within half an hour I had left the suburbs and saw ahead, in the moonlight, a stretch of fields on each side of the road. I squeezed through a gap in the hedge, unpacked my rucksack and discovered I was in possession of two sleeping bags, a frying pan, but minus a tent. The tent would be far away in the bus inside Nancy's rucksack. I decided that it was no great loss. The less I carried, the better. In the morning I would dump the frying pan and the stove. I wouldn't be frying anything anyway. So I settled down inside the sleeping bag, and with the other one rolled up as a bolster for my back, I fell asleep, still holding the bottle.

I was woken by the noise of a passing lorry on the other side of the hedge. I saw the sky was dull, but I thought the weather would be good enough for walking. I stood up to shiver in the cool air, pleasantly surprised to see that there was still whisky left in the bottle. Things weren't so bad after all. I packed my rucksack, leaving out the stove and the frying pan (though not, after all, without some regret) and set off along the road on the other side of the hedge, carrying the bottle in one hand. I had reached the temperance hotel where Nancy and I had been dumped by the woman in the car when I remembered I should have bought fags and some instant food like bread and cheese before leaving civilisation; but no way was I going to go back. I might be tempted to take the bus. The idea of arriving in the big city without Nancy was unbearable. I felt I had to walk back over this lonely space until I came to terms with my unhappiness – like Moses in the desert, who had been another screwed-up guy, I thought, smiling to myself at the unlikely comparison.

I walked on, endlessly it seemed, wishing I knew how far I had travelled. Two cars passed me on the road. One of them slowed down as if to give me a lift. I sat by the side of the road, yards back, to show that I wasn't interested. I regretted this immediately the car moved off. I could have asked how far I had come from Lornack. Yet, what did it matter? I wasn't heading for any place in particular. It was just hard to keep this in mind, I thought, as I took a swig from the bottle.

It took some effort to stand up and move again. I began to sing as I walked, composing my own tunes and rhymes and sipping from the bottle at intervals. By the time I reached the stony valley I was staggering from exhaustion and booze. I sat between the rocks, hunched up, clasping my knees, watching big black birds circling high above my head. Buzzards, I thought gloomily, and fell asleep.

This rest gave me the strength to reach the cliffs overlooking the sea. I put the whisky bottle to my lips, but found it was empty. Enraged, I threw it over the cliff edge. It smashed upon the rocks and the seagulls rose up screaming.

'I'm sorry,' I called to them, and sank to my knees. I felt tears stinging my eyes, which proved that I was at a very low ebb indeed. I decided to rest on this spot for the night, whenever that might be; but anyway, night or day, I could go no further. Though I was slightly deranged at that moment, I had the sense to put one sleeping bag inside the other to make sure of a warm bed. After crawling inside I fell asleep, lulled by the lapping sound of the waves on the rocks, and dreamt of Nancy.

The sky was clear when I forced myself out of my thick sleep to face the strong wind blowing over the headland. Down below the waves roared.

I turned away from the bleak scene and dragged my gear well back from the cliff edge in case a gust of wind blew it over. I wrapped it up, but it was a laborious business for I was weak with hunger as well as stiff with cold, and to make it worse my fags were crushed and sodden. I began to think I might die in this wilderness and no one would know. Anyway, no one would miss me, apart from my mother, and even that was doubtful. If Nancy thought of me at all, it would likely be as an association worse than the one she had with the Canadian guy. Strangely enough, it was at this desperate stage that an idea entered my head, in the way a drowning man in the sea below might clutch at a piece of driftwood. It was this: if I could manage it, I would head for the Auchenachen Inn, with its lounge of pale plastic divans and tumblers on the ceiling, where the buxom hostess Jessie might serve me with a plate of soup, or even two plates of soup. Despite her slap on my cheek before I was flung out of the inn, I was struck now with a clear impression that she had liked me up until that stage. Besides, I had money to pay for a meal, which might make a difference, and I was alone, another point in my favour. I laughed aloud and said, looking up at the sky, still being weak in the head as well as the body, 'Thanks for the sign.'

If I hadn't had the gumption to buy a loaf and a pint of milk from a suspicious-faced farmer's wife, I believe the buzzards would have got me in the end. As it was, I reached the reception desk at the Auchenachen Inn in a poor condition. I could hardly stand. I rang the bell three times before Jessie came through and said, looking over my head, 'Sorry, we're not open till six.'

I clutched the desk with both hands, saying, 'Can I sit doon somewhere? I think I'm gaun tae faint.'

Immediately she pulled me into the lounge, where I collapsed on one of the pale plastic divans. From a distance I heard her say, 'Are you the fellow who was camping with his girlfriend?' Then I passed out. I was returned to consciousness by the sound of Jessie placing cutlery on the table in front of me.

I sat up awkwardly and said, 'Sorry aboot the commotion. I'm thinkin' it wis because I hudny ate for a long time.'

'I'm thinking that too,' she said, without looking at me, and straightening a knife with deliberation. Then she marched off, swinging her hips in a businesslike manner.

Doubting that the cutlery was for me, I drank some water from a glass on the table. I thought this was all I would get, but she came back carrying a plate of steaming food.

'Eat this slowly,' she said, 'for I'm thinking that your belly will have shrunk and it would be bad for you to gobble.'

She watched me as I ate, tutting if I began to gobble. It was hard not to, the food was so fantastic. When I had finished, I asked her how much I owed.

'Pay me later,' she said with a smile. Then she became serious and asked why I had come to be in such a state, and why I was alone. I gave her a brief version of the affair, leaving out Craig and Dad, and saying more or less that my girlfriend had left me because I drunk too much booze. She shrugged and said that from what she remembered of my girlfriend, she had looked the type that would be hard to please on any score.

'Perhaps,' I said distantly, not wanting to pursue the subject.

'I'll tell you what,' she said later, when I had almost fallen asleep over the table as she spoke, 'go up to the room facing you on the first landing and have a lie down. You can't be sleeping here when the customers arrive.'

She led me by the hand out of the lounge and up the stairs, then shoved me in the direction of the room. I wanted to kiss her hand with gratitude, but she had vanished back down the stairs. Inside, the curtains were drawn, making the place dim, but I could see the shape of a bed. I stumbled towards it gladly, remembering, just in time, to take off all my clothes, except my underpants, in case I dirtied the sheets.

I woke suddenly. Something or someone had disturbed me. It seemed dark, as if it was late in the evening, though with the curtains drawn the room had been dark enough when I had stumbled into bed earlier. Then there was a sound, like a suppressed giggle.

'Who is it?' I asked.

'It's only Jessie,' came the reply.

A light was switched on. Now I saw the place clearly. I stared at a light oak wall unit, a writing bureau, a washbasin and the green velvet curtains that were closed – all very elegant, but it was Jessie who riveted my attention, standing next to a lampshade on the table beside the bed. She wore a black filmy garment which barely covered her chest. She leaned over me, her hair touching my cheek, and said, 'Are you feeling all right, dear?'

'Fine,' I said. 'I wis aboot tae get up,' and rose some inches off the bed to convey this.

'Now,' she said, pushing me down again, 'don't get excited. I've only came to give you something that will make you feel a lot better. In fact it will make us both feel a lot better. I've been a bit down in the dumps myself lately.'

As she headed for the writing bureau I saw the outline of her figure through the filmy garment, which made me agitated, though I wasn't sure exactly in what way. She opened a door in the bureau and brought out a fancy-shaped bottle, along with two glasses and a tray.

'It's some wine I've been saving for a special occasion, and I'm thinking this is as good an occasion as any.'

She put the tray and glasses on the table and began to pour. I saw it was a white wine and suspected it wasn't going to be strong enough for the occasion, as far as I was concerned. I drank it quickly and said, 'Very nice,' wondering how I could escape from the room without showing my nearly naked body as well as appearing ungrateful for her extreme hospitality.

'My, my,' she said. 'You are a quick drinker. No wonder your girlfriend took the hump.'

'Sorry,' I said, unable to look her in the eye, 'I wis chokin' wi' thirst.'

'Don't apologise,' she said with a throaty chuckle, 'I'm not short of a few bottles. But next time drink it slow.'

I was about to explain that I wasn't partial to white wine, when she said, 'Do you mind if I sit on the bed? It's not easy to drink standing up.'

Quickly I moved nearer to the wall, wondering what I had let myself in for. She sat with her back facing me. Her skin was very white and I noticed that there was a mole on her left shoulder, which I couldn't help admiring. There were a lot of things about her that I couldn't help admiring, but not so close at hand. Then she gave a big sigh, as if she knew what I was thinking, which moved me to ask if she was feeling OK.

'As a matter of fact,' she said, looking round at me, 'this is not comfortable either. I'll have to bring my legs in, otherwise I'll get a crick in my neck if I speak to you.'

Before I could answer she had swung her legs onto the bed, stretching them out so that we were lying side by side with only the blankets between us.

'That's better,' she said, and splashed more wine in the glasses. I drank mine, forgetting to be slow. Again I tried to think of some way of escaping, but I was becoming dazed. The wine was stronger than I had judged.

Then she said quietly, 'Perhaps you want me to go?'

This question confused me, for at that particular moment I hadn't been thinking of anything at all.

'No' really,' I said.

'What is it then? You're not saying much.'

I couldn't think of anything to say, being distracted by the sight of her plump but shapely legs and the red varnish on her toenails.

'Maybe it's because —' I began, unable to think clearly what it was because of.

'Because of what?' she said. 'Tell me. You're not afraid of me, surely?'

As she regarded me with concern I certainly couldn't think of any reason to be afraid of her. I could only say, 'Maybe it's because you're lyin' here with hardly anythin' on. Whit am I supposed to think?'

Her concern faded. 'You can think what you like, but I bet if your girlfriend was here you'd know what to think.'

'She wis different.'

'Different! I'm sure she was, leaving you the way she did.'

'I telt ye afore, it wis ma fault.'

'Hmm,' said Jessie, sounding bored.

After a strained pause I said, 'It doesny mean to say that because she wis different she was any better than you.'

At that Jessie moved closer to me so that her bare shoulder touched mine.

'I see that you've finished your drink again. What a terrible man you are.'

This time I drank only half of the wine she poured. It was getting more potent by the minute. Jessie put her glass on the table.

'Do you mind if I get under the blankets?' she asked. 'I'm fair freezing.'

By this time I had no qualms about anything. 'Get under,' I said and was immediately excited by the feel of her hips on mine when she moved in.

'I was beginning to think,' she said, snuggling close to me, 'that you only came here to be fed.'

I leaned over and put my glass on the table, saying, 'There was that, I admit, but I thought ye might have slapped me again if I tried for anything else.'

'Oh that,' she said. 'It was only to impress McFarlane who would have been in a terrible mood all night if I hadn't.'

I put my arms round Jessie's shoulder, not caring about McFarlane, and considering I could do a lot worse than to stay on here and settle down with Jessie until such times as the building trade took a turn for the better.

'What you need,' said Jessie turning towards me and wrapping her arms round my neck, 'is a great big cuddle.'

After that we came together easily. In fact we came together twice. I didn't quite make it the second time. It was spoiled by a fleeting memory of Nancy in my arms. Jessie didn't seem to notice.

'There's jist one mair thing I'd like,' I said later as we were finishing the last of the wine.

'Not again, surely?'

'I huvny had a fag for days and I'm fair gaspin'.'

'There's always something you're wanting,' said Jessie.

She rose from the bed, opened the door in the writing bureau and threw me over a packet of twenty Benson & Hedges along with a box of matches.

'That's a queer writin' bureau,' I said jokingly, surprised that she was making no move to come back in beside me. Not that I was bothering too much. At the moment I didn't fancy another session. But I didn't like the way she was looking at me very contemplatively.

'Whit's wrang?' I asked.

'Nothing really, but I'll have to get downstairs. It must be well past opening time and the customers will be furious.'

I thought she was starting to look a bit furious herself. I said evenly, 'Well, if ye must go, there's nae way oot o' it.'

I took a puff of the fag. It almost took the breath from me, I had been so long without one.

I said, as she continued to stare at me through eyelashes that had become gritty with mascara, 'but I'll come doon later if ye like and gie ye a haun'.'

'You can't stay here. I've to get the room ready for the next visitor.'

For a moment I thought she was joking; then I knew she wasn't when she added accusingly, 'And these sheets will need changing.'

'You mean, I've to go right now?'

'I'll give you ten minutes. Meantime I'm off to get dressed.'

'Wait a minute,' I called, as she turned to leave, 'is that a' ye've got to say?'

'And what am I supposed to say?' she asked with astonishment.

I knew there was no chance of it now, but I said anyway, 'I hoped you might gie me a job – barman, bouncer, or maybe collectin' tumblers, anything like that.'

'A job!' she said. 'And how could I give you a job, with the place not paying as it is, and it soon to be closed for the winter?'

Then she took a few paces nearer the bed and said in a more conciliatory way, 'Look, even if I could give you a job, I know you wouldn't stop long. I can tell you're not the hotel type and I do my own bouncing.'

'I could learn,' I said, encouraged by her softening attitude.

'You're much too rugged looking, if you know what I mean. Hotel staff, particularly the men, are required to be smooth.' She laughed, looking more like the Jessie I had lain with. 'Maybe that's why I wanted a shot of you in bed. It's not often I come across a rugged fellow like yourself.'

'Is that all it was – a shot?'

'Listen,' she said. 'I've got my business to attend to. I can't give it up for any young fellow who happens to come along. I've given you too much of my time already.' She sighed, 'But that's hotel life for you, never a minute to spare for pleasure.'

I nodded my head in sympathy, and told her I would leave immediately.

'Finish your cigarette first, and take my advice. Go back home and get on with your life. You look as though you'll be a big success one day. Make it up with your girlfriend, if you can. Likely it was only a lovers' tiff you had.'

As she left she said, 'Good luck, and keep the packet.'

After she'd gone I jumped from the bed, put on my clothes and gave myself a wash in the spotless washbasin. I left nearly all the money I possessed on the table, knowing Jessie would be back to tidy the room. When all was said and done, she deserved it. And anyway, the place wasn't paying. She would need it. She was right about me not being the hotel type.

Ten minutes later I was walking the pitch-black trail, hoping to find some hedge or bush where I could bed down for the night, and thinking that the best thing I could do was to become a tramp.

14

I was back home sitting in my mother's plastic easy chair, feeling like an intruder. Opposite me my mother sat frowning.

She said, 'I didny expect ye back sae soon. Whit's happened?'

I thought her appearance was as drab as ever, with her straight hair, crossover apron and slippers burst at the toes. Yet I've seen her look fairly spruce when she's been forced out to events such as weddings and funerals, with her hair frizzed and wearing the fur coat she got from the Oxfam shop, looking very impressive, and young for her forty-odd years.

'Are ye no' pleased tae see me?' I asked.

'Of course, but there's nothin' much tae eat, apart frae sausages, and I suppose ye'll be hungry.'

'Sausages will be fine.'

I had actually had nothing to eat for twenty-four hours, except for bread and cheese from a lorry driver. He had picked me up a few miles outside Grinstone and dropped me near my home town. At the time I had considered this a piece of luck. Now I wasn't so sure. If I had hiked it all the way I might have come to a sticky end, which would have been all for the best the way things were going. Or I might have, through necessity, been forced to become a poacher or a sheep rustler, like some guys have done, and finished up wealthy.

My mother disappeared into the kitchen. I looked around furtively. The room was shabbier than I had remembered. There was a fusty smell that I hadn't noticed before. Perhaps it had always been there. When she returned with a cup of tea and thick sausage sandwiches on a plate I said, 'It's time ye were gettin' a shift oot this place. It's rotten wi' damp.'

'So, it's no' good enough for ye,' she said as she thrust the cup into my hand, spilling tea on my denims.

'I couldny imagine bringin' onyone in here, even for a sing-song.'

'So,' she said, with her hand on her hips, 'ye've got haud o' some fancy wumman.'

'Don't be daft. I'm no' blamin' you,' I said, thinking I had gone too far. 'Ye dae yer best.'

'I should think so,' she said, then declared I was likely right about the state of the place. It badly needed decorating. She would buy paper and paint from the co-operative and I could get started first thing in the morning. That is, she added tentatively, if I had any money to spare.

'Hardly a bean,' I told her. 'The entire venture wis a washoot.'

'That's a pity,' she said, leaning back in her chair and looking worried.

'At least it wis an experience,' I said, with some defiance.

I sat back and swung a leg over the chair as she stared pensively into the unlit grate of the fireplace, her face sad but resigned.

'Cheer up,' I said. 'It might never happen.'

'The thing is,' she began, 'I don't know how I'm gaun tae manage noo that you're hame.'

'Don't worry. I'll get somethin' even if it's only broo money. Ye see, I had a job for a wee while up north, and I didny pack it in. I got paid aff. That makes a difference.'

'Does it?' she said quietly, and regarded me with the commiseration one gives an invalid.

'Whit's wrang?'

She sighed. 'I've often thought I should have had ye adopted when ye were a wean.'

'Adopted?'

'If ye'd been adopted by posh folk ye could have been a doctor or a civil servant by this time.'

'Whit's brought this on?' I asked angrily.

'There's nae chance for fellas like you nooadays. Ye need friends in high places.'

'Look,' I said sternly. 'I wid hate tae be a doctor or a civil servant. I'd rather be who I am, even if I am on the dole.'

'Is that right?' said my mother, smiling and flushed as if relieved. 'I've often thought aboot that –'

I interrupted her. 'Jist you get intae the kitchen and find me anither piece wi' something on it.'

The next morning I was dragging my footsteps on the road to the Labour Exchange when I accidentally came to the Paxton Arms, a pub I used to frequent. Its outer shade of faded pink was the same, perhaps flaking more than before, but the worst aspect about it was that it was closed. I asked a guy wandering past with a black dog on a leash if it was shut for good. He said, with a touch of hostility, 'It's only because there's nae giros delivered on a Monday. It'll be open the morra.'

I walked off in the opposite direction to conceal the fact I was heading for the broo because sometimes I have my pride. I arrived at the derelict drive where the squatters hang out, hiding behind smashed windows with the torn curtains blowing through the gaps like streamers.

Halfway along the drive I saw a gap in the building heaped with char, as if connections had been deliberately severed by fire. Then I came to a doorway where a guy was hunkered down spreading out fag ends on the step. It was big Mick, an acquaintance of mine who was very partial to the wine of South Africa. I remembered that I owed him a fiver from way back. It was doubtful if he would remember this. A lot of booze would have been drunk since then. I had no real notion for his company, but I was stirred by the thought that he might have a bottle of plonk in the pocket of his long black coat, which he wore in all seasons. I called his name. He stared up at me vacantly. Then he began to laugh in a wheezing manner, like Motley the cartoon dog. When he shook my hands his fingers felt like something retrieved from the earth, cold and clammy. There was no bulge in his pocket that I could see, so I told him that I was in a hurry; but he continued to grip my hand with surprising strength.

'Christ man, I thought you were aff tae Australia,' he said, pumping my arm and wheezing sorely. I asked him bluntly if either he or his mate Baldy, another acquaintance of mine, had any booze to spare, since I didn't feel so good. He rubbed his chin with an air of surprise. 'Baldy?' he said. 'He's been deid for a while. Did ye no' hear he wis burnt.'

'Burnt!' I repeated, having a fleeting image of a martyr at the stake.

'He lit a fire in the buildin' tae make some tea, and the place went up like a tinderbox. Luckily I wis away for a cerry oot at the time.'

Mick then took a fit of coughing, and asked me if I had a fag to spare to settle his throat.

'I haveny even got a match,' I explained.

He shrugged and turned back to his heap of fag ends. I knelt down beside him. He picked out two of the freshest and handed me one, then asked if I would like to come in for a drink.

'In where?' I asked, squinting upwards.

He kicked open a door behind. I followed him over piles of rubble into a room strewn with more rubble. A blanket was spread out in front of a fireplace heaped with ash. A strong smell of urine assailed my nostrils.

'No' very fancy,' said Mick, 'but it's cheery enough when I get the fire gaun.'

'I'd rather ye didny light a fire,' I said, thinking of Baldy.

He brought a bottle out from under the blanket and told me to have a gargle. It was a strange colour, a mixture of brown and green. I asked him if it was a home brew. He said that he wasn't sure as he had found it up the park. I said at that rate I wouldn't bother. He put the bottle to his mouth for a while, then told me it was the best stuff he had tasted for a long time. 'Go on, man,' he said, 'it'll no' kill ye.'

I wasn't sure about that but he was right about the booze. It was so strong that it brought the tears to my eyes. 'It's a liqueur, wan o' them fancy drinks that they serve in wee thin glasses big enough for a dwarf,' I explained.

After another couple of swallows each Mick became drunk. He began to sway and mumble.

'Are ye OK?' I asked.

'Sure I'm OK.' He fixed me with his bloodshot eyes. 'I've jist minded that you owe me a fiver. Ye borrowed it afore ye left for Australia.'

'You mean up north.'

'I don't care where it wis. Ye owe me a fiver,' said Mick, his voice thick but explicit.

'I thought it wis Baldy I owed the fiver.'

He thought over this remark and said, 'Maybe it wis so ye can gie me the money and I'll pass it on.'

'I thought ye said Baldy wis deid.'

'Who telt ye that?' he said, and took another swallow without offering me any.

'Is he deid or is he no'?' I asked impatiently. He was holding the bottle about an inch away from his eyes in order to gauge what amount of the liqueur remained. 'Maybe he's deid, but I'm no',' he said.

'Cheerio, Mick.' I turned away to find the exit. 'I've got better things tae dae than listen tae your ravings.'

He shouted, 'Fuck aff and leave me alane. Ye don't want me, but ye want ma drink.'

I thought, as I climbed over the heaps of plaster on the way out, that if I had any conscience at all I should report Mick to the social workers, or any kind of authority that took care of down and outs. But who was I to play God when I could scarcely take care of myself. Besides, he wouldn't thank me for it.

I didn't go near the Labour Exchange after that. The encounter with Mick had depressed me. When I returned to the house my mother asked me if I had been drinking. She was sure she could smell it off my breath. 'It's pineapple juice,' I said, 'it smells like drink.'

'Is that so?' she said, surprised.

I told her that there had been a long queue at the broo, but I would definitely go early the next morning.

'Jist as well ye didny wait,' she said. 'Duds Smith wants tae see ye. He might have a job for ye.'

'Duds the ragman. I canny see me shoutin' any auld rags through a tin trumpet.'

'Duds is in big business noo. He moved oot his council hoose intae a semi-detached. His wife walks aboot in a purple trooser outfit wi' her hair dyed blonde. It disny suit her.'

'Good luck to him, but I'm a brickie no' a hawker.' I turned up the television in order to finish the subject.

My mother turned it down again and said, 'Ye're no' likely tae be a brickie the way things are gaun nooadays, so ye'd better think again on Duds's offer. It's only because I'm pally wi' his wife that he's gi'en you the chance.'

'Did ye go crawlin' tae Duds on ma behalf?'

'I widny call it crawlin'. I'd call it havin' influence. It appears I'm the only one you know that has it.'

Duds Smith's scrapyard had stretched to double its original size. The old conglomeration of rags, copper, cookers and lawnmowers had been replaced by four big caravans, all painted yellow and with flowered curtains to match.

'Whit dae ye think o' them?' said Duds, brandishing a brush dripping with yellow paint. His style hadn't altered any. He wore the same dusty velour hat and baggy strides shoved into wellingtons. He was a wee fat man, with a nose and complexion typical of a son of the Levant race, though he maintained his origins were Irish.

'They're fabulous,' I said. 'They must cost a bomb.'

'Only three hunner quid. They're auld caravans tarted up a bit. I've selt two already.'

'Three hunner,' I said. 'Who's got that kind o' money aboot here?'

'Them that's got their redundancy money. Whit could be a better buy than a holiday hoose on the coast for only three hunner?'

'Right enough,' I said.

'And the beauty o' it is, if they canny keep up the site dues next year, havin' blown their cash by that time, I can buy the same caravan back for next tae nothin'.'

I was doubtful of his ethics, but I had to acknowledge his business sense.

I said, 'Ye could sell sand in the Sahara,' adding, 'I widny mind a caravan masel', though.'

'So,' said Duds after a pause, 'can ye drive? I need a man to deliver the caravans doon tae the coast on a low-loadin' truck.'

'Sure I can drive.' Actually I had driven an old banger once and had been stopped by the law. I considered the experience adequate enough. 'I haveny got a drivin' licence.'

'Nae problem. I can always buy wan,' said Duds.

He mentioned the amount of money I would earn. It was a lot less than what I had received on the building site. I told him this and he threw in the offer of a caravan reduced by fifty pounds, which I could pay for in instalments. I hesitated because I considered that it was a come down to work for Duds and I didn't really fancy driving a low-loader down to the coast.

'Let me know by the efternoon,' said Duds, 'otherwise I'll have tae send for ma brither-in-law.'

I entered the Labour Exchange and walked past the queue waiting on the bench as though I had an appointment. I banged on the counter. The clerk came through from the back premises yawning, and then asked me if I had waited my turn. 'Sure,' I said. 'I'm fed up waitin'. I thought ye were away for a kip.'

He frowned and asked me what I wanted.

'A job,' I said. 'Preferably as a brickie.'

He sighed and took out a form from a drawer. 'If you want to sign on, fill up this form.'

I asked him for a pen. He told me to sign it at home.

'How can I no' sign it here and save the footwear?'

'It's the rules,' he said wearily.

'I'll gie ye back yer pen, honest.'

He continued to shake his head as though he had some kind of palsy. Someone on the bench called, 'That guy's dodged his turn.'

'If that's true go and sit on the bench at the end of the queue,' said the clerk, suddenly alert and filled with fury.

I grabbed the form he held and tore it in two. 'Ye know whit ye can dae wi' that,' I said.

On the way out I gave the guys on the bench a V sign to which they responded with loud catcalls and jeers. Outside I stood on the steps, marked in black paint with the words FUCK THIS BROO, bracing myself for the only option ahead of me, and that was to accept Duds Smith's offer.

I nearly ran all the way back to his caravan yard when I started to consider that there were many possibilities in driving a low-loader. For instance, I could be sent up to the northern coast. It was possible I might bump into Nancy. It's a small world and this is a small country. I could even make a point of looking her up, come to that, all spruced up, the owner of a caravan and earning a weekly wage. She could only be impressed and overjoyed to see me again. As I strode rapidly along the road I laughed aloud at the extravagance of my thoughts. A woman passing, wearing a headscarf and carrying a bag of messages, gave me a startled look.

'It's a fine day for a chinge, missus,' I said.

Her face softened as she said, 'Aye, it's no' bad at a', son. We canny complain.'

A WORKING MOTHER

I

'I'll have to get a job,' I said.

My husband replied, 'To get away from me, I suppose.'

'We owe money. The kids need clothes, apart from the fact that we like to eat.'

'Do what you like. I'm tired of carrying you all.'

'You are tired of carrying yourself.'

He nodded. Ten years after the war he still looked as if he had just come home from the battlefield. Flags and bunting had hung from the windows in our street. I had helped to paste the letters reading WELCOME HOME ADAM, and immediately fell in love with his handsome, suffering face when he passed by our window.

'A fine lad,' my dad had said.

'He looks –' My mother broke off.

'Looks what?'

'Unreliable.'

I wanted to run out and touch him.

'Come back from the window, girl,' said my father. Then he ran up the street and shook his hand. The same evening he returned from the pub accompanied by Adam. Both were drunk, but drunk or sober I loved this war hero. Now I wanted to escape from him.

'I think I will go to the city for work,' I said. 'I should get something with no bother. I can type.'

'You're bound to be a success in an office with your laddered stockings and black fingernails.'

'It's only coal,' I explained. 'I can be smart when I want to.'

'Let's celebrate your new job.'

I emptied my purse and discovered I had enough for a bottle of the sweet, sickly, but lovely South African wine.

In a dingy street near the docks I located an agency, to reach which I climbed rickety wooden stairs.

'Could I see the manager?' I asked the young girl behind a window marked Enquiries. Her thin nose quivered.

'You mean Mrs Rossi?'

I nodded.

'I don't know. She might be engaged.'

'Will I come back?'

She sighed and turned down the corner of a page in a paperback on the ledge. 'Wait there,' she said.

Upside down I read the title *Love Came Too Late*. I turned the book round with no real interest and was caught in the act.

'She'll see you,' said the girl, grabbing the paperback.

'It looks good,' I said. She directed me sharply into the presence of Mrs Rossi.

'What is it you want to do, dear?' she asked me.

I sat down. 'Typing, I suppose.' I wondered if there were other possibilities.

'Do you have any legal experience?'

'Actually no – but –'

'It's not important.' She smiled and I was charmed by her eyes shining like two black beads in her plump, olive face. She scribbled something on a piece of paper. I admired the glittering rings embedded in each of her fat fingers. 'You will be fine with this firm. They are very nice. It's a lawyers' office.' She handed me over the paper in a delicate way. 'My commission is minimal,' she said.

'That will be great.' I felt like kissing her hand.

'It's for a fortnight. You can't go wrong.'

Leaving the room I collided with the ferret-faced girl on the other side of the door.

★

I located my employers, Chalmers & Stroud, in a street of polished nameplates. My legs dragged up the marble stairs. I had decided to ask if they required a cleaner, but was placed in a large room and seated at a heavy polished table before I could say anything. A kindly-faced old gent entered, shook my hand and said he was very pleased I had managed to come.

'I have no experience of legal work,' I said boldly.

'I'm sure you will manage.'

'It has been a while since I typed.'

'I'm sure typing is like riding a bicycle. You never forget how to do it.'

'I suppose so,' I said, looking at the shelves laden with heavy volumes. 'I can do shorthand too,' I added.

'That's marvellous. You wouldn't like a permanent job by any chance?'

I took so long to answer that he left the room. I closed my eyes in order to relax before I faced the marble stairs again, the bus ride home, then Adam's sneer at my lack of success. The old gent returned with a cup in his hand.

'There's nothing like tea,' he said.

'Thank you, Mr . . . ?'

'Mr Robson.'

I drank my tea slowly while he rummaged through a folder.

'Are you finished?' he asked considerately when I had drunk the dregs down to the sugary bit. Then he proceeded to dictate a letter with the words carefully articulated, reminding me of dictation in the primary school.

'I've got a job,' I told Adam.

'Good for you. I can now relinquish all responsibility for this household then?'

'And I can save up for a divorce.'

'So, let's celebrate,' said Adam.

★

'Where does Mr Chalmers hang out?' I asked Mr Robson.

'Mainly in the courthouse, to parry and thrust.'

'And Mr Stroud?'

'In a far, far better place.'

He gave me some dictation, during which I could scarcely suppress my yawns, and said at the end of it, 'I like your suit.'

'My husband calls it my Robin Hood outfit.' When he raised his eyebrows I added, 'Being green and kind of merry-like.'

'You are happily married then?'

'No.'

'Why is that?'

'Perhaps because my husband was a war hero.'

Mr Robson drew his chair closer to me. 'My wife is dead.' He placed one finger on my hand. 'Of course it happened a long time ago.'

I uncrossed my legs and drew them under my chair. 'That is very sad.'

'I've got used to it.' He coughed then said, 'Of course I don't bother with the opposite sex, but I like listening to their problems. It keeps me' – he smiled wistfully – 'young.'

'What do you think of old Robson?' a voice hissed in my ear when I was concentrating on an indecipherable word of short-hand. I looked round, surprised at being spoken to by any of the females in the typing pool.

'He's very nice,' I said.

'He's –' The owner of the voice tapped her head.

'Aren't we all?' I smiled shyly.

'Where do you go for lunch?'

'The cheapest place.'

The owner of the voice laughed. Her face was markedly pale in contrast to her short black hair and mascaraed eyelashes as long as spiders' legs.

'I know all the cheapest places,' she said.

★

'I lunched with one of the typists today,' I told Adam.

'I hope you're not wasting money on expensive meals.'

'Pie and beans is all I had, besides —'

'Yes, I know, you are earning money.'

'Can I get some sauce?' asked my ten-year-old son Robert, whose hair fell over his eyes in a maddening way.

'We can't afford sauce,' said Adam.

'Where are you going?' I shouted to my eight-year-old daughter Rae when she slithered off her chair.

'For a piss.'

'Don't dare use that word!' But she was gone.

Adam picked morosely at his black-pudding supper. Robert complained that he hated chips without sauce.

'My mother always maintained that meals should be a happy time, a time of unity and serenity,' I said.

'Your mother was a goon,' said Adam.

'She was right about you.'

'Do tell me.'

'She said anyone who was in the war was no use, and the only people who had any guts were conscientious objectors. It took guts to make a stand like that.'

'I don't know about that,' said Adam, picking off some frizzled paper from his black-pudding. 'I saw plenty of guts hanging from trees in the war. They must have belonged to someone.'

'I can't eat no more of this rubbish,' screamed Robert, and ran out of the back door.

'Never mind, kid,' said Adam, placing his hand on my shoulder. 'You're doing a great job.'

'I never would have taken you for a married woman with children,' said Mr Robson when he had finished his painstaking dictation.

I smiled deprecatingly. 'Especially with all the problems I have.'

'I thought as much,' he said.

'Not that I want to talk about them.'

He patted my knee ever so gently. 'A problem shared is a problem halved.'

'Not with my husband it isn't.'

Mr Robson looked expectant.

After a pause I said, 'He doesn't understand how difficult it is to manage.'

'You mean with money?' His mouth drooped.

'Mainly.'

'You can earn more if you become permanent.'

'I'll think about it, but – it's not only that.'

'Has it' – Mr Robson's voice was hushed – 'something to do with the war?'

'I can't talk about it.'

Mr Robson's face became flushed. 'I understand. Perhaps,' he said, taking out his wallet, 'I could advance you something until you get your wages?'

'Oh no, I couldn't,' I said, running out of the room with my pencil and pad.

'It's all balls,' said Adam.

'I don't like your language. What is?'

'You out working. The doctor said I was fit to go back to work. How can I, now that you're away all day? Someone's got to be in for the kids coming home from school.'

'Did he write you out another line?'

'Yes – but I don't want to stop in the house for ever.'

I kissed the top of his head where his fine brown hair was becoming thin. 'Take it easy. Your nerves are still shattered from that fireworks display when they opened the new town hall.'

'I couldn't help thinking it was gunfire. I must have dozed off.'

'Never mind, on Friday night we'll celebrate when I get some money. Perhaps we'll see Brendan. He appears to like our company.'

'Which is most unusual,' said Adam.

Much later in the evening the minister on the television said, 'Life after death is something we must contemplate very seriously.'

'I'd much rather contemplate some life before death,' said Adam. He added with a glance in my direction, 'There's not been much of it around recently.'

'Shhh,' I said.

We sat at each end of the settee holding a glass of sweet wine. The kids, protesting violently, were long gone to bed.

'Dying is natural and inevitable,' said the minister.

'Turn that crap off,' said Adam.

'God's ways are mysterious,' said the minister.

'It's peaceful and deep. I like it,' I said.

'I'll give you something peaceful and deep if you come to bed.'

'I'd rather not. I'm much too tired,' I said.

'You're not getting a bit on the side in that bloody office?'

'With Mr Robson?' I tittered. 'He must be sixty if he's a day.'

'The streets in the city are so hard,' I told Mr Robson, 'and the soles of my shoes are so thin. I don't know how they are going to last until Friday.'

'We can't have that,' he said, reaching for his wallet.

'It's only a loan —' I began.

'Certainly. Now draw your chair near and tell me more about that poor husband of yours.'

'I have told you about certain experiences during the war.'

'Yes, yes, but tell me how it affected him.'

'You mean mentally?'

He patted me in a fatherly way above the knee. 'I mean sexually.'

Hurrying along the crowded streets with Mai, the black-haired typist with the long eyelashes, was exciting, but also demeaning. All the men looked at her, but seldom at me.

'Why do you stare at everyone?' she asked.

'Faces attract me.'

'Only faces?'

'I'm always hoping to see a friendly one.'

'God, you're a scream.'

Whilst munching pies Mai said, 'I wish I could find a nice decent bloke with plenty of money.'

'There isn't any such thing,' I said, staring over Mai's head at a youngish-looking guy with horn-rimmed spectacles. He appeared to be looking at me, but I wasn't sure.

'You mean rich and decent?'

'I mean decent.'

The guy waved. I looked away, just in time. A female rushed past me and joined him.

'Oh well, I'll skip the decent and settle for the rich.' Pointing to the third finger of my left hand she added, 'I see you're married.'

I nodded and managed to swallow a bit of hard crust which stabbed the back of my throat.

'What's wrong? You look upset.'

'Some things can be painful,' I said vaguely.

'You can say that again,' said Mai, slurping her tea and leaving a smear of lipstick on the rim of the cup. 'I was once nearly married but the bastard took cold feet and left me holding the baby. Literally, I mean.'

'What a shame.' I decided that in future I would just take soup.

'It's not a tragedy. Thank God I've got my aunt to babysit.'

'With or without a husband, it's all the same. I've got two children, and here I am out working.'

'We'd be better off in a kibbutz,' said Mai. There was a smear of tomato sauce on the corner of her lips – it looked like blood. I felt squeamish. 'Can I have those chips?' she asked when I put down my knife and fork. 'As I was saying,' she said between munching, 'that old Robson's a queer hawk, isn't he?'

'He's not bad.'

'I notice he keeps you a long time in his office, yet you don't take long to finish the letters.'

'I'm a fast worker,' I said winking.

She laughed harshly. 'You're a right scream. Wait until I tell them in the office. They all think you're stuck-up.'

After that I was popular and included in conversations. I added very little to them, but what I did seemed amusing, and I always winked when Mr Robson buzzed for me.

'The typing pool ladies appear to like me now,' I confided to Mr Robson.

'Who wouldn't,' he said, placing his hand farther up my skirt.

'We are doing well for ourselves,' said Adam when I produced some pickled gherkins along with gammon.

'I borrowed some money from one of the women,' I explained, 'and I've got some drink for later.'

The kids looked over. 'Can we get it?'

'Yeah, yeah, you'll get, when you've finished your meal.'

'Isn't Mummy the greatest,' said Adam.

The gherkins were sour, but the colour contrasted nicely with the gammon and tomatoes.

Rain battered on my face on the way to the bus stop. I had no umbrella. I was upset by memories of lost umbrellas. I remembered a particularly nice one. It was mauve with dark-blue flowers – someone had left it on the train so I jumped off at the next stop with the umbrella in the shopping bag before it could be handed in to the lost property. For ages I had wandered around in the rain with a sense of pride. Inevitably I lost it. I don't know where, but I mourned for it like the loss of a friend.

'You're soaked,' said the women in the typing pool. 'Have you no umbrella?'

'I left it in the bus,' I said.

'It happens all the time. Try the lost property.'

'I doubt if it will be handed in. Not many people are honest,' I said.

'You can say that again,' said Mai. 'Someone pinched mine once before I could bat an eye. Expensive it was.'

I looked at her sharply and sneezed.

'I see you've got a cold coming on,' said Mr Robson.

'I got soaked this morning. I've lost my umbrella.'

'Poor thing,' said Mr Robson absently. 'By the way,' he added, 'I've an appointment with Mr Chalmers in ten minutes so we'll have to get a move on with the correspondence.'

'Of course, Mr Robson,' I said. 'I just hope I won't be off with this cold. I'm very subject to bronchitis.'

He looked at me slightly taken aback.

2

When we were married Adam wore his demob suit. My mother bought me a coat flared from the waist, princess style it was called, and a wide-brimmed hat with a ribbon hanging down the back, but she didn't come to the wedding. In fact no one did, but we wanted it that way.

'Some wedding,' she said. 'A hole-and-corner affair in a registrar's office and not even a best man or bridesmaid. I'm ashamed.'

'Give the lass a break. Besides, it saves bother,' said my father. He was sitting back in the armchair reading a paper with his feet up on a stool, his toes sticking through holes in the socks.

'I haven't even told anyone she's getting married, I'm that ashamed.'

'Leave it be,' said my father. 'It will be all one in the long run.'

'Imagine marrying someone that's just come out of jail.'

'He was only drunk,' I said.

'Broke into the post office and was only drunk?' said my mother.

'Stands to reason it was only because he was drunk,' I said. 'He was caught sitting on the post office floor throwing money in the air.'

'Stupid bastard,' said my father. He sniffed. 'Of course I blame the bloody war. They're all nuts.'

'To think I've scrimped to throw her away on a nut case.'

'I'll have to go now, Mum,' I said. 'Do I look all right?'

'You look a bloody treat,' said my father.

My mother burst into tears and handed me a fiver.

★

'He's just gone round for sugar,' said Adam's stepmother, who hated Adam. She leant out of her window, looking down on me from the second-storey flat.

'But he's getting married today. We've arranged it at the registrar's,' I called.

'Oh yes, I believe he mentioned something about it. He shouldn't be long.' She banged down the window.

I waited for twenty minutes outside the building before he showed up. 'Where's the sugar?' I asked. His face looked shrivelled.

'Sugar? I've been for a hair cut. What's that cow been saying?'

'Never mind. We are going to be late.'

'I think this is most unusual,' said the young woman we had approached in the street to ask if she would mind witnessing our marriage.

'It's definitely an honour,' said the young man who had been walking close behind her.

'We didn't want to make a fuss,' I explained.

'Her people don't approve of me,' said Adam.

'It's just that my mother doesn't trust men who were in the war,' I explained.

The couple shook our hands warmly after the short ceremony. They both hoped we would be very happy.

'I have never been so happy,' I said, as we journeyed back in the bus to our lodgings in a room belonging to Adam's stepbrother, who I later discovered also hated Adam. 'Aren't you happy too?' I added.

'I don't know,' he said. Then, 'Sometimes I wish I was back –'

'Back where?'

'Back in the army. I suppose it was hell, but at least it wasn't like this.'

Sandwiched between Adam and Brendan in the pub I felt very happy. It was easier to snuggle close to Brendan's bulk than Adam's boniness, though I tried to be impartial.

'Let me pay,' said Brendan.

'It's my turn,' said Adam.

'Bugger both of you,' I said. 'I've just got paid. I'll buy.'

'You're a kept man,' laughed Brendan.

I handed Adam a note and asked him to get the drink. I moved some inches away from Brendan for decency's sake.

'You're looking great,' he said.

'It's just the drink.'

'It isn't. You seem to get better looking all the time.'

Laughing, I patted my hair. 'It's my new hairdo. Underneath it's still the same old boring me.'

'You're never boring,' said Brendan, panting slightly.

Adam returned with the drinks. He looked stern.

'I was just telling Betty she looked great,' said Brendan.

Adam said, 'Hands off.'

Brendan's eyes bulged in his beefy face. 'Sorry, squire.'

'Move up a bit, old fellow,' said Adam, 'you're crushing my wife. She looks unnaturally hot.'

Brendan humped along the bench.

'You should have brought a girlfriend,' I said.

'I'm not stopping long.'

'Very huffy all of a sudden,' said Adam.

'Not me,' said Brendan, dashing over his drink. He stood up clumsily.

'For God's sake, man,' said Adam, 'you can't leave just like that. I was merely joking.'

'I don't know what's got into you two,' I said, pressing Brendan's foot under the table, 'but if you're both going to be like this I might as well go home.'

Brendan sat down. 'I should have tidied myself up,' he mumbled.

'Tidied up wouldn't suit him, would it, Adam?' I said. 'Being scruffy and nonchalant is his main attraction.'

'Besides he hasn't got anything else to wear,' said Adam.

'I didn't come here to be insulted,' said Brendan, laughing on his way over to the bar to get more drink.

At closing time we all tottered out of the pub. Adam marched on ahead very straight. Brendan's hand had brushed my cheek when he put his arm over my shoulder to hold open the pub door.

'I'd like to do something to you,' he whispered into the back of my neck.

We left him standing on the pavement, swaying slightly with his hands in his pockets. 'Bloody pest at times,' said Adam.

'He's your friend, after all,' I said.

'There's this fellow who fancies me,' I told Mr Robson, 'and he's a friend of my husband.'

'Does your husband know?' asked Mr Robson.

'He acts as if he's jealous when I'm with them both, but it's just an act. I don't think so.'

'Intriguing,' said Mr Robson. 'Was this fellow in the war?'

'No. That's what I like about him. He's younger than Adam, but anyway I think there's something wrong with him.'

Mr Robson raised his eyebrows.

'Backward. I don't mean retarded, just backward, but he attracts me somehow.'

'Has anything . . . ?'

'Oh no, but when he said that he'd like to do something to me I felt attracted to him.'

'He's not dangerous by any chance?'

'Brendan dangerous? Why he's got the sweetest nature. Mind you, he's a bit uncouth, but he has the most vivid-blue eyes.'

Mr Robson frowned. 'I wouldn't encourage him if I were you.'

'I haven't. It's Adam who encourages him.'

'How's your cold?' asked Mr Robson.

'My cold? It didn't come to anything, thank goodness.' I brought out some pound notes from a pocket in my skirt. 'Here's the money I owe you.'

His wrinkled hand closed over mine holding the money. 'Consider this a gift. You're a very sweet person – different from the others, if I may say so.'

After dictating a few short letters he said he was very proud to be the recipient of my confidences since he was writing a book about human behaviour in animals, and perhaps I might care to have tea with him at his semi-detached bungalow the following Sunday.

'I wouldn't go if I were you,' said Mai in the café at lunchtime.

'He's harmless,' I said.

'He's a creepy old bastard.'

I bent my head low over my soup. Mai pointed her knife at me.

'I don't get it,' she said. 'It's not natural inviting you out –'

I interrupted, 'It's quite simple. He's writing a book and he wants me to do a bit of typing.'

'Oh yeah?' She leered.

Her face, too close to mine, bothered me. I could see blackheads round her nose. 'You eat too much greasy food,' I said.

'So? What's that got to do with the price of a loaf? I'll say this,' she added, narrowing her eyes. 'He's got bags of money.'

'I'm glad to hear it.' I leaned back, perspiring from the heat of the soup.

'He made his money from the firm years ago. Should have retired, but he likes to nose around.'

'It's up to the firm what he does.' I shut my eyes overpowered by steam.

'They say he's got something on Mr Chalmers – why else would he be kept on?'

'As far as I'm concerned Mr Robson's a nice old man, and if he's going to pay me for doing some typing that's all I'm interested in.'

'You're quite right,' said Mai, and shut her mouth tight.

After a minute she opened it. 'I'm fed up with this restaurant. It's stodgy.'

Mrs Rossi telephoned me at the typing pool office. 'How are you getting on?' she asked.

'I love it,' I answered.

'And Mr Robson?'

'He's ever so nice.'

'Marvellous,' she purred.

'I might be kept on, but I'm not sure,' I said.

'If you make some arrangement come and see me,' she said. The word 'arrangement' lingered in my head like a whiff of orange blossom.

On Saturday it rained all day – a heavy torrential downpour with no sign of a break in the sky to allow it to clear up in the evening and give me the excuse for a stroll, if Adam happened to ask where I was going. Brendan and I had arranged to meet on the fringe of the woods – a good twenty-minute walk from the back of our house. With Brendan nothing was a certainty, and with this continual rainfall it was certain he would not be there – but I was compelled to make the effort, being a besotted fool. Adam retired early, worn out by his Friday-night binge, which was one thing to be thankful for. I donned an old mac which allowed the rain in as effectively as any other coat, but looked right for it.

'You're going out in this weather?' he asked when I glanced into the bedroom to see how he was.

'I must get some fresh air. All this cooking has given me a sore head.'

'Good luck to you,' he said, reclining against the pillow and viewing me across a library book.

'Perhaps you'd like to come?' I said, banking on there being no chance of it.

'Only fools or lovers would go out in a night like this.' His eyes were steady, but unsuspicious.

'I won't be long,' I assured him, inwardly aghast at my deceit towards this man whom I loved and hated with an equal intensity. Tonight I could easily have loved him, but I loved Brendan so much more. At that moment it seemed conscience does not necessarily make cowards of us all.

I could see a good distance along the path as I walked to the spot where Brendan should be waiting under the trees, though my vision was slightly blurred by the rain assaulting my eyes. I knew he wouldn't be there. Dismally I foresaw myself stumbling through sodden grass in a dripping wood with two pies and a bottle of wine in my bag, but when I reached the tree Brendan stepped from behind it and drew me into his arms.

'Thank God you came,' he said. 'I had no hope you would on a night like this.' He wiped the rain running off my cheeks like tears, adding, 'You must be crazy.'

Hand in hand we picked our way over the spongy grass until we found a patch between some bushes less sodden than everywhere else. I took off my coat (he had none on) and spread it on the ground. He took off his jumper, as rough as steel wool, and rolled it up to make a pillow.

'You'll catch cold,' I said.

'I've already caught it.'

Feverishly we made love, without much sexual satisfaction on my part, but I had the pleasure of making him happy. Afterwards I handed him the wine and a pie. As we ate and passed the bottle between us the rain eased off to a drizzle, but we still shivered in the wet undergrowth. I wondered if I really loved this man, an unemployed labourer, who possessed hardly anything. He was good-looking in a thuggish fashion, but I had seen better-looking – Adam for instance, but then Adam was an old and difficult story.

'Why do I love you, I wonder?' I asked Brendan.

'God knows,' he answered, wiping his mouth on the back of his hand as he finished off the pie. He replaced the cross and chain round his neck inside his jumper. It had been dangling in my face all the time he was on top of me.

'You're going to get ulcers one day,' I said.

'Who cares about one day? Today is what matters.'

I nodded. Perhaps it was his freedom I envied. It was on the tip of my tongue to say that it would be better if we didn't see one another again, when he asked, 'How's the big fellow?'

'Adam's fine,' I replied, angered and insulted by the question. 'Why do you ask?'

He shrugged. 'My conscience maybe.'

I jeered. 'So, afterwards your conscience bothers you, but never before.'

He didn't answer, but held his hand out for the bottle.

'You don't really love me. You just use me.' I was falling into the old trap again, just when I had the notion to break loose.

He gripped my arm, making me wince. 'I love you, I love you, I'll make a record of it, and send it to you so that when I'm dead and buried you can play it over and over, if that's what you want to hear.' He looked at me miserably and I was glad to have wrung the words out of him. He added, 'But sometimes love has nothing to do with it.'

I eased out the cross from under his jumper. 'Has it to do with this? Some pagan superstition, I suppose.'

He drew back as if I'd slapped him. 'I don't think so.'

Gently I took the bottle from him, satisfied I had hurt him. I drank a mouthful of wine and understood what Adam meant when he once said that it tasted as good as chocolate. The sun shone through the trees for a second, then vanished.

Brendan groaned. 'Don't tell me that it's going to clear up now that I've caught my death lying in this mud.'

'That's your precious God's way of doing things. Give them a taste of how it could be when it's too late.'

He grinned. 'Better late than never. At least I will have died making you happy.'

'Of course,' I retorted, 'you only make love to me out of the kindness of your heart.'

'One time you are going to make me hit you,' he said, gripping my wrist hard. I wished then he would hit me so that I could have more power over him.

'You make it sound as though it is pure hell for you being with me.'

'Most of the time it is,' he said.

'I wouldn't worry too much if I were you. You can always confess before we meet again.'

Perhaps I had gone too far. He said coldly, 'What makes you think we will meet again?' and rose to his feet.

When I stood up he helped me on with my very wet and crumpled raincoat. I found a damp handkerchief in my pocket and wiped the leaves and mud from his horrifying pullover and in turn he wiped my coat. We held hands again as we waded through the grass to reach the point of separation. We regarded each other sadly.

'I'll probably see you around,' he said.

I forced myself to smile. 'You know it's impossible to escape me.'

I ran back down the muddy path wondering if I might be the victim of some lurking maniac, and also thinking resentfully that if Brendan really loved me he would not have let me return by this sinister path on my own.

'I said that will be all for the time being.'

Mr Robson's cooing voice brought me back to the uneasy realisation that his ten minutes of dictation had been receiving scant attention from me.

'Be careful with that report. It's for the head office,' he added darkly.

'Yes, certainly,' I said, but thought, 'You'll be lucky.'

3

When war broke out I was thirteen years old. I was on holiday with my parents in an unspectacular seaside resort. The only thing I liked about it was the small window on the sloping attic roof above my bed. Everything else was boredom: long walks with my parents, sitting in a deckchair beside my parents, watching my parents play bowls in the bowling green set aside for visitors behind the church hall. I heard about the war from a conversation between my mother and the landlady, who was frying some ham for our breakfast. I was sitting in the toilet separated from the kitchenette by a thin wall when I heard my mother shout on my father. A radio was turned up and I stopped feeling bored. Quickly I flushed the toilet and joined them.

'Shall we all get killed?' I asked.

The landlady, who was ancient and wore a man's cap, put her finger to her lips as the three of them continued to listen to the sonorous voice of the newsreader. They appeared frightened. I left the kitchen and went upstairs to my parents' room. I took a ten-shilling note from the purse in my mother's handbag then returned to the kitchen. They were still listening to the radio in fearful concentration. I noticed the ham on the gas ring was frizzled.

'Can I go out to play?' I asked loudly.

My mother made a vague gesture with her hand as if to say clear off. I wandered into the main street and purchased twelve chocolate liqueurs from a distracted woman in the sweet shop. On a bench on the promenade I ate two of the liqueurs, feeling excited and slightly drunk. Apart from being sick I cannot remember much of the remainder of that day, except for my mother saying to my father as I went to my bed under the sloping window, 'I am positive I had another ten-shilling note. I wouldn't be surprised if that landlady pinched it while we were out.'

Later on I remember looking up at the red sky through the attic window and associating its splendour with the seven and six I had left in my knickers' pocket.

'You knew nothing about the war,' Adam was saying.

'I knew about Sidi Barrani, El Alamein and Tobruk. When we went to the Saturday matinée the names went through my head all the time like the dreary poems you got at school. Then there were the Desert Rats. We were hoping to see big rats in the sand. All we saw were tanks and guns. We used to stamp our feet and shout, "We want James Cagney. Give us the picture."'

'While men were dying,' said Adam.

'You didn't die. I wish you had.'

'So do I when I look at you and these brats and this dump.'

I smashed my empty glass into the empty fireplace. 'Don't dare call my children brats. Call me what you like, but not them. They are innocent.'

'Innocent – that's a laugh. They could teach the Arab kids a few tricks.'

'You'll know all about the Arab kids. Penny for my sister –'

'I'm going home,' said Brendan. 'I can't stand this.'

'Don't go,' said Adam and I almost simultaneously. 'We're not really fighting.'

'No, stay,' said Adam. 'I'll get another bottle. We'll be all right with another bottle.'

I raked in my bag and threw him some money. 'Don't be long and don't drink any before you get back.'

'Unlike you, I've got some decency,' he said, leaving the room.

'I can't stand when you argue like that – it does something to my brain,' said Brendan.

'I know,' I said, holding his head to my chest and stroking his hair. It was as tough as wire.

'Adam is my friend,' said Brendan, nuzzling closer.

'And I'm your friend too,' I said. 'We'd better be quick. He'll be running down the street.'

'What's the matter with him?' said Adam when he returned and was unwrapping the brown paper from the bottle.

Brendan was weeping in the chair.

'It's because we were arguing,' I said. 'He can't stand it. It does something to his brain.'

'Come on old chap,' said Adam, putting his hand on Brendan's broad shoulder. 'We won't argue again. We're pals now, Betty and I. We're all pals.'

In a low voice he hissed to me, 'See what you've done.'

My first meeting with Brendan had been one Saturday afternoon when Adam brought him back to the house after the pubs closed. He had the friendly look of a brigand from a Mexican film: swarthy, unshaven, and too young to be a war veteran. I perched on the arm of the chair where he sat and accepted a glass of cheap wine from his bottle.

'Meet the wife, Brendan,' said Adam.

Brendan's hand when he shook mine was strong and warm, the smile on his broad face with its flattened nose had melancholy charm, and I noticed his eyes, unlike a Mexican bandit's, were vividly blue. He didn't say much. Adam entertained us with some humorous war experiences I had heard before. The kids came in and hovered near Brendan. My son Robert studied the label on the wine bottle and asked Adam if he could have a sip, at which question I slapped him on the ear. He immediately howled, and my daughter kicked Adam's leg for the hell of it. It would have been a bad moment but for Brendan, who produced two separate shillings for them. They ran off, delighted. After that I put on a record called 'One Enchanted Evening'. Brendan and

I waltzed, or rather shuffled around the floor, while Adam sat with downcast head, silently crying, which was a bad sign. Not long after that Adam had Brendan by the throat and was pushing him towards the door. Brendan's powerful hands unlocked Adam's rather easily I thought. He pushed Adam back on the chair and punched him on the mouth. Adam wiped his mouth and looked vacantly at the blood on his fingers.

'It's the war,' I said. 'It's affected his brain, especially when he's drinking.'

'Are you all right?' said Brendan, wiping Adam's lip with the bottom of his pullover, which was ripped.

'I'm sorry,' said Adam, pulling on a bit of wool and unravelling it even farther. 'I didn't mean it. You of all people, my friend.'

He broke down again and Brendan cried too. I went into the kitchenette and made some tea.

'So you see,' I said to Mr Robson, 'Brendan has almost become part of the family. The kids call him Uncle Brendan.'

'Children invariably adopt acquaintances of the parents as relatives. It is a sign of insecurity,' he stated in a lofty manner.

'My children are very insecure,' I agreed.

'It seems to me this Brendan is also insecure.'

'Indeed he is. Being insecure myself I have noticed how much more insecure he is. He has no employment to speak of, apart from an odd gardening job here and there, because he feels so insecure.'

'Perhaps he's just lazy.'

'Oh no. Brendan would do anything for anybody. If you met him you'd know what I mean.'

'Hmm,' said Mr Robson. After a pause he said, 'Has he become your lover yet?'

'It's hard to think of Brendan as a lover. We are seldom alone together except for one time when Adam ran down the street for a bottle of wine. But to be honest I don't really want to be alone with Brendan for too long. He has no conversation.'

'It all sounds very intriguing,' said Mr Robson.

On Friday evening after leaving my employment I took a jaunt to the dock area to visit Mrs Rossi. The office girl raised her eyebrows when she saw me.

'Well,' she said.

'I would like to see Mrs Rossi, if you don't mind,' I said, staring her out. After a long pause she inclined her head towards Mrs Rossi's office. I could have sworn there was a smirk on her lips.

'You've come at a bad time,' said Mrs Rossi, stubbing a cigarette into a saucerful of ash. 'However.' She shrugged.

'It's nothing really,' I began. 'I just want to ask your advice.'

'Advice?'

'But if you're busy –' I said.

'I can spare ten minutes.' She lit a cigarette and looked at me enquiringly.

'I have been offered a permanent position with Chalmers & Stroud and I wondered –'

'Well that's just fine, dear.' Delicately she blew a smoke ring into the air, a study in sophistication. Her black earrings matched her black eyes and contrasted well with her bejewelled hands.

'I hate being tied down,' I said.

'Tell me,' she asked, 'are you a Gemini?'

'Come to think of it, I am.'

'Geminis are like that – always on the move, easily dissatisfied, but often very talented.'

'Fancy that,' I said.

'You've got me going now,' she said, casting the papers on the table to one side. Then she brought out a pack of cards from a drawer and dealt out six of them face downwards. One by one she turned them over with great concentration. I scarcely breathed. She closed her eyes for so long I thought she had dozed off. I coughed nervously. Her eyes when opened were so black she appeared to have no irises.

'There are three men in your life,' she said, 'one of whom you have great doubts about. Cast your doubts aside, for this man is good for you and he will improve your circumstances greatly.'

I asked timidly, 'Does this mean I should stay on at Chalmers & Stroud?'

'Oh dear me,' she laughed, looking quite normal now. 'You'll have to make up your own mind about that. I can only convey a general impression from the cards. Any elaboration could be misleading.'

'You have been most helpful, Mrs Rossi. It's been very inter-esting to discover you can tell fortunes.'

'I don't do it in a big way, just now and then when I get the urge. Come and see me again. Who knows, I might get another urge.' She laughed unusually loudly.

The office girl shoved her ferret face round the door asking, 'Did you shout?' and looking at me suspiciously.

'Yes,' said Mrs Rossi, suddenly appearing hostile. 'There are letters for posting. Get a move on with them.'

'Goodbye,' I said, heading for the door, but neither of them answered.

'Tells fortunes!' exclaimed Mai as we sat pressed close at the table of McFenny's Food Service Cafeteria, which we were sampling for a change. 'Sounds dodgy to me,' she added.

'Everyone sounds dodgy to you,' I said, trying to get some spaghetti to my mouth with my right elbow wedged in her side.

'There's a lot of dodgy people around and I consider fortune tellers very dodgy.'

'She's not a professional, just reads the cards when she gets the urge.'

'Gets the urge?' Mai repeated giggling. 'This spaghetti's marvel-lous, isn't it?'

'It's very long. They should cut it up in smaller pieces. It reminds me of worms.'

Mai dropped her fork. 'You've put me off. I can't take another bit.'

'It's disgusting anyway.'

We sipped our tea with heads close to the cups.

'Honest to Christ, I'm really fed up with everything,' she burst out.

'Sorry,' I said.

'I don't mean the spaghetti – just everything.'

'How's that?'

'I can't go on like this, forever sitting in with the baby all week then going to the dancing on a Saturday and meeting no one, no one that's interesting, that is.'

I shrugged. 'At least you go to the dancing.'

'What do you do on Saturday nights – watch the telly?'

'Actually I go out for a drink with Adam and his pal Brendan, and leave the kids to the telly.'

Her head swivelled round. 'Brendan, eh? What's he like?'

'He's hard to explain. You wouldn't like him.'

'Try me. Three's a crowd, four's company.' Her eyes were pleading.

'It's a good distance. Oh well,' I said, 'I'll give you the name of the pub and directions later in the week, if you want.'

'Marvellous,' she said, and clapped her hands.

'Did you know that Geminis are always on the move, easily dissatisfied and often talented?' I asked Adam.

'No.'

'According to Mrs Rossi they are.'

'Who's Mrs Rossi?'

'The woman who runs the agency.'

We sat round the table looking down on burnt mince.

'I hate mince,' said my son.

'I hate burnt mince,' said my daughter, and banged her spoon down on the plate with a dollop of mince stuck to it like cement.

'It's not easy to burn mince,' I told Adam.

'I fell asleep. I'm always tired nowadays.'

'Doing what?' I shoved a lump of rock-like substance in my mouth. When I got no reply I went on, 'Anyway, between Mrs Rossi saying that Geminis are talented and Mr Robson wanting me to come to his house on Sunday and do some typing for him – for which I will get paid extra – I am quite pleased with myself.'

'I'm glad you're pleased, because we're not – are we, son?' he said to Robert, who was by this time staring at his meal with intense hatred.

'So go and take a banana!' I screamed, at the same time catching hold of Rae, who was sliding down her chair to escape. 'And you, miss, don't move!'

All was ominously silent for five minutes. Then Adam said, 'Next week I'm going back to work and you can stay at home.' He picked up Robert's banana skin from the table and threw it at me shouting, 'This definitely can't go on.'

'You forget,' I said, catching the skin, 'that you were sacked last week by post, so it will have to go on, and furthermore I will be going out on Sunday to earn some more money.'

'Can we come with you?' said Rae, who had been in a fit of giggles over the banana skin.

'I'll take you both out on Saturday, to the seaside perhaps, if you're good.'

'Is Daddy coming?' asked Robert.

'Of course he is, if he's good.' I put my arm round Adam's shoulder. He now sat slumped with his mouth moving strangely. 'Won't that be a good idea?' I said, 'to get away from everything?'

'Is Uncle Brendan coming?' asked Rae.

'Uncle Brendan has no decent suit to put on. Besides he once said he didn't like the sea. It makes him want to drown himself.'

'I'll come,' said Adam, shaking his head. 'I'll come and drown myself instead.'

'It will be nice,' I said, patting the back of his fist lying clenched on the table, 'for the four of us to have a trip by ourselves for a change.'

'Betty is taking us to the seaside,' Adam told Brendan in the pub on Friday, while my eyes were glued on the door looking for Mai.

'That will be nice,' said Brendan.

'Sorry old chap, it's just me and her and the kids. It was her idea.'

Brendan recoiled and wiped his mouth as if it was all crumbs. 'Of course. I wasn't suggesting. I mean I wouldn't intrude on a family outing.'

'Especially you not being one of the family and not possessing a decent suit even,' said Adam.

Brendan looked down at his pullover, which looked as if it had been knitted with black rope. 'Bit of a mess,' he said ruefully, 'but I'm getting some new gear from my mother's catalogue.' He added sadly, 'Can't stand new clothes. They never fit me.'

'It's not that, Brendan,' I said. 'You told me once you hated the sea. I didn't think you'd want to come.'

He blinked. 'That's true. I don't really like the sea. Can't remember much about it though. Don't know if I was ever at the sea. I don't think I should like it,' he added hastily, giving me one of his vivid-blue stares.

'Come if you want to,' I said casually. 'Oh look,' I shouted. 'Here comes my friend Mai from the office.'

She was pushing her way through a crowd near the door wearing a purple dress and a black hat with gold metal buttons round the brim.

'There you are,' she said all breathless and sportive. Her mouth fell open when I introduced her to Brendan. She simpered at Adam, saying, 'I've heard a lot about you.'

'You have?'

'Nothing but the sweetest things,' she said. She was like an actress in a silent film except for the sounds she was making.

'Can I get you a drink?' said Adam in a dignified way which made me proud. Brendan looked flushed and worried. I squeezed his hand behind Mai's back.

'Get us all a drink,' I said loudly, 'so we can all get drunk.'

Brendan laughed as if it was a great joke I had made.

'Isn't she terrible?' said Mai waving her hands about. 'That's why I like her though.'

When we were seated Mai sat between me and Adam. Brendan was on my other side. By the slant of him he appeared to have half a buttock on the seat.

'Move over,' I said. 'Brendan's arse is not the size of a pygmy's.'

Adam's nostrils distended. He does not like me being coarse in company.

'I'm fine,' said Brendan, holding on to the table for support. Mai and I were jammed as close as Siamese twins, and the fumes from her perfume seeped through my pores.

'Hope you don't mind me coming,' she hissed into my ear, reinforcing the vapours.

'I'm glad you came,' I said.

Brendan from his position half over the table called across to Mai, 'Any friend of Betty's is a friend of mine.' I could feel the heat from his flushed face.

'Er – yerrs.' She turned to Adam and said something, to which I saw him stiffly nod.

For the rest of the evening Mai spoke to Adam between the drinks that were ordered by me, Brendan and Adam, but never by Mai. I couldn't hear what they were saying and when I did look enquiringly at Adam his eyes were downcast on the floor. Brendan said, 'Your friend is very lively,' and I jabbed him hard in the side. After that he said nothing. The drink seemed to be having very little effect on me, so when we got up to leave I was surprised to find I could scarcely stand. I grabbed the table to steady myself and discovered I was alone. Brendan was waiting outside, Adam and Mai were arm-in-arm moving onwards.

'They're a couple of bastards,' I said, clutching Brendan's arm.

'I don't like her much,' he said. 'She didn't say one word to me all night.'

'You weren't missing anything.'

'You're a lot better looking than her,' said Brendan.

Now I felt more steady and sure of myself. 'Let's walk along by the river and let them do whatever they want to do.'

'Are you sure?' said Brendan.

'Sure I'm sure. I don't want to go back to the house and find them banging each other on the floor or up against the wall.'

'Adam's not like that.'

'You don't know him,' I said darkly.

When I got home three quarters of an hour later, Adam was in bed.

'Where did you disappear to?' he asked.

'Looking for you,' I said. 'I went to the toilet and when I got outside you'd all disappeared.'

'What happened to Brendan?'

'How should I know? What's more to the point, what happened to Mai?'

'Her?' he said. 'I was never so glad to get rid of anyone in all my life. I made sure she got on a bus right away.'

'So you say,' I said, taking off my shoes and surprised to see that they were thick with mud.

'I just hope Brendan's OK,' he said before turning round for sleep.

'Who cares?' I said, feeling sick.

4

On Saturday morning I lay in bed as long as I could, praying for rain while Adam snored. I consider him an attractive man, although he no longer attracts me, but when he snores I have an intense aversion for him. I long for a bed of my own. Rae burst through the door.

'Mummy, get up. It's all sunny and you said you would take us to the seaside.'

Adam sprung up as if he'd been spattered by grapeshot. 'What is it – what's happening?'

'We are going to the seaside,' I said joylessly. I arose and shuffled downstairs to face the litter of yesterday's unwashed dishes. It was incredible how much litter could gather in one small house in one day. It would have been simpler to burn the place down and start afresh, but the insurance policy had run out. By the time I had washed up and made toast and marmalade Adam was stumbling around the kitchenette, displaying a bleeding chin from a blunt razor blade while he searched dementedly for his tie.

'Perhaps you strangled Mai with it,' I suggested.

'Who is Mai?' he said, emptying out a pile of dirty linen on the floor.

'It's all right, Daddy,' said Robert triumphantly. 'I found it under your bed. It's all stinky.'

We had a sniff at the tie and came to the conclusion the smell was stale alcohol.

'Just put it on,' I said. 'It gives you a certain aura.'

One hour later we were as ready as possible to leave when we discovered we had lost the key.

'We can't go until we find it,' said Adam.

'Let's forget it then. We won't bother going.'

The kids wailed, stamped their feet and punched the wall.

'All right, we'll go,' said Adam. 'Anyone that breaks in will die of fright.'

'There's only the record player that's worth taking,' I said.

'It's broken anyway,' said Rae.

Outside the house we peered about, our eyes dazzled with the sun.

'I could do with a drink,' said Adam.

'Better not,' I said, watching the kids sprint along the road. 'The train could be due any minute.'

We waited in the station for fifteen minutes before the train left. The kids hopped in and out of the toilets and scampered close to the edge of the platform.

'You never realise how much you detest your kids until you take them somewhere,' said Adam.

'I used to hate going places with my parents when I was a kid,' I said. 'We should be glad they want to come with us.'

'From what I can remember of your parents I don't blame you.'

'At least they gave me a sense of security. Our kids don't have any.'

'For Christ's sake,' Adam shouted, 'I don't know where you get your ideas from –'

The train slid into the platform and we rushed on like lemmings heading for oblivion.

Later, with our backs resting against the shore wall, Adam and I drank small sips from a bottle purchased from the licensed grocer's.

'I suppose it was worth it,' said Adam.

'I knew it would be nice.'

'Yes nice, an apt description – reminds me of your mother somehow.'

I stared at the silhouettes of the kids poised on the rocks far in the distance. 'I've always liked being on the beach,' I said.

'I was on the beach once – for three months, trapped. I didn't appreciate it much.'

'Don't let's talk about the war,' I said, 'not now.'

'Sorry.'

I let the sand trickle through my fingers. A wind sprang up and I shivered.

'Have a drink,' said Adam.

I reached for my cardigan. 'Why does everything remind you of the war?' I asked.

'It was the only time I felt alive.'

'So you enjoyed it.'

'You wouldn't understand,' said Adam. His eyes stared towards the horizon like a castaway.

I snatched up the bottle saying, 'I've never made you happy, have I?'

'I'm happy enough.' He sounded uninterested.

'Me too,' I said, appreciating the heat of the liquor reaching my stomach.

He rose to his feet and headed towards the rocks, then scrambled up beside the kids and pointed seawards. They all stood still like totem poles. I closed my eyes and was disturbed by the recollection of Mr Robson and the book he was writing. It didn't seem right. Afterwards we wandered through a park high on a hill behind the town. We sat on a wooden bench behind some bushes and munched doughnuts washed down with lemonade for the kids and sips of alcohol for Adam and me. A blanket of cloud dimmed the sun.

'It's been a nice day,' I said, possessed by an urge to leave.

'Very nice,' said Adam, with the sly look of one who knows better.

'What's wrong?' I asked.

'Everything's perfect.'

Robert ran over with a pair of sunglasses he had found. I put them on.

'How do I look?' I said. The rims were broken and the perspex cracked.

'Like a film star,' said Adam. He handed me the bottle saying, 'Finish it off.' When I put the bottle to my lips he said, 'Watch out. Here come the bizzies.' It was only a doddering old park keeper, who gave me a strange look when he passed.

'We'll have to be going,' I said.

The kids made sounds of agony. 'Just when we were enjoying ourselves!'

'That's the best time to leave,' said Adam.

'Perhaps we should stay a while longer,' I said. 'It's still early.'

'I want to go home now,' Rae snarled. 'I'm fed up.'

Adam laughed as if he had heard a joke. The effect of the alcohol lay like a tight band on my head. I placed the empty bottle in a litter bin and walked away from them. The journey back in the train was passed in silence. The kids looked sullen and disappointed. I closed my eyes to blot out their faces.

Brendan turned up on our doorstep at nine o'clock in the evening, holding a black bottle and bulging out of a grey pinstripe suit.

'You're a sight for sore eyes,' said Adam.

Brendan looked down at his legs. 'It's not too tight is it?'

'You look terrific,' I said. 'Like a business executive.'

'More like a top Mafia man,' said Adam.

'Mafia?' repeated Brendan.

'Have you never watched Mafia films?' said Adam. 'They all dress like city slickers.'

'It's from my mother's catalogue – delivered this morning. Did you go to the seaside then?'

'Yes, and we had a lovely time,' I said.

'You should have come,' said Adam.

'I thought about it, only –'

'Why didn't you?' I said, pouring wine into glasses.

'Can I sit on your knee?' said Rae, dashing in and tugging Brendan's jacket.

'Get away,' I screamed. 'Your fingers are all jam.'

Brendan stood in the centre of the room with a beautiful soporific smile on his face while we all admired him. After the subject of his appearance was exhausted I asked him how his mother was keeping.

'Fine,' he said uneasily, adding, 'She thinks I should look for work, now I've got this suit to pay for.'

'What about a factory?' I suggested.

'I wouldn't advise working in a factory,' said Adam. 'It's too claustrophobic.'

'I don't like being indoors – except in pubs or houses when I'm drinking,' said Brendan, winking at Robert who was still admiring him.

'A building site then?' I said.

'Hmm,' said Brendan. 'I worked in one for a few hours. The ganger kept shouting and swearing at me. I wanted to hit him with my shovel, but I just walked away instead.'

'You should be a bank robber,' said Robert. 'That's the best thing to be. That's what I'm going to be.'

Brendan ruffled his hair. 'Good idea. We'll be partners in bank robbing when you get older.'

'What about the gardening work? You're good at that,' said Adam.

Brendan nodded. 'Don't mind digging gardens. The last place I was at the woman was always asking me in to fix things. I got fed up.'

'Fix what kind of things?' I asked.

'Like plugs or taps and things. I'm no use at fixing things,' he said, turning away as if to drop the subject.

'Maybe she wanted you to fix her,' said Adam with a guffaw.

'Brendan could fix anybody if he wanted to,' said Robert, looking fiercely at his father.

'You two kids – off to bed,' said Adam, gesturing with his thumb in a menacing manner.

'Sure would like to fix a lot of people,' said Brendan, giving me one of his vivid glances.

Next morning I slept almost to midday. I remembered too late about my appointment with Mr Robson. The effort of dressing was too much bother. I slopped around in my dressing gown listening to Nat King Cole records and handing out coffee and cheese sandwiches as a sop to dispirited appetites. Brendan lay on the sofa most of the day looking like a whale cast up to die. At four o'clock he rose and left us without a word. Three hours later he returned with bottles of booze. I don't know how he manages it.

On Monday morning I didn't want to rise. I didn't want to cook the breakfast, or go to Chalmers & Stroud, or see Mr Robson, or lunch with Mai. I wanted to sleep until I was tired of it, then rise and sip coffee and eat rolls, then stroll through the park and sit when I felt like it or walk when I felt like it. I wanted to be alone and free.

'Time to get up,' said Adam, turning off the alarm.

'Yes, darling,' I said in tones of loathing. 'Do you want one slice of toast or two?'

'Nothing,' he said.

I dressed furtively with my back to him.

'By the way,' he said, 'I shall be gone when you get back.'

'Will you, darling?' I said, adjusting my suspender belt.

'I can't stand you anymore.'

'I'm not surprised,' I said, feverishly looking through a drawer for a blouse which would certainly need to be ironed.

'Why is it,' he said, 'you always try to drag me down when there's an audience?'

'I wouldn't call Brendan an audience.' I viewed a crumpled blue article with extreme despondency.

'What would you call him then?' He sat bolt upright against the pillow. In a brief glance I noticed he looked slightly deranged.

'A halfwit,' I answered.

'In all my experience –' he began.

'Would that include the war?' I said sarcastically, hoping to shut him up.

'I've never met anyone as chilling as you.'

'What did I do?'

'What did you do?' he laughed. 'What did you do? It would take all morning to describe what you did – laughing, crying, kissing Brendan, the poor fellow was completely confused – and screaming how I'd never been anywhere during the war, that is anywhere farther than Aldershot –'

'I'm sorry I can't stop to hear all this, I've got to work you know.'

'So I'll be gone soon. I can't take any more.'

'Sorry I'm late,' I said to Mr Robson, smoothing down my crumpled blouse. 'I've had a terrible weekend.'

'Dear, dear,' he said. He was reaching up for a book on one of the shelves called *The Joys and Fears of Extra-Marital Bliss*.

'I thought I wasn't going to make it this morning,' I added.

He opened the book at a particular page, studied it for a moment, then closed it. 'What happened?' he asked.

'It's my husband's friend Brendan.' I paused, folding my hands and looking blankly ahead. Mr Robson gave a barely perceptible nod as if he could anticipate something ominous in connection with Brendan. 'The last time we saw him, which was on Saturday night, he appeared slightly deranged, and –' I paused again.

'Yes?' Mr Robson tapped his fingers on the table, then coughed.

'He accused my husband Adam of being a fraud. He said he knew for a fact that Adam had never been farther than Aldershot during the war because he had spoken to someone who had known Adam when he was in the army. This person had told Brendan that because of Adam's high degree of intelligence they had kept him in a special unit to decode enemy communications.'

'It all sounds very commendable,' said Mr Robson.

'When Adam heard this he nearly took a stroke. He was literally foaming at the mouth with rage. He tried to strangle Brendan, who fortunately has a strong, thick neck and came to no harm, but Adam was in a bad way all day Sunday; that's why I couldn't manage to come to your house. He paced about swearing vengeance on Brendan, saying over and over again that he had been a complete dumb-cluck during the war; that's why he'd been sent abroad to fight and die for his country along with a million other dumb-clucks. I said I believed him, but now I'm not sure. He is very intelligent you know.'

Mr Robson puckered his bottom lip with his fingers. 'I must say the situation has taken a strange turn, but it sounds to me as if it is your husband who has acted in a deranged manner.'

'That's where you are wrong,' I said. 'It was predictable that Adam would act like that under the stress of Brendan's accusation. But for Brendan to make the accusation is completely out of character. I doubt if he has even heard of Aldershot, and even if he had it would be beyond him to concoct such a story.'

'Then,' said Mr Robson with a sigh of impatience, 'he has spoken to someone who knew Adam during the war, as he said.'

'It's hard to say.'

Mr Robson opened his book again and peered hard at the writing as if looking for a solution, or perhaps a distraction from my network of probabilities.

'I hesitate to say this,' I said shyly, 'but do you think Brendan could have a split personality?'

Mr Robson looked up and opened his eyes wide, showing his milky irises. 'That would be beyond my judgement, but' – he smiled in his fatherly way – 'do you know what I think?'

'What, Mr Robson?'

'I think it all boils down to sex. It's all in this book you know, the lengths a person will go to when he or she is foiled by a member of the opposite sex for whom they have a great desire.'

'Sex?' I repeated.

'It is obvious that they are both jealous of each other because of you. Animals are much more direct. They fight it out straight away and the best animal wins. Brendan and your husband are complex humans who have no idea what they are about. Human behaviour, my dear' – he squeezed my hand which lay listlessly on the table – 'is very complicated.'

'You were in old Robson's room a long time this morning,' Mai hissed into my ear when I was placidly typing my rather dull correspondence. 'It's getting beyond a joke.'

'What are you talking about?'

She shrugged and gestured backwards with her thumb. 'It's them. You know what they're like. They see bad in everything.'

I regarded the assortment of females sitting at their desks in casual attitudes of employment. 'Perhaps I should leave,' I said.

'I didn't mean that,' she said as I brushed past her to stop at the desk of a very nice woman called Miss Benson, who had confided to me recently how worried she was about her nephew who was doing badly at university.

'Tell me,' I asked her in a voice audible to everyone, 'do you really want me to leave?'

She threw up her hands as if I was holding a pistol to her head. 'Why should I want you to leave?'

'It has come to my ears there is a lot of talk about the length of time I spend in Mr Robson's room taking dictation, which does not appear to be justified by the amount he gives me. Well,' I continued in my very audible voice, 'this is because he spends most of the time reading his mail before he replies to it.' From the corner of my eye I saw Mai creep out of the office. I continued,

'What seemed a joke at first is getting beyond a joke, or so I'm told.' I waved my hands in a despairing fashion. 'Perhaps it's better I should leave.'

After a minute's silence the females twisted and turned in their seats and looked at each other with concern, then at me with concern. Mrs Grimble, a fat, homely female who had been with the firm for thirty years or so and who, according to Mai, had no time for Mr Robson, having described him as an overbearing old fool, said, 'My dear, I think this is too utterly ridiculous, and I for one would like to make it known that if anyone is suggesting there is some sort of – er –'

'Hanky-panky?' said Miss Partridge, a youngish typist who sat behind Mrs Grimble.

Mrs Grimble frowned. 'Don't be offensive. What I mean to say is if we're going to make something out of the amount of time that is spent over Mr Robson's dictation then I think we're all potty.'

'Exactly,' said Miss Benson. She gently led me back to my desk, saying, 'I don't know what to make of people nowadays. Before the war everyone was much kinder. Now they have no sense of decency. I blame it on the cinema.'

'I would simply hate Mr Robson to have any inkling of –' I broke off and sat down shakily. 'He's such a kind man.'

Mai was unnaturally subdued at lunchtime when we sat on stools, side by side in the new Wimpy Coffee Bar.

'It's a lot dearer in here,' I said.

'Yes.' She chewed half-heartedly on her beefburger.

'Appetising though.'

'Yes.'

'Not hungry?' I asked.

She put down her beefburger on the plate. 'You didn't have to make such a commotion this morning. I was really embarrassed.'

'And how do you think I felt? I mean if people are going to tittle-tattle what am I supposed to do?'

'You exaggerate everything,' she said, having another go at her beefburger.

'I'm a very sensitive person.'

She gave me a black look from her blackened eyes. 'You're so sensitive it isn't real.'

I laughed and said, 'Did you enjoy yourself on Friday?'

'It was all right,' she said. 'That Brendan looks a proper weirdo.'

'I hope you're not going to start talking about my friends.'

'Sorree. I'd better watch it, hadn't I, otherwise you'll be leaving again.'

'I can't go through the same act twice in the one day,' I pointed out.

'God, you're a scream,' she said, tucking into the remainder of her beefburger.

'It's strange that you didn't take to Brendan. He's the sweetest person really,' I said. 'He's not a weirdo at all, otherwise we wouldn't bother with him. I mean if you're going to judge people by the clothes they wear or how charming they appear you're easily impressed.'

'I just don't fancy him, that's all. Matter of fact he gave me the creeps,' said Mai.

'Have you ever noticed his eyes?'

'No,' she said, leaning back and giving out an unbecoming belch. 'Though it sounds as if you fancy him.'

'Brendan's not the type one fancies. He's someone you can rely upon when the chips are down. That's why I admire him.'

Mai blew through her lips as if it was all beyond her understanding. 'I must say I much prefer your husband, not that I fancy him either. And even if I did, I wouldn't encourage him. I don't believe in encouraging married men; it's not fair to the family.'

'I don't care if you encourage him or not,' I said coldly. 'I haven't found him attractive for years.' Distastefully I stared around the Wimpy Bar. 'Considering the prices they charge in here it's extremely dingy. I don't think we should come back.'

She raised her heavily pencilled eyebrows. 'What do you expect for two and sixpence? The Imperial Hotel or something?'

I closed my eyes to blot out the sight of her offended, moon-shaped face. 'I expect to get value for my money.'

We left the Wimpy Bar yards apart. Outside we became parallel.

'I don't feel so good,' she said. 'I don't know what's wrong with me nowadays.'

I looked at her with a touch of pity. 'I've noticed your breath smells bad. I didn't want to say, but remarks are being passed in the office. Perhaps you are eating too much greasy food, or perhaps it's constipation. I'll say this much for Brendan. He might be a weirdo but his breath doesn't smell.'

At home Adam and I sat at the table by the window looking outwards, which was preferable to looking inwards. The room was a riot of dust and clothes scattered around like empty cushions.

I said, 'Do you know, I believe that Mr Robson is a Jew. Do you know why I think that?'

'No,' he said.

'Because for one thing he has a big aquiline nose and his eyes are very dark brown.'

'Hmm,' said Adam.

'I never noticed this before, probably because being kind of old and white-haired you don't notice much about him. Though I suspect Robson could be a Jewish name.'

'For Christ's sake!' said Adam angrily.

'I hope he pays me. I mean you can never tell with Jews.'

'Pays for what?'

Wearily I said, 'He wants me out to his house this Sunday to do some typing. I was supposed to go last week, but I couldn't be bothered.'

'Who's going to make the Sunday dinner?' said Adam, his interest snapping to attention.

'Can't you make it on a Sunday for once? It will only be for you and the kids. Probably I'll get something at Mr Robson's.'

'For once!' said Adam, staring wild-eyed at the kids, who were throwing stones over the fence at the cat next door. He banged on the window, then turned to me still wild-eyed. 'I can't stand Jews.'

'You can't mean that,' I gasped. 'After all they've suffered it's blasphemy!'

'Don't start on about what they've suffered because it doesn't mean I have to like every Tom, Dick and Harry of a Jew who asks my wife out to some penthouse for supposed typing and is up to God knows what.'

'Penthouse!' I laughed.

'Apartment, bungalow or mansion, it's all one. You're not going.'

'I don't understand you,' I said, at the same time hearing the man next door call the kids a couple of sadistic little bastards. 'You didn't bother too much when I told you before. Is it because he's a Jew next?' I became angry. 'Is that what it is?'

The kids clashed by the window, laughing. Adam banged his fist on the table, then stood up and towered over me with hands on his hips, reminding me of my father's intensive inquisitions when I was a child and he was about to thrash me. I stood up also to be in a less vulnerable position. We faced each other with what amounted to bared teeth.

'I am going anyway,' I said. 'We need the money.'

'So,' his voice sank, 'you need the money, and with a Jew too. It has come to this.'

'You're completely mad. I'm going to do a bit of typing for an old man who is writing a book called "The Study of Human Behaviour in Animals", and who probably isn't a Jew. It was only supposition.'

'Animals? By God that's rich. Who the hell is he to study anything? Does he experiment on them as well, does he?' he shouted as he shook me vigorously.

Robert ran in and kicked Adam on the shin. 'Leave my mum alone,' he ordered.

'Big pig,' shouted Rae at his back.

Adam sat down. He looked exhausted. 'Please yourself,' he said weakly. He explained to his attackers, 'It's all her fault. She prattles on a lot of shit about Jews and animal behaviour. She's trying to drive me crazy. What do you think, kids?' He smiled pathetically. 'Do you think she's trying to get me into a nuthouse?'

Robert turned on me. 'Don't talk any more shit to Daddy. Anybody that's been in the war can't stand it. Leave him alone.'

'What time's Uncle Brendan coming?' asked Rae. 'He doesn't talk shit, does he, Daddy?'

'I'll just leave things the way they are,' I told Mrs Rossi after she remarked that I looked distraught and did I want a transfer. At this point the office girl, whose name was Poppy, came in with a pot of coffee on a silver tray that also contained a silver milk jug and sugar bowl. Two fine cups and saucers were already on the table.

'It's just that I didn't want to feel tied down.' I had been explaining about Mr Robson.

'You need to have an escape route?' she asked. 'Is that it?'

'An escape route? Yes — well — I see what you mean. I wouldn't say that exactly.'

'Everyone should have an escape route,' she said in her unfathomable way. 'Do you like my silver?'

'It's lovely — so elegant.'

'It's from Poland — the Germans would have loved it, even though they have no flair for elegance.'

'I thought you were Italian. You look Italian.'

'Fortunately I do, and to make it appear a certainty I married an Italian soldier who was with a German unit. He also thought I was an Italian.' She laughed in her heartless fashion. 'He never found out. He was blown to bits by a bomb placed in an army truck by the Polish resistance, which was a great relief to me. All the same, he was my escape route.'

'You've had an exciting life,' I said, filled with uneasy admiration for this resourceful woman.

'It's all very placid now.' She sighed as if regretting life's placidity.

'My life's very boring. I long for some excitement,' I said, sipping the coffee and liking its nutty flavour. 'This coffee is excellent,' I added.

'It's only Maxwell House instant,' she said. 'Shall we have a look at the cards, then?'

She studied the cards she dealt out with all the intensity of a scientist studying life through a microscope. The hairs on the back of my neck rose. Then she picked up one and said, her face rigid and unfamiliar, 'Beware of a dark-haired man. He means you harm.'

Adam, Brendan, they were both dark-haired, and Mr Robson undoubtedly had been dark-haired before he turned white. Did that count, I wondered. Which one of them meant me harm? Perhaps I had not met this particular dark-haired man.

'How can you tell?' I asked.

She picked up another card without looking at it and waved it in front of my nose. 'You will evade this harm because this card denotes there is a force for good on your side.'

I received this information with boredom, since it amounted to nothing. The next card apparently conveyed that there was money involved somewhere, but it was difficult to say if it was to my benefit. I sensed Mrs Rossi was losing her power when she rubbed her eyes and yawned. The card she now showed me was the ace of spades.

'Death?' I asked.

'Not necessarily,' she said, 'but I can go no farther. Sometimes it has to do with persons themselves. It's hard to tell.'

'Perhaps it's the cards.'

'No,' she said, boxing the cards and returning them to the drawer. 'It's never the cards.'

'I'm sorry,' I began.

'Not at all, my dear.' Her eyes looked puffy. 'We can't expect results all the time.'

At that point Poppy entered and told Mrs Rossi there was someone for her on the outer telephone.

'How annoying,' she said, giving me a look of regret.

'I'm going anyway,' I said, rising.

'Don't forget to call on me if you have any problems.'

5

'I don't want you to have anything to do with these Yanks,' my mother used to warn me. It was the fourth year of the war and I was sixteen, all dolled up and ready to head to the amusement arcade with my pal.

'I hate Yanks,' I said, which was only part true. I liked their thick, drawling accent, their ochre-coloured skin and their brashness. I didn't know what brashness meant in those days, but their eyes embarrassed me, as all-knowing as if they could see through to my bra padded with bits of cotton wool. My pal appeared quite at ease as they watched her play the pinball machine while I stood by her side drooping with self-consciousness. I wanted to be noticed by them but if they did happen to give me a sidelong glance I flushed up like a chameleon. My pal's strident laugh at everything they said was a challenge I could not match with my feeble, forced titter.

'Regular little sad apple,' said one of them contemptuously, when he spied me mooning over his black slicked-back hair and black moustache reminiscent of Clark Gable. I turned my usual beetroot red, then walked away from them to hide my distress.

'Where are you going?' my pal yelled.

I turned and stuck my tongue out. 'Big Ears,' I called, since the Yank also shared that feature with Mr Gable.

She caught up with me. 'What's wrong with you?'

'I wouldn't be seen dead with these Yanks,' I said. 'They would rape you as soon as look at you.' I wasn't sure what the word 'rape' meant in those days, but I sensed it was about the worst thing that could happen. However, when my dad brought two of them home from the pub one evening I was quite happy to loll around with one leg over the arm of a chair and view their gratitude at being seated round the dining table, which was an old-fashioned kitchen effort varnished over. Surprisingly my mother gave them a plate of spam sandwiches and Dad opened bottles of beer.

'It must be terrible, being such a long way from home,' my mother said to them, at the same time pushing my leg down.

'We're only too happy to be here,' said the small one with slant eyes, who had introduced himself as Aza. The other one, who had told us to call him Buster, beamed all round the room, saying, 'Gee whiz what a swell little place – what swell folks,' and guzzled down his beer in two gulps. My mother brought forth a bottle of port from the sideboard drawer and gave everyone a drink from the small crystal sherry glasses she only used at the New Year – everyone except me. When she left the room and returned minus her wrap-over apron I poured and drank a half cupful of it before she could notice. I immediately felt groggy, hot and cheerful. It came to me that this Aza one was very attractive, and I was possessed with an urge to kiss his thin, manly lips.

'Where's the er –' He gestured backwards with his thumb.

'You mean the bog,' said my father, leering.

My mother tutted and led Aza out of the room. It seemed they were gone a long time. When my mother returned I saw her hair was dishevelled and her lipstick smudged. I think I was the only one who noticed. Buster was wolfing down sandwiches while my father talked about the battle front like one who has inside information. I saw my mother in a new and unpleasant light. With her knitted V-neck jumper drawn tightly over her big chest, and her short tweed skirt clinging to her pot belly, she looked as sluttish as Mary Kelly from down the street, who walked about squiffily arm-in-arm with anyone in uniform. I darted out of the room and collided with Aza who was buttoning up his fly. He gripped my arm, pushed me up against the wall of our hall (as mother called it) and shoved his hand up my skirt. For a split second

I had quite a pleasant sensation before I was sick over his tunic. In the next second I saw his face turn ugly before I ran into the toilet and was sick again down the pan. Five minutes later, when my mother barged in and said, 'Have you been at the port?' I was on my knees retching. Finally I stood up and faced her, water streaming from my eyes, relieved to see she looked like my normal waspish-faced mother again.

'That American tried to rape me,' I told her.

'The dirty bastard,' she said. I went straight to bed and fell asleep to the sound of abuse coming from the kitchen.

'During the war an American soldier asked me to marry him,' I told Mr Robson in a moment of abstraction.

'Perhaps it was wise that you didn't,' he said. We were drinking our morning tea drowsily. The heat from the radiator plus the heat from the sun streaming through the glass pane was clouding my brain.

'Shall I open a window?' I asked.

'Afraid it is not possible. The window cord has snapped.'

'It is so hot in here,' I said.

'I find it very comfortable,' he said with a touch of asperity.

I stifled a yawn, saying, 'Perhaps it's just the way I feel.'

'It can't be the menopause yet,' he laughed, his leathery skin lying in folds round his neck like a chamois cloth. I shuddered at the word menopause.

'Hardly,' I said, my voice cracking a bit.

He tapped my knee in his fatherly way. 'You were saying about this American?'

'I wish I had married him. People are much better off in America. But my mother wouldn't allow me because I was too young.'

'Being better off isn't everything,' said Mr Robson reprovingly.

'I suppose not.' My eyes drifted to his pinstriped shirt, red satin tie and gold tiepin. I sighed. 'It wasn't meant to be.'

'It's interesting that you say that,' he said, lighting a cigar. I closed my eyes to appreciate better the aroma from Havana. It suggested golden sands, drifting canoes and the magic name Copacabana.

'What did I say?' I had a compelling urge to place my head on his shoulder and sleep.

'It wasn't meant to be.' He shook my arm. 'Wake up, my dear. I believe I'll have to turn this radiator off after all. Now,' he said after he had done so and sat down again, 'you should not believe that things were either meant or not meant to be. It is a superstitious attitude and not worthy of your intelligence.'

'Perhaps I'm not intelligent then,' I said.

'Of course you are, otherwise we would not be discussing such matters. It is the intelligence and awareness in your eyes that appeal to me.'

'Really?' I sat up straight, widening my gaze.

'You' – his forefinger stabbed a bone in my chest – 'are the master of your fate. It's up to you to decide whether events are meant to be or not.'

'I don't see how I can alter anything,' I snapped. 'It's so bloody difficult –'

'Tsk, tsk,' he exclaimed gently. 'Perhaps I could help. Visit me on Sunday and we shall discuss things at greater length.'

'What about the typing of your book?'

'That too.' He added, 'My house is an Aladdin's cave – full of treasures.'

'I'll have to skip going for lunch today,' I explained to Mai.

'Oh,' she said. 'Hope it was nothing I said.'

'Don't be stupid. I've got to buy something –' I waved my hands about. 'I'll have no time to eat.'

Her stupid, accusing face twitched. 'I could come with you.'

'It's not possible.' I turned my back and called out to Miss Benson, 'How is Andrew doing now?' That was the name of her nephew in the university, who was of no interest to me.

'I think he's settling down to his studies again,' she began.

'That's marvellous.' I flashed her a sympathetic smile and listened to her long enough to dispatch Mai from my side. 'I hope I haven't made an enemy of Mai,' I interrupted Miss Benson.

'Why do you say that?' she asked, dropping the subject of her nephew like a hot potato.

'She is beginning to take over my life,' I said plaintively.

'She's a funny one,' said Miss Benson. 'Doesn't really belong here. She uses far too much make-up for an office.'

When I returned home in the evening Rae tugged my coat before I could take if off and said the teacher wanted to see me to discuss her work at school, then Robert informed me that he had torn his jacket and would I sew it right away, and Adam stated that we had run out of potatoes. Wearily I sat down and said I was thinking of packing in my work because everything was getting on top of me – added to the fact that Mr Robson expected me to go to his house and do typing for him, but since I couldn't stand the strain of the row it would cause I'd better leave.

'And then what?' said Adam.

'What do you mean – then what?'

He shrugged, smoothed down his hair. 'How will we manage?'

'You can sign on the dole like everyone else. We're bound to survive.'

'What's the dole?' Robert asked.

'It's a big building where they hand out money.'

'I don't believe that,' said Rae, 'or else why didn't we go before?'

'You have to be very poor and unable to work, and they only give you enough to buy bread and corned beef and wear old clothes and shoes from a rag store.'

'Cut it out,' said Adam. 'Don't listen to her. If your mother wants to pack her job in, I'll get one – don't worry.'

'I'm glad to hear it,' I said. 'In the meantime is there anything to eat?'

'There are some old bits of gammon and a few squashed tomatoes,' said Adam.

'If you look properly you will find sausages in the cupboard. Do you think you could manage to cook them? We can have bread and sausage at least. In the meantime I am going to lie down on the settee.'

Rae woke me up later with the meal and a pot of tea on a tray. 'Daddy thinks you should go to work,' she stated.

'Why should I?'

The thick sandwiches were excellent and the tea most refreshing.

'Because we need sweeties,' she explained.

'Perhaps you'd better keep working meanwhile,' said Adam, 'but come next Monday I'll look in at the paper-mill. They're bound to start me —'

'So in the meantime I've to carry on whether I like it or not —'

'No one is forcing you. Do what you like —'

'Exactly. That's what I'll do.'

I retreated to the bathroom to spend some time applying what make-up I could lay my hands on.

'Going somewhere?' asked Adam, when I passed him on the stairs.

'I have arranged to visit my friend Mai,' I said on the spur of the moment. I had no intention of visiting her. It was just an excuse.

'You mean that one —'

'Yes, that one.'

'I didn't like the look of her —'

'I don't like the look of your pal Brendan. I have to put up with him just the same. Make sure the kids are in bed before I get back.'

'You're not leaving me with the kids again?' said Adam, aghast.

'For God's sake, they're your kids too!'

'I can't stand another minute of them.'

'No doubt Brendan will come round and comfort you in your hour of need.'

'At least let me have the price of a drink.'

Thin-lipped I put some money on the table and departed with what I hoped was an air of purpose. Outside I gave a fleeting thought to Mr Robson's address, but prudently decided not to go there. After all, it wasn't Sunday. I waited at the bus stop unsure of what to do. When a bus came along I jumped on with a feeling of relief and sat down beside a fat, jolly lady, who immediately opened up a conversation on the pecadilloes of buses and bus drivers, which I listened to with a deep sense of appreciation. This was replaced by a sense of dismay when I had to get off at the terminus. The jolly lady turned round and waved me goodbye. I was forced to walk away smartly to create a good impression. In actual fact I didn't know where I was going. I wandered around for twenty minutes, avoiding the glances of lonely males cruising the city aimlessly like tourists in a non-conducted outing. Master of my fate indeed, I sneered to myself. One nod of the head to any of those wayfarers and I could finish up floating along the city river face downwards. Heedlessly and needlessly I had blown good money on bus fares when I could have been at home sharing Adam's bottle in the discomfort of my own home. Then it came to me that I had Mai's address in my jacket pocket. With something like joy I brought out the scrap of paper and there it was: M Paterson, 12 Angelio Street. I liked the name Angelio. It sounded romantic.

It turned out that she lived in the top flat of a three-storey dark and dingy building reminiscent of the apartment we shared with Adam's stepbrother in the early years of our marriage. The title of 'Mrs' was on the nameplate to fool the neighbours, no doubt, and likely fooled no one. She took a while answering the door, though I knew she was in. I could hear a baby crying. She opened it with the child in her arms, her face bleak.

'Oh,' she said, brightening up, 'it's you. Come in. He's been howling since I came home.'

I followed her into a room and sat down on a floppy divan beside a cot.

'He's a lovely baby,' I said, peering at his distorted, enraged face. 'What's his name?'

'Anthony,' she replied, pacing up and down and shaking him in a futile manner. I wondered how long I should wait for decency's sake. 'I'm glad you came,' she said, just as I was edging off the divan.

'Let me hold him,' I said without meaning to. 'Perhaps a change of arms might do something.'

She passed him over and the child, either in shock or surprise, stopped crying. He was as fat and soft as a pig and smelled of sour milk. He pulled my hair and made a gurgling sound.

'That's marvellous,' said Mai. 'I couldn't do a thing with him.'

I dandled Anthony on my knee while Mai produced weak milky tea and custard creams and breathed warm smiles upon me and chattered about Anthony's weight, teeth and so on. To keep myself awake I concentrated on the painting-by-numbers picture of two flamenco dancers on the wall behind her head.

'Have another biscuit,' she said.

'No thanks. I'm not hungry. Do you mind taking Anthony? I think he's wet me.'

'The little ratbag.' Mai laughed. 'He does that all the time.'

'You haven't got a drink of something?' I asked when the damp bundle was taken from me.

'Drink? Oh you mean drink. I'm sorry, nothing at all.'

'It doesn't matter,' I said carelessly, 'but I'm afraid I can't stop long. I just happened to be passing.'

'Oh, what a shame. I've been so fed up. I was simply dying for a chat with someone.'

Swallowing a mouthful of the tepid milky tea I said, 'OK, chat away. I'll stop for a half hour.'

'Good. Just a sec until I change Anthony.'

'Change him for what?' I called as she dashed off to leave me with the flamenco dancers.

I sank back on the floppy divan, trying to create in my mind an impression of progress towards some goal, but this eluded me. My life seemed to be a vacuum of desperate nothingness. Surely there must be a reason why I was sitting in a floppy divan in the house of a woman I had nothing in common with, married to a man who was my enemy most of the time, and the mother of children I merely tolerated. And Brendan, yes Brendan. What was he to me? A lover? An ally? Or simply a distraction, with his vivid-blue stare which saw nothing or everything? I must break free, I thought, panicking.

Mai entered. 'I think he'll go to sleep,' she whispered. 'And now' – she sat down beside me, breathing hard with the exhaustion of a long-distance runner – 'I can relax.'

'So,' she added after a two-minute silence, 'where are you going?'

'Nowhere,' I said.

'I thought you were just passing.'

'I wasn't passing to anywhere in particular. I just wanted to go somewhere, but I don't know where exactly. You see –'

'You poor thing,' said Mai, her face looking nondescript without her make-up, 'I know just how you feel.'

'I don't usually feel like this, but Adam gets on my nerves at times. You know how it is when you live with someone –'

'Don't I just. I lived for six months with someone.'

'What happened?' I felt better now that we were rid of Anthony.

'I told you. He buggered off when I became pregnant.'

'Men are swine,' I said.

'Do you know,' she giggled, 'I quite fancied your Adam.'

'I'm not surprised,' I said with a kindly smile. 'Most women do.'

'Not that I am serious,' she assured me. 'It's like you know when you fancy a film star, it's simply –'

'Fantasy?'

'Yeah, fantasy.' She giggled again. 'Imagine telling someone you fancy their husband!'

'Don't worry.' I winked. 'I'm trying to get rid of him.'

We laughed and joked a lot after that and I began to feel I had benefited from my visit; so much so that I invited her to come to our house the first Saturday she could manage and bring Anthony. When I left she stood on the landing with Anthony in her arms.

'Wave to your Auntie Betty,' she said. He hid his head in her shoulder and howled. On the bus I calculated whether I had enough for a half-bottle of sherry, which I would drink alone in the toilet. It was quite nice to be going back.

'Handsome is as handsome does,' my mother had said of Adam.

'At least he is handsome,' I had retorted.

'Leave the fellow alone,' said my father. 'She could have done worse.'

'His family were a funny lot,' said my mother. 'His mother's first husband hanged himself.'

'He was no relation to Adam,' I said.

My mother said, 'They say she drove him to it.'

'She didn't manage to drive Adam's old man to it.'

'Well, he was a big man,' said my mother. 'He took a good bucket every Friday, and when he returned from the pub Adam had to wait at the bottom of their stairs so he could help his father up to the door – a wee skinny thing Adam was then. I felt sorry for him.'

'I don't remember that,' I said.

'Well, he was a lot older than you. Besides you weren't allowed near their place – very low-class people in that district.'

'Many's the drink I had with Adam's old man; clever he was, self-educated. Was gassed in the first war. Told me he spent a lot of time reading – said he believed in communism, but not in the party members.'

My mother sniffed. 'Communism indeed. I might have known.'

My father took off his Woolworth's spectacles and shook them at my mother. 'Don't you get uppity over Adam's old man. Many's the letter he wrote to the papers exposing the government for what it was.'

'And I could never understand a word of them,' said my mother.

'I don't know why I bother to come and see you both. You're always arguing.'

'And I suppose you and Adam never argue.'

'Not as much as you two.'

This was true but I didn't mention the heavy sullen silences that had hung on the air like a thick fog in the early days of our marriage. It was only when I began to share the drink with Adam that my tongue was eventually released.

'Anyway,' said my father, 'Adam's old man wrote a fine letter for me when I was sacked from Langton's sausage factory, and we couldn't get a penny from the means test. A fellow called on us after the letter was sent and gave us some money.'

'Ten shillings,' said my mother.

'We would have got bugger all otherwise.'

'I saw Adam's father when he was dying. I don't think he liked me.'

'Christ Almighty,' said my father, 'if you've got cancer I don't expect you like anyone.'

'He was always moody even without cancer,' said my mother. 'And I know for a fact he didn't like me.'

'He thought I'd no character,' I said.

'See what I mean,' said my mother. 'That's what happens when your daughter marries beneath her. They try to bring her down to their level.'

'He was right,' I said. 'I had no character in those days.'

'Ah well,' said my father, 'character's only another name for cheek and you've always had plenty of that.'

I asked my mother for the loan of five bob until I got my wages.

She sniffed. 'I notice you only come round nowadays when you need something.'

'Give her five bob for Christ's sake,' said my father. 'She's your daughter, not some bloody Arab.'

'Or communist,' I added.

'So long as it's not for drink,' said my mother, delving into her purse.

'Drink?'

'You've been seen in the licensed grocer's.'

'I don't think our Betty would take to drink when there are kids to be fed,' said my father.

'I was in the licensed grocer's for Adam, not for myself.'

My mother threw her hands in the air. 'See what I mean, he sends her for drink!'

'At least he doesn't booze in the pub,' I said with heat. 'It's not as if the odd bottle of sherry costs that much.'

'Nothing wrong in going to the pub for a pint with the lads,' said my father, lifting up his newspaper. 'Can't stand furtive drinkers, though.'

'If you two are finished with the snide remarks I'll be off – unless you want your money back in case I drink it,' I said to my mother.

'So long as you pay it back, I don't care what you do with it,' she answered. She walked me to the outside door and stood with her arms folded while I shut the gate of their council garden as neat as a giant postage stamp. 'Give my regards to Adam,' she called, possibly for the benefit of the neighbours.

I bought some sherry with the five shillings. It wasn't much, only a half-bottle, but it might placate Adam, who hadn't been speaking to me recently.

'Taking to drink, are you?' he asked.

'If you can't beat them, join them.'

I saluted his glass with the greatest of aplomb and after one drink became flushed and garrulous, interrupting him when he started on the inevitable topic of his army days.

'What about that one you met in Italy?' I asked.

'What one?'

'The Christina one.'

'What's brought this on?'

'I just remembered how you spoke about her before we were married. I haven't heard much about her since.'

'Did I? What did I say?'

'You apparently had a big thing going with her. You said something about helping her to climb a gate and putting your hand up her skirt.'

Adam groaned. 'If I had known I was going to be lumbered with you I would have kept my big mouth shut.'

'Well, you didn't – so tell me about her again.'

'There's nothing more to add. Over the fence, onto the grass, and then what every man does.'

'I want you to go into detail.'

'Is this what gives you a kick?'

I laid down my empty glass and pushed myself onto his knee. 'I don't know. Tell me so that I can find out.'

I stroked his hair and kissed his eyes while he went into the graphic details.

'You're a dirty bastard,' I said when he stopped talking.

'I made it up to please you.'

'No you didn't.' I punched his chest with my fists.

'God's sake, kid, what do you expect? It was before I met you. It was the war.'

'It's always the war.' I was crying, but something inside me was enjoying it.

'I love you – only you,' he said. 'Come to bed and I'll prove it.'

So I did.

Life's full of surprises. Tonight Brendan did not come. We set off for the pub, if not arm-in-arm at least companionable, but we are always companionable at this stage. Half an hour passed as we sat toying with beer and waiting for Brendan. We felt it unfair to start guzzling before he arrived – besides he always bought the first round. We mentioned the heat, the flat beer, the weather, then gave up. The study of human behaviour in animals came to my mind, a promising subject, but dangerous. I let it pass.

'What the hell's keeping him?' said Adam.

'He's not obliged to come,' I pointed out.

'It's not like him.'

'He could have something else to do.'

'Brendan doing something else? He'd be lost without us.'

'It's not normal though. He's not even in our age group and he clings to us as if he was our son. Wonder what he does for sex,' I said reflectively.

'What any man does when he has to go without.' I sensed bitterness in Adam's voice.

'Perhaps his mother is ill,' I said.

'Perhaps.' Adam approached the bar and returned with two short drinks. I scowled at the glass he placed before me.

'What's wrong? Don't you want this?'

'We should have stayed at home.' The image of home increased my depression.

'I thought you liked getting away from home,' said Adam, staring at me like a hawk. His face looked gaunt and the old acne marks from adolescence made him look like a smallpox victim. Perhaps it was the angle of the fluorescent lighting.

'You never know what the kids will be up to,' I said.

'We'll go home then.'

I narrowed my eyes and looked around at all the well-occupied tables.

'Pubs are lonely places,' I declared.

'Lonely — Jesus, what next?'

'You can't say they are friendly. No one ever speaks to us — except Brendan.'

'People are just minding their own business,' said Adam.

'Why bother to drink to mind their own business?' I smiled wildly at a woman at the table opposite who had caught my eye. Her lips creased slightly before she turned to her companion.

'OK, let's go,' said Adam. He swallowed his drink, stood up and marched outwards. I paused for a second, but aware of the ignominy of appearing discarded I rushed after him.

When we opened our backdoor Brendan was standing in the kitchenette with his back against the wall. The kids sat on the kitchen chairs studying him as if he was on show. We also studied him. There was something wrong.

'Look at Brendan's trousers,' said Robert, pointing.

We looked. One trouser bottom was torn and his exposed ankle looked bloody.

'Your good suit?' I said.

'Been in a fight?' asked Adam.

'It's ruined,' said Brendan, 'and I haven't even made the first payment.'

I said, 'Perhaps it could be sewn. What happened?'

'A fucking dog. A vicious rat of a thing that came out from nowhere and pounced on me. Then it bit my ankles before I could as much as turn. Look at that!'

We both looked.

'It's not the end of the world,' Adam said jocularly, eyeing the bottle Brendan had placed on the table.

'Your ankle is in some mess with all that blood,' I said. Brendan smiled as he surveyed his ankle. I was glad to see him cheer up.

'That's not my blood,' he said. 'It's the dog's. I kicked its head in and threw it over the hedge. It's dead.'

Adam and I regarded each other, slightly open-mouthed.

'You rotten pig,' said Rae, her face all crumpled.

'Don't be a stupid bitch,' said Robert to his sister. 'It was a big dog. It attacked Brendan.'

'Was it an Alsatian?' Adam asked.

Brendan thought for a minute. 'It wasn't an Alsatian, it was one of those small, white, furry dogs.' His forehead puckered. 'What do you call them again?'

'A poodle,' I suggested.

'Perhaps,' he said, examining again his trouser bottom.

Adam opened the bottle and poured out three glasses. I looked at Brendan's torn trousers with his podgy white legs showing and shuddered.

'Perhaps you could sew it up,' said Brendan, 'so that my mother won't notice it. She's going to be real mad.' He gave me one of his vivid-blue stares.

'Sew it yourself,' I said, expecting Adam to butt in and tell me off, but he didn't.

He said, 'Don't you think you went a bit far, killing the animal? I can understand a kick, but –'

'It ruined my suit,' said Brendan firmly.

'I don't like you any more. You're cruel to animals,' said Rae.

'It's not that when you're throwing stones at the cat next door,' I told her.

'But we've never killed it,' said Robert. 'We always aim to miss.'

Rae went into the cupboard and brought out a bottle two inches full of milk. 'I'm going to feed that cat, and you' – she pointed to Brendan – 'had better not kill it.'

'That's all the milk we've got,' I began, but she had gone out the door with Robert following.

Brendan looked sad. 'They don't understand.'

'Neither do we,' said Adam.

'Let's forget it,' I said. Then I told Brendan I would sew his trousers later on.

Brendan beamed. 'Thanks, Betty. You're a pal.'

Adam said reflectively, 'You must have put the boot in real hard to kill it.'

I said, 'It wasn't that when you shot down a German pilot bailing out of his plane. You killed a man. That was worse.'

'That was different,' said Adam. 'It was the war. We didn't know what we were doing half the time.'

'Yeah,' I sneered. 'There is still a good difference between a man and a dog.' But it took another two drinks for me to look Brendan full in the face.

When eventually I did I told him to go and wash his ankle in the bathroom, but that I was sorry I just remembered I had no thread. He shuffled off limping.

'What a state to get into,' said Adam.

'Killing a dog like that gives me the creeps.'

'Probably lost the head.'

'It's obvious he lost the head, but it still gives me the creeps.'

'Have you any iodine?' Adam asked.

'No, we don't,' I snapped.

'I'm sure we had some thread.'

'I'm damned if I'm going to touch his trousers, stiff with some animal's gore. Anyway I can't be bothered. Between one thing and another it's been a rotten night.'

'It doesn't give you the creeps to take his drink.'

'If I have to put up with you and him I'm due to take his drink.' Defiantly I poured myself out a glassful.

'Steady on,' said Adam. I handed him the bottle and he poured himself one with the look of a person who is merely being obliging. 'Anyway,' he added, 'if a guy loses his head once in a blue moon he's entitled to. He doesn't have much of a life at the best of times.'

'Who has, but we don't go around kicking dogs to death.'

Brendan came into the room at that moment.

'OK now?' asked Adam.

He held out his foot. There was nothing to see. He had pinned the torn cloth together. 'Nips a bit – hope it isn't poisoned.'

'I'm trying to forget all about your ankle,' I said in a cold voice, 'so let's drop the subject.'

'She's in a bad mood,' said Adam. 'Probably her time in the month.'

Brendan looked at me puzzled.

'Here, take a drink,' I said to him to avoid any more complications.

'You're not still angry with me?' Brendan asked, some time later, when Adam had gone to the toilet. Then he did a strange thing. He went down on one knee and kissed my hand. 'Please forgive me,' he said. 'I can't stand you being angry with me.'

I kissed the top of his head. His hair was thick and greasy, unlike Adam's fine growth. 'Of course I'm not angry with you any more.' How could I be angry with Brendan in such a position of worship?

'I see you two have made it up,' said Adam, entering. His voice was finely sarcastic. Brendan got to his feet clumsily. I tapped my head at Adam to indicate I was humouring an idiot.

On Sunday afternoon I sat in Mr Robson's study, looking around and faintly surprised, but then Mr Robson is a surprising man. The walls of his study were decorated everywhere with photographs. Some of them were framed and some were only snapshots pinned on. At a quick guess there must have been around two hundred of them.

'Memories,' he said.

'Is your wife . . . ?' I felt duty bound to ask.

He pointed to one of the larger framed ones. The features were indistinct like an early silent movie – smudged eyes and bushy hair.

'She was a lovely woman,' I said.

'Not really,' he said. 'She was quite plain in fact.' His finger moved quickly away from his wife and stabbed the print of a young man with a steadfast gaze.

'Your son?'

'I have no family. This face is not one I wish to see in my dreams, but I feel obliged to record his memory. He was hanged, you see.'

'Hanged,' I repeated.

'It was a long time ago. I was his lawyer, one of my early cases, but my engagement was only a formality. The evidence against him was too damaging. He had cut the throats of his parents and his young sister while they were asleep. I tried for insanity, but since he was so obviously intelligent it did not come off.' Mr Robson sighed. 'I rather liked him. As I said he was very intelligent, and it was not often I had to deal with intelligent people.'

'But what he did was horrible.'

'I agree, but it's unreasonable to expect everyone to be reasonable or rational. Now and then the mind keels over from some apparently trivial cause. It could be compared to the sudden emergence of a pimple on the face. One doesn't want the pimple, but there it is.'

'Perhaps he had a pimple on the brain,' I said with a feeble stab at humour.

'Who knows, my dear – that is a very good comparison; but in his case the pimple vanished as quickly as it came, leaving no evidence of a disturbed mind – which was unfortunate for him.'

We stood for a moment deliberating on the steadfast gaze of the hanged man, then Mr Robson took off his spectacles and wiped them assiduously with a small piece of yellow cloth, saying, 'Before we start I wonder if you would be so kind as to partake of a cup of herbal tea with me. It tastes quite excellent and is beneficial to the health.'

I said that I'd love to, mainly because I wanted to escape from the photographs.

'We'll take it in my kitchen. It's much cosier.'

The kitchen was brightly tiled and a wonder of gleaming equipment. I could happily have spent my life in that shining order. With neat, precise movements he placed two cups and saucers, probably china ones, on a polished kitchen table beside the window. The tea, which had evidently been prepared beforehand, was poured from a silver teapot, and two plain digestive biscuits were produced to enhance the ceremony. I wasn't keen on the herbal tea but said it was very nice when he asked me what I thought.

'Some people have to acquire the taste,' he explained. 'Like music, poetry, painting and all works of art.'

I thought he was going on a bit about what was only a cup of tea, after all. 'I understand what you mean,' I said. 'I never used to appreciate Beethoven, but after I listened to him once or twice I enjoyed it immensely.' This statement was fabrication as I never listen to any kind of classical music if I can help it. I changed the subject quickly lest he began to discuss Beethoven. 'You have a lovely house.'

'It's modest, but peaceful,' he admitted.

I reflected on our house with its tatty, stained furniture and frayed carpets. 'Yes, it's very peaceful.' Hastily I swallowed the last of my herbal tea and regarded him expectantly for the next course of action, but his eyes were straying out the window.

'It was different when my wife was alive. Flowery and frilly, it was. I've had it refurnished to my taste.'

'I see. I suppose,' I said, 'you will miss her?'

'Who? Oh you mean my wife. Yes, I suppose I did, at the time. Now I'm quite happy to be alone. It lets me do what I want. Not,' he said with a wink, 'that I do very much, at my age.'

I tittered uneasily. 'Still it's nice that you are —'

'Yes, isn't it?' He now sounded bored with the subject. 'Shall we retire to the study?'

I jumped up, glad to be moving, but feeling more uneasy with Mr Robson in his house than I did at the office, which was probably because of the strange surroundings. He gave me pages of meaningless data to type, or if not quite meaningless, extremely boring, and rather like a social worker's study of various clients; but as it was a study on social behaviour it was bound to be like that. I had typed three reports on individuals named John, Timothy and Maurice. I paused at a bit where it stated Maurice had sexual aberrations which were similar to those discovered in white mice after injections of hormones. 'Sounds fun,' I said aloud, and wondered how much I would get paid for all this bumf. Lunch was another formal affair in the kitchen with Mr Robson. The chicken salad and boiled beetroot were enjoyable, but sharing it with him gave me claustrophobia.

'Would you care to see my garden?' he asked. He looked eager and timid at the same time.

'I'd love to,' I said, glad to get out in the fresh air. Making appropriate appreciative noises I looked at the neat flowering borders.

'I've just been thinking,' he said, tapping me on the shoulder, 'that you would make a delightful study for one of the chapters in my book.'

'I would?' I stepped back in surprise, the heel of my shoe sinking into the earth. 'Oh dear,' I said, looking at the hole I had made.

'Don't worry. The gardener will soon sort that out.'

'You have a gardener?'

'Yes, but he's been off for three weeks with a bad back, an affliction common to gardeners. I expect him to return next week. He only comes for a couple of days anyway.'

'A gardener,' I said. 'I wonder if –'

'Don't worry about the garden,' he said impatiently. 'Now, as I was saying, I think you would make a delightful study –'

'Yes, Mr Robson, I know what you said, but what does that mean exactly?'

'It's really quite painless.' He laughed waggishly. 'I ask certain simple questions and you give me certain simple answers from which I draw certain conclusions.'

The words 'sexual aberrations' hung on my mind. 'Would I have to take drugs or injections?'

He laughed heartily. 'My dear, I am not exactly Dr Frankenstein. Of course not. The questions would be less than embarrassing, but sometimes with female conclusions I am often working in the dark, so to speak, and any data I have gained in the past from the female species was never conclusive enough, for reasons I will not go into. So what do you say? I will pay you adequately, if not handsomely.'

'I will have to consider this, Mr Robson, if you don't mind.'

'Naturally, my dear. Take your time. At the moment I'm happy enough with the typing.'

Before we turned into the house I said, 'By the way, I can get you a gardener if you are stuck for one.' Before Mr Robson could open his mouth I said quickly, 'He's very dependable and strong and very good at his job and he doesn't charge all that much.' I had no idea what Brendan charged.

Mr Robson said, 'Well, this fellow that usually comes –'

'It would only be until he came back.'

Mr Robson looked at me quizzically. 'This gardener wouldn't be your friend Brendan by any chance?'

'It is.' I made my eyes wide and candid.

'I see.' He walked ahead of me into the study slightly hen-toed. I noticed, being taller than him, that though his scalp shone through his thin hair he sported a double crown. I also have a double crown, which my mother always maintained was unlucky. I sat down at the desk with its pile of papers. Mr Robson peered at the papers I had typed.

'You are getting along nicely,' he said.

'It's interesting work.'

'Do you find the subjects interesting?' he asked eagerly.

'Totally absorbing,' I said. 'In fact,' I added, 'the part about Maurice – the one with the sexual aberrations – was fascinating, although I wished I had more time to go into it deeply.'

'Did you really?' said Mr Robson. He bestowed on me an approving glance as if he had discovered a talented pupil. 'Why were you fascinated?'

'I don't know really.' I paused, then continued, 'I believe Brendan has sexual aberrations.'

Mr Robson pondered, then stated, 'From what you said about him I'm not surprised, but then,' he patted me on the shoulder, 'most of us have.'

'Perhaps,' I said, moving about to dislodge his warm old hand. 'Though some may have more than others.'

'Tell him to call on me any time after six o'clock,' said Mr Robson. 'The weeds are getting out of hand.'

I thanked him, then told him there was something else on my mind that was rather disturbing as well as embarrassing.

'Spit it out, my dear. You need not be embarrassed with me.'

'The women in the office are beginning to talk.'

'Talk? You mean talk about us?'

'Well,' I said, blinking my eyes, 'it's one of them in particular. She's trying to make something out of me coming here to type for you.'

Mr Robson's small eyes twinkled. 'An old man like me and an attractive young woman, that is flattering.' To my annoyance he ruffled my hair.

'Nevertheless, it's very upsetting.'

'Who is the woman who is causing the talk?'

'The one called Mai, with the black hair and painted face.'

'That one! Yes, well, I could never take to her – looks like a streetwalker to me.'

'Perhaps she would make a good study,' I said mischievously.

'No depth to her. She'd be no use to study. Besides, I wouldn't trust her the way I trust you.'

'She's not a bad person really,' I said. 'She likes to create situations.'

'A troublemaker, in other words,' he said sternly. 'We can't have that.'

'You won't get rid of her,' I said anxiously. 'She has a baby you know, and –'

'An unmarried mother!' said Mr Robson in a scandalised way.

'Please don't let on I told you that. I'm really sorry for her.'

'You are simply too sensitive, my dear.'

He left the room and I typed on for another two hours. After that he called me up to his bedroom, which was a simple affair, containing a double bed covered with a heavy brocade quilt, a small set of drawers and a large screen. He stroked my hair, my

face and my breasts for some minutes, then retired behind the
screen. I sat on the edge of the bed hearing small panting noises,
then a low painful groan, but as I wasn't involved in this I considered I had been let off lightly.

He emerged from the screen quite composed and asked me if
I could manage the following Sunday, handing me a ten-pound
note.

'Certainly, Mr Robson,' I said. 'And what about Brendan?'

'Yes, by all means,' he said.

At lunchtime there was no sign of Mai anywhere. I was neither
surprised nor curious about that. Good riddance, I thought. I
would go and see Mrs Rossi instead. Who knows, she might be
in the mood to read my cards.

'Sit down,' she said. I thought she looked surly, but I was encouraged by Poppy's friendly glance as she brought in the silver tray
with all its accessories, including biscuits, though actually I longed
for a sandwich.

'That will be all, dear,' said Mrs Rossi.

Poppy winked at me before she left. I would have liked to wink
back but Mrs Rossi was watching me.

'Impudent bitch,' she said when the door banged shut.

'Why do you employ her then?' I asked.

'She's my niece. I like to keep things in the family. Is there
something in particular you want to see me about?'

'I was wondering if you could read my cards to find out if
there's anything good happening in the future. I feel as though
I'm going through a dark patch.'

She looked at me closely and said, 'I notice you've got a widow's
peak.'

'Is that significant?' I asked.

'Could be.'

'But why do you think it's significant?'

'My, you're a one for the questions.' She placed her forefinger on her lip and closed her eyes. The effect was very impressive. She opened her eyes suddenly, catching my fascination with her solitaire diamond ring. 'More often than you would think,' she added.

'I wouldn't want anything to happen to my husband,' I said.

'Of course not, but whatever is going to happen will happen.'

I could see she wasn't going to bring out the cards. I thought I'd change the subject.

'Mr Robson has two crowns. Is this unlucky?'

'It depends.' She added with a cautious glance, 'Is he still as weird?'

'Not all that much.'

'Self-centred then?'

'Maybe. Do you know him well?'

'Well enough. He once asked Poppy round to his house to do some typing.'

I kept my voice flat. 'Did she go?'

'Not that I know of, though you never know with her. She keeps a lot to herself.'

'Does she?' I said, thinking of Poppy's conspiratorial wink.

'Besides,' Mrs Rossi added, 'she can't type for nuts. I don't know why I keep her on, family or not.'

She brought the cards out from a drawer under her desk and asked if I wanted a quick gaze at the future.

'Oh yes,' I said. 'That's why I came.'

The cards were dealt. Mrs Rossi gave a long serious glance at each of them in turn while I sat holding my breath.

'What do you see?' I asked, unable to stand the tension.

She waved my question aside as though it was interfering with her concentration. She dealt another one and said, 'This is interesting.'

'What is?' I asked.

She meditated on the card for a while, then confronted me with eyes glowing like hot tar. 'You'd better watch your step.'

'Why?'

'I don't know; there's a kind of black shadow here. I can't be specific.'

'If you can't be specific how can I be careful? I can't shut myself up in a room all day.'

'Don't get angry,' she said. 'When it comes to it you will know what to beware of. Just a warning, my dear.'

I wanted to tell her I didn't believe that she saw anything in the cards, and was simply making it up, but wisely I said nothing.

In the afternoon, when I was sitting at my desk in the office stuffing myself with a roll and cheese purchased from a snack van, Mai came over and asked me to come out to the toilet.

'What for?' I asked with a show of resentment, though inwardly I felt apprehensive and guilty.

'Just come,' she said. 'I can't talk here.' This was reasonable enough. Faces were beginning to turn in our direction.

In the toilet she was wiping off the mascara from her smudged eyes. Without the black stuff they looked surprisingly small. 'I've been sacked,' she said.

'You've been what?' I wished she would put the mascara back on. She looked vulnerable without it.

'Didn't you notice I was in Mr Robson's room for a full hour?' Her eyes brimmed with tears.

'I wasn't paying any attention. I thought you had gone home. Why has he sacked you? He's not your boss anyway.'

'I know he isn't,' she burst out peevishly, 'but he seems to have the power to sack people.'

'But why?'

'He said it had been brought to his attention that my work has been careless of late.' Her shoulders heaved with short sobs. 'It hasn't been any worse than usual.'

'That's rotten,' I said, 'but you shouldn't worry about it. This place is a dumping ground for old women anyway. You'll get another job easily.'

'It's the disgrace of it.'

'Why didn't you see your own boss?'

'That old bitch Benson? I did, and she said my timekeeping was bad. It's no worse than anyone else's. Yours is much worse come to think of it.'

'Come now, Mai, it's not my fault,' I said.

'Someone's got it in for me anyway.'

'Are you sure you didn't tell anyone else about your baby? You know how they are in here.'

'Only you.' She was reapplying the mascara. Now she looked more like her old self.

'I didn't say anything,' I said. 'Anyway, I'm thinking of chucking it myself. Old Robson's getting on my nerves. I think you're lucky in a way, being forced to move on. Wouldn't it be great to work for someone handsome and sexy?'

'You're right,' said Mai, brightening at the mention of sex. 'This place is a dead end. When do you think you'll leave?'

'I'll give it another week. The agency hasn't got anything to offer right now. I've already asked them.'

'Perhaps I should try your agency.'

'I suppose you could,' I said doubtfully. 'So long as you're prepared to wait. Mrs Rossi is always fully booked up.'

'Pity,' said Mai, gathering her make-up spread before her like a theatrical kit. She smoothed down her skirt and looked at the back of her legs to make sure her stocking seams were straight, then she squared her shoulders and sighed.

'I might as well go now. At least I've got two weeks' wages to blow – that is if I get another job at once.'

'I'm sorry to see you leave,' I said, truly regretful.

'I'll phone you as soon as I get something and we can meet again for lunch.'

'Oh God,' I groaned. 'I'll have no one to talk to over lunch now.'

She squeezed my hand in sympathy. 'Don't worry, I'll get in touch.'

She whisked out of the toilet leaving me vaguely depressed. I hadn't thought she would get the sack, only a reprimand, perhaps, for spreading gossip. Mr Robson had certainly taken my point. What was I getting into anyway with the old goat? But when I thought about it there wasn't much I could do except to play the cards dealt me as well as I could.

Adam and I had not been on speaking terms, apart from uttering the barest requests like, 'Pass the salt,' or, 'What's for eating?' The funereal atmosphere even affected the kids, who crept around like orphans in the custody of a hostile foster-parent. A bottle of wine would have remedied the silence but it went against the grain to make any overtures. It was boring to sit at the open window after the dreary business of eating, watching Adam dig the garden with the air of a martyr, but boredom has always enveloped my life like a continually recurring cloud. I heard Robert rummaging in the kitchen cupboard.

'What are you looking for?' I shouted.

'Daddy says I've to get a trowel to dig up the weeds.'

'There is no such thing in this house.'

'Well Daddy says –'

'Pull them out with your hands.'

The rummaging continued with a lot of noise. I joined Robert crouched in the cupboard, looking through an assortment of items which would have depressed a rag-and-bone merchant.

'I have told you –' I began, and broke off. Robert had dislodged what appeared to be an old, empty wine bottle, but I had the feeling it wasn't empty. I pulled it out. It was three-quarters full. The cloud lifted immediately. 'Tell Daddy there is no trowel,' I said gently. 'Tomorrow I'll buy one.'

'Tomorrow is no use,' Robert said bitterly, backing out of the cupboard.

After a glass of the wine I was in a brighter mood. 'Adam,'

I called out of the window, displaying the bottle. At first he looked insulted and continued to dig. Five minutes later he entered.

'What?'

'Look what I've found,' I said, handing him a glass.

'You found it?'

'Among the junk in the cupboard when Robert was looking for a trowel.'

Adam wiped his hands on his trousers, saying it was an ill wind et cetera. We sat down in the warmth coming from the open window, sipping the wine with dainty appreciation. I drew marks on the dusty table. 'At least we are speaking,' I said.

'Are we?' His face was friendly.

'You know there is no harm in my typing for Mr Robson. After all I did get five pounds.'

'I suppose not,' he admitted. 'What did you do with the fiver anyway?' he added. 'I never saw much sign of it.'

'I'm saving up.'

'You are?'

'It's not for myself. I thought we might go for a holiday, some-where near the sea. The kids would love that, wouldn't they?'

'Suppose so,' he said slowly, 'but how many more fivers do you have to earn to accomplish that?'

'I can only do my best. At least it's a start.'

'I'll say this much for you, kid' – he caught my wrist as it reached out for the bottle – 'you're a trier. You deserve something better than me.'

I laughed. 'I know, but at the moment I've only got you.'

When the bottle was finished I purchased another. We sat in the garden on a blanket with the bottle and the glasses. The kids ran around chasing the cat next door with Adam's spade. The man next door viewed us over the hedge. We waved at him. He turned away sullenly.

Adam said, 'This is the life.'

'Just like the poem,' I said.

'Of course. A loaf of bread, a flask of wine and thou —'

'Beside me singing in the wilderness,' I added. I looked at Adam affectionately. I would really miss him if he went out of my life, but some day he would have to go.

When I was very young, before the war, I took it for granted that if my parents were not exactly rich they were not poor; that is, poor in the sense that you didn't get twopence for the Saturday matinée, a penny for sweets, and a penny for a comic. The fact that the comic cost twopence and I always had to steal the extra penny from my mother was nothing to do with being poor, since she never missed it — sometimes not even missing as much as twopence.

'Now don't get the sausages at fourpence a pound or the ones at eightpence, get the ones at sixpence,' she would instruct me. I would get the ones at fourpence, and that was a penny straight away from half a pound of sausages. I loved when I had to go for sausages, but to be sent for threepence worth of mixed vegetables gave me no room for manoeuvre, unless I arrived home tearfully explaining I had dropped a halfpenny down a drain. Another thing that proved we weren't poor was the fact that I had cornflakes for breakfast. My friend across the street had never heard of them. It was when I was sent to the Secondary Academy, a twenty-minute bus journey out of town, that I discovered we were poor. I didn't wear the appropriate clothes with the appropriate school colours, and worse still I had to borrow a hockey stick from the school pavilion when we played the ghastly game.

'Hockey stick!' my mother said in a scandalised voice. 'I'm damned if I'm going to buy a hockey stick when you can borrow one from the school.'

'Everyone else has their own hockey stick.'

'That's too bloody bad.'

On the subject of school colours she relented by knitting me a jumper with a blue and grey collar and waist band. A month later the colours were changed to red and yellow. It was out of the question to tell my mother this, so I retreated into a shell for the three years I attended Morton Academy, and waited at the bus stop yards apart from the giggling girls in red and gold blazers. I once told another unpopular girl with buck teeth and woollen stockings that if she hung about with me I would give her sixpence every week. 'Sez you,' she said, and wandered off with an unholy smile on her face.

Once when we were reminiscing about our childhood I told Adam all this.

'Serves you right for being at that bloody snobbish place.'

'My mother sent me because I was clever.'

'Clever – Jesus, what's that got to do with it? You were a lot better off than me. My old man was always drunk out of his skull.'

'So I heard,' I said coldly.

'At least he knew what life was about.'

'Getting drunk?'

'You've got to get through it the best way you can.'

'That's what I intend to do.'

'I don't know where you get your big ideas from unless it's from your mother.'

'Look, Adam,' I shouted, 'just because I'd like things to be nice – just because I'd like to dress nice and have a nice house – just because I'd like you to be different from your father –'

'My father was his own man. I wish I was like him.'

'You are like him. Is that why you drink so much?'

He hadn't answered, but I remember saying, 'Of course, I forget – it was the war. That's what made you drink.'

He continued to say nothing. I don't mind his drinking now since it's about the only thing we have in common, apart from

Brendan and the kids. But I'd still like things to be nice. Mr Robson's house is exceptionally nice.

When Brendan appeared on the scene on Friday night as usual I told him I could get him started at the gardening. He didn't look enthusiastic.

'It's extra money,' I pointed out. 'It will help to pay for your suit. I notice you haven't got it on. Didn't your mother sew the trousers?'

'I chucked it in a cupboard. Can't be bothered with it any more.' He added listlessly, 'I prefer my old rags – don't feel right in a suit.'

'That's not the point, old man,' said Adam. 'You've still got to pay for it.'

'Not unless,' I said, 'he expects his mother to pay for it.'

Adam looked at me balefully, then asked Brendan, 'How's the ankle – healed up?'

'It was only a scratch,' said Brendan, shifting from one leg to another, with hands in his pockets.

'Poor dog,' I said.

'No sense bringing the dog up,' said Adam. 'It's long gone.'

'But it's so irritating,' I said. 'To think a dog has been kicked to death because it tore Brendan's trousers, which he's chucked in a cupboard, and his mother will have to pay for them when he could have a job and at least pay for them himself and have a bit extra to spend at the same time.'

Adam laughed. 'That's like the old woman who swallowed a fly.'

'I'll think about the job,' said Brendan. 'Are you two coming out to the pub?'

'Supposing I said no?' I said.

'That's fine. Brendan and me will go ourselves.'

'We can't leave Betty,' said Brendan, giving me one of his vivid-blue stares.

'Who can't?' said Adam. 'She'll only nark at you all night about this job. You know it's for the same old guy she types for, not only at the office mark you. She goes to his house to type.' He uttered this in a significant way to Brendan.

'I didn't know that,' said Brendan, as if I had been keeping secrets from him.

'Mr Robson is a very nice old man. I put in a good word for you about doing his garden – thought you would be pleased.'

'But I am pleased. It was good of you. You're right – I could pay up the suit easily. Maybe I could get something else out of the catalogue – something that would suit me better, ha ha.'

'You're some guy,' said Adam, smiling and shaking his head.

'Well I hope that's settled then so that I can tell Mr Robson you'll start on Monday evening after six.'

'Will you be there?' asked Brendan.

'No, but don't worry. I'll tell him you're a good worker.'

'What about getting me a job at the gardening?' asked Adam.

My eyes widened. 'I didn't think you would take it, but if you like –'

'Forget it,' said Adam. 'He's not going to want two gardeners.'

'I wish you had said –' I began.

'Let's go,' said Adam. 'I'm fed up with all this yacking about gardeners and so on. Are you ready, Brendan?'

He walked out while I was searching for the new handbag bought with some of Mr Robson's money. 'Wait for me,' I called, running after them. Brendan was looking round anxiously like a dog that is torn between two owners.

Lunchtime was lonesome without Mai. I almost choked over my food in the hurry to get away from the diners around me. Not many people, it appeared, eat alone. Outside in the clammy drizzle of a summer day it was less claustrophobic, though shop windows taunted me with displays of garments I couldn't afford. I walked through Woolworth's and managed to sneak a manicure set into my bag. I was filing my nails in the office cloakroom when Miss

Benson entered tutting about the rain. Then she said, 'Aren't you early?'

'Just one of those days when you're glad to get back inside.'

'Perhaps you're missing your friend?' she said, her eyes as bright and as knowing as a squirrel's.

'I think it was a rotten thing to happen.'

'What was?' She shook the rain from her plastic coat fussily.

'To get her books like that. She thinks someone had it in for her.'

'Well, it wasn't me,' she said, her voice unnecessarily shrill.

'I never thought it was you. I've always considered you a fair-minded person.'

'I am,' she said in a grateful tone. 'I've never known anyone to leave so quickly. I'm not sure what happened. Do you?'

I sighed. 'Not really, but it just goes to show.'

'Show what?'

'That no one's safe here. I'm glad I'm only temporary.'

'I've been here for twenty years, and I've always been treated with the greatest consideration. If you do your work well there is no question of your position being unsafe.'

I shrugged. 'I'm sure you know this firm better than I do. Twenty years is a long time.'

'I think we'd better get back to the office,' she said in a fractious tone as she studied her watch.

I stood in the cloakroom for another two minutes after she'd gone. I wasn't going to do what she told me. I was independent, after all.

Later I sat in Mr Robson's room, waiting while he checked the letters I had typed in the morning. He nodded while peering along the words like a hen pecking on gravel. I considered he was being unnecessarily particular. Usually he simply signed the letters after a brief glance.

'Everything all right?' I asked.

'One or two small errors.' His face creased into a reproving smile. 'And look, there is a smudge at the top of this one.' He pulled out the offending letter.

'I see,' I said, staring at his pointing finger.

'Nothing to worry about, my dear.' He coughed apologetically.

I stared into his face, which reminded me of a tortoise with all its creases. 'Perhaps it was thinking about Sunday that made me careless.'

'Sunday,' he repeated, frowning, as though he could not recall anything about it.

'Yes, Sunday,' I said, with a darkening suspicion he might be suffering from amnesia. 'You remember Sunday?'

'Certainly I remember Sunday.' He drew his chair close in to the table, his knees touching mine. 'You did very well on Sunday and I trust this Sunday you will do equally well.' He coughed again saying, 'But if you would just take out this smudge with your rubber I would be very much obliged.'

'What about the other small errors?'

'There's nothing much. I'll let them pass.'

'If I'm to stay on permanently –' I began.

'Yes?' he said, fixing me with his rheumy eyes.

'I only said if, but if I do stay on permanently do I get any more money?' I asked this gently so as not to startle him.

'Certainly, you will get a little more money. Anyone who pleases me is always rewarded.'

'I don't suppose I would get as much as Miss Benson, since she has been here for twenty years.'

'Miss Benson,' he said with a wink, 'has never pleased me at all.'

Before I left I told him that Brendan had promised to come and dig his garden.

'Teacher says you've to give me money for wool,' said Rae. We were having pies and beans for the meal, which was popular with the kids, but not with Adam. I had run out of ideas.

'Wool,' I repeated, trying to cut the hard, burnt crust of the pie.

'Take it in your hands,' said Adam, 'like a chop, which I have dim memories of eating long ago.'

'Yeah, and teacher says the collar of my shirt is dirty,' said Robert.

'Christ's sake,' I said. 'Who does teacher think she is?'

'My teacher is a man.'

'He must be an old poof if he notices your collar.'

'What's a poof?' asked Rae.

'Something you sit on,' said Robert.

I had to laugh, but Adam was frozen-faced. 'That's right, something like your father.'

'Are you going to start?' I demanded, pushing aside the pie.

'With all the money you earn, I expect something better than this.'

'Do you now?' I shook with loathing for him. 'So this is what it's all about? What the hell do you expect with all the boozing you do?'

'And you,' he said.

'And who pays for it?' I had a terrible urge to throw my plate against the wall, but I would only have to clean up the mess.

'Tell you what I'll do,' said Adam, standing up and pushing back his chair. 'I'm going to see someone.'

'A man about a dog,' I sneered.

'No, a man about a job.' He picked up his jacket draped over the chair and slammed out.

'See what you've done,' I blasted the kids, 'talking about wool and dirty collars. Now you've given him the excuse.'

Rae started to whine.

'Shut up you,' said Robert.

'Who are you telling to shut up?' I said to him.

'You're always nagging,' snarled Robert and ran out of the room.

If only I could pack up and leave it all I thought, but I had no suitcase, no clothes and, worst of all, no money. I must save up, not for a holiday, but for a change of address. I could send for the kids after it was all fixed. Adam could do what he liked. Our marriage was a ghastly mistake, always had been. No use expecting miracles to happen. He wasn't going to vanish. Meantime I must wash the dishes and tidy up a bit before I could do anything.

'Stop crying,' I told Rae. 'I'll get your wool tomorrow.'

'Where's Daddy gone?' she said, her snivelling dying down to sniffs.

'You heard him. For a job, so he says.'

'He's not leaving us, is he?'

'I shouldn't think so. Go and play. I've got things to do.'

I washed the dishes, then located one of Robert's shirts and scrubbed the collar while my mind was afire with plans that faded as soon as they formed. Finally I sank into a chair worn out by the contention inside my head. 'I know I've plenty of faults,' I told myself, 'but I do think I've tried my best to be a good wife and mother, and while I understand I shouldn't drink so much, the fact is if I didn't drink when Adam drinks I would go out of my mind. As for Mr Robson, I have done nothing to be ashamed of, nothing that anyone can prove anyway, and as for Brendan, if I've done anything to be ashamed of it was more out of pity than anything else. Surely it is only fair that I leave all this confusion for a better life. After all, we're only here for a few fleeting moments, as Adam often says. Why not make the best of them?' My mind swivelled back to the question, where was the bastard and what was he doing? What right had he to do anything? I was the victim, not him. I went outside to look for the kids but they had vanished. Walking along the street I saw them leaning on the fence with some other kids. They seemed happy. I was glad. I could leave them any time. Turning the corner I met Adam.

'Where are you going, kid?' he asked. He looked concerned.

'Anywhere away from you.'

'I've a present for you.' He shoved something into my hand. It was a five-pound note. 'It's all right,' he said as I stared at the money. 'I sold the gold watch.'

'It was your dad's. You'd no right to —'

'Are you coming for a drink?'

'You sold your father's watch for a drink?'

'We'll do something else if you want. I'll buy you something —'

'Don't bother.'

We were walking along the street. 'What do you want?' he asked, breaking the silence.

'Nothing really.'

We entered the pub and ordered two drinks.

'You shouldn't have done it,' I said.

'What use was the watch to anyone? It was no use to my father.'

'It had sentimental value.'

He laughed. 'To you — not to me. A watch means nothing. I can remember my old man without a watch.'

'I suppose so.' I sipped the whisky carefully.

'Drink up. I'll get another, not unless —' He spread out his hands as if he could offer umpteen choices.

'Just get another drink.'

'At least,' he said when he had fetched more drink, 'we can be alone for once. I mean' — he winked — 'without Brendan.'

'I thought you liked Brendan.'

'I do like him, but he's always around. We never get to talk about anything when he's around. I think that's our problem. We don't talk much about anything.'

'What's there to talk about?'

'Now and again I'd like to say something like I love you.' He broke off as if embarrassed. My mind was blank. I sat dourly as if

I had been insulted. 'You hate me, don't you?' He gulped down his drink.

'I don't hate you, it's simply –'

'I know what it's simply,' he said. 'It's simply that you'd like to be shot of me.'

It was my turn to toss the drink. 'It's nobody's fault,' I said. 'I still love you. It's the life we lead. It's so pointless. All we do is drink.'

'Is there something else you want to do?' His voice was reasonable. 'Would you like to go for a walk? Or perhaps the cinema? I've two or three pounds left. Or would you like a meal? Or a box of chocolates? Just say what it is.'

I looked at my empty glass. 'Just get me another drink.'

'You know, kid,' he said, touching me under the chin, 'you're a lush. Why not admit it.'

'If I am,' I answered with a sardonic smile, 'it's because you made me one.'

'That's more like the girl I know and love – always blaming someone else, but it doesn't bother me. Thank God you didn't want to go to the cinema.'

'Of course I don't,' I said. 'So get me another drink.'

I don't remember clearly what happened when we got home. As usual we were the last to leave the pub. I awoke suddenly and Adam wasn't in bed. I thought I'd heard something fall. When I crept downstairs Adam was crawling round the floor like an animal or a gigantic baby, moaning and grinding his teeth and muttering words that were unintelligible. Then he shouted, 'Fire! Fire!' and began to thump the floor and weep. I turned away and crept back up to my bedroom to lie awake waiting for the dreaded creak on the stairs. It was a while since he'd been like this. I knew the war had a lot to do with it. But I had no sympathy. He should go and get treatment, but of course the first thing they'd do was tell him to keep off the drink.

★

On looking back on that particular summer it could have been described as a long hot one, or at least that is how I remember it. At the very least it seemed a long one, though the end of it was swift. I could say it was the last summer I remember being happy in, though I don't think I was aware of it at the time. But when was I ever aware of being happy? It seemed then that Brendan would always be there at week-ends, irritating me, boring me, sometimes exciting me for no good reason I could think of. One evening when Adam lay on the settee in a drunken coma Brendan and I went outside and made love on the back green in the warm dark. I never reached a climax because Brendan was inept and apologetic, but I enjoyed the risk.

'Am I the only one you've done this with?' I asked him afterwards.

'No.' He fumbled with the zip on his trousers. Before I recovered from my surprise he added, 'I did it once or twice with my cousin.'

'You don't perform very well, do you?' I didn't know why I felt angry about his cousin.

'I've had too much to drink,' he said.

'I'm really quite ashamed of myself,' I said, staring up at the kids' bedroom window. 'I shouldn't be drinking at all.'

'It was all my fault,' he said. 'I took advantage of you.'

'Wouldn't it be terrible if Adam ever found out?'

'I'd kill myself if he ever found out,' said Brendan.

'If you're going to keep coming round we'll have to stop doing this.'

He was contrite. 'All right, but give me one last kiss.'

I allowed him to kiss my cheek. 'Was your cousin very young?'

'Sixteen. But I don't see her any more. She moved away.' He sounded ashamed.

'I'm a bit disgusted with you. A cousin? It seems incestuous somehow. Did you only do it once?'

'Don't keep on about it,' said Brendan. 'I didn't love her, like I love you.'

'Love,' I repeated, smiling in the dark. 'Tell me,' I asked, looking up at the red burning sky, 'if I got a divorce from Adam, would you marry me, and take care of the kids?'

'But I couldn't face Adam.'

'Are you frightened of him?'

He didn't answer. I pulled on his arm when he stepped forward.

'So you love me?' I followed him into the house. Adam still lay on his back with his mouth open. 'Look at him,' I said. 'If he was sick he could choke to death.'

Brendan's eyes wavered from me to Adam, his eyes far from vivid. 'Would you want that?'

I looked at him and laughed. 'You take everything I say far too seriously. Do you want a cup of coffee before you go?'

He followed me into the kitchen. 'I'm not coming back,' he said as he sat down on a chair and wiped the mud from the knees of his trousers, which now looked as if he'd worn them for years. I shook my head in disbelief. When he was drinking his coffee I asked him if he had started on Mr Robson's garden. He nodded. I said that was good and asked what he thought of him.

'He's all right,' said Brendan, looking into the cup.

'Does he pay you well?'

He shrugged. 'Well enough.'

'I don't know why you look so miserable. Extra money, and no worries. You've a better life than most.'

'I wish I was Adam,' he said.

'Adam? You can't mean that. He's not right in the head.'

Brendan's face relaxed. 'That makes two of us.'

'You know, Brendan,' I said, 'you'd be much happier living with Adam than with me, if it came to it.'

'You're in a funny mood tonight,' said Brendan rising. 'I think I'll go home.'

'Do that.' I swiped the coffee cups onto the floor smashing one of them. 'That's how I feel about the both of you.'

'Do you believe in God?' I asked Mrs Rossi after she had read my cards and told me that someone close was under the black shadow of death, which did not necessarily mean this person would die soon, but still the shadow was there.

'Certainly not,' she said haughtily.

'But aren't you a Jew? Didn't you imply it?'

'I didn't imply it. I implied I wasn't an Italian. But you're right. I'm a Polish Jew, though I don't like admitting it.'

'I don't blame you. They have to put up with a lot.'

'The way I see it,' said Mrs Rossi, 'they're too unsociable for my liking, and all that stuff about kosher food is very unreasonable, don't you think?' She fixed me with her black eyes as if I might disagree.

'For me it is unreasonable, but then –' I shrugged.

'Of course you gentiles have always the best of everything.'

'Catholics eat fish on a Friday,' I said.

'Sometimes they do, and sometimes they don't, but' – she spread out her hands in her fascinating continental manner – 'what have kosher food and fish got to do with God?'

'Not much,' I agreed.

'It came to me one night when I was thirteen years old that there was no God. I was sitting on the steps outside the house eating a pork pie. I was very hungry you know, and I had stolen it from a baker's tray, which was a very dangerous thing to do in those days. My mother caught me when I was swallowing it down in great ecstatic gulps. She snatched what was left from my hands and stamped it into the ground. Then she pulled me by the hair into the house and locked me in the bedroom, giving me nothing to eat all night, which was a good excuse for the rest of my family to have a little extra watery soup and bread. In my room I cursed my family and God. But then as I shivered in the cold and dark it came to me in the midst of my despair that there was no God, so I merely cursed my family and felt much better.'

'What happened to your family?' I asked.

'I've no idea. I ran away from home the following year. I worked in a brothel, and did quite well all things considered. As you know, I married an Italian and eventually after many years of doing things my way, without the help of God, here I am, and as you can see, still going strong.' She laughed merrily in her infectious way and immediately I forgave her for seeing the shadow of death in my cards.

'So, my dear,' she said, wiping the tears of mirth from her eyes, 'if there is a God, which I have seen no evidence of or have had any reason to think there is, I would say God helps those who help themselves.'

'Your sentiments correspond exactly with mine, but then there was no religion in our house, apart from going to the Sunday school once a week in order to get to the Christmas party and the summer picnics.'

'There was some sense in that,' said Mrs Rossi.

We both laughed again. Poppy entered with the coffee. She looked grim. 'There's that sales fellow out there wanting to know how many letter headings you need. He looked kind of suspicious about all that screeching.'

'He can look as suspicious as he likes. Tell him I'll take fifty.'

'But we need more than that,' whined Poppy.

'Well, he'll just have to come back again when we need them.' Poppy banged the door on her way out.

'That one is in for a surprise one day,' said Mrs Rossi.

'She does seem a bit familiar,' I said, 'but I suppose being one of the family –'

'Families are not important to me. I may just up and leave this place if I've a mind to.'

'Will you?' I said, feeling depressed. 'What about the agency?'

'You can't stay in the one place for ever, my dear. When something tells me to move on I pay attention. I have instincts, you know, which is nothing to do with God. It is to do with —' She tapped her forehead.

Sadly I left her office, reflecting that if Mrs Rossi's agency folded up I would have to throw my lot in with Chalmers & Stroud and become permanent.

My encounters with Mr Robson when he gave me his letters were now as mundane as his big, sanctified room. Gone were the innuendoes and the pats. His letters became more complicated and his dictation faster. He appeared enshrouded in a surge of work, and I began to wonder about that. I ventured to ask him, 'How is Brendan suiting you?'

'Brendan?' he repeated, as if the name was foreign to him.

'The gardener,' I said with a touch of apprehension.

'Oh yes, of course, yes. He is doing his job quite well.' He stated this in a distant manner as if I had intruded into something private, then carried on with his dictation.

When he'd finished I sat up straight and said haughtily, 'About Sunday. I don't know if I can manage.'

He blinked as though I'd slapped him. 'But, my dear, I urgently require you to come. I am on the verge of a very important discovery in my studies which may elude me if it is not set down right away.' He smiled at me ingratiatingly.

'I'll try,' I said, 'but I have a lot of things on my mind.' I added, 'Perhaps you had better get someone else.'

'But, my dear,' he said, and I was glad to see his lips quivering, 'there is no one as suitable as you.'

'How is that?'

'I thought you understood.' Now he looked pathetic.

'I am not a clairvoyant,' I said.

'But I can trust you,' he said. 'There are not many people I can trust.'

'Yes,' I said doubtfully, 'and there are not many people I can trust either when it comes to problems.'

'You can trust me.' He put his notes to one side with a slight sigh, I noticed. 'Now tell me, what is wrong?'

I proceeded to tell him, with the right degree of reluctance, that my husband was drinking heavily and we were getting into debt.

'It's not really his fault,' I concluded. 'As you know he has come through a lot; not that being in the war is a good excuse for drinking, though I can understand it in a way. But now he doesn't seem to care about anything any more. He never has any money to give me, and it's getting to the stage that I'm thinking of moving in with Brendan just to get away from it all.'

'I must say,' said Mr Robson sympathetically, 'I consider Brendan a pleasant enough fellow from what I've seen of him, but he doesn't seem very well endowed either with money or brains. How would he be any better?'

'I've thought of that too, but when one is desperate –' I broke off, biting my lower lip.

'How much do you need?' Mr Robson asked.

'It's an impossible sum. I don't want to discuss it any more.'

'Perhaps I could make a small advance.'

I confessed it was around thirty pounds, then broke down covering my face with my hands.

'Quite a bit,' he said severely, 'but if I advance you this amount will you pay me back with your Sunday earnings?'

I looked at him through grateful tears. 'Oh yes, Mr Robson. I promise I will pay.'

He dismissed me with a wave of his hand. 'Run along, my dear, and stop worrying. I'll see you on Sunday as usual.'

'Singing, are we?' said Adam when I arrived home clutching my plastic bag of groceries and humming 'Lili Marlene'.

'I hope it's not a crime.'

'No. It's nice to see you in a good mood. But I just can't help wondering what you've been up to.'

'Lamb chops, that's what I've been up to. Lamb chops for supper and a bottle for afterwards.'

Adam and the kids regarded me with blank stares.

'There's no pleasing you lot is there?'

8

Being an only child I should have been a lonely child, but loneliness did not afflict me in my early years, since I had two friends. Susan and Ina I called them, figments of my imagination, but very satisfactory ones for I could conjure them up at any time. I did not like Ina as much as Susan. In my mind she was always poorly dressed with a runny nose while Susan was beautiful and blonde-haired, like a doll with china-blue eyes. Susan and I whispered things about Ina, who usually walked six paces behind, pleading with us to be allowed into our company. Sometimes we let her. She was useful for games like mums and dads, or nurses and patients, when we needed a child to be slapped or a patient to be poked. Now I can see that Ina and Susan were based on myself. Susan was what I wanted to be. Ina was the real me – shy and awkward and without friends. I wonder if all lonely children play this game or only those with split personalities.

When the struggle for survival began in the primary school playground I lost trace of them altogether. I had real children to play with and yet they were always less satisfactory than my imaginary friends. It's always been like that with me. I've never taken up with anybody who is anywhere near rational. That is men, not women, for I don't rate women very highly. Adam is certainly not rational. Brendan has no intelligence whatsoever and Mr Robson is weird. But they're all I've got to work on. God helps those who help themselves, said Mrs Rossi. Perhaps she had better material to work with, or perhaps she was more skilful than me, or perhaps it is a matter of perseverance.

'I hope you are not thinking of giving your gardening job up,' I said to Brendan. The three of us were sitting in the pub.

'Did I say I was?'

'I hope you are saving some money, and not wasting it all on drink.'

'Leave him alone,' said Adam. 'He can do what he likes. It's nothing to do with you.'

'Perhaps she's right,' said Brendan, giving me the anxious eye.

'The day Betty is right we'd better all jump off a high cliff,' said Adam.

'You don't like hearing good advice?' I asked.

'Advice coming from you is dangerous, not good. I should know.'

'Since when have you ever listened to me?'

'Don't start fighting, you two,' said Brendan. He jabbed me in the side with his elbow, and I jabbed him back.

'If you like I'll put money in the post office for you,' I told him. 'Since you managed to drink before, you can still do that and save the extra.'

'I've got my suit to pay up,' said Brendan in a weak manner.

'Even with that you should still have something left.'

'You want to get your hands on Brendan's money as well,' said Adam, tapping the table with his empty glass.

'As well as what?' I asked.

'As well as the money you could paper the walls with.'

I turned to Brendan. 'Because I am trying to save a little for a holiday, which I considered would be very nice for him and the kids, he's trying to make something of it. He makes me sick.'

'Shut up and give us some money for a round,' said Adam.

When he went off to the bar I explained to Brendan, 'I'm not really going on a holiday, I'm saving to get away from him. Why don't you do the same? With some money we could make plans.'

Brendan leaned back with a frightened look on his face. 'What kind of plans?'

'You exasperate me, Brendan. Without money there can be no plans. We'll both have to save up before we can make any.'

'I've never made a plan in my life,' he said with force. 'I don't feel up to it right now.'

I said very coldly, 'Don't intrude into my life then.'

'What's up with you two?' said Adam, returning to the table.

'Nothing at all,' I replied.

'I've been thinking,' said Brendan, 'if I saved up some money, I could come a holiday with you all. That is,' he said diffidently, 'if you don't mind.'

'Been at you again, has she?' said Adam.

Disdainfully I looked away. The bartender caught my eye and winked. His hair was so flat and black it was like shoe polish. He looked as if he was a guy who knew how to live it up. However, he must have received my message of not being available for the moment, for he turned his head the other way. I felt a pang of regret.

'You can forget about holidays,' I said to Brendan. 'Next year I shall be gone.'

'Begone?' repeated Adam. 'That's a good one. Begone fair maid.'

'I don't blame Betty,' said Brendan in a firm tone of voice, as though he'd done a lot of thinking about this. He gave me a conspiratorial glance.

'Who the hell are you not to blame her?' Adam spluttered over his beer, while I stared at them both as if I was watching a particularly poor play.

'She is a fine woman,' uttered Brendan, his florid face and bulky shoulders emanating the strength of a bull who spies the red cape.

'You don't say?' said Adam, fascinated. 'I've no doubt you fancy her.'

'Carry on,' I muttered to myself.

'So what,' said Brendan, flexing his shoulders. I felt a shot of admiration for him.

'Calm down,' I said, but neither of them paid any attention.

'You're getting out of hand,' said Adam, wiping the froth of beer from his mouth.

'You sneer at her far too often for my liking,' Brendan interrupted. 'You don't know how to treat women.'

Adam laughed so much he nearly fell off the seat. Heads turned to us with quizzical expressions. Adam's laughter dried up. He said to me, 'Do you, Betty, take this lump of shit to be your ever loving lover?' His voice was loud.

I decided it was time to leave. 'You can both get stuffed,' I said, and walked out with a sidelong glance at the bartender, who gave me another wink before I departed.

I had a phone call from Mai at work, or occupation as they preferred to call it in Chalmers & Stroud. Miss Benson's eyes were wide and curious when she handed me the receiver.

'I've managed to get something,' said Mai. 'Quite a good situation as it turns out. How about meeting me for lunch at the usual place?'

'Love to,' I said, and put the phone down.

'Was that Mai?' asked Miss Benson, standing a foot away from me.

'Mai? Oh you mean Mai. I'm not sure,' I said vaguely, walking back to my typewriter.

'It's really very good, and the money's a lot better,' Mai explained while I champed patiently through mashed potatoes. 'You should get out of that place,' she advised me at the end of a rambling account of her new wonder job, 'otherwise you'll become old before your time.' Her make-up was toned down a lot and her hair a lighter shade of black.

'I'm still working for the agency, just waiting for something better to crop up.'

'And why doesn't something crop up?'

'As a matter of fact,' I said with the air of one who has decided to come clean, 'I am in a quandary. I've been offered such a big rise by Mr Robson I don't know whether to accept it or not, but money isn't everything.'

'How much?' she asked, puckering her forehead.

I mentioned a substantial amount. Mai raised her fork to her mouth unhappily.

'I wouldn't like to work for that old creep no matter what he offered.'

'I know,' I said. 'Money's not everything. What's your boss like?'

'Very attractive and a real gentleman and good at making you feel at ease, if you know what I mean.'

'Lucky you,' I said. 'I've read of bosses like that. Unfortunately I've never met them. Perhaps if you play your cards properly –' I winked.

'Come to think of it,' said Mai, 'I wouldn't mind a night out with him, but,' she sighed, 'he's married.'

Hiding my pang of envy, though I suspected it was ill-founded, I said, 'What difference does that make?'

'Why don't you make love to me?' I whispered into Adam's ear. He was lying in bed with his back to me. I had figured that it was almost a fortnight since we had had sex. The contact was more necessary for me than the actual deed.

He half turned towards me. 'I can't switch on when it suits you.'

'You don't love me any more?' I asked.

'I'm not sure what I feel about you,' he grumbled softly.

'Neither am I sure about you.'

'You're very devious,' he said, stroking my hair.

'My mother used to say I was too deep for her liking.'

'Forget your mother.' Our arms were touching now. 'I don't want anyone else, that's for sure.'

I smiled, staring up at the ceiling.

'I suppose I'm difficult to live with. It's not been easy for you,' he said.

'It's not been easy for you either.' Our voices sounded wooden, like the first stages of a prayer meeting.

'In what way?' he asked.

'Perhaps the war —' I began.

'I drink too much,' he said.

'So do I.' Now we were facing, but it was dark. He was like a stranger. 'We don't drink all that much.' I stroked his cheek. It was like a stranger's cheek.

'I'm thinking of giving it up,' he said.

'Sex?'

He laughed, like a stranger. 'I thought I had. I mean drink.'

'The kids would miss it; I mean us stopping the drink. They wouldn't recognise us.'

'What a terrible thing to say.' He was now stroking my breast, which strangely enough I couldn't stand. It made me feel as if I was being insulted or assaulted, unlike any other part of my body.

'We could make it up to them by buying lots of fancy gear.'

'Or holidays,' he added.

'They'd likely prefer us to drink on holidays, otherwise we'd be no fun.'

'One thing,' he said, squeezing my nipple, which made me want to scream. 'Without drink Brendan would vanish like the proverbial rose of yesteryear.'

'You're not jealous of Brendan, by any chance?' I asked.

He withdrew his hand, saying, 'Should I be?'

'You're such a fool, Adam,' I said. 'You deliberately encourage him, make him feel as if we were his foster-parents, then for no good reason want to get rid of him.'

Adam moved round and lay straight on his back with one arm under his head. 'We have drifted into a situation with Brendan which frankly is getting on my nerves.'

'He's like a child, isn't he? I don't know what to do about him either.'

Adam gave one long sigh. 'Fuck Brendan,' he said. Roughly he pulled me close then moved on top of me.

'Fuck me,' I said. Normally I don't like the word, but I was excited.

Afterwards Adam said quietly and sincerely, 'No more drink then?'

'Right,' I said, wishing I could have one long pull on a bottle of wine to set me off to sleep. The act had done nothing for me.

On Sunday when I was in Mr Robson's kitchenette I noticed there were two five-pound notes lying under the coffee jar. I looked quickly away and asked him if I should pour.

'Please do,' he said as he laid an embroidered linen square under my cup.

'That's pretty,' I remarked.

'My wife was a beautiful stitcher,' he said.

I looked through the window at a patch of upturned earth. 'I noticed Brendan has been busy,' I said.

'He has uprooted some of my plants,' said Mr Robson darkly, 'but I don't think he will do it again.'

'Perhaps he's not suitable.'

'He's careless, but I think he's learned his lesson.'

'Lesson?' I repeated stupidly.

'Don't worry, my dear, Brendan and I understand one another. He's not a complicated person, but let's say being acquainted with the criminal mind I have a way of talking to him.'

'Brendan's not a criminal,' I said, putting my cup down on the saucer with a clatter.

'I shouldn't think so, but he has a behaviour pattern which could be associated with crime. He interests me.'

'I'm surprised to hear this, Mr Robson. I certainly would not have spoken for anyone if I'd thought they were the criminal type.'

'I'm sure you wouldn't, my dear. What I should have said is that Brendan is the kind who has a direct approach to life, a simple type who views situations in black and white rather than in various shades of grey like you and I. But let's not worry about him,' he said hurriedly. 'There is much to be done.'

The notes headed 'Capabilities of Human Behaviour in Animals' were spiced with a lot of jargon I could not understand. Some parts that I could understand held my attention for seconds, but I mainly plodded through it with a feeling of boredom and a feeling that Mr Robson, though not exactly crazy, was very eccentric. When I visited his toilet at one point in the day I noticed for the first time a small circular hole above the cistern. Viciously I plugged it with an old biscuit wrapper from my pocket. Later I followed him up to the bedroom, reassured by the fragile set of his shoulders and the way he tottered like an old man uncertain of his footsteps.

'I fear you may think this is all very strange,' he murmured when I was seated in front of the mirror of his dressing-table, 'but you understand I don't require you to do anything other than –' He broke off.

'Yes,' I said, staring at my pale, strained reflection in the mirror.

'Now my dear, just undress very slowly while I go behind the screen. As you know it's the only way I can –'

'Yes, I know,' I said sighing, thinking at least he might have heated up the room.

He coughed and vanished behind the screen.

On the way out I picked up the two fivers lying under the coffee jar.

'Is this . . . ?' I said, waving them in front of his face.

'It is, it is,' he said, nodding his head as if he had discovered more human behaviour in animals.

'Can't you get me something else?' I asked Mrs Rossi. 'I'm not keen on my situation now. Frankly I can't stand Mr Robson. He is very difficult.'

'Most people are,' she said, languidly popping a dark chocolate into her mouth. She offered me the box. Impatiently I waved it away.

'He's crazy,' I said, adding, 'possibly worse than crazy.'

'But generous,' she said.

'He's sick,' I pointed out.

'But generous,' she said again.

'He's a creep, maybe dangerous.'

'You'll not get a better position,' she said, putting the chocolates back in the drawer, and feeling about in it as if looking for something.

'Don't bother with the cards,' I said. 'I've no time to spare.'

'Other than that I can't help you,' she said. 'Besides, I'm winding up all my affairs. I'm tired of living in this country. People are not interested in the occult. They'd rather believe in God and all that rubbish.'

'Fortune telling doesn't sound too secure,' I agreed.

'I'm tired of security. Death is preferable at times.'

'I know how you feel,' I said. 'I thought money might be a good reason for sticking to Mr Robson, but I can't stand it when he goes behind the screen. He's old and he smells.'

'Behind the screen?' Her eyes shone blackly and she laughed. 'What does he do?'

'I don't know but I have my suspicions.' We both laughed at that.

'I knew him quite well when I was younger,' she said, wiping her eyes.

'Nowadays he studies human behaviour in animals.'

'Don't tell me any more,' said Mrs Rossi, now holding her heaving sides. 'I'll do myself an injury.'

'But you see what I mean?' I said after she'd calmed down and brought out her long cigarette holder. 'I'm still young and it's no life for a working mother.'

Mrs Rossi's laughter was threatening to surge up again.

'Look,' I said, 'can't you find me something to do in the fortune telling line? I could be your receptionist.'

'I've got Poppy for that.'

I hung my head despairingly. 'That's that then,' I said.

'Wouldn't you like to try the cards?' she asked. 'They might help.'

'If the future is so certain, I can't do anything about it.'

'True,' she agreed. 'Listen,' she said suddenly. 'I'll see what I can do for you once I get established somewhere else. Meanwhile throw in your lot with Mr Robson. He's generous and not such a bad old stick really. He might snuff it and leave you a fortune.'

9

'How much have I got now?' Brendan asked as he handed over two pounds for me to put into my savings account in the post office.

'You mean how much have we got,' I corrected him. 'Well, between you and me we have seven pounds ten shillings.'

He was sitting with his elbows on the kitchen table, hands cupping his face. 'Not bad,' he said, looking impressed.

'I think it's wonderful,' I said, tying a chiffon scarf on the side of my neck. 'How do I look?'

'Stunning. What's it for anyway?'

'My scarf?'

'The money.'

In a low voice I said, 'I get so tired of you at times. I've to keep explaining things. You remind me of that Lennie guy in *Of Mice and Men*.'

'What guy's that?' He brought his arms off the table and stared at me wildly.

'Look, when we get enough we can set up some little business between us. There's this woman I know. She's marvellous at telling fortunes and that's something that people are always keen on hearing. But she needs some capital to rent a good place, and a couple of assistants for various duties –'

'I thought you said we were going a holiday; me, you and Adam.'

'I think I'll give you your money back. I see it's no use.'

He stood up and grabbed my hand. 'Please don't. I'm really all for going into business.'

I kissed his forehead, which was damp. Brendan sweats a lot, probably because of his weight. 'Before you do that,' I said, 'you'll have to get your hair cut and your suit cleaned. It's full of stains.'

I stopped talking when Adam came into the kitchen rubbing his hands, his face nicely pink from shaving. Compared to Brendan he looked admirable.

'All ready I hope.' He beamed. Arm-in-arm we sauntered down to the pub as jolly as the three musketeers.

On Sunday morning I opened my eyes with the sensation they had been stuck together with paste. Adam lay face down on the pillow making gurgling noises. I glanced despairingly at the alarm clock and pulled the sheet over my head. Then the kids came in and sat on top of us, jumping up and down as if they were on ponies.

'We want breakfast,' shouted Rae.

Adam lifted his head and croaked, 'Go and fry some sausages.'

I considered pleading a terminal illness, but Mr Robson hovered on my mind like the peal of a church bell to the faithful.

'Last time we made sausages they got burnt,' declared Robert.

'Only on the outside,' I said. 'Inside they were raw.' I addressed Adam's back. 'Why can't you make the breakfast? You're not doing anything else.'

'Apart from the washing, the ironing, the cooking and the cleaning.'

'Not the ironing,' I said, adding gently, 'You know I've to go out and earn money.'

'For doing what? That's what I'd like to know.'

'Is Mr Robson a nice man?' Rae asked, most inappropriately.

'Not particularly, but he gives me money for typing.'

Adam laughed like a dog barking. 'Don't believe a word of what she says.'

'Can we have some?' asked Rae.

'Go and make cornflakes and I'll give you a shilling each.'

They scampered off. Adam turned round and said, looking dangerous, 'All this money you earn, we don't seem to be any better off. What do you do with it?'

I closed my eyes and clasped my hands as if praying. 'I am saving up.'

'For what?'

'Because,' I said carefully, as if he was a child who did not take things in easily, 'I am going to start a business, if you must know.' Hastily I swung my legs out of the bed and donned an old coat which I used as a dressing gown.

'Business?' He sat bolt upright. I half expected his hair to stand on end.

'Yes, business,' I repeated, relieved that I had uttered the word.

He jumped out of bed and grabbed the front of my raincoat as if I had said something vile. 'What the hell are you up to?'

'Calm yourself,' I said. 'It was to be a secret. I was going to tell you once I got the thing going. I have plans for us, great plans really, but I might have known you wouldn't understand.'

'You're mad,' he said, and threw himself back on the bed looking exhausted.

'So that's why I work through the week and on Sundays: to save money.'

'What kind of business?' he asked listlessly.

'You'll never believe it,' I laughed, dressing rapidly at the same time.

'Try me.'

'Remember that woman Mai who came out to the pub not so long ago?'

'The one that looked like a whore?'

'Really, Adam. She's a nice, sensible person, who had too much make-up on, that's all.'

'Go on – about the business.'

'Well. I hope you are listening closely.'

He nodded his head. His mouth looked slack.

'The lady at the agency, Mrs Rossi, you've heard me mention her –'

He shook his head and closed his eyes.

'And myself, and Mai, are all going into the agency line –'

'Call girls?'

Ignoring this, I continued. 'Mrs Rossi wants to expand but she needs two more partners like Mai and myself.' My brain couldn't invent any more, so I finished off by saying, 'Take it or leave it, Adam, but I've got ambitions and I don't want you standing in my way.'

'Right,' he said, 'that's fine.' He yawned. I thought he looked pale. When I left the room he called, 'I too have my ambitions. I'll be gone when you return.'

I shook my head and looked at him sympathetically. I had heard it all before.

Not being in much of a hurry to encounter Mr Robson I dallied on his garden path, admiring the fuchsias, rhododendrons, roses and other blooms with the uneasy feeling that Mr Robson could be peering through the net curtains. I spent another five minutes round the back of the house staring at reddish-brown upturned earth where apparently Brendan had been digging. I admitted it did nothing for the look of the place, but no doubt there was a reason for it. I saw a string vest hanging on the washing-line, harmless but suggestive of Mr Robson's old body. I shook my head to cancel the image and knocked hard on the backdoor. It was ajar, so I entered. In the kitchen I ran my hand along the marble table-top alongside the sink unit and touched the silk lacy curtains on the window. I opened the cupboard above the sink unit and took down two cups and saucers, in readiness for the coffee. Then I decided I had gone far enough with Mr Robson's utensils so I waited for him, sitting on the kitchen stool. After five minutes I called, 'Mr Robson – I have arrived.' I tiptoed into the large room where I studied the photographs on the wall, particularly the steadfast face of the hanged man, but my mind was distracted by the absence of my employer. I left the room and climbed up the stairs to Mr Robson's bedroom, calling, 'Are you there, Mr Robson?' I entered the unoccupied room, was unable to resist looking behind the screen, but found nothing more than a desk with some sheets of paper. 'Mr Robson!' I called again, and picked up a sheet which was marked with my name. I read the contents with a sense of surprise, relief and anger. This was due to one paragraph which said, 'It would appear that this subject is a reckless young woman who will readily enter into a situation without any thought of consequences. Given certain factors she could be a danger to society. Without any qualms she sits on the other side of the screen with an air of expectation which would be frightening if it were not so interesting. Such simple tests have proved –'

I stopped reading when I heard a noise from below, but on running downstairs into the kitchen I found a draught had caused the door to bang. I closed it forcefully. The activities of this deluded old man made me want to puke. It seemed I had displayed my soul to him for a few paltry pounds. On the way back home I calmed down. There was no harm done really. I would display a lot more than that if the price was right. That's how desperate I had become.

Adam's bed was unmade. The kids' room looked as if it had been burgled with all the drawers left open. Spilled cornflakes littered the carpet. Downstairs on top of the radio I found an envelope. The message inside read:

'Goodbye, Betty. Have taken the kids with me. Sorry things didn't work out. Hope you succeed with your business arrangements.'

My first reaction was shock, then anger, then relief. I could now do what I wanted without Adam breathing down my neck. I expected he would leave the kids with his stepmother, who'd be glad to take them in. She always spoiled them rotten whenever she got the chance. 'Poor neglected lambs,' she described them. My main problem was how to get in touch with Brendan. He never usually showed up on Sundays.

On Monday morning Mr Robson did not appear.

'Any word from him?' I asked Miss Benson. 'He wasn't at home on Sunday when I called to do his typing.'

'Ah yes, your typing,' she said, smiling mysteriously. 'No, we have heard nothing.'

I sat around all morning, yawning and filing my nails with my neat little manicure set. I offered to do some typing for one of the other women for the sake of passing the time. This offer was refused. I became keenly miserable about everything. I pined for Mr Robson's return or for a sign he would be back. At lunchtime I was thankful to see Mai inside the coffee bar. She listened to me with an air of abstraction when I told her about Mr Robson.

'Probably has the flu and can't be bothered phoning,' she said.

'But he wasn't around on Sunday.'

'Perhaps he decided to take a holiday.'

'Could be,' I said. After that we had nothing much to say. Suddenly we'd become strangers with only the weather to talk about.

'I meant to tell you,' she said when we had moved out onto the street. 'I've had my lunchtime altered. Can't say when I'll see you again, but I'll give you a ring.'

'Yes, do that,' I said in a similar distracted manner before I caught the bus back.

I'm looking over the veranda of the cottage hospital to where a bus shelter stands covered in graffiti. I can make out the words 'Fuck the Pope'. Lady Lipton is asleep. She's been asleep for most of my tale. I'm surprised when she says with her eyes still closed, 'Is that all?'

'All what?' I said, wishing I was sitting in the bus shelter talking to some wino with a bottle to share.

'You said you caught the bus back. What happened after that?'

'Weren't you listening?'

'I heard most of it, though I may have dozed off at the boring parts. Please do go on.'

'It's not true anyway,' I said off-handedly.

'It sounds to me like a whodunit where you have to plough through a lot of red herrings before it gets to the point. Believe me I've got a pile of them in my locker and I know the set-up off by heart. So what happened after you caught the bus? I suppose your husband and children returned and Mr Robson wrote you a letter to say he didn't require your services any more. Is that it?'

'I never saw Mr Robson again. And as a matter of fact my husband's got another woman.'

My hand tightened on the rail of the veranda. I wondered if I should jump over and land with a splatter on the street below. On the other hand the railings were too high for me to climb. This was a pity I thought at that moment. I turned away from the old woman. I'd said enough.

I stayed away from Chalmers & Stroud to allow Mr Robson plenty of time to worry about me. At home I washed and polished everything I could lay my hands on, appreciating the peace and quiet of the house as well as the money I saved on food now Adam and the kids were gone. There was no loneliness in the double bed at night. I could stretch and toss and turn without encountering Adam's stiff animosity. It was like a holiday when the sun shone through clean bedroom windows in the morning. The kitchen too had an unfamiliar foreign look about it: tidy and tasteful with a bunch of stolen roses from the garden next door on the centre of the table, while I daintily munched toast and marmalade for my breakfast. Later I remember a fine drizzle of rain as I went to the post office and lifted some money from the savings account. The first blow fell when I called round at Mrs Rossi's and found the door locked. I rattled and banged to no avail. A man came out on the landing below and shouted, 'Don't you know she's scarpered?' and added, 'Funny business!' in a questioning way.

I walked down to him and said, knowing it would be useless, 'Any idea where she's gone?'

He shook his head. 'Owes you money does she?' Then without waiting for an answer he went back inside.

I was sad about Mrs Rossi's departure, unlike Adam's and the kids', which at the time I thought was only temporary. I called at Chalmers & Stroud to be told by an excited Miss Benson that they had heard nothing from Mr Robson, though this was not unusual since he was known to go off to foreign holiday resorts whenever he took the urge.

'Very inconvenient for you I suppose,' she said, her voice thinly insincere.

'That's all right,' I said. 'I don't mind the rest.'

'I'll let you know when he gets back, but –'

'I've no doubt he'll let me know himself,' I said, giving her a wave.

Brendan appeared just after I had shovelled most of my meal of tinned tuna and beetroot into the dustbin, replacing it with a glass of vodka. He followed me into the kitchen. I told him to sit down and poured him a glass. He drank it over as if it was water.

'That's vodka and lemonade,' I informed him.

He nodded, wiped his mouth, looked behind him in a troubled way and said, 'Very nice. Can I have another one?'

'Don't be so greedy.' But I refilled his glass and mine, adding a splash of lemonade. The hand reaching out for it was dirty, his fingernails engrained. 'You're a mess, Brendan,' I said. 'Worse than usual. You might have washed.'

He stared at me as if I was speaking in a foreign language.

'By the way,' I said loudly as if he was deaf, 'Adam's gone.'

'Gone where?'

'Left days ago. Took the kids with him.'

There was a noise from Brendan's throat which could have been a hiccup or a sob. His face crumpled and he cried like a child.

'For God's sake, it's me he's left, not you.'

'What will I do?' he wailed, pressing his face on the table.

'Have another drink, that's what.' I surveyed his bowed head with disgust. 'Go and wash yourself and brush that suit. It looks as if you've been sleeping in a byre with it on. We might as well go out and enjoy ourselves.'

Brendan looked up, his eyes like small pools of mud. 'It's not the same without Adam.'

'I agree, but since I've been alone in this place all week I want out.' I hauled him off the chair and shoved him into the bathroom. It definitely was not the same without Adam, but that would pass. Freedom was the thing.

I felt much more optimistic in the pub, being squiffy from the vodka we already had. Brendan was giggling now.

'Alone at last,' I said, trying to match his continual vivid-blue stares.

'Here's to Adam.' He held up his glass squintily, spilling some of the drink.

'Tell me,' I said after some more desultory talk, 'what's happened to Mr Robson?'

'Who's that?' He giggled uncontrollably.

'You're drunk,' I said.

He wagged his finger close to my nose. 'You're beautiful. Will you marry me?'

'You're a fool,' I said, warming to his fatuous, beaming face, 'but I'll always love you.' I traced a cross on his forehead. 'What about Mr Robson though?'

'Fuck the old bastard, that's what I say.'

I was impressed by the touch of violence. 'You're dead right. He owes me money.'

'Don't worry about money. Look!' He showed me a ten-pound note. 'I've got more where that came from.'

It was a pretty sight. I'd never felt so happy as I did at that moment. I was like Irma la Douce finding her true lover. 'Tomorrow we will go to the seaside,' I said, 'and sit outside a hotel at a table with an umbrella, and sip Martini.'

'And we can go to the races and back horses,' said Brendan excitedly.

'While I watch through binoculars,' I added. We held hands and made outrageous plans, laughing aloud. The barman came over and wiped our table.

'Where's Adam?' he asked reprovingly.

'Gone,' I said.

'Gone with the wind,' Brendan added, now almost hysterical.

'Take it easy with the drink,' said the barman. 'I don't want to have to put you out.'

I winked at him. 'It's Brendan's birthday. We're just celebrating.'

The barman walked away, looking as if he'd rather hear no more about it. Brendan's mood changed. 'I hope he comes back,' he said anxiously. Two drinks later he was crying.

'Let's go,' I said when I saw the barman staring over. Passing the licensed grocer's I purchased some sweet wine. Every so often I had to return and drag Brendan along the road. Like a dog he was wavering at every lamppost. Inside the house I had a drink while he was sick in the toilet. After that he sat in Adam's chair, pale and lumpy and unhappy.

'Go to bed,' I said. He lumbered off like a wounded bear. There was a lot of crashing on the stairs, but I couldn't be bothered to investigate. No news was good news the ways things were going. After that I let down the pulley and began to fold up the clothes – a skirt of Rae's, a shirt of Robert's, and some socks of Adam's. In a drunken, dramatic way, I said aloud, 'This is all that remains of my family,' then I drank some more wine with the happier thought that tomorrow Brendan and I would go to the seaside. On Monday I would search for Adam and the kids and we would all start afresh. Clearly it was impossible for me to pass the rest of my life with Brendan. I discovered him later sprawled across the bed with his clothes on. He had not even taken off his boots. I tried to push him over to get under the covers, but he was as heavy as an ox. I staggered into the kids' room and lay down on Rae's bed, falling asleep with the smell of Johnson's shampoo, which a friend had given her for her birthday.

On Saturday I awoke feeling uneasy. I looked at the small Walt Disney clock on Rae's set of drawers. Half past one, it read. Surely it had stopped. I held it to my ear and in disbelief listened to the steady tick tick. 'Brendan!' I shouted, rushing through to my room, surprised that I had all my clothes on. Apart from rumpled blankets and a dirty smear on the bedcover there was no sign of him. 'Don't leave me, Brendan,' I sobbed, nearly falling down the stairs to reach the kitchen, but I knew he wouldn't be there. The front door was slightly open. He couldn't even shut it properly, I thought bitterly. I drank coffee while I tried to figure everything out. It was like a badly produced film where you try to put two and two together, knowing that the murderer is the one you least suspect, while thinking the script writer must be crazy because the plot is so bad. The fact was that all the people I was connected with were disappearing. I thought I'd better start praying for them to come back, but that seemed like giving in or going against my principles. Besides, maybe Brendan had gone home to change for the outing. 'We can go to the races,' he had said, though I couldn't see him worrying about appearance. Anyway, he had very little to change with. Perhaps he was merely checking in with his mother. Perhaps this, perhaps that. I took off my crumpled dress, washed my face, and sat around in my underskirt waiting for him to return, as there was nothing else to do but finish the remainder of the wine facing me on the table. This took the edge off things. It was clammily hot. I would have liked to lie down on the grass in the back green. Instead I lay on the settee in the living room singing snatches of songs like 'See What the Boys in the Back Room Will Have' and 'The Isle of Capri'. I had conversations with people like Adam and Mrs Rossi, who were with me in spirit if not in reality. I actually had a good time before I fell asleep, hearing in my head Brendan sing, 'Gwine to run all night, gwine to run all day, I'll bet my money on de bobtail nag –' He does have a humour of a kind, I thought drowsily.

I can't remember too much of the rest of the weekend, but I must have dressed later on in the evening and fetched another bottle from the licensed grocer's. I have a vague recollection of sitting in the back green in the dusk with the rain cooling my forehead. I think I was very happy until the man next door loomed up in front of me. 'Mind your own business,' I said, but sensing trouble I withdrew indoors clutching the bottle. I slept most of Sunday but was forced up by a blinding thirst for water. In the shadows of the kitchen I groped to the tap and realised I was completely alone.

IO

I gave Lady Lipton a nudge. She was nodding off again.
'Do you hear what I said,' I shouted in her ear. 'I was
completely alone.'

She jumped a bit and said, 'Because I am closing my eyes does
not mean I haven't been following what you say. I find this Brendan
fellow very drab. I don't know what you saw in him. I'm more
interested in Mr Robson, a strange fellow perhaps, but at least he
had some kind of breeding. What became of him?'

'Ah, Mr Robson,' I said, smiling. 'I'll come to that. All in good
time.' I leaned back in the chair and shut my eyes, rocking myself
to and fro.

She nipped my arm painfully. 'So what became of him?'

'Well –' I paused once again. My head felt almost worn out by
the details of what was history to me now.

'Come on,' she said, her skinny fingers reaching out for another
nip. I went on.

After that things became a bit hazy. For a week I remained in the
house, sozzled most of the time. I had enough money in the savings
account to buy drink. I don't remember eating. Again I was having
a good time. They all came in and listened to me. They never did
much talking, being only there in my mind. But they listened; Adam,
Brendan, Mr Robson, sometimes Mai and Mrs Rossi. I admit I was
probably off my rocker. I'm certain Adam came back once in reality.
As usual he was shouting various accusations, and I pulled a blanket
over my head to shut out the voice. Finally a social worker came.
I believe I have him to thank for that, the swine.

When he visited me later in here he sat on the edge of the bed examining his fingernails. I told him he didn't look well and asked if he was still drinking.

'Not really,' he answered. 'Perhaps that's why I don't look well.'

'I feel marvellous,' I said, struggling to sit up. I looked down at the rough white hospital nightdress and told him when he came next time to bring me a decent one.

He said, 'Have you got any? I don't remember you ever wearing one.'

I told him for God's sake to buy one, and asked if he didn't care how I looked.

'I'll get you one,' he said quickly.

I asked how the kids were.

'Happy.' He looked away, as if he could not stand the sight of me.

I asked how he was managing without me and he said, 'Very well.' I said that I hoped he was keeping everything tidy, as I had left the house very clean.

He looked at me so miserably that I yearned to forgive him, then he said the house was no longer his responsibility, and, 'It's over a month since I left you. Don't you remember?'

'Oh,' I said, 'how time flies.'

After a long pause I asked why he had come to see me. He said because I had been very ill and was the mother of his children. I laughed, which hurt my chest a bit.

'The mother of your children! That sounds like the pen of my aunt. We got that in French at school.'

'I never took French,' he said with the martyred look he had on his face the day he came home from the war and passed our window.

'Welcome home, Adam,' I said.

He took this literally. He said, 'It's no use, Betty. I'm not coming back. I'm not saying it was all your fault, but after what's happened I couldn't face it.'

'Fuck you,' I said and closed my eyes. The bed creaked as he lifted his weight off. I opened my eyes, aware he was about to leave.

'What happened anyway? I got drunk for a time. So what's the big deal?'

'The big deal is' – his eyes bored into mine – 'that Brendan has been arrested for murder.'

I closed my eyes to hide the shock and said I was not surprised.

'Aren't you the clever one?' said Adam. 'You're not surprised. Did you arrange it like you arranged everything else?'

I shook my head. I was too tired to argue. I wanted him to go. He reached out and gripped my wrist hard. It was painful.

He said, 'You put it into his head to work for Robson.'

I told him it was only a suggestion.

'And the money he saved on your suggestion, what happened to that?'

I told him I had drunk it, which was why I was in here, and to let go because he was hurting me. He released me with a look of contempt, or hatred, or both.

'So he murdered Mr Robson,' I said, putting my hands under the blankets as they had become very cold.

He said, 'And you gave him the idea.'

I told him to go away as I couldn't think properly. He stood up looking like an apparition. Could I be dreaming all this, I wondered. But no.

He said, 'It was a nasty business. He smashed Robson on the side of the head with a spade. The body was scarcely recognisable when they found it in the garden shed. Doesn't that shock you?'

'I'll think about it later,' I promised. 'Just go away or I'll ring the bell for the nurse.'

I buried my face in the pillow listening to the sound of his receding footsteps. When the nurse came I asked for a sleeping pill. She said, 'Not now, dear,' so I told her to get my clothes, that I was not stopping here, that I must have a drink, that my husband always upset me. Finally she gave me something in a glass.

'Promise you won't let any visitors in again,' I said, 'especially him. It's because of him I'm in here. I like it here. I like it here. I wish I could stay here for ever.'

The nurses appear to like me, perhaps because I take their pills without any bother. I'm not one of those who complain, saying we're being turned into junkies. I don't care. I like helping to hand round tea and scones before climbing into bed for the afternoon snooze. It's a lovely feeling. In the evening before they dim the lights the pills give me a nice woozy, relaxed sensation like a good gargle of wine. This is one of the best times I ever had.

Today Lady Lipton appears to be in a trance. Her eyes are open but unblinking. I move my hand up and down in front of her face.

'Don't do that, you bitch,' she says.

'I thought you were in a state of coma.'

'I was merely thinking that the tea was late.'

'Is that all you were thinking?'

'Actually no. Did you really encourage that Brendan fellow to kill Mr Robson?'

'As a matter of fact I didn't,' I snapped. 'What use was Mr Robson to me dead?'

'Revenge perhaps?'

'Revenge for what? Jesus Christ, he wasn't my lover.'

'People can lie,' she said, giving me a withering glance.

'That's true. I don't believe you are a Lady.'

'It doesn't matter what you believe,' she said. 'It's what's in my head that counts, and I know it's true.'

'So, you were one of the upper class?' I sneered.

'Near enough, when I look back on it. It was only after my husband died everything went wrong.'

'You mean when you took to the bottle?'

'If you like to put it that way,' she said, her face untroubled. 'But I had my good times,' she added.

'Adam once said to me we were put into this world to look at a picture, and it was up to us whether we liked it or not. But,' I added, 'the picture he got was one of war. He was a disturbed man.'

She stared at me with a glance of incomprehension. At that moment a nurse came forward with tea and fairy cakes. 'Here you are, dears,' she said with a charitable smile.

When she turned away I gave her the two-finger sign.

'You're very rude,' said Lady Lipton, shoving a tiny cake into her mouth. It made her choke. 'Oh dear,' she said when she regained her breath, 'I can't seem to swallow properly nowadays.' In the same breath she asked, 'Did they hang Brendan?'

'Capital punishment has been abolished. Besides, the lawyer put forward a case of diminished responsibility.'

'It makes me sick to think of all the thugs going around. There's no decency in the young people nowadays.'

'Brendan wasn't that young. Over twenty he was. And you didn't know Mr Robson.'

'From what you say he was a gentleman, eccentric I dare say, but a gentleman for all that.'

'Have my fairy cake,' I said. 'It's a bit stale. But not so much you'd notice.'

'I suppose you will visit him in jail.'

'Of course not. Why should I?'

'Weren't you fond of him? I thought he was your boyfriend.'

'Brendan?' I laughed. 'He was so stupid he was no use to anyone, not even himself. It was because of him Adam left me. I could never forgive him for that.'

'It couldn't have been all his fault,' said Lady Lipton, 'if your husband was carrying on with another woman. He would have left you in any case.'

I became so angry that I shook her by the shoulder. 'How do you know what he would have done? Supposing I told you I made the whole thing up?'

'Then why are you so angry?' she said, rubbing her arm without any look of pain.

'Only some of it's true,' I said, regretting having opened my mouth. 'I am married to a man called Adam, who had a pal Brendan. He happened to kiss me one day when Adam was out of the room, nothing more than that. I didn't fancy him, he was so awful. But he died a long time ago in very dull circumstances.'

'Was there no Mr Robson?'

'Oh yes, but' – I shrugged – 'he was a dotary old lawyer who I typed for now and again. That was all. And while I'm at it, Mrs Rossi did not tell fortunes. In fact I don't think the woman who ran the agency was called Mrs Rossi; something like Smith or Brown.'

Lady Lipton looked doubtful. 'It seems to me you don't know what the truth is. From now on I won't believe a single word you say.'

'And you'll be right,' I said, finishing off the sweet, milky tea. 'When you're in here everything gets so jumbled up it's hard to know the truth.'

'I know what you mean. I can scarcely remember what the estate looked like, but I dream about it.'

'I never dream about anything.'

'Not even your children?'

'Not even my children,' I told her, with a hard stare.

'Oh well,' she said, 'it's time for our rest soon, thank God. I'm worn out with all this chatter. Talk, talk, all talk. I would give anything to be back home on my estate, but –' She threw her hands up in the air in a delicate manner, then rose and walked back into the ward.

It must have been about a fortnight after Brendan disappeared that the social worker called.

'How are you keeping, dear?' she asked.

'Fine,' I said. 'But I've no money and nothing to eat unless you

260

count some blue-moulded bread and potatoes with shoots growing out of them.'

She gave me three pounds, explaining that it would be deducted from any money the Social Security might allow me. I listened to all this with a sense of despondency, then I asked if there was any chance of me getting the kids back since I didn't trust my husband to take care of them properly. When she looked at me doubtfully I explained that he had been in the war and was not responsible for himself, let alone children. I tapped the side of my head to give her a clearer picture of him, but all she said was that she'd make enquiries. Meanwhile, she added, the best thing for me to do was to take it easy and not worry myself too much about anything. She was sure the children would be all right. The important point was that I attend the clinic on the date stipulated on the card.

'Nonsense,' I said. 'There is nothing wrong with me. I simply had too much to drink. But I'm all right now.'

'That's fine, dear, but I still think you should attend the clinic if you want to get back on your feet.'

'I am back on my feet!' I shouted. 'I want you to find out where my husband and kids are! I want them home!'

'That,' she said firmly, 'is not to be considered at present.'

I told her to fuck off. After she had left with a tightened mouth I looked out my Robin Hood suit, as Adam called it, applied some make-up and headed for the licensed grocer's. I was careful with the money, only purchasing a half-bottle to help me think about what I was going to do.

About a week later, which seemed like a month, I spied Adam pushing a trolley along the Co-operative floor. Mai was with him putting tins into it. They both looked cheerful until they saw me.

'Adam,' I said, confronting him and wondering why Mai of all people should be helping him with the shopping.

He looked at me woodenly but said nothing.

'I'm not working any more,' I explained gaily, winking at Mai. In a way it was good to see her. She would back me up and take the edge off Adam's truculent mood.

'I'm glad to see you looking so well,' he said at last.

'Please forgive me,' I said with a catch in my voice.

'I forgive you.'

'Has Mai' – I gave her a look of gratitude – 'been looking after you then?'

Mai responded glumly, 'You could say that.'

'Look, Mai,' I said, 'could you leave us alone for a few minutes. It's not going to be easy –'

'Mai is staying where she is.'

A twitch came into my eye which I found embarrassing.

'You mean you two are –' I stopped, strangely surprised. She wasn't his type.

'Yes, we are,' said Adam, looking over my head.

'Are what?' I wanted to stamp my feet and spit on them both.

'Going to get married once Adam gets the divorce,' said Mai, searching his face as she spoke.

'You can't,' I shrieked. 'He's a nut case. I'm the only one who understands him.'

'I'm afraid we'll have to go now,' said Adam politely, as though he was talking to a Jehovah's Witness.

'Yes, the kids will be wondering where we are,' said Mai. 'We don't like to leave them too long on their own.'

They both turned and practically ran out the Co-operative. Adam was carrying the shopping bag. I wondered if there was drink in it. I felt like shouting, 'You bastard. You never carried shopping bags for me.'

They were gone when I got outside. It was raining again. Without thinking, I brought out from my plastic bag the bottle of sherry which I had just bought, unscrewed the top and took a long swallow. After that everything was a blur in my head.

*

Lady Lipton said I was in a bad state when they brought me in, shouting and screaming and acting like a madwoman. I don't particularly believe her. She's the type that exaggerates. But I put up with her. She's the only one worth talking to in here. I haven't seen Adam since he told me about Brendan. You'd think he'd come and visit me now and again and bring the kids. It would be nice for us to be together again. After all, I am their mother.

FOR THE LOVE OF WILLIE

Foreword

Two patients sit on the veranda of a cottage hospital run by a local authority for females with mental problems, some of them long-term and incurable. Peggy, stoutly built, middle-aged, and with a hard set to her jaw, rises and stares down through the high railings at a bus shelter below.

'A man in that shelter resembles someone I once knew,' she tells her companion.

'Really?' says the companion, elderly and frail but known as the duchess because of her imperious manner. 'It beats me how you can remember anything.'

'I remember lots of things. That's why I'm writing a book.'

'A book? You never told me. What's it about?'

'About my life before they put me inside,' says Peggy. She adds wistfully, 'I had one, you know.'

'I can hardly imagine it,' says the older woman, whether referring to Peggy's earlier life or the book not being clear. 'Anyway,' she says snappishly, 'if you do manage to write a book who will read it? They're all simpletons here, including the staff.'

'I was hoping you might read it,' says Peggy, 'you being a highly educated woman with a superior knowledge of the frailties of the human heart.'

Her irony is lost on the duchess who says with a condescending smile, 'I might, if I've nothing else to read. But wouldn't it be better to get it published? Otherwise the whole thing could be a waste of time.'

'What does it matter?' asks Peggy. 'I've plenty of time to waste.'

I

'Wake up!' cried Peggy's mother, shaking her sleeping daughter in the bed recess of the kitchen where most of the house activity took place.

'Bloody well waken up, I said!' her mother cried louder as Peggy pulled the quilt over her head. From his bed on the other side of the wall her father shouted, 'What's all the racket about this hour in the morning?'

'She won't get up. She's supposed to start a paper round, but she can bloody well forget it if I've to go through this every time.'

Peggy jumped from the bed and stood shivering with her feet on the linoleum and her hands crossed over her chest. In place of a nightdress she wore her mother's black satin evening dress, a relic from the good old days before the war. It was too big for Peggy in every direction but she liked to stroke it under the covers. Her own tattered nightdress was now used for a duster. She began raking the ashes in the fireplace, hoping to ignite a flame.

'Heat yourself over the gas ring,' said her mother. 'There's still some of last night's tea in the pot. Pour it out for yourself and make some toast. I'm going back to bed. I'm worn out getting up in the middle of the night to waken you, and don't touch the curtains or we'll be in trouble with the blackout people.'

'You mean the wardens,' said Peggy.

'Never mind what I mean. You get a move on or you'll be late. Personally I don't think it's worth the bother for the sake of a few bob –'

'I'm hurrying,' said Peggy.

She wriggled out of the evening dress and reached for her

jumper. The sight of her daughter groping about in black school knickers and a dingy grey vest drove her mother to say, 'You might change your underwear once in a while.'

As Peggy stood over the gas ring waiting for the tea to heat up she lost all desire to leave the house and deliver papers in the cold and dark. Yesterday it had seemed a good idea when she spied a card in Willie Roper's shop window asking for a paper boy.

'Will I do instead?' she had asked him, excited by the smell of broken toffee in a tin on the counter. She could have nicked a piece if he had turned away.

'But you're a girl,' he had said.

'I can deliver papers as good as any boy.'

He had stroked his chin, looking her up and down. She had smiled back diffidently. It was easy to smile at Willie Roper with his reddish-brown curly hair and blue ingratiating eyes. He was slimly built, possibly in his late thirties and not much taller than herself.

'I suppose you could, but the papers have to be fetched from the railway station to the shop.'

'That's no bother.'

'It's only six shillings a week.'

'That's fine.'

She was overwhelmed by the sum of money. She would tell her mother it was four shillings and keep two.

'All right,' he said. 'Start tomorrow.'

She held out her hand to clinch the deal. The action seemed appropriate.

'Tell you what,' he said. 'Seeing as you're a girl I'll let you off with going to the station.'

He then handed her a bit of the toffee and she felt she was floating on air.

That had been yesterday. At this deathly hour she no longer felt like walking about in the blackout without meeting a soul.

On the other hand Willie was now depending on her. At five to six she rushed along the dark empty street to the paper shop wearing her Sunday coat with a red pixie hat (one of a series she had knitted, huddled over the fire in the long winter evenings), also her mother's new suede shoes.

Two hours later she deposited the suede shoes under her parents' bed and returned to the kitchen where her mother stood over the stove stirring something in a pot.

'How did you get on?' she asked.

'It was OK,' said Peggy.

'Was Willie Roper pleased with you?'

'I think so. He was nice to me.'

'Oh yes, Willie's nice enough, but don't let him take advantage of you. He's a fly one, is Willie.'

'How do you mean?'

Her mother, not feeling able to discuss matters of a delicate nature with a daughter who appeared to move through life in a trance, said, 'Just keep your eye on him. No man's as nice as he looks.' She added with her eyes on Peggy's stocking soles, 'I hope you weren't wearing my good suede shoes.'

'Why should I? They're too big.'

'It's not the first time,' said her mother, frowning into the dried-egg mixture.

Her father entered the kitchen and said, 'Don't tell me it's *that* stuff again.'

'You're lucky to get anything,' said her mother. 'There's a war on.'

Peggy ate her breakfast with an air of contentment which had nothing to do with the food. Willie Roper had accompanied her on the paper round: 'To show you the ropes,' he had said with a grin. From his nods and smiles she thought she had managed well, though slightly discouraged by the way he blew his nose into a handkerchief then rubbed it hard as if to erase the snot. She forgave him when she remembered how her father picked

his teeth with a matchstick and cut his toenails on to the carpet.
Her mother said all men were like that, with habits worse than
dogs. There had also been a boy called Boris in the shop, who
gave her a wink as they sorted out the papers before leaving to
deliver them. He was tall, sallow-skinned, with jet-black hair;
foreign-looking, she considered, but when she shyly asked Willie
Roper if the boy was Italian, he had said with a contemptuous
laugh, 'Irish.'

'I've to get four shillings,' Peggy told her mother.

'I thought it was five.'

'It's because I don't have to collect the papers from the station.'

'What did I tell you? Already he's taking advantage. You shouldn't
stand for it.'

After a glance at Peggy's sullen face her mother added, 'Oh
well, it's up to you. I'll save the four shillings until there's enough
to buy you a pair of shoes when you get your next lot of clothing
coupons.'

'Give her a shilling for herself,' said her father, wrapping a
woollen scarf round his neck before leaving for the munitions
factory. Her mother told him to mind his own business and get
on his way, and after he left told Peggy, 'That was to save *him*
giving you the shilling a week. He thinks I can't see through his
little tricks.'

'Mother!' screamed Peggy. She sprang up in bed, looked round
the ward, then sank back, dazed, against the pillow.

'What's wrong?' said the duchess, swinging her legs slowly over
the side of her bed and sitting panting with a hand on her chest.

'I was dreaming.'

The old woman straightened her body and moved her head
from side to side as if testing it for faults. She said, 'I dream a lot
myself. It's like going to the cinema in a way.'

'Cover your legs,' said Peggy. 'They're like bones washed up by
the tide.'

'The nurses say that for my age I've the best legs in the ward,' said the duchess, stretching them out to study them.

'At that rate when you're six feet under you'll have the best skeleton in the cemetery, if anyone cares to dig it up.'

Peggy jumped from her bed and reached out for the striped hospital robe saying, 'I'm off for a bath. I can't stand the smell of pee in this ward, especially first thing in the morning.'

The rest of the day was one of Peggy's bad ones. Days were mostly passed in static, stupefying boredom broken by exchanges of words, usually contentious, with the duchess. On her bad days she paced up and down the ward like a caged tiger.

'She reminds me of the woman in that film when she was about to be hung,' said a patient to the duchess. This raised no interest as she invariably said this when Peggy paced up and down.

'Never knew her,' snapped the old woman, immersed in a Mills and Boon romance.

She was more annoyed when Peggy stopped pacing to tell her, 'I wish someone would blow up this place and put us out of our misery, don't you?'

'Oh yes,' said the duchess without taking her eyes off the paperback and hoping Peggy would pass on. It was not to be. Peggy sat down beside her and asked if it was anywhere near the time for the sleeping pills, otherwise she might just slash her wrists.

The duchess looked at her own wrist (which had no watch on it) and said, 'It's early yet,' and added she didn't believe in taking sleeping pills since they were bound to be addictive.

'As if I care,' said Peggy. 'And is there any reason why I shouldn't be addicted?'

'None,' said the old woman, closing her book with a sigh. It was impossible to read with Peggy at her side. 'Especially when you're addicted already.'

'Who gives a shit?' said Peggy, throwing the book on to the floor. 'I'd rather be addicted to something than be a fraud like you.'

The old woman bent down and picked up the book.

'I don't know what you're talking about,' she said, searching for the place where she'd left off.

Peggy grew used to facing the cold and dark with the paper bag slung over her shoulder and had a distinct feeling of giving the public an essential service. Noisily she opened and closed gates and banged letter boxes when shoving the papers through, hoping someone would come out and give a tip. All she received were angry words from the bedroom window of an irate customer, and a threepenny bit from an old woman who gave her a fright by waiting for her inside a porch. Her fingers were sometimes so cold that she heated them by putting them round her neck. When her mother told her to knit a pair of gloves Peggy said gloves were much harder to knit than pixie hats. Her mother then suggested cutting up a pair of old socks and making them into mitts, but Peggy said she wouldn't be seen dead with old socks on her hands. She also thought that, when she returned to the shop with her empty bag, the joy of warming her frozen fingers in front of Willie Roper's one-bar electric fire almost made the cold worthwhile.

'You'll get chilblains,' he would say, slipping her a chocolate-coated caramel and adding, 'Mum's the word.'

'I think Mr Roper's a smashing boss,' she confided to Boris one morning as they left the shop together.

'He's OK, I suppose.'

Detecting a note of disparagement in his voice she said, 'Don't you think he's smashing?'

'He's a boss, and you can't trust bosses.'

'He didn't say anything when you were late on Monday.'

'He knows better,' said Boris, as though he'd some sort of upper hand.

'How does he?' she said, then added inconsequentially, 'He says you're Irish.'

'I'm not,' he said. 'I'm the same as everybody else.'

'What does it matter?' said Peggy. 'So long as you're not a German.'

She offered him a caramel which had lain in her pocket since yesterday.

'Where did you get that?' he asked.

'Mr Roper gave me it.' The words were out before she remembered him saying, 'Mum's the word.'

'He did?' said Boris, surprised. 'Keep it. I've got something better.'

He brought out an oblong piece of tablet wrapped in newspaper.

'Did you get that with coupons?' she asked.

'I stole it when Roper wasn't looking,' he said, then broke it in two and handed her half. The next moment he leapt over a fence and through a garden to deliver a paper.

Peggy went in a different direction, thinking that he wouldn't be pleased to know she was given a caramel nearly every day.

In its second year the war was her parents' main topic of conversation, though each had a different interest in it. With her father it was the battle front. On coming home from work he repeated for their benefit all the reports they'd heard on the wireless and disregarded. With her mother it was the shortage of food and clothing.

'Isn't it ironic,' she said, 'that after all these years of being unemployed your father's got a good job in munitions and we can hardly buy a bloody thing?'

'Just thank your lucky stars they haven't called me up,' said her father.

'Yes,' said her mother doubtfully, thinking that a husband in the army earned more respect than a husband working in the munitions factory.

Peggy had no interest in the war. She had either her nose stuck in a book (as her mother described it) or was knitting her pixie hats with wool ripped out of old jerseys. An accumulation of pixie hats gave her a feeling of prosperity. The reality of the war only hit her when she was forced to accompany her mother into a cupboard under the stairs when the air-raid siren blew. They could have gone into the brick building across the road which was supposed to be a shelter, but some said it was so fragile a strong wind could blow it down.

'Why can't we stay in bed,' said Peggy. 'I've to get up early for my papers.'

'Do you want us killed because of your bloody papers?'

'I'd rather get killed than suffocate here,' said Peggy. But after five minutes in the cupboard Peggy was usually asleep under a pile of coats, while her mother remained wide-eyed and praying for the all-clear.

One morning the train carrying the papers didn't arrive in the station. The line had been derailed, not bombed as the paper boys were hoping, but a great cheer arose amongst them when Willie Roper told them to go home. On the spur of the moment, fearing she might not get paid for lost time, Peggy asked Willie if she could sweep out the shop. He frowned, scratched his head and said, 'All right, and while you're at it you can pack some shelves and put out the rubbish.'

The words rang like music in her ears, particularly when he added, 'If you do it right I'll give you an extra sixpence.'

'Sneaky bitch,' said Boris as he walked by her, but Peggy didn't care. She felt as if she'd been singled out for promotion.

2

Peggy and her parents lived in what would once have been described as a humble row of miners' cottages, but the gas mantle replaced the paraffin lamp, and some years later electric light replaced that, and with the installation of an inside toilet and bath they were much less humble and almost as good as modern council houses. If Peggy protested about having to bring a shovelful of coal from the outside bunker her mother would remind her how her grandfather had died along with twenty other men digging the stuff from below the ground when the old mine had been flooded years ago.

'Do you remember your da?' Peggy had asked.

'Of course I do. He was killed when I was no older than you. I remember him always black with the coal dust embedded under his skin even after soaking himself in the big tin bath in front of the fire.'

'I would love to have a bath in front of the fire instead of that freezing bathroom.'

'You wouldn't be so keen if you had to boil pots of water and run back and forward for twenty minutes to fill the bath, then run back and forward for another twenty to empty it.'

'I wouldn't care.' A thought struck Peggy. 'Did he sit in front of everyone naked?'

'He was covered up to his waist in water. Ma used to hold out a towel in front of him when he stepped out.'

Peggy giggled. 'You must have seen his bum.'

'Don't be so dirty. As if we cared about seeing our da's bum. It was hard times then. A lot harder than now, even with a war on.

276

Anyway, bums were always on view in our family, getting leathered with a heavy belt. That's what you should get to knock some sense and respect for your elders into your head.'

'I'd run away if I got leathered.'

'Words are easy. Besides, your da is too soft with you. So am I for that matter.'

'Did you get leathered often?'

'Certainly. So did my two brothers and sister.' Peggy's mother smiled as if softened by a pleasant memory. 'I remember the time,' she said, 'when I accidently poured boiling water over his back before cooling it. He was reading his paper too.'

'Imagine reading a paper in the bath,' said Peggy.

'He always read the paper in the bath while either me or my sister scrubbed his back. When I poured the boiling water he nearly hit the roof like a scalded cat. Then he chased me round the room naked. I saw more than his bum that day. When he caught me he whacked me on the cheek so hard that I had a black eye for over a week. He was a hard man and I hated him most of the time, but I suppose he kept me in check.'

'Were you glad when he was drowned?'

'Good God, no! To think of my da's body floating in the oily water of the mine was more than we could bear. It took a long time to find him. All we remembered about him then were his good points. How he used to give us a halfpenny every week, which was fine in those days. In particular I remembered how I was the one who got his chop bone to lick when he was finished with it, and don't make a face, my lady, a chop bone then was better than a lollipop to us.'

To Peggy he sounded like a grandfather she had done well not to know, but she was impressed by the manner of his death. When she told Boris about it he wasn't.

'My great uncle got stuck up a chimney when he was cleaning out the soot. He choked to death and he was only sixteen.'

'That's strange,' said Peggy.

'What is?'

'If you think about it they both died because of coal. When I look in the fire I'll remember my grandfather and your great uncle. I might see their faces in the flames.'

'Like ghosts?'

'Especially with the light off and the flames flickering round the room.'

'Don't get me all spooky,' said Boris. 'It's bad enough having to deliver to the house on top of the hill, and just when you're pushing the paper in the letter-box a tall man dressed in black opens the door and snatches the paper out your hand like a maniac.'

'I bet you it's only a butler.'

'They don't have butlers in bungalows.'

'How would you know if you've never been in one?'

'Anyway I hate the colour black,' said Boris. 'In all my life I'm never going to wear black.'

'Not even to funerals?'

'Not even.'

'What about your own funeral? Other people will be wearing black then. You can't stop them.'

'Shut up and don't talk about my funeral. You'll be dead long before me. Wait and see.'

He left for his paper route, hunched and hostile. Peggy hoped he wouldn't keep up his bad mood since she reckoned that she might have to marry him one day. He was the only boy she knew.

The duchess kept to her bed most of the time, except when forced out to the toilet. As she clung to Peggy's arm for support she murmured in a weak voice that she was sure she had suffered a stroke.

'Well, you don't look any different to me,' said Peggy.

'I was told that I fainted. How do you account for that?'

'I don't know about fainting. I remember you tried to attack me.

278

Then you fell and banged your head on the locker. Is that what you call fainting?'

'That's not true,' said the duchess, stopping to pluck at her lip. 'You're saying that to make me feel bad. You know I have a weak heart. Even the nurse said that it was touch and go.'

'You can fool the nurse but you can't fool me,' said Peggy. 'I don't believe you. You'd say anything to get sympathy.'

She began pulling the old woman along.

'Don't walk so quick. You're making me breathless.'

'You're always breathless. There's nothing wrong with your heart or they wouldn't allow you up.'

'Oh leave me alone,' said the old woman, shaking herself free from Peggy in a spurt of energy. 'You're nothing but a cruel evil woman.'

'Evil?' said Peggy, with her hands on her hips. 'I like that. Who is it runs your errands and takes you to the lavatory and sits beside you when no one else will? Who does that, may I ask?'

With surprising spirit for someone who'd just had a stroke the duchess said, 'And who is it hides my walking stick so that I can't get about, and who is it reads my mail when my back is turned?'

'What mail?' interrupted Peggy.

'And who was it stole my jotter?'

'Stole your jotter?' repeated Peggy, her face a study in bewilderment. 'Why, you gave it to me! Don't you remember the orderly told you she would bring in writing paper and envelopes which were more suitable for a person in your position, as you pointed out, instead of making do with a mouldy old jotter. You must remember that. Surely you're not in your dotage already?'

The duchess blinked in confusion. She placed her arm on the wall for support. A nurse came down the corridor.

'What's the problem, dear?' she asked.

The duchess was unable to think of an answer.

'It's OK,' said Peggy quickly. 'I'm taking her to the lav.'

She grabbed her companion's arm and they progressed slowly

towards the toilet with the old woman staring backwards at the nurse as if there were things she had wanted to tell her.

'I don't know what's come over me recently,' she said. 'I can't seem to remember a thing.'

'Senility, that's what it is,' declared Peggy. 'It comes to us all, but if you know what's good for you you'll try and buck up, for I don't want to go around with somebody that's in their dotage. You're bad enough the way things are. Anyway,' she added, 'I've got pages of my story done while you were snoring your head off.'

'What story?'

'My life story. Don't you remember me telling you about it?'

'Oh that.'

'Not that I expect you to appreciate it. Mills and Boon is more your line.' She squeezed the old woman's thin arm to make sure she was paying attention. 'Isn't it?'

'Not really,' said the duchess. They entered the toilet area which Peggy called the gas ovens and she hastened to add, 'I'm looking forward to reading your story, especially the bit about the man who was the father of your son.'

She broke off, partly because it was a sensitive subject but more because they were alone. Peggy, however, spoke quite blandly while shoving her into the toilet. 'I'm nowhere near there. You'll have to be patient.'

After carefully snibbing the door inside the duchess sat nodding her head with a mild form of paralysis.

An hour before the lights in the ward were dimmed Peggy looked over what she had written. Despite scorings out and possible misspellings she thought she had the start of a good story. It was a pity her only reader was a crazy old woman, but no one else in the ward seemed able to read, except herself of course, though she had never found anything worth reading in the hospital. She handed the jotter to the duchess who sat propped up on her pillow sucking a mint imperial from a secret store in her locker.

'Let me know what you think of it,' said Peggy, 'and don't sticky the pages with those mints you think I don't know about.'

The duchess suppressed a sigh. She had been looking forward to reading a tropical romance about a doctor and a nurse in a South Sea island hospital. It had as much in common with her surroundings as a cathedral has to a henhouse.

As the weeks passed the mornings gradually became less dark and cold, making the paper deliveries easier, but she missed the anonymity of darkness. People were inclined to get up early in the good weather and reprimand her for leaving their gate open, or not pushing the paper far enough through the letter-box, or (if she happened to be daydreaming) delivering the wrong paper. When such mishaps resulted in a ticking off from Willie Roper it made her cheeks burn. But on the whole Peggy was happy in her job until the morning Boris told her that a dark-haired woman who occasionally hirpled through to the back shop on crutches was Willie Roper's wife.

'Wife?' said Peggy, drawing in her breath, as it had never occurred to her he had one. 'I thought she was his mother.'

'That's because she's got arthritis. My ma says he married her for the shop.'

'She owns it then?' said Peggy with a sense of doom.

'Yes, and their house above it, but she doesn't take anything to do with the shop. She leaves all that to him.'

'Thank goodness. I wouldn't like her to boss me around.'

'She's not all that bad,' said Boris. 'She gives me a sixpence if I get her a message.' He added meaningfully, 'No wonder.'

'What do you mean, no wonder?' said Peggy, annoyed and dismayed that no one had told her about Willie Roper's wife.

He hesitated then said, 'She always sends me for the same thing, a bottle of sherry. Sometimes she gives me a sip.'

Peggy was shocked. 'Gives you a sip of sherry?'

'I don't mind,' he said defiantly. 'She's opening the bottle anyway. I expect she's only wanting somebody to talk to.'

'Poor Mr Roper.'

'What's so poor about him? If she dies he'll get the shop. My ma says she wouldn't be surprised if he puts poison in her sherry one day when she isn't looking.'

'I wouldn't believe that.'

'That's because you've got a crush on him,' jeered Boris.

'I have not,' said Peggy, flushing. 'But I don't think it's right that they're married.' She added with a furtive look at him, 'Especially if they sleep in the same bed.'

He shrugged. 'So what. I sleep with my big brother and I can't stand him.'

'It's not the same.'

'You mean,' he said, his eyes growing round, 'they might do dirty things?'

'You're a pig,' said Peggy, white at the idea of it. 'I don't want to talk to you any more.'

Sometimes she had fantasies about Willie Roper kissing her when a blast from a bomb had thrown them together on the floor of the shop, but nothing more. From furtive discussions with girls in the playground she knew vaguely what went on between men and women but couldn't relate it to Willie. She saw him more in the light of a saviour, or a tough guy with a heart of gold as depicted in the films.

'You started it,' said Boris angrily. 'I expect you're jealous.'

They parted cold and silent. Peggy decided that he wasn't the one to marry when he talked so dirty about Mr Roper. But that had happened a week past, and the subject was forgotten, especially when she hadn't seen Willie Roper's wife since. She had allowed herself one small image to make everything right in her head: Mrs Roper drinking alone from her bottle of sherry while Willie lay asleep in his bed in another room with an arm flung over his forehead, perhaps dreaming of a better life in which Peggy had a big part. Outside these preoccupations of the heart Peggy felt that in lots of ways things were looking up. For a start she had acquired a new pair of shoes.

'Don't think I haven't noticed that you're wearing mine,' said her mother, handing her a pair of clogs which were in fashion because they required no coupons. She could even afford to go to the pictures twice a week, and pay for a friend.

'Do you ever go to the pictures?' she asked Boris.

'Only gangster ones.'

She told him that she liked gangster pictures too and added, unable to stop herself, 'I think Mr Roper looks a bit like James Cagney, don't you?'

'All you ever think about is Willie Roper!' he groaned.

Once again they fell out over their employer, ruining Peggy's chances of asking him if he would accompany her to the next gangster film. She wanted this less out of affection for him than the status of being seen with a boyfriend.

When bombs fell on nearby cities Peggy told her mother that she would sleep permanently in the cupboard under the stairs because there was no way she could get up to deliver papers if every night she had to run back and forward to the air-raid shelter.

'I don't understand how you're so keen on that rubbishy job that you'd risk your life for it,' her mother grumbled, but without much emphasis. The air-raid shelter was something she now looked forward to. She'd wait up half the night for the siren to go, a flask of tea and sandwiches on the table, and her hair swept up into an elastic band which was the latest style. Peggy's father was now permanently on night shift. Part of his day was spent in the home guard which meant leaving the house in a khaki uniform and long boots he took an hour to polish.

'We have inspections just like the army,' he would say with an air of importance. If Peggy wasn't busy knitting her pixie hats she gave him a mock salute as he went out the door. Once he said, 'I hate leaving you two to the mercy of these German bastards.'

Her mother replied bravely, 'Don't worry about us, Robert. Just you do your duty and remember we are all in the hands of God.'

Peggy had stuck her tongue inside her cheek in order not to laugh, though she supposed it was wise not to incur the wrath of God in the shape of a German bomb. Once inside the cramped space of the cupboard she felt safe because here was no room for the ghost she had once seen in the flames of the fire when sitting in front of it knitting a pixie hat. It was the face of an old man regarding her balefully. Realising this must be the face of her grandfather, she told it to go back to hell and prodded the coal with a poker.

'In the name of God, have you gone mad?' said her mother, slapping her cheek.

Peggy didn't answer. She knew she wouldn't be believed if she said what she'd seen. Besides, she had the feeling that she might be one of those people singled out to see what nobody else saw, somebody like Joan of Arc, for example. To talk about it would spoil everything.

3

For some peculiar reason all patients in the ward were served meals in bed, as if moribund or on the verge of it. The meals were predictable. Every weekday had its own speciality. Today being Tuesday it was liver. The duchess complained as if she was seeing liver for the first time.

'I can't eat this!' she said in a faint but peevish tone.

Peggy said, 'I don't care what I eat. It's all one to me.'

This was not true because if she didn't like what was on her plate she went to the veranda and threw it through the railings. Rats had been seen scampering in and out of the rhododendron bushes. The old woman cut her liver into small pieces then moved them round the plate with a fork as if playing a game of miniature chess.

'Back in your second childhood again?' asked Peggy.

The canteen woman passed back down with her empty trolley, paused at the duchess's bed and ordered her to stop messing about and get the food eaten.

'I'm not hungry. I've had a stroke, you see.'

'Liver's good for strokes,' said the canteen woman.

'Actually she's more used to a servant dishing her up venison,' said Peggy.

The canteen woman took this seriously.

'Oh she is, is she?' she said in a threatening tone.

The duchess dropped her knife on the plate and said timidly, 'If I could just have a cup of sweet milky tea —'

'You'll get that when you eat your liver! It's ridiculous wasting good food.'

The duchess shrank back on her pillow, blinked away tears in her eyes and put a small dice of liver in her mouth.

When the canteen woman left Peggy pushed her tray to the bottom of the bed, swung her legs on to the floor and said, 'You really ask for it, don't you?'

'Ask for what?'

'The way you draw attention to yourself all the time. It's a wonder they haven't done you in long ago. Give me that liver and I'll get rid of it.'

She grabbed the plate out of the old woman's shaking hands and pattered out to the veranda.

'I don't know what I'd do without you,' said the duchess when she returned.

'Always keep that thought in mind then,' said Peggy sternly.

When they were drinking tea afterwards the duchess said she thought what she'd read of Peggy's tale was most interesting and unusual. Peggy raised her eyebrows, staring hard at her companion.

'I mean it. It's really very interesting.'

'Don't overdo it,' said Peggy, looking pleased all the same. She added, 'It can't be any worse than those trashy books you read.'

'By the way,' said the duchess after a pause, 'have you seen the novel I was reading yesterday? I was going to lend it to one of the nurses.'

'I chucked it in the bin. It's the best place for it.'

'I suppose so,' said the duchess, turning away as the tears threatened to brim again.

'Don't worry. I'll try and have another chapter ready for you this evening,' said Peggy. 'Meantime I'm going out to the veranda to get a breath of air that doesn't have the smell of shit in it.'

One morning Willie Roper asked her to fetch a big ball of string from the back shop to tie up some old newspapers. She complied eagerly, always happy to oblige him and liking to study the shelves in there which were stacked with custard, tins of prunes, beans and all the food that didn't need coupons, besides ordinary stuff like sauce, salt, soap and soap powder. What most interested her was the perfume and make-up and combs and kirby grips on the shelf at the bottom. Lately she had bought a lipstick called Pink Cyclamen which she only wore outside the house. Boris said, 'God, your lips have gone a funny colour,' but Willie Roper never gave a sign he'd noticed. While bending down to pick up a paper that had fallen on the floor, one of the paper boys came in and put his hand up her skirt. Peggy spun round, pale with affront.

'I'm telling Mr Roper on you.'

'Telling me what?' said Willie, appearing in the doorway.

'He pushed me,' Peggy mumbled, her face scarlet.

Willie looked at her intently then said to the boy, 'You get through to the front. You've no right being in here.'

Then he asked Peggy if she was sure that was all he did. Peggy thought she was going to faint with embarrassment, especially when he put his arm round her shoulder and said, 'Maybe he did something else?'

She shook her head and stared down at the floor, hiccuping with nerves.

'Look,' said Willie, his mouth close to her ear, 'don't worry about it. It's not your fault you're turning out to be a right pretty one.'

For a second she thought he was going to do the same as the paper boy but when she finally managed to look round at him his face was all concern. At that moment she thought she'd never loved him so much. This made the blow harder when next morning he told her Mrs Haddow had cancelled her papers because Peggy had left a garden gate open, and as a result her dog disappeared for three hours and returned with an ear chewed off by another dog.

'But I did close the gate! Perhaps it was the postman.'

'It's no good blaming the postman. The dog had disappeared before he arrived. You've lost me a customer.'

Peggy was appalled by the cold and stern look on his face. She was about to walk out rather than wait for the sack when he said less severely, 'Try and be more careful about closing gates in future. The woman's a complaining old bag but that's beside the point.'

Peggy, close to tears, nodded and began folding up her papers. Not even a sympathetic nudge from Boris who stood beside her folding his own cheered her up. Outside the shop she told him, 'I know I closed that gate. Why did he have to believe Haddow and not me?'

'I told you bosses were like that,' said Boris. 'One minute all sugar the next minute all shite. He took sixpence off my wage last week when I slept in. As if it made any difference. I still had to deliver the same amount of papers. I tell you he's as mean as get out. You should hear what my ma has to say about him —'

'I don't want to talk about it any more,' said Peggy, her anger against her boss evaporating when she remembered the shivery sensation in her spine as he put his arm round her shoulder. 'Anyway there's no point in him being a boss if he can't tell people off.'

'Oh yeah?' said Boris scornfully. 'He's a pig. If it wasn't for Mrs Roper he would have got rid of me long ago. Do you know I've to sneak up the back stairs when he isn't looking to give her the sherry? The less he knows the better, she told me, and that's his wife.'

'I thought she'd the final say in everything.'

'Not about the sherry. He thinks it's a disgrace for women to drink.'

'And so it is.'

'If you were in pain with arthritis maybe you'd want to drink. She says it's the only time she feels well.'

Peggy gave an exaggerated shudder. 'I'd hate to have to go for sherry.'

'That's because you're a snob. By the way, she once asked me about you.'

'Asked about me?' said Peggy, scandalised. 'What did she say?'

'She asked me why you don't collect the papers at the station the same as everybody else.'

'What did you say?'

'I said maybe it was because you were a girl, but I wasn't sure.'

'And then what?'

'She just went "Mmm" –' He broke off. 'Look, I'm away before the customers start complaining about me next. Not that I'm bothering.'

Peggy watched him go, feeling uneasy at the thought of Mrs Roper asking about her.

In the same week an incendiary bomb fell near a bus stop where her father was waiting after leaving his work. He died instantly with a piece of shrapnel in his head and that finished Peggy's paper job. At the funeral service her mother had sobbed into a handkerchief at the loss of a husband whom previously she had considered no great asset, while Peggy sobbed at being removed from Willie Roper's newsagent's.

Her mother had said, 'I won't have you leaving me alone in this house while you go skedaddling all over the place in the early hours of the morning. You could get killed the same as your dad and then where would I be?'

Peggy felt that if she couldn't see Willie Roper again she would like to get killed. Later that evening her mother came into her bedroom and told her to cheer up. She would get over her father's death in time.

The duchess slept badly that night, tossing and turning and calling out the names of people Peggy had never heard her mention before. Finally she sat up and asked Peggy to get her a bedpan.

'Get it yourself,' said Peggy, punching her pillow in temper.

'I can't. If I move I'll wet the bed.'

'Wet it then and give us all peace.'

'The nurse will hit me. You know what they're like.'

Peggy stabbed her forefinger into the bell above her head.

'They're going to hit you anyway when they find out you've wakened half the ward.'

Further along the ward a woman had begun to shriek and another one was banging her head on her locker. A nurse came whirling in to ask what the racket was about.

'It's her,' said Peggy, pointing to the next bed. 'She wants a bedpan.'

'A bedpan?' said the nurse, raising her thinly pencilled eyebrows at the duchess who sat cowering. 'Surely she's not so incapacitated that she can't walk to the toilet?'

'I think I'm going to wet the bed any minute,' the old woman quavered.

'Why didn't you go earlier?' said the nurse, jabbing her on the chest.

'It came on me all of a sudden.'

'And let's face it,' said Peggy, 'it's not easy to go for a piss in this place. You're liable to get beaten up for walking along the corridor.'

'You mind your own business,' said the nurse, staring down the ward to where patients were either sitting up in bed or walking in circles weeping and wringing their hands. She took off towards them at a run and after a good deal of persuasion and threats managed to get them back to their beds. She returned to the duchess flushed and dishevelled.

'Listen,' she said. 'I'll get you a bedpan this time but I warn you, try it with me again and I'll give you such a smack on the bottom you won't be able to sit down on anything, let alone a bedpan.'

When she left Peggy turned to her companion and said, 'I like the way you stuck out for that bedpan. For once you got the better of her.'

The duchess said nothing but stared sorrowfully at the ceiling while a warm stream of urine spread over her thighs and down her legs.

'You're surely not going out?' Peggy's mother called from her bedroom as Peggy passed the door.

'I need some fresh air. My head's stuffed up with being indoors all the time.'

'You know I can't bear being left on my own,' said her mother in the plaintive tone she'd adopted since the funeral. Peggy looked at her mother flicking through the pages of a woman's magazine with a bored expression on her face.

She said, 'If I was at school you'd have to be on your own.'

'But you've only a few weeks to go. They won't be expecting you back now under the circumstances.'

'I'm going out,' said Peggy defiantly.

'All right then,' said her mother. 'We'll both go out and visit your father's grave. It will be nice to look at the marble headstone again.'

'I don't count that as being nice,' said Peggy, who could not connect a marble stone with the last sight of her father polishing his boots before leaving for the home guard. In the cemetery her mother had looked at the inscription *Forever in our Hearts* and said, 'So tasteful!'

'Is it?' Peggy had said, looking with detestation along the row of similar inscriptions on similar stones.

'All right, go out,' her mother now said with a sigh. She was tiring of her role as a grieving widow. Resentment had become what she mainly felt at a husband's death which had not been exactly in his line of duty.

Once outside Peggy approached Roper's shop with a sinking

heart. What if he had somebody else in her place? She went round to the back of the shop and to give herself time to think sat at the bottom of the stairs leading up to Willie Roper's house. Suddenly a voice called from the top of the stairs saying, 'Will you come up a minute?'

Peggy looked upwards and was shaken to see Willie Roper's wife on the landing.

'Come on,' shouted the woman. 'I won't eat you.'

Peggy climbed slowly to confront the woman who from close up was quite attractive. Dark eyes contrasted well with a pale complexion and black curling hair gave her the appearance of a gypsy.

'Would you mind going a message for me?' she asked.

Peggy wanted to refuse but she couldn't find the words. Mrs Roper must have taken her silence as agreement. She said, 'Come in.'

The room was surprisingly clean and cheerful for a woman who couldn't move about easily. A bright fire burned in the grate and there was a vase of flowers on the table. She took a purse from a drawer and handed Peggy silver saying, 'Are you the girl who used to deliver the papers?'

'Yes,' said Peggy hoarsely.

'I don't see you coming any more. Did he give you the sack?'

'If you mean Mr Roper, no. My da got killed with a bomb and I couldn't leave my ma alone in the house.'

Mrs Roper tutted and shook her head. 'What a tragic thing to happen. But it's always them that's needed that gets snatched off and them that isn't that's left to rot.'

She showed Peggy her hands with the knuckles twisted and enlarged.

'Arthritis,' she said.

Peggy gave her a thin smile of sympathy, wishing she was far away from this woman with the knowledgeable eyes. She looked at the silver in her hand and said, 'What is it you want me to get?'

'A bottle of sherry,' said Mrs Roper. 'If you don't mind.'

4

'**M**y, my, you're a stranger,' said Willie Roper when she walked into the shop and bought a *Schoolgirl Weekly* with the sixpence his wife had given her. 'I thought I would have seen you before this.'

'It was my da,' she began. 'He died and I –'

'I know,' he said, becoming serious. 'It's been a rotten time for you and your ma. If there's anything I can do, let me know.'

She took a deep breath and asked him if she could have her job back. He frowned and scratched his head.

'It so happens I had to get someone else when you didn't come. I kept the job open for a week but when Boris left to join the army cadets I was in the soup. So you see –'

'It's all right,' she said, turning away as a customer came up to the counter.

'Hey, wait a minute,' he called. 'When do you leave school?'

'In two months.'

When he told her to come back then and he would give her a part-time job behind the counter she couldn't believe her luck.

'You're not going,' said her mother.

'Why not?'

'It's only common types who work in shops. Your father and I always wanted you to work in an office where you meet a better class of people.'

'I don't want to work in an office,' said Peggy. 'Only snobs work there. I've always wanted to work in a shop and it's my life, not yours.'

Her mother regarded her with a look of pity and said, 'Normally I wouldn't care where you worked, but I do draw the line at working for Willie Roper. Maybe you don't know this but he gets the name of being fond of young girls, and I don't mean in a nice way. I thought it was bad enough when you were going with his papers but I let it slide because I knew it wouldn't last for ever, and now here you are going to work in his shop. Well I –'

'I don't care what you say,' said Peggy. 'Willie Roper is a gentleman and I know him better than you. I'm going to serve in his shop and you can't stop me.'

The duchess was moving around better than she'd ever done before. She'd discarded her walking stick and didn't ask for help when going to the toilet. Her manner had also become studiously polite to everyone, particularly the patients. She went round them asking how they were keeping, even though they backed away from her in alarm. Peggy viewed this change with suspicion.

'Are you all right?' she called out, seeing her companion nimbly approach the swing doors, presumably to go to the toilet.

'Of course I am all right. Why shouldn't I be?'

'I don't know. It's just that you seem to have got a new lease of life and I'm damned if I know why.'

'I feel much better than formerly,' declared the duchess with a cheerful laugh.

'I'd watch out if I was you. They say a light bulb flashes its brightest before it goes out.'

'I'm not interested in light bulbs,' said the old woman, nipping through the door.

Peggy got hold of the nurse who was dishing out the evening dose of sleeping pills.

'Listen,' she said, 'you'd better watch out for the duchess. She's gone out the door as fast as a two year old. I wouldn't be surprised if she's on the verge of a breakdown and slashes somebody with a dinner knife.'

The nurse gave an inane laugh somewhat similar to some of the patients'.

'Don't be silly. She hasn't got the stamina.'

'Well, she had the stamina to stab her husband to death,' said Peggy. 'At least that's what she told me.'

'She doesn't know what she's saying,' said the nurse. 'She's crazy.'

'I know that,' said Peggy. 'And now she's crazier than ever. Aren't you going to do something?'

The nurse tutted and walked down the ward shaking her head. Then the duchess returned to the ward and asked Peggy what month it was.

'March, I think.'

'Good, I'll be getting out soon. My husband's coming to take me away at the beginning of April. It's all been a ghastly mistake me being in here, you know.'

'I thought your husband was dead,' said Peggy.

The duchess stared at her, exasperated. 'I don't know where you got your information, unless it's from the staff who are all pathological liars, but I can assure you my husband is alive and well and is coming for me soon and I'll have to have all my wits about me when I walk down those high stone stairs. That's why I'm not taking any sleeping pills. However I don't want to discuss it at present.' She gave Peggy a bright smile. 'So how is your writing coming on, dear?'

'Not bad,' said Peggy.

'That's the spirit. Keep writing and get it all out of your system, and don't forget to let the world know what is going on in here, how they keep us doped up most of the time so we won't complain. You tell them –'

'That reminds me,' said Peggy. 'Have you any writing paper to spare? My jotter's almost used up.'

The duchess's face became hostile. 'Excuse me,' she said. 'I'll have to go and ask the nurse to give me something for a sore head. An aspirin will do.'

★

Willie Roper kept his word and Peggy got the part-time job of stacking shelves, sweeping the floor, folding papers and making tea for them both in the afternoon. They did not take it together, but Peggy was glad. It saved her the embarrassment of eating in front of him and making conversation. She was still in love with him, she supposed, but not as much as the day he'd put his arm round her shoulder, which likely hadn't meant a thing. He'd only been trying to comfort her. Some men were like that, 'the fatherly type' they were called, so now she found it easy to face Mrs Roper on Friday night when fetching her sherry. She had inherited Boris's job.

One morning a box of loose custard was delivered to the shop and Peggy was asked to stay through lunchtime to help make it up into small bags, for which she would be paid an extra two shillings. This turned out to be a messy business. Her blue angora jumper, actually her mother's, became covered with the stuff. She tried to wipe it away but it became all the more engrained. Noticing this, Willie took a brush from a drawer and began brushing her down, first at the back, then at the front, going very carefully over her chest. Peggy's face was burning. She hoped he didn't notice.

'That's better,' he said, standing back to survey her. Peggy closed her eyes and tried to think of buckets of ice in order to cool down. The next thing his arms were round her waist. She pulled herself away.

'I'm sorry,' he said, immediately contrite.

'That's all right,' she said, amazed that her voice sounded so composed when inwardly she was shaking. The following morning he asked her to stay on again at lunchtime. She wondered why. All the custard had been packed. But it was no surprise when he came into the back shop and kissed her on the cheek, saying he was mad about her and couldn't help himself and would she forgive him?

'Of course,' she said, smiling at him tenderly then going on to say that she'd always been mad about him from the first day she'd delivered the papers. After that there was no need for them to say any more.

A week later he bought her a black handbag and promised her a ring, nothing too flamboyant, he said. Just a plain silver one to plight their troth. She thought the words 'plight their troth' were the most exquisite she'd ever heard, though he explained in the next breath she'd have to wait until they could slip away to a jeweller's out of town so that she could get the right size. She said she didn't mind waiting.

'What's come over you these days? You look as if you're sleep-walking half the time,' said her mother, putting on her coat. She was going out with a friend to the pub as she usually did on Friday after coming home from the munitions factory.

'I'm tired, that's all,' said Peggy.

'I don't know why. You only work half a day and do damn all the other half as far as I can see. I hope you manage to wash these dishes before I get back.'

Peggy nodded, her eyes fixed somewhere in the distance.

'Another thing I've noticed,' said her mother. 'You're never outside the house except to go to that job of yours. Why don't you join something like the badminton club? It would give you an interest instead of sitting in here moping. It's not natural.'

'I thought you didn't like me going out.'

'That was just after your father died. You could hardly expect me to be on my own then. But it's different now. You should be out enjoying yourself.'

That's because you're out all the time and feeling guilty, Peggy thought, but didn't much care. Her mother could do what she liked as long as she kept her nose out of Peggy's affairs. But some-times her mother's words struck home. Perhaps it wasn't natural staying in so much and listening to the wireless. She'd stopped knitting pixie hats. But mostly her mind was occupied by Willie Roper and what they did on the floor of the back shop during the lunch break.

When he came to the door one evening she nearly fell down with shock and pleasure.

'Willie,' she breathed. 'What are you doing here?'

'Is your ma in?'

'No.'

'That's what I was hoping.'

As she showed him into the living room it struck her the place looked a mess. Clothes lay over chairs, an ironing board stood in the middle of the floor; for the first time she noticed the dust on the sideboard.

He planked himself down on an easy chair and told her to come and sit on his knee. Shyly she complied, thinking how handsome he looked in his grey pinstripe suit and more like James Cagney than ever. She asked if there was anything wrong.

'No, my love,' he said. 'I just happened to be passing on my way to a boring committee meeting at the bowling club and thought I might as well look in.'

He took a flat-sided bottle from his pocket and offered it to her.

'What is it?' she asked.

'Gin. It's good for you in small doses.'

'I don't know,' she said, remembering with wonder how Willie didn't like his wife drinking.

'A spot won't do you any harm.'

'All right,' she said, thinking, why not? This visit was as good as anything she could wish for. She took a sip and shuddered. He laughed and whispered in her ear, 'How about going into the bedroom?'

'All right,' she whispered, the bottom of her spine beginning to tingle.

Twenty minutes later they were back in the living room. Willie looked at his watch and said he would have to fly.

'Can I come with you?' she asked on an impulse.

'To a committee meeting?' he said, aghast.

'I could wait outside until it was over. Then we could go somewhere and –' She broke off when she saw the angry look on his face.

'If people saw us together outside the shop they'd put two and two together and then what do you think would happen?'

She shook her head shamefacedly.

'I could go to jail. You must know that you're considered a minor if you're under eighteen, though God knows you could pass for eighteen any day.' Then he added, 'Don't look so despondent, darling. Do you still love me?'

'You know I do,' she said. 'I didn't realise what I was asking. Do you still love me?'

'Of course I do, you silly girl,' he said. He tweaked her nose and was gone.

5

Mrs Roper asked Peggy if she was in the habit of reading books.

'Sometimes,' she replied, dreading what was coming next and wanting to get away as quickly as possible. She hadn't minded fetching the sherry when it was just a matter of purchasing it and handing it over but the woman now persisted in asking her in.

'I've got this terrific novel called *The Plague* by a man called Camus,' she said. 'You should read it. I'm sure you'd like it. A good book helps you to understand yourself as well as others.'

Before Peggy could say anything Mrs Roper had thrust the book into her hand.

'I know everyone hasn't got the same taste when it comes to books but –'

'Thanks,' said Peggy, not wanting to prolong the subject and finding it difficult to look her in the eye. She'd once asked Willie why he didn't buy sherry for his wife. He had said that he didn't want to encourage her to drink, which seemed strange since he drank himself.

'Besides,' he'd added, 'she likes seeing you. It breaks her day.'

From Peggy's point of view that made it all the worse.

'Though perhaps you've better things to do with your time than read a book,' said Mrs Roper, unscrewing the bottle top.

Peggy turned red, sensing some kind of implication.

'Not really.'

'I thought you might have a boyfriend?'

'No,' said Peggy, becoming agitated.

'I'm surprised. You're a pretty girl. Still, I suppose you're better not to rush into things. I did, and look at me.'

'You mean you got married?'

'Don't take me seriously,' Mrs Roper had said. 'My husband's a good enough man. He doesn't like to see me drinking, and who can blame him? But you see it's the pain. I always have this terrible pain.' Then she broke off. 'But I shouldn't be talking like this. I'm sure you won't repeat anything I say.'

'Oh no,' said Peggy, and said she would have to leave, her mother would worry if she stayed out too long.

'Of course she will,' said Mrs Roper, 'and she's quite right. Young girls are always so vulnerable.'

Peggy wondered if there was a hidden meaning in her words. Was it possible she knew what was going on between her and Willie? Her fears were dispelled when Mrs Roper called over the railings that she hoped to see her the following Friday.

As weeks turned to months she grew more and more dissatisfied with the way they had to be furtive about everything, even the single glance that might betray them to a customer. Yet she knew it had to be this way for her mother would kill her if she found out. But despite her mother's poor opinion of Willie Roper she remained strangely unsuspicious. Once, in connection with Peggy's stopping on at lunchtime, she said she hoped Peggy was being paid for the extra hour and if so why didn't she hand over the money? Peggy's answer was to leave the room suddenly as if she had something urgent to do. After that the matter seemed to be forgotten.

One day, being in a particularly anxious mood, she asked Willie if he still slept with his wife.

'Of course not. What kind of a person do you think I am?'

'Then why don't you put in for a divorce? By the time I've turned eighteen we can get married.'

He looked at her, frowning. 'How do you know you'll still love me when you're eighteen?'

302

'I'll always love you.'

'That's easy to say now but you might not say it then.'

She didn't argue about this as she could see he was becoming annoyed. The next time the subject of divorce cropped up he said that there was no way he could abandon his wife when she was in such poor health.

'Besides,' he added, 'the shop is hers and without it I'd have nothing.'

When Peggy said she didn't care as long as they were together as man and wife he said she must give him time to think about it. In the meantime they would just have to carry on the way they were.

A day came when they were bold enough to take a journey into the country, travelling in separate buses then meeting on the outskirts of a field where there was not a soul in sight except some distant cows. Peggy thought it was wonderful to lie on the grass like any other courting couple. They ate Spam sandwiches she had made up at home and drank beer out of bottles. She disliked the beer's bitter taste and would have preferred lemonade, but drank it anyway. It made her head spin. It also made Willie belch a good deal, which he did loudly and without excusing himself. She disliked that. When he tried to push her down on the grass she told him to leave her alone as she was feeling sick, then she got up and walked aimlessly round the field. He was sitting on the same spot when she returned, his face red and angry.

'What's wrong with you?' he said.

'I told you beer made me sick.'

'At that rate we'd better go home.'

Before they separated to go back on different buses they made it up again. Yet at the same time she felt as dismal as though they hadn't. Over and above that she had a splitting sore head. She put this down to the fact that her period was late.

★

For two days the duchess had either been sitting in a trance or dozing off except when hauled to the toilet by Peggy, who got a certain amount of satisfaction from seeing her old friend dependent on her. Now in the late afternoon of a cold spring day she sat on the veranda with Peggy who stood with her back against the railings saying, 'It serves you right for refusing your pills. You should know by this time they'd only make you swallow double. Whatever made you do it?'

'Mind your own business,' said the old woman, 'and take me inside.'

'Take yourself inside,' said Peggy. She turned and looked through the railings, then became excited. 'Look, he's back again. I knew he'd come back.'

'Who's back?'

'The man that was there before.'

'Oh,' said the duchess. 'If you'll just give me your arm I'll manage once I get inside. I don't know why I came out in the first place.'

Peggy wasn't listening. She was shouting through the railings, 'Come on up. We're in ward A, first on the left.'

'I'm sure I don't want any undesirables visiting me,' said the duchess.

Peggy became more excited. 'He's on his feet and looking up here. I do believe –' Then she sagged and said, 'Damnation and blast. He's walking away.'

The duchess said, 'That's because you frightened him off. One look at you and anybody would be frightened.'

'If anyone frightened him off it would be you,' said Peggy.

They both went silent after that. A drizzle of rain began to fall.

'Funny thing,' said Peggy. 'I usually feel better when it rains.'

'Well, I don't,' said the duchess, pulling the shawl up over her chin. 'I'm likely to catch my death out here.'

'Go in then and give us peace.'

'If I do they'll pick on me. They're always picking on me.'

'They pick on everybody.'

'They pick on me the worst. God, I wish I was dead.'

'You will be one day.'

'And you'll be glad, I suppose.'

'I won't know until it happens.'

'And I thought you were my friend too,' said the old woman, wiping her watering eyes on a corner of the rough material.

Peggy gave her an odious look. 'How can I be your friend when you won't give me one little shitty piece of your writing paper, and me good enough to lend you my grandma's shawl?'

'Take the filthy thing back,' said the duchess, throwing it on to the veranda floor. 'It only makes me itch.'

Another dismal silence fell. Peggy picked up the shawl and draped it round the old woman's shoulder. Then she looked through the railings to stare at the view she'd seen a thousand times before.

'To think I used to stay somewhere down there,' she said, 'and I don't even remember the name of the street. I expect it will be gone, though. It was during the war.'

'Ah yes, the war,' said the duchess, shifting restlessly in her seat. 'I remember the war. All those bombs falling. It was terrible.'

'And all those brick shelters. I remember refusing to go into them.'

'And all those American soldiers. Weren't they lovely?'

'I hated them,' said Peggy. 'They were ugly and loudmouthed.'

'Did you ever go out with any?'

'I didn't ever go out with any kind of soldier. I only had one boyfriend and that wasn't for long. Well, two if you count my boss.'

The duchess blinked as if she was on the point of a great discovery. 'Why, I believe I got married during the war,' she said. 'I distinctly remember going to the church, for some reason. It must have been that.'

'So you did have a husband?' said Peggy. 'Well, it's more than I did. Though they say you don't miss what you've never had.

What I miss is dancing. I would love to have done a waltz round a floor in a dancehall you sometimes see in old-fashioned films. I always thought I was cut out to be a dancer.'

The old woman stared at her blank-eyed as she went on, 'I remember tap dancing on the floor of our scullery. Being a stone floor it was good for that. I was only fourteen at the time and I thought one day –' She broke off. 'What's the point of talking about it. It doesn't do any good and anyway it won't be long now.'

'What won't?' said the duchess.

'Until they turf us out. I heard from the canteen woman this place is going to close soon and she's usually right about everything.'

'I don't understand,' said the duchess. 'How can they put me out if I've nowhere to go?'

'She said they'll give us a flat to share with someone. How would you like that?'

'I wouldn't like it at all,' said the duchess. 'I can't eat, I can't walk and now they tell me I've got dementia. How can I possibly share a flat?'

'Don't ask me,' said Peggy. 'Ask the sister. You know how she always listens.'

'I won't bother,' said the duchess, detecting a note of sarcasm in Peggy's tone. 'I know you're just trying to get me into trouble. I think you're a very wicked woman.'

Peggy had just left the shop to go home when she saw Boris cycling down the main street towards her. She might not have noticed him if it hadn't been for the rattling of his bicycle chain. The next moment it fell off and he was lying on the pavement beside her.

'Are you OK?' asked Peggy.

'Sure I'm OK.'

He scrambled up and gave the machine a kick. Peggy stared at him, mesmerised by his maturity. His face was thinner and paler and seemed to be all nose, yet he was still better looking than he used to be.

'Don't you remember me?' she said.

'Of course I do. You were the paper girl at Roper's.'

He knelt down to fix his chain. Peggy had the feeling of being dismissed. When she walked on he called out, 'Hold on a sec, I won't be long.'

She waited while he fiddled with the chain. When it was fixed she told him he had a grease mark on his cheek. He rubbed it off then stared at her in a puzzled way.

'You look different from when I last saw you,' he said.

'So do you.'

He stood frowning as if something worried him, then finally asked if she was doing anything in particular later on, and if not he'd like to take her out somewhere, but if she couldn't make it that was all right with him.

'I'm not doing anything,' she said.

'Then I'll meet you outside old Roper's shop at half-past seven and we could try that new ice-cream parlour that's opened up in the High Street.'

Peggy was affronted at Willie being called old but said, 'All right.'

There was no sign of Boris when she reached the shop, though his bicycle stood up against the building. Five minutes later he appeared from round the corner.

'I was just about to leave,' she said crossly.

'I was visiting Liza,' he explained.

'Liza?'

'Roper's wife. I thought I might as well pay her a visit while I was here. She was always good to me, not like him.'

Then he said he was going to put the bicycle behind the shop in case somebody stole it.

'Hurry up then,' said Peggy. 'I don't want to hang about here all night.'

She was worried that Willie might come out and see her with Boris, though she suspected he was more likely to be at the bowling club than with his wife.

'So where do you want to go?' Boris asked when he rejoined her.

'Didn't you say that new ice-cream shop?'

They sat inside the ice-cream parlour without speaking. Apart from two schoolboys giggling in a corner the place was empty. Peggy suspected they were giggling at her and Boris. Forcing herself to speak casually she asked him where he'd been since she last saw him.

'I'm in the cadets, training,' he said from the side of his mouth.

'Training for what?'

'The war. I'm going to join up when I'm old enough, like my brother.'

'Maybe the war will be over by then.'

'I hope not,' he said fiercely.

Another silence followed. Peggy's discomfort became acute when the schoolboys made explosive sounds behind their hands. In a distracted way she told Boris she now worked as Willie Roper's shop assistant.

'You do? I never would have thought that.'

'Why not?'

'It was bad enough delivering his papers.'

Peggy regarded him coldly. 'You never liked him, did you? I suppose it was because he was a boss.'

'He was a creep as well. He should be in the war like other folk.'

Peggy sneered. 'First you call him old, and now you say he should be in the war. Make up your mind.'

'He's not too old to fight.'

Peggy finished her orange juice then stood up and said she was going.

'Hey, wait a minute!' he called after her. 'What's the matter?'

'It's the way you go on about Willie Roper. I would have thought you'd grown out of it. Why do you hate him so much?'

'I don't hate him. I don't even want to talk about him. I thought we might have gone into the amusement arcade, but –' He shrugged. 'All right, I'll come.'

'Listen, I can't stay at lunchtime. The gasman's coming to read the meter.'

'The gasman?'

Willie waited until the customer he'd been serving had left then he turned and told Peggy he'd never heard of a gasman working during his dinner break.

'He left us a note saying he'd call at that time. Maybe he thought it was the only time he'd catch us in.'

'Oh well, I suppose if that's it –' He sighed and walked into the back shop, his face petulant. Peggy felt guilty but had no intention of missing going to a special picture-house matinée with Boris at one-thirty. For the rest of the morning Willie went around with a scowl on his face.

'Cat got your tongue?' said one of the customers, who came in every morning for ten Woodbine, a paper, and a chat on either the weather or the war or both if he could manage it.

'It's the wife,' said Willie. 'Her arthritis is worse than usual. I doubt she'll have to go to hospital one of these days.'

'I'm sorry to hear that,' said the customer.

Later on when they were alone Peggy said, 'How do you mean she's getting worse? She was all right when I took up her bottle of sherry last Friday.'

'All I can say is that I couldn't get a wink of sleep for her moaning all through the night.'

Peggy's brain immediately became alert. 'How do you know that if you weren't sleeping in the same room?'

He regarded her with a wounded expression. 'Is that all that bothers you? She could be heard moaning throughout the building, if you must know.'

'I'm sorry. It's just that –'

'Just that what?'

'I get so fed up with all this secretiveness.'

'It's not any better for me,' he said, running his finger up and down her bare arm. 'Must you really go home at lunchtime?'

'You know I must,' she said, though part of her mind was already thinking she could wait on for half an hour at the least and it would still give her time to meet Boris. 'All right,' she said. 'I'll stay until one o'clock.'

When she got to the picture house, hot and flushed and ten minutes late, there was no sign of Boris or his bicycle. She waited for another three-quarters of an hour but he never appeared.

6

An incident took place in the ward that jolted the patients out of their usual apathy, even those who were practically comatose. For no apparent reason a normally unobtrusive patient had thrust a fork into the chest of a nurse during breakfast. Luckily the fork was of the cheap variety and did not much penetrate the skin, but it was enough to create a high state of tension in the rest of the staff. Five gathered round the erring patient and whisked her so fast from the ward her feet scarcely touched the ground.

'To think I've wanted to do something like that for years,' said Peggy, doing a few steps of the highland fling.

'Better watch or they'll have you off too,' said the duchess.

'I'm sure I wouldn't mind. These jags they give you are as good as a stiff drink. They put you out like a light and that's something I could be doing with nowadays. Even a couple of sleeping pills would be better than nothing.'

'I thought you'd stopped taking them because you wanted to write.'

'I'm fed up trying to write,' said Peggy. 'I can't get peace for people screaming and groaning. If it's not that they're snoring like troopers, you included. Anyway I've no paper left.'

'I don't snore,' said the duchess.

Peggy laughed. 'You snore worse than anybody. You snore so loud you waken yourself up.'

'You snore like an elephant,' said the old woman, determined not to be outdone.

Peggy shook her head, exasperated. 'The point I'm trying to

make is if I don't get any peace to write and have no paper I might as well get doped up the same as everybody else. Understand?'

'I don't understand,' said the duchess. 'Everything you say is so totally absurd. I think you talk like that for spite.'

Then she began to chew on her lips and roll her eyes round her head like a frightened horse, which Peggy took to be a bad sign.

'Take it easy,' she said. 'The nurse will be along in a minute and you'll soon get your pills.'

'I'm not bothered about that,' snapped the duchess. 'What I want to know is where is my *True Romance*?'

'I told you before, I chucked it out. Anyway you don't want to read stuff like that at your age. You want to read something sensible.'

Without warning the old woman reached out and fastened her long bony fingers round Peggy's throat.

'Cunt!' she screamed. 'I'm going to kill you.'

A nurse rushed up and loosened her fingers by giving her what looked like a karate chop on the wrists.

'Is there something in here that's catching?' she said.

'She stole my *True Romance*,' sobbed the duchess.

'What's she talking about?' the nurse asked Peggy, who was feeling her throat tenderly with one hand.

'God knows,' said Peggy. 'She hasn't been herself lately.'

'I see,' said the nurse, looking from one to the other then crooking her finger in the old woman's direction. 'You come with me,' she said, 'and we'll soon sort everything out.'

'You know where my *True Romance* is?' said the duchess eagerly.

The nurse gave her a slight nod then took hold of her arm and led her out of the ward. Peggy watched them go with a slight twinge of guilt.

On Friday evening instead of fetching Mrs Roper's sherry she went straight to the amusement arcade hoping to see Boris again, not because she cared about him, she told herself, but because she wanted to be taken out.

The arcade was half empty. She saw at a glance he wasn't there. She hung around the entrance in the hope he'd show up. Two American soldiers walked past her. She'd heard that a squad of them were in town. One of them turned and said, 'Hello, doll.'

She blushed, intimidated by his bland good looks. He stopped and asked her what her name was. The other one kept walking.

'Peggy,' she said, thinking he might do instead of Boris.

'Peggy,' he said. 'That's a pretty name. You wanna come along with us?'

She was about to say yes, when the other soldier looked back and called out, 'C'mon man. Leave the kid alone.'

'But she wants to come along,' said his companion.

'No way. She's a sad apple. I can tell.'

'Sorry kid,' said the other one. He went up and joined his mate and they began to play the machines. Peggy left the arcade hurriedly with the words 'sad apple' ringing in her ears. At the last minute as she was about to go home she turned and went in the opposite direction to delay going in to an empty house.

'You're late,' said Mrs Roper, opening her door. 'Not that it matters. The shops are still open.'

Peggy followed her, thinking that contrary to what Willie had said his wife looked no worse than usual. Once inside the woman told her she was glad to see her. She couldn't have stood going without her sherry, especially on a Friday.

'Why on a Friday?' Peggy asked.

'I suppose it's because Friday is the night most people go out to enjoy themselves. Even Willie has his bowls.'

'I know what you mean,' said Peggy sadly.

'At your age?' asked Mrs Roper, surprised. Then she added looking into her face, 'Are you all right? You look pale.'

'I'm all right,' said Peggy, and burst into tears.

'Oh dear,' said Mrs Roper, handing her a handkerchief from somewhere within her cardigan. 'Would you like a cup of tea?'

Peggy shook her head, wishing she'd never come. She vowed to herself that she would never come again. The woman unnerved her.

'Or a glass of port? I might have some somewhere.'

'I don't want anything, I'm fine,' said Peggy. 'I'd better get to the shops before they close.'

'There's plenty of time,' said Mrs Roper, still staring intently into Peggy's face. Then she asked, 'Are you pregnant?'

Peggy gasped. 'What makes you say that?'

'I don't know,' said the woman. 'I suppose I get a feeling for these things.'

When she asked her gently who the father was, Peggy just managed to blurt out, 'A soldier,' before she fainted.

The duchess leaned over the side of her bed and jabbed Peggy with her walking stick.

'Wake up.'

Peggy sat up, startled.

'What's happening?'

'Nothing. I only wanted to tell you I'm thinking of going on a hunger strike. It's the only way to get things done.'

Peggy looked down the ward where the patients were either asleep or comatose.

'You woke me up for that?' she said angrily. 'Just when I was getting to sleep?'

'Anyway it's time you were up,' said the old woman, poking her again. Peggy leapt out of bed, grabbed the stick and threw it on to the centre of the floor, wakening several patients who sat up startled.

'I've had enough of your carry-on,' said Peggy. 'Don't talk to me again.'

She walked out the ward and into the toilet area where she stood holding on to the rim of a wash-hand basin for support.

'Good God,' she said, catching sight of her face in the mirror. She'd never got used to how much like her mother's it had become. She could well imagine her saying, 'If only you had done what I told you everything would have been different.'

'Yes, Ma,' said Peggy. 'But how was I to know?'

At that moment a nurse came charging in.

'Oh there you are. I've been searching everywhere.' She peered in at an empty cubicle. 'Who were you talking to?'

'Nobody.'

'I heard voices.'

'That's because you've become like the rest of us.'

'Don't give me any of your lip,' said the nurse, gripping her hard on the fleshy part of her arm. 'You're in enough trouble as it is.'

'How's that?'

'You've been stealing the matron's writing paper. We found a bundle of it in your locker. I suppose you've been writing letters to the management complaining about the treatment. Well, if you think –'

'I'm writing a novel.'

'A novel?' said the nurse. She let out a peal of hysterical laughter then calmed down. 'What about?'

'Myself.'

'Yourself?'

'Yes, I've got plenty to write about with all the things that go on in here.'

'We all have plenty to write about,' said the nurse. 'I could write a few things about what goes on with the patients if I could be bothered.'

'But you can't be bothered,' said Peggy. 'That's the difference between you and me.'

The nurse opened her mouth to say something then shut it again, finally saying, 'I don't know why I'm listening to all this nonsense. Tell it to the matron when she sends for you, which she will be shortly. Meantime get back to bed and lay off the duchess. She doesn't know what she's doing any more.'

Wondering what had happened to Boris made Peggy vaguely unhappy. She couldn't resist asking about him amongst the paper boys. None had seen him, though most didn't know what he looked like anyway. Then one of them told her he'd heard that he'd been caught breaking into a shop and stealing cigarettes. She could hardly credit this. She was about to say it couldn't have been the same person when Willie Roper came into the back shop and said that if it was the Boris who'd worked in here he'd better not show his face and what was she wanting to know for.

'Somebody asked me for his address,' she said casually. 'You don't happen to know what it is?'

'I don't,' he said, giving her a glare which made her wonder if he'd seen them together on that last occasion. The rest of the morning he'd scarcely a word to say to her.

'Is there anything wrong?' she asked him when the shop was empty.

'Not really,' he said, and muttered something about having a lot on his mind.

'Is it something in connection with your wife?' she said, panicking in case Mrs Roper had mentioned she was going to have a baby.

'Worse than that,' he said. 'I'm expecting to get called up.'

'You are?' said Peggy, relieved. 'Aren't you too old?'

'I'm only thirty-seven, for Christ's sake.'

'I didn't mean that you're really old,' said Peggy, positive he'd told her he was forty-two. 'I only meant –'

'It's not that I'm scared to fight. It's the shop I'm thinking about and what's going to happen to Liza.'

'Liza?'

'You know how she depends on me. Who's going to look after her?'

Peggy turned away to serve a customer. Who's going to look after me, she thought, when I'm having your baby. She knew she'd have to tell him sometime, but there never seemed a right moment.

'I thought you were never going to serve me,' said the customer, a young and pretty woman who was flashing her teeth at Willie. Then she asked if there were any prunes in. She'd been hunting high and low for them.

'They'll be in soon,' said Willie, giving her back a wide admiring smile which made Peggy want to weep. She hadn't been getting very many smiles from him recently and it made her wonder if he no longer loved her.

7

The recreation room in the hospital was more like an old waiting room in a railway station, with torn brown leather chairs and a big ugly wooden table pushed against the wall. The only difference was a television set showing an old film with William Powell and Myrna Loy. The patients were either watching with rapt attention or were simply dazed. Peggy and the duchess sat further along the table playing cards.

'It's my turn to go first,' said the old woman.

'Are you sure?' said Peggy.

'I'm sure. You went first the last time.'

'I'm not sure I did,' said Peggy.

'Naturally,' said the duchess. 'I'd be surprised if you were sure of anything, considering the time you've been out for the count.'

'How long?'

'I should say about three days, off and on.'

Nothing was said for a while, then they began to play cards, Peggy's face grim and the old woman's expressionless. After Peggy had won three games the duchess said she'd rather watch the film.

'Do what you like,' said Peggy, boxing the cards together and putting them in her pocket, then going over and taking a drink of water from a tap in the wash-hand basin. 'I can't get rid of this thirst,' she explained to the duchess, who asked her what she'd done to anger them. Peggy frowned.

'I can't remember exactly.' Then her face cleared. 'By God, I do. Didn't I go berserk when I discovered they had taken the manuscript out of my locker?' Bitterly she added, 'I suppose they'll have burned it by now.'

'Maybe not,' said the old woman weakly. Then she coughed once or twice before saying, 'If I tell you something, will you promise not to be angry?'

'How can I promise anything when I don't know what it is?'

'It was me who took it.'

'You took it?' said Peggy, her eyes bulging.

'I did it because you threw away my stick, remember. I was going to put it back but, when they came and searched your locker, I thought I might as well hold on to it for a time.'

'Why, you old cow.'

'At least it was safe with me. If I hadn't taken it it would have been in the furnace by now.'

Peggy thought for a bit. 'Maybe you were right but I don't think I'll bother going on with it. I don't have any paper for a start.'

'I'll give you some of mine if you like.'

'That's good of you,' said Peggy, humble for once. 'But I've lost interest. Who would want to read about an old trout like me, in a nuthouse too, and not even mad enough to be interesting?'

'I think people might want to read it if you put some romance into it,' said the duchess. 'I mean if you wrote about falling in love with someone. Women always like to read about things like that.'

'For God's sake,' said Peggy, 'you should know by this time that there's no such thing as falling in love. It's only sex with a sugar coating round it. I once thought I was in love, but on looking back I can see it was nature's way of getting the female pregnant. We're just like animals, you know. Do you think *they* fall in love?'

'How can I tell what they're thinking?' said the duchess haughtily. 'But I'm quite sure they do in their own way.'

Her mouth closed firmly as she turned her attention to the film on the television. Peggy shook her head and went into a reverie which had nothing to do with her present circumstances.

★

One evening at teatime Peggy's mother paused with her cup halfway up to her mouth and asked her daughter if she was correct in thinking that she'd put on weight recently.

'I'm pregnant,' said Peggy, the words out before she could stop them.

'Pregnant?' said her mother, putting her cup down and spilling tea all over the table.

'You don't have to worry,' said Peggy. 'It's my problem.'

Her mother stared at her in disbelief.

'Your problem?' she repeated. 'When I won't be able to face the neighbours or the people I work with or my friends? In fact I won't have any friends when this gets out. Who's the father?'

Peggy remained silent and her mother said, 'If you don't tell me I'll burn all your clothes.'

'Willie Roper.'

'My God,' said her mother, reeling back with her hand to her mouth. 'I might have known.'

'He doesn't know about it yet,' said Peggy, hardly thinking what she was saying, 'but anyway we're going to get married once he gets a divorce. He told me so.'

Her mother shrieked. 'Married to a man more than double your age who's already got a wife! It's disgusting.'

'I'm sorry,' said Peggy.

'Sorry?' said her mother. 'You don't know what sorry means. All your life you've been deaf to everything I've said. Now look what's happened. Pregnant at sixteen. If your father was alive this would never have happened. Oh Robert,' she moaned, 'if only you were here to help me.'

'Shush, Ma,' said Peggy. 'Willie's going to marry me. It's just a matter of time.'

'Time?' said her mother, as if she'd been reminded of something equally horrible. 'How far on are you?'

'Three or four months, I think.'

Her mother rose up, distraught. 'Then you've no time at all. Give me my coat. I'm going to see that bastard.'

'Wait a minute,' said Peggy, becoming equally distraught. 'He might not be in. He usually goes to the bowling green after his tea.'

'Then I'll talk to his wife. Wait until she hears about this. That'll give her something to think about. She always was stuck up, though I don't know why when she's only a cripple.'

But she must have thought better of it for she didn't make any move to get her coat. Staring at Peggy thoughtfully she said, 'Do you honestly think he'll divorce her to marry you?'

'He said he would,' said Peggy, unable to remember exactly what he'd said on the subject.

Her mother sat down looking more composed.

'Mind you,' she said, 'it wouldn't be such a bad idea if he did. That shop must be a regular gold mine.'

Peggy refrained from saying it was Willie's wife who owned the shop, lest it started another row.

'One way or another,' her mother added, 'he'll have to pay.'

'Pregnant?' said Willie Roper the following morning. 'Jesus Christ, since when?'

'I'm not sure. Three or four months.'

'In the name of God, why didn't you tell me sooner?'

'What difference would it have made?' said Peggy miserably. She'd been banking on him taking the news a lot better than this. She'd even thought he would have been pleased. Now she wondered how she could have been so stupid.

'Of course it would have made a difference. It would have been easier to get rid of it. As it is —' He broke off when a customer came in. 'Go into the back shop,' he hissed. 'I'll talk to you later.'

Five minutes later he came into the back shop and asked if anyone else knew.

'My mother,' she said, deciding not to say anything about his wife. He was in a bad enough mood.

'Your mother?' he said with a sharp intake of breath. 'What did she say?'

'I don't remember exactly. Something about making you pay.'

'She wants money from me. Is that it?'

Peggy became flustered. 'I don't know –'

'Well, she'd better not try to blackmail me if that's what she's thinking or I'll get the police to her, and bugger the consequences.'

Peggy tried to keep the tears back, aware how easily her face got swollen nowadays.

'I don't care about my mother,' she said, 'so long as you still love me. That's all that counts.'

'Love,' he said dismissively. 'I don't think this is the time to talk about love. The important thing is that your mother doesn't get it into her head that she can get at me through my wife. I know for a fact Liza will stick by me. She always has.'

'Always has?' said Peggy in a hollow tone.

He glanced at her slyly. 'There have been others, you know.'

If Peggy's hand had been chopped off the statement couldn't have hurt her more. Her voice shook. 'Are you telling me that because you're angry with me?'

'No, it's true,' he said somewhat sheepishly. 'But I'm not so much angry with you as at myself for not taking precautions. Still,' he added in a more cheerful voice, 'it's no good crying over spilt milk. We'll just have to face up to the facts.'

His kindlier tone encouraged Peggy to come close to him so that they were almost touching.

'I don't care about the others,' she said. 'I'll always love you.'

Gently he pushed her away. 'I'll have to go back to the counter. There must be a pile of customers waiting. Stay there and I'll be back shortly.'

She waited for what seemed like ages. When she did finally look into the front shop he was leaning over the counter reading a newspaper. Blindly she reached for her coat and left through the back door.

While sitting on the veranda again Peggy said to her companion, 'Strangely enough, it's only when I'm writing that certain aspects of my life come back to me, otherwise my mind is usually a blank. For instance, it came to me just now there was a time during the war when I looked for him in pubs and railway stations, especially in railway stations. I always expected to find him coming off one of the trains with his uniform on. When I found out he'd got killed cycling in front of a bus I was almost glad. It saved me looking any more.'

The duchess said, 'I'm not sure who you're talking about.'

'That's because you never listen,' said Peggy. 'I was talking about Boris. Don't you remember I mentioned him earlier on?'

'Perhaps you did,' said the duchess. 'It's just that you keep jumping from one subject to the other. With all these men in your life it's a wonder you never contracted a disease.'

'Sorry,' said Peggy, 'but I only had two men in my life who meant anything to me, and you couldn't really count Boris as he was only a childhood sweetheart.'

'They do say that disease was caught mainly in the foreign brothels,' said the duchess, who hadn't been listening. 'I recall my husband mentioning this. Not that he went into any great detail, knowing how it would upset me. He was a very considerate man.'

'I'm sure he was,' said Peggy, 'though it's a pity he never visited you all the time you were in here.'

'Indeed,' said the old woman peevishly. 'But then he could have died, couldn't he? It was a long time ago.'

Peggy stuffed the writing pad she'd been reading from into her pocket. 'I don't think I'll write any more. My mind's gone blank.'

For some reason this seemed to anger the duchess. 'Give me that paper back. There's no use in having it if you're not going to use it.'

'Why, you old devil, you insisted I take it and it isn't even yours if you remember. You told me you stole it from that new patient, remember?'

The duchess blinked rapidly. 'I don't recall saying that.'

'Well, you did. Do you want me to go and tell her?'

'Don't bother. It will only cause trouble. Keep the paper if it means all that much to you.'

'I don't know that I want it,' said Peggy. 'There's not much point in writing anything if you're not going to listen. You're the only audience I've got.'

'But I will listen,' said the duchess eagerly. 'Please tell me about the man who was killed in the war. Were you very fond of him? I'm really interested.'

'I don't want to talk about it,' said Peggy. 'I'm going in now.'

'Please don't go,' said the duchess. 'I know I'm always saying the wrong thing, but I am interested in what you write, especially now that I haven't got anything else to read.'

'There you go again,' said Peggy. 'I suppose if you had something else to read you wouldn't be interested. Is that it?'

'No, it isn't,' said the old woman. She began to cry weakly. 'It's just that I don't feel well and I think I'm going to die.'

'Oh yeah,' said Peggy, with a sardonic smile. 'Well, before you die listen to this.'

She took out the pad from her pocket and began to read aloud.

'I've had a long discussion with Willie Roper,' said Peggy's mother, 'and we've come to an agreement. You'd better understand that you can't keep it, and you'll have to stay indoors until arrangements can be made.'

'What's going to happen?' said Peggy, guessing what the answer would be.

'Adoption,' said her mother, smiling encouragingly. 'It's the only way. Between the money I've got left from your father's insurance and what Willie is putting towards it, we'll be able to get you into a place three months before you're due, then when the baby is born it will be handed over to a nice couple who'll give it a home. And I hope you appreciate what we are doing for you,' she added earnestly.

'I'm not having the baby adopted,' said Peggy.

'You'll do as you're told.'

'It's my baby,' said Peggy. 'You can't make me.'

'Look,' said her mother, trying a softer approach, 'you've got your whole life in front of you. You don't want to start it as the mother of a bastard child.'

'I'm not going to listen to you,' said Peggy. 'I'm going to see Willie Roper for myself and hear what he says.'

'I told you. He wants it adopted. He's willing to pay,' said her mother.

'I want to hear him say it then.'

'You can't leave the house,' her mother shrieked. 'People will notice that you've put on weight as well as those black shadows under your eyes.'

Peggy walked out while she was still shouting.

'Your mother is right,' said Willie, ushering her into the back shop. 'You shouldn't come here in that state. It'll look suspicious if Liza walks in and catches us. She's been acting very funny lately. I'm just hoping it's her time of life.'

'I thought you said she was practically dying.'

'Not so much dying as chronically ill. And why did you tell her you were pregnant and the father was a soldier? She didn't have to know anything.'

'She guessed I was pregnant and I had to tell her something, didn't I?'

'Yes, but why a soldier?' He gave her a sidelong glance. 'Unless it's true.'

'Of course it isn't,' she cried. 'I've never been with anybody but you.'

'All right, keep your voice down,' he said. 'The customers might hear.'

'Is that all you care about, your customers?' she said bitterly.

'Now you know that's not true,' he said, putting his arm round her shoulder. 'It's you I'm concerned about. Can't you see that?'

She moved away from him and said she was going to keep the baby, no matter what. His face hardened.

'If you do I'll wash my hands of you altogether and God knows what will happen to you. Society doesn't look kindly on young girls who have illegitimate children. God knows, I didn't mean you to have a child but now that it's happened we can only do our best to rectify the situation. The only other alternative is an abortion which could be messy and dangerous. So go home and think about it.'

She turned and left the shop, his words ringing in her ears like a death knell.

8

'Wake up, lazy-bones, and get up so that I can make the bed,' said the nurse, towering over the duchess who lay so small and thin under the covers that she scarcely ruffled them.

The old woman opened her eyes and said, 'Leave me alone. Can't you let me die in peace?'

'You can die in peace after I make the bed,' said the nurse, hauling at the blankets, then sniffing the air. 'Why, I do believe you've wet it again. I can smell it from here.'

The duchess swung her thin legs on to the floor.

'It's not my fault that I've a weak bladder,' she said piteously.

'It's not a weak bladder,' said the nurse, heaving the blankets on to the floor. 'You just can't be bothered to get up. That's what it is.' She stared at the offending sheet. 'Look at that. Damned well soaking and it was only changed yesterday.'

Swaying like a reed in the wind the duchess said, 'You haven't by any chance seen my slippers? I need the toilet.'

Not deigning to answer her the nurse called on Peggy who was helping to serve the porridge.

'What's she done this time?' said Peggy.

'Get her out of here,' said the nurse. 'She wants to go to the toilet. As if it's not enough that she'd already wet the bed.'

'I want my slippers,' said the duchess querulously.

'Look under the bed,' said Peggy.

Once out in the corridor Peggy asked the duchess if she couldn't walk any faster as she didn't want her porridge to get cold.

'It's my heart,' said the duchess. 'It beats too fast and I can't take much more of the aggravation these nurses are giving me.'

Inside the toilet cubicle she began to complain that she was having difficulty moving her bowels. Peggy turned on the tap to avoid hearing this, while trying not to look in the mirror in case she saw her mother's face again. At last the old woman came from the cubicle explaining that she hadn't made her will and must do so soon or the estate would go to a distant relative she hardly knew.

'That's right,' said Peggy. 'One of those rich bastards in Australia with a sheep farm.'

'How did you know?' said the duchess, wiping her perfectly dry hands on a towel.

'It usually happens that way, doesn't it?'

'I know what I'll do,' said the duchess. 'I'll leave everything to the hospital. The money can be used to build a new wing, and there might be enough left over to put a plaque up with my name on it.'

Peggy's mouth fell open. Even in fantasy the idea was out-rageous.

'You'd leave your money to the people who run this horror camp for the sake of having your name on a plaque?'

'Well, I've no one else to leave it to,' said the old woman huffily.

'What about me?' said Peggy. 'Or that husband you're always talking about?'

The old woman regarded her steadily. 'Why, my dear, I don't have a husband, and never had. You should know that by this time.'

Peggy rolled her eyes in mock despair. 'That's right. I keep forgetting nothing is real with you. You could be Alice in Wonderland and me the White Rabbit for all you know.'

During the day Peggy had to stay indoors. When it was dark she walked the back streets to get some fresh air, wearing a slack coat to hide her figure, though there was little to hide at this stage. When she pointed this out her mother said, 'But you can't be too careful.'

The months dragged on until the time came for Peggy to go to the home.

'I've spoken to the woman on the phone,' said her mother. 'She sounds very nice. All she requires of you is to do a little light housework, nothing strenuous.'

'Will I be the only one there?' Peggy asked, resolving to run away at the first opportunity.

'Of course not,' said her mother. 'There's more than you gets into this kind of mess, but mind you, they're usually a lot older, so thank your lucky stars you've been accepted. At your age they could have turned you down.'

'I wish they had,' said Peggy under her breath.

The evening before she left she wrote a letter to Willie Roper informing him about her departure and saying that if he didn't help her to keep the baby she was going to tell his wife. She was sealing the envelope and wondering how she could get a stamp when her mother came in to the room shouting at the top of her voice that she'd just heard Willie Roper had been called up, which would likely mean that they wouldn't get a penny out of him if he was in the army.

'Does that mean I don't have to go to this home?' said Peggy.

'Oh no, you're going,' said her mother, 'even if it leaves me a pauper. I'm not going to have any bastard child in my house.'

The journey in the tramcar took an hour, during which Peggy stared blankly out the window while her mother looked stonily ahead. She'd hardly spoken a word to her daughter except to say how Willie Roper had skedaddled off to the war to avoid paying out the money and that she blamed Peggy for everything.

The big house might have been grand in its day but had a neglected air. Bushes in the front garden had been allowed to grow wild and the path to the door was covered in weeds. The woman who opened it was tall with thick wiry hair and protuberant eyes. She introduced herself as Lily and led them to a clean but drab room with faded linoleum, two single beds, a wardrobe and a wash-hand basin with a pail under it. Peggy wondered about that pail.

'Very nice,' said Peggy's mother with a fulsome smile.

'We do our best,' said Lily, then told Peggy, 'Take your coat off and hang it in the wardrobe with your other stuff.'

She went out with Peggy's mother and closed the door, leaving her inside. Peggy was hanging up her things when there was a knock and a voice said, 'Can I come in?'

Peggy turned to see a woman with short red hair, neither young nor old-looking, her face a mass of freckles.

'I'm Annie,' she said.

Peggy was reassured by the woman's plain but friendly features.

'And I'm Peggy,' she said. 'Have you come to show me what to do?'

'Not yet,' said Annie. 'I came to let you know tea is at six and I'll give you a call then.'

Peggy was dismayed to learn she would have to wait in the room for all that time.

'Is there no heating?' she asked.

'There's an electric fire there,' said Annie, pointing to a space between the beds. 'We're not supposed to use it through the day. If Lily comes in don't tell her I told you about it.'

Peggy nodded. Her feet were numb. At that moment an electric fire was her idea of heaven.

'Am I sharing this room with you?'

'No, I'm in another room,' said Annie. 'There's nobody else in here but yourself, but you never know who's going to come in beside you. It's that kind of place.'

She looked at Peggy curiously.

'You're in for three months, I hear.'

'At least that,' said Peggy with a tremor in her voice.

'I know it will seem bad at first,' said Annie, 'but you'll get used to it. I've been here for five months.'

'That long?' said Peggy, surprised. 'Isn't your baby adopted yet?'

330

'Two months ago,' said Annie, and fell silent. Then she said that she'd only stayed on to give Lily a hand until she got a job that suited her. 'I prefer cleaning houses,' she added.

Peggy found it hard to believe anybody would want to stay on any longer than was necessary.

'That woman in charge, Lily, what's she like?'

'She's not bad if you take her the right way.'

'I see,' said Peggy, wondering what the right way was. She pointed to the pail and asked what it was for.

'It's for when we need the lavvy,' said Annie. 'We're not allowed to use the proper lavvy in case of germs. The midwife is very particular about germs.'

'But I can't use a pail,' said Peggy, aghast. 'I'll die if I have to.'

'Well, you'll just have to,' said Annie. 'It's one of the rules.' She regarded Peggy with concern, then said, 'I must go now or else she'll be wondering where I am.'

Peggy had used up all her writing paper and, being possessed by the urge to set down her life story before she lost the thread of it, she asked the night nurse in the ward if she could possibly get her a jotter and she'd pay for it out of her meagre allowance. The nurse raised one eyebrow and said she would see. Peggy sensed by her tone she'd either forget or had no intention of seeing, so when the duchess shuffled down the ward to find out what was going on at the bottom she began to search in the old woman's locker on the off-chance of finding something to write upon, even if it was only a piece of toilet roll.

For her part the duchess had stopped to watch a group of patients playing gin rummy round a patient's bed, which wasn't allowed, but the night nurse was quite often out of the ward either having a smoke or a blether. The game reminded the duchess of the times when she was a young girl and people came to the house on Sundays to play cards with her parents. Strangely she couldn't remember her parents too much and hardly anything else about her childhood or even her later years. Sometimes she had the impression she'd been born an old woman.

One of the card players beckoned her over and whispered something in her ear, which caused her to turn round and shuffle back up the ward tapping her stick as she went.

'What are you doing?' she said to Peggy who was hunkered down on her knees searching the back of the old woman's locker, her imperial mints rolling all over the floor.

'Looking for something to write on,' said Peggy. 'What do you think?'

'How dare you!' said the duchess, poking Peggy in the back with her stick.

Peggy immediately rose up and took the stick off her then strode out on to the veranda. A nurse came at her back.

'I hope you're not going to do anything foolish,' she said.

Peggy pointed towards the duchess who was wringing her hands and giving a good impression of someone severely demented.

'She attacked me with this stick and it's not the first time, so I'm going to get rid of it.'

'Over the veranda?' said the nurse.

'Where else?'

'Tell me,' said the nurse, squeezing the soft part of Peggy's arm in a vice-like grip, 'do you often throw things over the veranda?'

Peggy clamped her lips together as the nurse escorted her up the ward, passing the duchess who was clawing at her hair, then out into the small room with no windows and no furniture except for a medicine chest on the wall. After locking the door she slapped Peggy hard on each cheek and asked her what was bothering her.

'Nothing,' said Peggy. 'I only wanted paper to write on and I thought she had some in her locker.'

'So you thought you'd the right to help yourself to it.'

'She said I could.'

'Roll up your sleeve,' said the nurse. 'Let's see what your blood pressure's like.'

Before Peggy could refuse she'd unlocked the medicine chest from which she brought out a syringe then stuck it into Peggy's arm saying, 'This is for your own good.'

Peggy slept all the next day until teatime. When she woke up there were two jotters on top of her locker. The duchess called from the chair at her bedside, 'Look what the nice nurse left you after I told her you were writing a novel.'

'Fuck you and the nice nurse,' said Peggy. 'And don't do me any favours in future. I was in the punishment room because of you.'

'You brought it upon yourself,' said the duchess. She added, 'I've been reading more of your story while you were sleeping. It's actually quite interesting in parts.'

Peggy touched an eye that was turning black. 'To think you've been as crazy as a coot for the past two days and now you're acting as if butter wouldn't melt in your mouth. What's the matter with you?'

The duchess came over and whispered, 'I want you to know that there's not a soul in this ward I'd talk to except yourself. They're all too ignorant. At least I can appreciate what you're trying to do. They wouldn't have a clue.'

'Is that right?' said Peggy. 'Well, I won't be doing any writing tonight. My head feels like it's crawling with worms.'

'Never mind,' said the duchess. 'We'll sit out on the veranda later on and watch the street lights. We might see that man again. What's his name?'

'I don't know,' said Peggy.

9

Peggy was on her way back from the dairy with a shopping bag containing six pints of milk over each arm.

'The even weight should balance you up nicely,' Lily had said before Peggy set off. In theory this might have been true but in practice her arms felt as if they were being wrenched out of their sockets. She stopped halfway to unbutton her once slack coat that was now so tight it was making her sweat. Resisting the impulse to stop for longer she carried on into the lane that led to the back of the house. She'd been warned not to come in the front door in case the sight of a pregnant woman gave the place a bad name.

Annie opened the door, shaking her head. Needlessly she said, 'You shouldn't be lugging all that weight in your condition,' since they both knew Peggy had no choice in the matter. In the big kitchen Lily was stirring a pot of porridge on the kitchen range. She ordered a plate to be put out for the new client who had come in the previous night.

'Is that who it was? I thought I heard something,' said Annie.

'Yes, at half-past ten,' said Lily. 'Some people have no consideration.'

At that point a woman entered in an advanced state of pregnancy and stared around as if wondering if she'd come to the right place.

'Sit down, please,' said Lily, pointing to the table, and then placing a bowl of porridge in front of her. The woman said she didn't eat porridge since it made her sick just to look at it.

'You won't get anything else,' said Lily.

'Not even a cup of tea?' said the woman.

'Not at the moment. You'll have to wait.'

'I'll wait,' said the woman. She took out a cigarette from a packet she'd been holding in her hand and asked if anyone had a match.

'Smoking?' said Lily, scandalised. 'And you expecting any minute.'

'I've been smoking for nine months,' said the woman. 'It's a bit late to start worrying about it now.'

'Well, you still want to chuck it,' said Lily. 'It's a filthy habit and I'm not having you smoking in my kitchen.'

Peggy and Annie listened to the conversation with interest. It was a change from the usual silence if Lily was in the kitchen. Then a bell rang which meant the midwife wanted her.

'Who does that cow think she is?' said the woman when Lily had gone. 'She needn't tell me what to do. I paid good money to come here.'

'She's not that bad,' said Annie. 'Her bark's worse than her bite.'

'Well, if that's her bark I wouldn't like to see her bite,' said the woman, tearing a strip off the newspaper and sticking it in the fire to light her cigarette. 'By the way,' she added, 'my name's Cathy. What's yours?'

'I'm Peggy.'

Annie frowned as she stared at the torn newspaper. 'She'll have something to say about that.'

'She can say what she likes,' said Cathy. 'I hardly think she'll fling me out.' She added, 'Is there any chance of getting a cup of tea now she's gone?'

Annie put on the kettle and said they might as well all have a cup of tea. Peggy then told Cathy she'd been here for two months and would likely be here for another two.

'You've got my sympathy,' said Cathy. 'I couldn't stick this place for more than a day. I'm only in here to have the kid and then I'm off.' She stared at Peggy curiously. 'Aren't you a bit young to be having a kid? You don't look more than fourteen.'

'I'm sixteen.'

'You're still too young at sixteen. Was it some old married man that did it? It's usually the case now that all the young men are being called up.'

'We don't discuss our personal affairs in here,' said Annie stiffly.

'Pardon me,' said Cathy, after taking a long tense pull at her cigarette. 'I don't care who knows mine. I'm in here to have a kid for my sister since she can't have one herself.'

'That's good of you,' said Annie. 'I know I wouldn't like going through all the bother for somebody else, even my sister.'

'Well, you see,' said Cathy, 'the man involved was her husband and when she discovered I was having his kid she thought it best to keep it in the family.'

'I see,' said Annie a trifle coldly, while Peggy tried to figure it all out.

Lily came in and sniffed the air suspiciously, but said nothing. She told Peggy to polish the furniture in the front room after she'd washed the dishes, and Annie to change the beds in the rooms that were not being used.

'And you,' she said to Cathy, 'bring in coal for the fire. You'll get it in the bunker outside.'

Cathy said she'd no intention of doing anything, she hadn't come here to be a servant. Besides, she thought she was going into labour since she was having pains in her back. Lily said in that case she'd better go to her room and stay there until the midwife came.

'But it's freezing in there,' said Cathy. 'I'll catch my death, sure as God.'

Lily opened the kitchen door wide and beckoned her to leave.

'I'm afraid we can't have you in the kitchen if you're in labour. So please go or I'll have to remove you by force.'

'Oh no you don't,' said Cathy. 'I'm getting out of this dump and I want my money back.'

'Dear me, no,' said Lily. 'You can't have it back. You signed an agreement.'

'What agreement?' said Cathy. Then she went chalk white and sank into a chair. 'Jesus Christ, I believe I am in labour. I've just had one hell of a pain.'

'I thought you might be,' said Lily. 'Come along and I'll fetch the nurse.'

They both left the kitchen with Cathy hunched and shaking all over.

'I doubt we'll see her again,' said Annie.

'But she's right,' said Peggy. 'Why does Lily treat us like hired help when we're paying for it?'

'Because it's cheaper than some of the other places. It saves us money and them as well if they get their help for nothing.'

'Like you and me.'

'Exactly,' said Annie. 'There's no union rules here.'

'I suppose not,' said Peggy, regretting that she wouldn't see Cathy again. Annie was all right, but too meek and mild and always sided with Lily.

During the early hours of the morning the duchess called out for a bedpan, which request was ignored until Peggy stamped out the ward and down the corridor and into the room where all the bedpans were kept in neat rows.

'Didn't you hear old Violet shouting?' she asked two nurses who had been talking to each other in a desultory manner. They gave her a blank stare and walked away.

'Never mind,' Peggy called after them. 'I see you're busy.'

Back in the ward she discovered the old woman sitting up in a lopsided manner with her mouth hanging open.

'Here's your bedpan,' said Peggy, shoving it into her face, but the old woman didn't move a muscle and when Peggy shook her lightly on the shoulder she toppled over.

'Nurse,' called Peggy, running out of the ward.

Ten minutes later a nurse came through to check the duchess's pulse and finished up sending for the sister who took one look at the patient and arranged for a screen to be put round her bed. It didn't stop Peggy from shouting over it that if they'd got the old woman a bedpan sooner she'd probably have been OK.

'If you don't shut your mouth I'll shift you to B ward among the advanced cases,' said the sister, coming out from the screen. 'Meanwhile go and take a bath so that we may be allowed to give this patient proper treatment.'

When Peggy returned half an hour later the duchess and her bed were gone. Later in the morning she was told by one of the friendlier nurses that she might not last the day.

'I bet she won't,' said Peggy angrily. 'They'll have been giving her one of those lethal injections to finish her off.'

'Get that woman out of here,' said the matron, who happened to come into the ward to do her morning rounds, accompanied by two orderlies for protection, and an elderly male doctor who appeared to be half asleep. Once again Peggy was locked up in the small padded room, but this time without the injection. When she got out next morning she went to the veranda to get some fresh air and was in time to see a coffin being taken to a limousine by two men in bowler hats. She guessed the coffin was the duchess's.

'Coo-ee,' she shouted, in the hope the men would be startled enough to drop it. It wouldn't do the duchess any harm if she fell out in front of the traffic but it wouldn't look so good for the hospital. However they didn't turn as much as a hair, not even when she added, 'Murderers.'

Back in the ward she took from under her vest the jotter and pencil she always kept and read aloud the chapter she had written in the punishment room.

Every Saturday Peggy's mother came to the home and paid the weekly fee, then Peggy accompanied her back to the tram stop by way of a park with a pond where children threw bread to the ducks. Peggy always wished she had sneaked some bread out.

It would have been a cheerful thing, feeding the ducks, but by the time she'd finished all her chores and got herself ready she'd forgotten about the bread. In any case her mother was always in a hurry, though whatever for Peggy couldn't think.

'I wish you'd keep up with me,' her mother was now saying. 'My feet are freezing with having to walk so slow.'

'I'm going as fast as I can,' said Peggy. To point out that her increasing weight was holding her back would only have provoked her mother into making some kind of bitter comment. She was never encouraged to speak about her condition. Therefore it was a shock when she said, 'It won't be long now until the little bastard's born and I won't have to come here and pay a third of my wages to that greedy bitch, and as well as that I won't have to tell any more lies when people ask about you.'

'I'm sorry,' said Peggy.

'And so you should be. Do you know some parents would have put their daughters in an asylum for what you've done. Think yourself lucky that I didn't.'

'I do.'

'Another thing, when this is over you'll be taking a job in an office even if it's only to make the tea and you'll stay away as far as possible from Willie Roper's shop.'

'I thought he was in the army,' said Peggy, startled at the mention of his name.

'So did I but I heard he got a discharge on account of having varicose veins or something equally ridiculous. And it appears his wife is dying, and his business is not doing so good. If it had been I would have been on to him like a shot for the money he owes me, but I suppose you can't get blood out of a stone.'

Peggy had a fleeting recollection of Mrs Roper thrusting a book into her hand and telling her a good book helps you to understand yourself as well as others. Tears of sorrow and shame came into her eyes. She gave an involuntary sob.

'What's the matter with you?' said her mother. 'I hope you're not thinking of that Willie Roper.'

'If you must know I wish I was dying.'

'Well, you'd better not be. I've enough to contend with.'

They left the park and came out into a short street of tenement buildings with a public house at the end of it.

'I think I'll nip in for a small port while I'm waiting for the tram,' said her mother. 'I need something to buck me up after all this –' Her voice broke off as though there was no need to explain.

'Yes, you should,' said Peggy, and was going to add, 'See you next Saturday,' but her mother had disappeared through the swing doors.

'I'll be leaving at the end of the week. I've got a job,' Annie whispered, though there were only she and Peggy in the kitchen. For the past few days there had been no clients. Lily had explained they were taking in no one else meanwhile, since the midwife wanted a break over Christmas.

'That means I'll be here on my own,' said Peggy in a tone of dread.

'Surely you can put up with that? You don't have long to go.'

'How do I know how long I've got after the birth?' said Peggy. 'And it's plain that Lily hates me. It's going to be worse if you're not here.'

'She doesn't hate you. It's only her manner.'

Peggy began to cry. 'I know she hates me. If you go I'll kill myself.'

'For goodness sake, stop it,' said Annie. 'You are making me feel bad and I thought you would have been glad for my sake. After all, I've been here for months on end.'

Peggy wiped her eyes on her sleeve.

'I am glad for you. It's just that I'm going to miss you terribly. So what kind of a job is it?'

'It's cleaning a dentist's surgery,' said Annie. 'I had a notion of working in a shop, but I'm no good at counting. Cleaning's all I know.'

'It's easy to work in a shop,' said Peggy with a touch of scorn. 'I did.'

'So you did,' said Annie, 'and look what happened.'

Peggy bit back an angry retort and said instead, 'My mother's almost fifty and she works in a munitions factory. You should try that. It's more money.'

'So I should,' said Annie in a sarcastic voice. She went over to the sink and filled a basin with water. 'If we don't get a move on we'll both be getting it in the neck from you know who and I don't want to annoy her in case she doesn't give me a reference.'

So much for sticking in with Lily, thought Peggy. She began to wipe the table while Annie went down on her knees to wash the floor. Nothing was said as they worked, until Peggy was struck by a notion. She asked Annie if she ever regretted having her baby adopted.

'What a question!' said Annie, squinting up at her. 'What brought that on?'

'I only wondered, because I'm sure I would. In fact when the time comes I'm going to keep my baby.'

'You think so?' said Annie in a sneering sort of way, which made Peggy wish she hadn't said anything. Changing the subject she added, 'What's the midwife like, I mean when you're in labour? I hope she's not anything like Lily.'

'She does what she has to do, if that's what you're asking.'

'I see,' said Peggy, not reassured by this statement. The one time she'd seen the midwife was when she was standing in the doorway of the kitchen watching them while they cleaned up. She was fat all over with piggy eyes and bare arms that looked as strong as a man's.

'Is there anything else you want to know?' said Annie, rising to her feet with a scowl.

'No, nothing,' said Peggy, now almost in tears at the way

Annie spoke. 'I didn't mean to annoy you,' she added. 'It's just that I feel so miserable about you going.'

Annie's face softened. 'You didn't annoy me. Just don't be too upset, that's all. It's not as if I won't be in touch. I'll write to you as soon as I'm settled.'

'That'll be great,' said Peggy, forcing a smile and knowing it would be most unlikely. In her place she would have wanted to forget everything connected with the home.

10

'Don't make so much noise,' said the midwife, bending over Peggy who was screaming with pain. 'You're not co-operating. Press when I tell you.'

Peggy scarcely heard her. She thought she was going to die.

'And keep on pressing until I tell you to stop, otherwise I'll have to use forceps and I don't think you'll like that.'

The word 'forceps' galvanised Peggy into giving one almighty push and the baby's head appeared.

'Now press again,' said the midwife.

Peggy thought definitely she was going to die. She screamed and pressed at the same time until the rest of the baby emerged. Then she passed out and woke up in a different room with a black dog at her feet which she took to mean she'd died and gone to hell. Lily entered with a bundle in her arms.

'You've got a fine boy,' she said, 'and now you'll have to feed him.'

'I'm too tired,' said Peggy, only wanting to return to oblivion and never waken up again.

'You'll feed him whether you're tired or not,' said Lily, thrusting the child into Peggy's arms so that she was forced to look at him. He didn't look human, she thought, more like a fledgling with his wrinkled skin and beaky nose.

'I've no milk,' she said.

'You'll have milk,' said Lily. 'Put him on your right nipple for five minutes then change to your left.'

Peggy fumbled at the buttons on her nightdress, affronted at having to expose her chest to Lily's grim gaze. It was painful at first when the infant began to suck. After a few minutes the pain eased off.

'Didn't I say you had milk?' said Lily.

Peggy asked what she was to do with him when he'd had enough.

'Keep him beside you. I'll bring in a cot.'

'Is he to be with me all the time?'

'Oh yes,' said Lily. 'Up until the time he's to be adopted, and as for that dog,' she added, pointing to the animal who had made itself comfortable at the bottom of the bed, 'keep him out of here. He's supposed to be guarding the house.'

The days passed slowly and Peggy never left the room except to go to the toilet. Being no longer pregnant she didn't have to use the pail. All the other rooms in the house were locked including the kitchen and Lily came in only twice a day to leave Peggy a meal and make sure the infant was being fed and changed properly.

'We don't want you neglecting him,' she said. 'That child's valuable.'

Although more or less a prisoner Peggy wasn't too unhappy. The baby took up all her time and during the night she took him into bed beside her, while the dog lay at the bottom. It was a cosy arrangement and although she still planned to escape with the baby the sameness of the everyday routine lulled her into a false sense of security.

One morning Lily arrived with the breakfast, toast and a boiled egg, porridge being too much trouble to make for one, and asked her if she had a name for the child.

'Robert,' said Peggy. Then after a slight hesitation, 'It's my da's.'

She would have liked to call him William but it didn't seem appropriate when his father would never know him.

Lily nodded. 'It's only for the records. Whoever adopts him will likely change it.'

Peggy's heart sank. She'd have to make her getaway soon but how could she when the front door was always locked from the outside? And if she did manage to escape where would she go?

'Somebody has sent you a present,' said Lily, arriving on Christmas Day with a small parcel and throwing it on to the bed. For a wild moment Peggy thought it might be from Willie Roper, but on opening it she discovered it was from her mother, a red headscarf with black dots.

'Very nice,' said Lily sarcastically. 'I'm sure it must have cost a fortune.'

Peggy felt insulted on her mother's behalf. 'She can't afford much when she's got to pay for me,' she said.

'Maybe, but she could have at least visited you, considering it's Christmas, instead of sending it on.'

Peggy dropped her eyes. She wasn't going to run down her mother to this woman. Lily shrugged.

'Still, I dare say it's none of my business. How about a slice of apple crumble with your dinner tonight? Will that make you feel any better?'

Peggy nodded to convey that it would, then encouraged by Lily's unusually sympathetic tone she asked if she could go outside for a walk.

'Outside?' said Lily, flabbergasted. 'And who's going to look after the baby?'

'I thought you might,' said Peggy, not daring to look at her in case she went into a rage.

Surprisingly she agreed. 'Only for half an hour,' she said, adding that she'd enough to do without looking after somebody else's child.

'Do you think I could have some bread to feed the ducks?' said Peggy. 'I've always wanted to feed them and the pond's not far.'

'Dear Christ, whatever next,' said Lily. She stamped out of the room then came back with some bread in a poke. 'Mind,' she said, 'no more than half an hour.'

Peggy walked around the pond, with the ducks following her, glad there was no one else to see her in the slack coat. Twice she went round the pond with the ducks at her back until the bread was finished.

'No more,' she said, shooing them away, then headed back towards the house, positive she hadn't been gone for as much as half an hour, but somehow she had the feeling her child was crying out for her. She began to run.

Lily was waiting for her in the hallway.

'Thank God you're back,' she said. 'A couple came about the baby around twenty minutes ago and as you weren't in they said they'd come back tomorrow. I knew I shouldn't have let you go out.'

The matron sat staring at the folder in front of her then finally looked up at Peggy and said, 'I want you to know you're going to be discharged soon. As to the date I cannot say exactly –' Then she stopped, struck by Peggy's blank face. 'Did you hear what I said?'

Peggy nodded her head.

'Well, aren't you pleased?'

'Not particularly.'

The matron looked surprised.

'Don't you want to leave?'

Peggy shook her head.

'For goodness sake, why not?'

'I want to stay and finish my writing.'

'Your writing?' said the matron, peering at the pages inside the folder. 'There is no mention of writing in here.'

'I can't help that,' said Peggy. 'I'm writing a novel and I don't want to be distracted from it. Being discharged would distract me so much I might not be able to continue.'

The matron looked annoyed.

'It's not up to you to decide whether you leave or not. This isn't a holiday camp where one can lounge about writing novels, and I'm sure you'll have fewer distractions in a place of your own than in here.'

When Peggy remained silent the matron said, 'Perhaps you're distracted already by the death of your friend?'

'What friend?'

'Why, old Mrs Smith, better known as the duchess. She was your friend, wasn't she?'

'She was in no condition to be anybody's friend,' said Peggy.

'But still you must miss her. Anyway,' she added impatiently, 'whether you like it or not you're going to be discharged into a nice little flat where I'm sure you'll be very happy and you'll be able to come and go as you please, provided you conform to the rules.'

'So there are rules?'

'Naturally. We must all abide by rules.'

'Is that so,' said Peggy, holding the matron's gaze steadily. 'What about my pills?'

'Your pills?'

'If I don't get them I'm liable to break the rules.'

'But you don't need pills,' said the matron. 'That's why we're sending you out. You're cured.'

Peggy leaned forward and hissed into the matron's face, 'I'm no more cured than you are.'

Immediately the matron put her finger on a bell under her desk and an orderly appeared.

'Everything all right?' the orderly asked, looking from the matron to Peggy then back again.

'Everything's fine,' said the matron. 'Just take this patient away and give her the usual pills. We'll get no peace otherwise.'

Peggy's mother bought her a coat two days previous to the adoption.

347

'We can't have you coming home like a tramp,' she'd said. 'I've told everyone you were working in London, so remember, if anyone asks you where you've been –'

'I'll remember,' Peggy said. At the last minute she pleaded with her mother to let her keep the baby – they could say she'd got married in London and her husband was away to the war. Her mother became so angry that she slapped Peggy's face saying, 'You must be joking.'

It was then Peggy gave up all hope of a last-minute reprieve to keep the child. As for running away, she pictured herself collapsing in a field from exhaustion and the baby dying in her arms. She couldn't let that happen to him.

'Put on this new blue suit I bought him,' said Lily in a cheerful mood for once, 'and make sure his nappy's not soiled. We want him to look as perfect as possible.' She added, 'Leave your suitcase in the hall before you go. It'll save you going back to your room to collect it, for there's no point in hanging around.'

Peggy thought that was very true.

The couple arrived on time but had to wait ten minutes before Peggy came into the hall carrying the child.

'What kept you?' said Lily, trying to keep her voice low as the woman smiled nervously at Peggy.

'He was crying and I had to get him quietened down,' said Peggy, handing over the baby wrapped tightly in a shawl.

'Well, he's quiet enough now,' said Lily with a brief glance at the child and a fawning smile at the woman who gazed at him in wonder and said, 'Isn't he beautiful?'

'He is,' said Lily, glaring at Peggy who stared dully ahead. The husband came forward to gaze over his wife's shoulder.

'He's certainly a fine boy,' he mumbled, as though slightly embarrassed by the whole affair.

The next moment they were leaving with Lily waving them goodbye. When the taxi had gone Peggy hurried to the door, relieved that Lily had walked past her without speaking. She couldn't have stood it if she had. The dog followed her and would possibly have come down the path and out the gate with her if she hadn't told it to go back. And only now that she was safely on the tram did she allow herself the luxury of wondering how long it would take the couple to discover the baby was dead.

Postscript

Peggy had finished the last chapter of her novel, but wasn't entirely satisfied with it. She wondered if the ending was too abrupt, if perhaps there weren't enough details. She couldn't remember much of what had happened, only the judge saying that she'd murdered an innocent child and therefore was capable of murdering again. She was a danger to society and should be put away for the rest of her natural life. She'd been surprised at that. She hadn't thought she was capable of murdering again – she'd only killed her child to stop someone else having him. But apart from all this there was no one whose advice or opinion she could ask now that the duchess had gone. The duchess had not been good on advice but she'd always been strong on opinion.

'I'm going to donate my manuscript to the hospital,' she informed a patient in the day room who'd been watching television all morning with a baffled look on her face.

'Donate what?'

'My life story.'

'Oh I see. Are they going to make a film of it?'

'I don't think so. They haven't read it yet and I'm leaving today.'

'You're quite right,' said the patient. 'I'd leave too if I got half a chance.'

'The snag is I'll have to share a flat with someone.'

'That'll be nice,' said the patient, looking back at the television as if she'd said too much.

Peggy walked on to the veranda and remembered the duchess. She could imagine her sitting in her usual chair.

'They're letting me out,' she said, as if the duchess could hear her. 'After thirty odd years of being shunted from place to place for what I did they say I'm no longer a danger to society. Well, let's hope they're right.'

Then she went over and stared down through the railings. The bus shelter was empty. Just as well, she thought. She wasn't missing anything. Back in the ward she was handed the battered cardboard suitcase she'd come in with.

'I take it you're all packed and ready,' said the ward sister in a jolly tone.

Peggy said, looking confused, 'What do you mean, packed and ready? I'd hardly anything to pack.'

'It's a figure of speech,' said the sister. 'Don't pretend you're not glad to be leaving us. I'm sure you must be jumping with joy.'

'So I am,' said Peggy flatly, 'but I've been thinking, maybe I should take my manuscript. There's bound to be bits I should change and if I leave it behind I might forget what they are.' She broke off, adding anxiously, 'I can always send you a copy later.'

'Oh yes, your manuscript,' said the sister, barely suppressing a smile. 'I wouldn't worry about it if I was you. It will be fine the way it is and we're all dying to read it. Hurry now, the taxi's waiting.'

Before Peggy could say another word a young man took hold of her arm and led her out the back door of the hospital, explaining he was her social worker and would make sure she was all right. She scarcely listened. It had dawned on her she'd never see her manuscript again. They would have chucked it in the bin; that's why the ward sister had smiled. But she couldn't take it for granted.

'I'll have to go back,' she said and the young man's grip became tighter.

'I told you you'll be all right,' he said, pushing her into the back seat of the taxi then moving into the front beside the driver. The next thing they were off at what she considered an outrageous speed. She sank back and closed her eyes to stop feeling sick. When she opened them the taxi had stopped.

'Here we are,' said the young man. 'You can get out now. You're home.'

Laboriously she got out and stared up at a building whose height made her dizzy. She said, 'It doesn't look like home to me.'

'You'll love it once you're settled in. It's only a matter of getting used to it.'

He took the cardboard suitcase from the boot of the car. Peggy felt like telling him to throw it away but was too ashamed. Instead she asked him how far up the flat was and he told her the fourteenth floor, but not to worry, the lift was easy to manage and near her front door. Peggy stumbled towards it, her head spinning. The young man came at her side and pressed a button to open the doors. Inside the lift she told him not to come up with her, she would manage if he showed her where to press.

'Are you sure?' he said. 'I don't want you to get stuck halfway.'

'Don't worry, I'm not daft,' she said.

They both smiled at that then he handed her a key.

'Once you get out you'll see the number facing you, forty-four. You can't go wrong.'

After he'd gone she suddenly pressed the button, deciding that on the fourteenth floor she would throw herself from the first window she came to. There would be no more anxiety or pain. She'd reached the end of her tether.

But when the lift stopped and the door opened she saw another one facing it. A white-haired old lady with the gaze of a child stood there saying, 'I'm Dorothy,' and holding out her hand. 'Are you my new flatmate?' she asked. 'The other one disappeared. I think she was run over.'

Peggy, speechless, could only nod, return the handshake then follow the woman into the flat. The comfortable look of it pleasantly surprised her despite the slightly soiled sofa where a cat reclined on a cushion. A wilting bunch of flowers hung over a vase on the table.

'I hope you don't mind cats,' said the woman shyly. 'This one was a poor soul that didn't have a home.'

'Hmm,' said Peggy, sniffing the air. 'Judging by the smell in here we'd better get it a litter box or it'll be homeless once again.'

'Oh yes,' said Dorothy, clapping her hands like a child that's been promised a treat. 'I knew there was something I'd forgotten to get.'

'I suppose there will be other things as well,' said Peggy, punching a cushion from which the dust flew.

'There will be!' said the woman almost ecstatically. 'I'm always forgetting things and once I get up here I can't be bothered going out again. But now I'll make us a cup of tea. I expect you're dying for one.'

She dashed away leaving Peggy to stare round the room thinking that she was going to have her work cut out getting this place in order, but somehow she didn't mind. It was obvious the woman needed someone to look after her, as well as the cat. For a start it would learn to sleep on the floor. If this was to be her home, she certainly wasn't having a sofa covered in hairs.

BAD ATTITUDES

Foreword

Peter Dawson, a skinnily-built boy of fifteen, came back to the terrace for a look at his old home before it was demolished. He walked with his dog along the cobblestone lane feeling that eyes were watching him from behind broken window panes, though this was unlikely as all the previous tenants had left for council houses. All, that is, except Shanky Devine, who was cursed with a bad squint, a nature that endeared him to no one, and who had stubbornly refused the council's offer of a flat. Hurrying past Shanky's house (since he might have gone mad by this time), Peter arrived at his old home and stood staring up at the window half expecting to see curtains and a geranium plant, but there was only a jagged black hole where the glass had been. Taking a deep breath, he climbed the stairs and opened the door.

The living room seemed smaller than it used to be, maybe because there was nothing to break the bareness of it but a fireplace overflowing with burnt paper, particles of which floated up into the air when his feet struck the floorboards. He raked amongst the ash to see what he could find, a bit of jewellery or foreign coins or even a knife he had missed for months. But he only got black smears on his hands which wouldn't rub off. That and the strong whiff of damp from the walls, which were now the colour of green cheese, made him feel like gagging.

When the dog began pawing the floorboards as if for something buried under them he said to it, 'Let's go. This place stinks.'

Once outside the dog bounded ahead, probably glad to be free for it had been shut indoors most of the day. Peter caught up with it and put it on a lead, warning it not to bark when they got back to the flats, or it could be a goner one of these days.

I

Old Mrs Webb reckoned she hadn't had a minute's peace since the Dawsons moved in. From the time they carried their furniture upstairs to the flat above she had sensed they would be trouble. The man, the woman, the two youths and even the large dog running beside them had that seedy, untrustworthy look. She was sure the man was the worse for drink. He came towards her with a wardrobe on his back, telling her if she didn't get out of his road she was liable to be flattened. She scurried inside, insulted by the rough way he spoke, and then told Frances Brown in the flat opposite that she'd be informing the caretaker about the noise.

'Is that so?' said Frances, a drab fifty-two-year-old spinster. 'I must admit I never heard a thing.'

'Then you need your ears cleaned,' said Mrs Webb, annoyed her neighbour wasn't supporting her in the way she'd expected.

'Maybe I do,' said Frances, going back into her flat with a huffy look on her face.

Next morning when the Dawsons' youngest son came down the stairs bouncing a ball Mrs Webb was at her door to tell him he wasn't allowed to bounce balls.

'Another thing,' she added as he ran out, 'I hope you know you're not allowed to keep a dog in the flat.'

She was pleased to see him look round startled and later in the day she noticed he had the dog on a lead. But that would make no difference. She was still going to complain.

On another occasion when she was emptying her rubbish the Dawson woman appeared in the back green with a basinful of washing, which she began to peg out.

'That's not your washing line,' said Mrs Webb. 'Yours is the one further back.'

'Is it?' said the woman. 'And how am I supposed to know?'

'You're supposed to enquire.'

'I'll try and remember that in future,' said the woman, continuing to peg out her clothes on the same line.

Mrs Webb was so angry she felt like pulling the line down and jumping on it, but that would have definitely put her in the wrong. She'd just send another letter of complaint to the caretaker, though so far she'd had no reply to her first.

As time passed the Dawsons had the impression they were living on a volcano ready to erupt. When the boys passed Mrs Webb's door she often stood in it, glaring. Once the youngest one called her an old cow and she threatened him with the police.

'Fancy him calling you a cow,' said her neighbour with a slight smile.

'Maybe you think it's funny,' said Mrs Webb.

'No, it's just that –'

'Just what?'

'I don't know.'

Mrs Webb got the feeling she couldn't trust Frances any more, but there was no one else she could talk to. All her neighbours were either too old or too dumb or too unpleasant.

'I hope not,' she said, 'for it's no laughing matter.'

Harry Dawson was furious when he received a letter from the council stating that if he and his family didn't stop persecuting the tenant in the bottom flat they were liable to be evicted. At first he called Mrs Webb all the names he could think of then he began to blame his youngest son for taking the dog round the back green to do its business.

'That's not true. I always walk the dog in the fields,' said Peter.

'It's beside the point,' said Harry, glaring at the Alsatian sitting on the couch. 'It'll have to go.'

'But he's no bother,' said Peter. 'I'll take him out in the dark and nobody will know we've got him.'

'Don't worry,' said his mother. 'We're not getting rid of the dog to suit that old bitch. I just wish somebody would get rid of her.'

'You may have a point,' said her husband. 'But on the other hand I'm not getting put out of this flat because of a bloody dog.'

He lifted the newspaper as if to end the subject then put it down when he saw his wife Rita had on her coat.

'You're not going to that bloody bingo,' he said. 'You must spend a fortune on it.'

'Not as much as you spend in the pub.'

She then searched in her bag for money, which she gave to Peter so that he could have something to eat.

'Thanks, Ma,' he said, pleased to see it was enough for cigarettes.

After she'd gone Harry stood up and said he might as well leave since what was good for one should be good for the other.

'So what will I do here all alone?' said Peter.

'Do what you always do, watch the television or take the dog a walk.'

Peter was glad he'd said that. It meant he could smoke in peace.

Next morning at the crack of dawn Mrs Webb was up at their door.

'Never in all my life did I put in such a night,' she told Rita who answered it. 'All that shouting and bawling, it was terrible.'

'See my husband,' said Rita, pointing backwards with her thumb. 'He's the one to blame.'

'I will,' said Mrs Webb with a bravado she didn't feel.

Harry Dawson came to the door with only his vest and pants on.

'Well?' he said, looking down at her as though she was a mess on his doorstep.

She took a deep breath. 'It's like this, I simply can't put up with the noise from your flat. I've been on tranquillisers since the day you moved in and if you don't quieten down I'll have to do something about it.' She omitted to say she was already doing all she could.

Harry continued to stare at her from under lowered eyebrows. He was trying to assemble his wits, having been so drunk the night before that he couldn't remember a thing.

Finally he said, 'Do what you fucking well like,' and slammed the door in her face.

Mrs Webb stared at it for a moment then in a state of shock turned and went slowly down the stairs, stopping at the bottom to knock on Frances's door.

When Peter got home from school on Monday he found the dog stretched out on the carpet. His mother was talking to a man in a tweed suit but broke off to say she was sorry, the dog had to be put down, since it got out and into Mrs Webb's back garden. 'And you know what she's like about her vegetables,' she added.

Her voice trailed off as Peter tried to lift the dog, but it was so heavy that he had to let it fall back with a thud.

When the vet pointed out that nothing could be done now, as the dog was dead, Peter kicked him on the leg.

'What did you do that for?' said Rita. 'He's only doing his job.'

'It's all right,' said the vet. 'I know how he feels.'

Inwardly he too was upset. He disliked getting rid of healthy animals.

Peter ran out of the room shouting, 'Bastards,' and after that the dog was never mentioned.

2

Mrs Webb was delighted when she heard the dog had been put down. Another letter to the council should see the Dawsons off altogether. It was a pity she couldn't get Frances to write one too, but she had to face the fact Frances was too mealy-mouthed to do anything.

'I wouldn't be able to sleep at night,' she'd said when Mrs Webb asked her.

Mrs Webb had said that was all very well but she couldn't sleep either. However, as Frances made no comment on this, Mrs Webb knew she was wasting her time.

It so happened her triumph over the dog was short-lived when a brick came hurtling through her window one afternoon as she was dozing in front of the television. Immediately she was on her feet and up the stairs like a shot to bang on the Dawsons' door. It was the older son Jim who opened it.

'Is your mother in?' said Mrs Webb, her face twitching so badly she feared she was going to take a stroke.

'No, she isn't,' said Jim sharply, making to close the door but unable to do so since Mrs Webb had stuck out her foot.

'I'll wait until she comes in then,' she said.

Jim was about to say something when Rita appeared. 'What is it now?' she asked.

'Your son has just smashed my window.'

Rita's face hardened. 'It's no use blaming my son. He's not in yet.'

'No, because he's out smashing windows, and mine in particular.'

'How do you know it was him? It could have been a number of kids.'

'I know as sure as the nose on my face.'

Rita gave her a look of disgust then went back inside.

Mrs Webb decided to get the police involved, but first of all she thought she'd tell Frances about it in case there was the slightest chance she'd back her up.

'I wouldn't get the police,' said Frances. 'They'll only say they can do nothing without witnesses.'

Mrs Webb turned pale. 'But surely they'll have to pay me for a new window?'

'Only if you've got witnesses.'

Mrs Webb thought for a minute, then she said, 'How about going as a witness?'

'I couldn't, it would be against my principles to lie.'

'Balderdash,' said Mrs Webb. 'I know it was him and I can't let them get away with it.'

'I've an idea,' said Frances. 'See Councillor Healy. He is easy to talk to and has a sympathetic manner.'

'It's not sympathy I need. It's more like a hit man for quite honestly I think that family is trying to put me into an early grave.'

As if to verify her words the next morning as she was taking in her milk she saw a swastika painted on her door.

She dashed round to the back of the building guessing the Dawsons would still be in bed and began to shout, 'Get up, you lazy shower, and see what your son has done to my door.'

They either didn't hear or pretended not to. As she turned away she was hit with something so sharp and painful she thought she was going to be sick. Then she almost collided with Frances who'd come to see what the commotion was about. When she asked Mrs Webb what had happened the old woman showed her the blood on her hand before she fainted.

'Are you trying to get us put out?' Rita asked her son Peter, who was staring ahead with a blank look on his face.

'The bugger's been trying it since we moved in,' said Harry.

'And burn that,' he added, picking up the catapult lying on the table. 'He should never have had one in the first place.'

'It's only a kid's sling,' said Rita. 'And it was likely an accident. He didn't mean it. Did you, Peter?'

'An accident?' said Harry, his voice rising. 'When the old bitch could have died of a heart attack or something, and your precious son up on a murder charge.'

'It was an accident,' said Peter, coming out of his trance. 'And I bet she wasn't hurt that much or she'd be in hospital.'

'See what I mean, he's not even sorry,' said Harry.

'Why should I be sorry when it was an accident?'

'That settles it,' said Harry. 'I'm going to sort you out once and for all.'

He unbuckled his belt then took a step towards his son who backed off saying, 'I hope you don't think you're going to hit me with that belt?'

'It's the only way to teach you a lesson,' said Harry.

Rita broke in at that point. 'You can't hit him. The law says it's an offence to hit your kids.'

'Well, I say fuck the law,' said Harry.

He raised the belt but before he could bring it down on his son Peter was out the door and down the close stairs as quick as a flash with Harry following, hampered by his trousers that kept falling down.

'Wait until you get back,' he shouted at the empty stairway.

By this time Peter was running along the pavement at a great speed.

When Harry came back into the living room breathing hard Rita said to him that surely there were much better ways of dealing with problems than using a belt.

Harry flung himself into the armchair saying, 'Is that right, well, I'd like to know what they are.'

3

Peter had stopped going to school. At present he was looking over the landing of his old home in the terrace hoping to catch a sight of the girl he'd seen in the lane the previous day. He guessed she was one of the tinkers who'd moved into the house across from Shanky's. When he mumbled a hello to her she'd run off and that was the last of her he'd seen. Now he was hoping she might show up again, but it was becoming too cold and wet to hang around for long so he went inside to strip paper off the walls and burn it in the grate. By this time the ash was almost halfway across the floor.

Then he heard a voice from behind him saying in a strangled sort of tone, 'What the hell do you think you're doing?'

He turned round to see Shanky Devine squinting at him through a roomful of smoke.

'Nothing much,' he said.

'Nothing much?' spluttered Shanky. 'You're tearing all that wallpaper down. Is that nothing much?'

'All right, I'm tearing it down and burning it for a heat,' said Peter. 'If that's all right with you.'

'No, it isn't all right,' said Shanky. 'This is private property.'

'I thought everything was going to be pulled down anyway.'

'Well, you thought wrong,' said Shanky, staring hard at Peter. He added, 'Don't I know you from somewhere?'

'I used to stay here at one time.'

'That's right,' said Shanky. 'You're the kid who threw stones at my door.'

'I don't remember that.'

'Well, I do. You used to get me out of bed just when I needed to sleep.'

'Maybe it was another kid you're thinking of.'

'I don't think so,' said Shanky. Then he changed the subject by asking Peter why he'd come back.

'I like it here. I didn't want to leave.'

Shanky's face softened. 'Then you should have refused to go like I did.'

'How could I when my parents left?'

Actually he was wishing Shanky would go away. He thought he could be crazy if not downright dangerous. He remembered the time when he'd very near strangled a kid on the terrace who was taunting him about his squint. The kid never told his parents in case he got the blame for starting it.

'You can come here any time,' Shanky was now saying, 'so long as you don't mess up the place any worse than it is. It's bad enough trying to keep it in shape with these tinkers around.'

'I won't,' said Peter, trying to keep a straight face. 'But I'll have to go now. My mother expects me in at the back of four.'

'It's nowhere near that time,' said Shanky.

'I don't want to risk being late or she might get the idea I'm not at school.'

'Come early next time so's you can visit me,' said Shanky, 'and I'll get in lemonade and biscuits. You'll like that, won't you?'

'Sure thing,' said Peter, knowing there was no way he would visit Shanky, not even if he was paid to.

As he walked along the cobblestoned lane he could feel the big man's eyes following him right up until he turned into the main thoroughfare.

His father was asleep on the floor when he got into the flat.

'What's the matter with him?' he asked.

'Drunk. You should know by this time he gets drunk on a Friday.'

'He must have got away early when he's that drunk.'

'I wouldn't be surprised if he's got his books and spent the money,' said his mother.

'Neither would I,' said Peter.

She regarded him balefully for a moment then said, 'The school board's been up at the door and says you haven't been to school. What do you say to that?'

'I have been at school. He must have been mixing me up with somebody else.'

Rita shook her head in despair. 'Why do you lie to me all the time?'

'I don't lie to you all the time and when I tell the truth you still don't believe me.'

'No wonder,' she said. They went silent for another while then Rita told him that if he went through his da's pockets to get the pay envelope she wouldn't say anything about him not being at school.

'You won't anyway,' said Peter. 'You couldn't stand the row it would cause. Why don't you get it yourself?'

'Because I'm no good at picking pockets,' she said. 'I'd be bound to waken him.' She added, 'If you do it I'll give you a pound.'

'OK. I'll do it.'

'But I don't want you wasting it on fags.'

'What should I waste it on then?'

'Just get on with it,' said Rita with a sigh.

The pay packet was eventually found on top of the mantelpiece where his father had left it when he came in.

'Thank God for that,' said Rita. 'If I'd only known –'

'Don't forget you still owe me a pound. I had to go through his pockets, remember.'

Rita gave him the money in a grudging manner warning him not to get into trouble since it would be her that got the blame.

★

Later the same evening Peter sat on Shanky's bottom stair smoking a cigarette. It was the best place to go to without being seen, not that he cared too much about being seen, but he didn't want to be in when his da woke up. Besides he'd changed his mind about Shanky. The guy was all right, just a little bit crazy, and that kid he'd nearly strangled probably deserved it.

He crouched low when he heard a door open up above, but not before the tinker had spotted him.

'Hey you, whit are ye daein' doon there?' he called. 'Spyin' on us. Is that it?'

Peter stood up and explained he'd only come to visit a friend but when he found out he wasn't in decided to hang on for a bit.

The tinker said, 'If you're referrin' to that guy who lives ower there, then ye'll hae a long wait. He'll no' be back until the morrow.'

'Then I might as well go home,' said Peter.

Before he could move away the tinker asked him how it was he'd never seen him visiting the guy before.

'I don't visit him that often.'

'I'm surprised you visit him at a',' said the tinker. 'I'd soon as visit the devil.'

Peter blew upon his hands that had become cold. 'He's not as bad as all that. They say his bark's worse than his bite.'

'Maybe so,' said the tinker, then he asked Peter in a kindlier tone would he like to come up and get a drink of something that would heat him up for he looked fair frozen.

'Thanks, but I'd better not.'

'Is oor company no' good enough?' said the tinker, his voice turning harsh again.

'All right, I'll come.'

The room was lit up by candles and a big log fire. In front of the fire the tinker's wife sat with her child.

'Who's this?' she asked when Peter came in through the door with the tinker.

'He says he wis waitin' on the guy next door,' the tinker explained. 'Gie him a drink o' that wine. Ye can see he looks frozen.'

The woman poured out some dark liquid into a cup, which Peter found surprisingly sweet and easy to swallow.

'And so how well dae ye know the guy next door?' the woman asked him suspiciously.

'Not all that much,' he said, thinking it best to say as little as possible. 'I knew him better at one time.'

'Then how were ye visitin' him?' she asked in a demanding tone.

'I was running away and there was nowhere else to go.'

'Dae ye hear that?' she said to her husband. 'He wis runnin' away.'

The tinker shook his head in disbelief and took a gulp from the bottle.

The woman said to Peter, 'I widny advise you to hae onythin' tae dae wi' yon fella. My daughter has just newly disappeared and I'm positive he had somethin' to dae wi' it.'

'There's nae proof,' said the tinker. 'So haud yer tongue.'

'I don't need proof,' said his wife. 'I jist have tae look at his ugly face and I can tell he's a bad wan.'

She poured more dark liquid into Peter's cup, which he drank over too quickly then felt as if he was going to pass out.

But when the woman asked him if he was willing to put money towards another bottle, considering he'd drunk a third of what they had, he sobered up and told her he would have to go to the toilet before he counted out his money but instead when he left the room he quietly opened the front door and ran down the stairs as fast as he could.

The following morning his mother woke him up to say he was going to school whether he liked it or not.

'I can't,' he said, pulling the covers over his face. 'I'm ill.'

'I'm not surprised considering the time you got home. It's a good job your father didn't hear you, but anyway you're going, ill or not.'

'But I am ill, really ill. I'm not kidding.'

This wasn't a lie. His head felt as if it were made of lead and his eyes filled with grit. He doubted he had the energy to stand up.

'I don't care how ill you are,' said Rita. 'You're going to school and to make sure you do I'm coming with you.'

Unable to think of a reason that would put her off he got out of bed and stumbled about looking for his clothes.

In the classroom the teacher remarked on his continual yawning.

'It's not natural,' she said. 'Is there something wrong with you?'

'Yes, I'm tired.'

When the pupils began to titter the teacher told him to see the headmaster and ask to be given two of the belt for distracting the class. He nodded as if that's what he was going to do then walked straight out through the main entrance in order to head for the terrace hoping Shanky would be in by now.

'It's you,' said Shanky when he opened his door without making any move to let him pass.

Peter blinked nervously. 'I thought you said I could visit you.'

'Did I?' said Shanky, shaking his head as if in denial of this, then, noticing the tinker's wife staring at him from across the landing, he added, 'All right, come on in. I don't want these tinkers listening to every damn thing we say.'

Peter followed him inside at the same time explaining how the tinkers weren't that bad when they'd invited him into their house last night and given him two or three glasses of wine.

Shanky was aghast. 'Well, I wouldn't have went in or drank their wine for a fortune. It could have been poisoned.'

'You can see that it wasn't, for here I am,' said Peter.

'They'd no right giving you strong drink,' said Shanky. 'They could have got the jail for that.'

'Maybe they thought I was a lot older than what I am,' said Peter. 'Anyway I only went in the first place thinking I would see the daughter.'

'What daughter is that?'

'The tinkers' daughter. You must have seen her yourself when her folks stay right next to you.'

'Well, I've never seen her,' said Shanky, 'and that's a fact.'

As if to change the subject he turned round and lifted a silver-framed photograph off the mantelpiece then began to study it so intently Peter was obliged to ask whose photo was it.

'My mother's,' said Shanky. 'You can see she was a fine-looking woman.'

Peter thought she bore a close resemblance to Shanky.

'I take it she's dead?' he asked.

'Yes, but she can still come back and tell me when folk are planning to rob me.'

'You mean in your dreams?'

'She tells me when I'm awake.'

Peter stared close into Shanky's face to see if he was kidding but he looked deadly serious. All the same he didn't believe this about his mother. It might be Shanky's idea of a warning. Folk who weren't right in the head could be very cunning.

'I hope you don't think I'd rob you,' he said. 'It's the last thing on my mind.'

'I wasn't meaning you,' said Shanky. 'It's these damned tinkers I was meaning. My mother's already warned me about them. She thinks they intend to rob me.'

Peter thought it wouldn't take a dead person to figure that one out, but apart from anything else he began to think that Shanky must have money stashed away somewhere in the house when he was so worried abut tinkers robbing him.

'She could be right,' he said.

4

'**A** woman to see you,' said the councillor's wife, putting her head round the door of the study then adding in a waspish tone, 'she says it's urgent.'

'Show her in,' said the councillor, wishing people would stick to the surgery hours instead of coming to his house and giving his wife the opportunity to be sarcastic.

The woman entered, clutching her handbag. 'I'm sorry to bother you,' she said, 'but I simply had to see someone.'

'Do sit down,' he said, pointing to a chair, and adding, 'but take your time.'

She sat facing him over the table, breathing hard, he noticed, by the rise and fall of her chest, then she handed him a letter explaining it was from the housing manager threatening to put her and her family out because of their bad behaviour, which, she added in a burst of anguish, wasn't true.

He read the letter slowly. Apart from some minor details it was similar to ones he'd read before.

When he'd finished he said, 'What isn't true, Mrs er —?'

'Dawson. Rita Dawson. It isn't true we make a lot of noise. We only make the usual noise anybody would make if they had two boys in the house. And if my husband and I have the occasional row and happen to raise our voices, what couple doesn't?'

What indeed, he thought, recalling the noisy rows he used to have with his wife that ended in grim silence for days. Now they'd got beyond that stage and hardly spoke at all.

'Granted,' he said. 'But it also states your husband was abusive to one of the neighbours, namely a Mrs Webb.'

373

She looked at him helplessly. 'I know what you're saying, but I can't do anything about that.'

'I see,' he said, puzzled by the remark, which appeared to be the opposite of what she'd said before.

He returned his attention to the letter. 'It's also written that one of your sons hit this same neighbour with a stone and she had to go to hospital. Isn't that a bit drastic?'

'It was an accident,' she said dully. 'He was aiming at a bird.'

'Even so,' he said, stroking his chin thoughtfully.

She gave him a sigh then said, 'You have to understand this old woman's never had a family living above her. Any kind of noise upsets her. I think she expects us to go about on our tiptoes all the time.'

'No doubt,' he said, 'but while I do understand your problems and would really love to help you, this kind of situation does not come within my jurisdiction. You'd be better to see the housing manager.'

'I've tried to, but he's never in.'

'I see,' he said, becoming irritated. 'Well, I'm afraid that –'

He suddenly stopped talking when she leaned over the table and said in an urgent tone, 'Actually I want a divorce.'

'A divorce?' he said, drawing back and thinking she could be slightly deranged. 'You'd have to see a lawyer for that.'

'Yes, but I can't get a divorce if I'm living with my husband, and I can't move away until I get another flat and what with the council threatening to put us all out I don't know which way to turn. I mean they'll probably send us to some horrible housing scheme where we'll be stuck there for years.'

She blinked her eyes as she spoke and he thought between that and her face all flushed she looked prettier than he'd thought at first.

'So it's not really about your neighbour,' he said. 'It's about you wanting a divorce.'

'Something like that,' she said. 'If I could only get a place of my own I'd know what to do and I was so sure that you'd help me. I've been told you're a great man for helping the people.'

'Have you indeed?' he said, trying not to look smug. 'Well, I must admit I do try my best for people. It's my job.'

'So will you do your best for me?'

He tapped his lip with his forefinger apparently deep in thought then he said, 'All right, I'll talk to the housing manager at the next meeting and see what I can do, but of course I can't promise anything.'

'You will?' she said, her lips parting with surprise and pleasure. 'That's really awfully good of you.'

'So,' he said with a slight tremor in his voice, 'if you meet me outside the county buildings next Tuesday evening at nine o'clock I'll let you know what's happening.'

He saw her to the door, careful not to stare at her openly, but he could tell she had a good figure under her coat. Back in the study he poured himself out a stiff drink of whisky with the feeling that he needed it somehow.

Mrs Webb threw a rasher of bacon into the frying pan then cracked in an egg to go with it. The doctor had said that too much fried food was bad for her, especially after the shock, but she had decided she never felt so good as she did at the moment with all that rest, and fried food was the only kind she'd ever liked.

She'd just finished her meal and was wiping the crumbs from her cheeks when she saw Rita Dawson pass her kitchenette window to go into the back green. By the time she'd returned Mrs Webb was standing at her door.

'Excuse me,' she said in a timid sort of voice, unlike her usual brusque tone. 'Do you think you could do me a favour?'

Rita was surprised. She'd never expected the old bitch to ask her for a favour especially in the light of what had happened with the catapult.

'What is it?' she asked doubtfully.

'Well, if you're going to the shops at any time this morning, do you think you could bring me back a pint of milk? I haven't been able to manage out after all the trouble I had.'

Rita had the grace to look embarrassed. 'I always meant to tell you how sorry I was, but it was an accident, and Peter will never be allowed to have a sling again.'

Mrs Webb said stiffly, 'If it was an accident there's nothing much I can say about it except I hope it doesn't happen again.'

'It's good of you to look at it like that,' said Rita. 'Did you say a pint of milk?'

'Yes, if it's not too much bother.'

'Of course not. Is that all you need?'

'Well, there might be one or two other things. If you come in a minute I'll give you a list.'

Frances, who'd opened her door when she heard the voices, couldn't believe her eyes when she saw Rita Dawson enter Mrs Webb's flat. After all that had been said about the woman it was like a stab in the back. What were they saying that was so private that they had to go inside? They must be talking about her. She couldn't see it being anything else.

5

Early on Monday morning Tom Ashton entered the social work department and asked for the report on Peter Dawson.

'I haven't finished it yet,' said the typist with a flirtatious glance in his direction. Tom was single and not bad-looking, his main fault being, as far as the office staff were concerned, that he was far too serious.

'I'm in a bit of a hurry,' he said, trying to keep the irritation out of his voice.

His problem was that he hadn't been in the job long enough to keep cool about such things as clients who barricaded themselves in, children neglected near enough to death, and delayed reports. Sometimes the way he worried about everything made him suspect that he wasn't cut out for the job but then most of the other social workers he'd met didn't appear to be cut out for it either.

The typist said icily, 'I'll be as quick as I can, but you're not the only one who expects everything to be done on the dot.'

'Sorry,' he said, not wanting to cause offence since typists had been known to lose reports out of sheer spite. 'I know you've a lot to do.'

Ten minutes later she handed him the report saying, 'Don't say I'm not good to you.'

'Thanks a million,' he said, smiling at her widely and deciding not to bother checking it in front of her in case she'd got the names of the clients wrong and he'd be forced to let her know.

'I'd be careful of that last client,' she said as he was going out the door. 'They say he's a bit funny and even dangerous.'

'So what should I do then?'

'Act as though he's normal.'

Tom said, 'All my clients are normal. It's their lives that aren't.'

The typist looked down at her typewriter. She didn't want to talk about his clients. She wanted Tom to ask her out.

Half an hour later Rita opened her front door, then tried to close it again, guessing the man confronting her was a social worker.

'You may as well let me in,' said Tom. 'I'm not going away.'

She allowed him to come in then asked him in a truculent manner, 'So, what's he done now?'

Tom didn't answer, thinking it was best to wait until he was well inside.

Harry, who'd taken a day off work due to migraine brought on by his family, looked up at him with loathing.

'Who the hell are you?' he asked. 'Not a cop, I hope?'

'I'm a social worker.'

'Christ, that's about as bad. Is it about him?'

'Him?'

'My son Peter, who else?'

'You might as well sit down while you're here,' said Rita.

Once he'd sat he took out a sheet of paper from his briefcase and said, 'What I want to know is why your son has been at school only once in the past three weeks. What's his reason?'

'He doesn't need a reason,' said Harry. 'It's more like a belting he needs.' Glaring at Rita he added, 'The fact is he's been mollycoddled since the day he was born. But of course I'm not allowed to say anything or she goes off her head.'

'Listen to him,' said Rita. 'You can tell he's back in the Victorian era when kids got belted for nothing.'

'That boy would never get belted for nothing,' said Harry.

Tom decided to intervene. 'I don't think belting solves anything. What you both should do is sit down with Peter and find out why he stays off school. Perhaps he's getting bullied, or perhaps being a new pupil he feels out of things. I know it can be diffi-cult but –'

'You're bloody right, it can be difficult,' said Harry. 'I've tried talking to him but he doesn't listen. His eyes go blank and he stares into the distance. He's supposed to be my son but I some-times wonder.'

'He doesn't listen because all you do is nark,' said Rita.

'And what do you do, give him money for fags so as you can go to the bingo.' He looked at Tom. 'Do you know, nearly every night she goes to the bingo? That's a lot worse than narking.'

Tom thought it a waste of time to continue with the discussion but he said anyway, 'The thing to keep in mind is that parents have a duty to see that their children attend school, because if they don't the children will be sent to an approved school where they'll be kept in most of the time. Over and above that the parents themselves will either be fined or sent to jail. In this case it would be the father.'

Harry threw the newspaper he'd been holding across the room.

'I'm not paying any goddamned fine,' he said. 'I'll go to jail first, and as for him being sent to an approved school, that suits me down to the ground.'

Tom decided at that point it was time to leave.

Rita saw him to the door saying, 'Don't listen to him. He's all mouth. He doesn't know what he's saying.'

Tom nodded as though agreeing then gave her a card. 'Tell Peter to see me at this address after school hours,' he said. 'Not that I expect he will have gone.'

'Right,' she said, watching him go down the stairs, then posi-tive she heard Mrs Webb's door close after he passed.

A few days later Peter was standing at the close entrance with his hood turned up to keep out the rain. He'd got back from the terrace at the usual time to find his mother wasn't in, yet the door had been left unlocked and it wasn't like her to leave it like that.

At first he thought she had gone to the afternoon bingo and it had continued longer than usual. But as time passed he began to think she had gone for good.

He went into her room to see if the clothes were still in the wardrobe and the empty space inside it struck him like a sudden death.

Despite this he went back out into the close to wait for her in case there was some other explanation.

Mrs Webb, whose ears were always attuned to the least little sound, opened her door and asked him what he was doing standing there with his hood up. Was he planning to paint her door with more disgusting words or perhaps smash a window or two? He didn't answer this, hoping she'd go away, but when she enquired in an insinuating tone if his mother wasn't even in yet he was stung into saying she'd probably left home and if she had it was all Mrs Webb's fault for complaining about them to the council.

'My fault?' she said, outraged. 'Why it was only the other day your mother was good enough to fetch me a pint of milk and there was no mention of complaints then. If you ask me she was more likely to be driven away by yourself and your horrible drunken father.'

'Everybody knows you sent letters about us to the council,' said Peter. 'And I hope you die and rot in hell.'

'I don't know what you're talking about,' said Mrs Webb. 'I've never complained about anybody in my life.'

By this time Peter had walked out the close into the lashing rain.

Half an hour later Harry Dawson came home from his work surprised to find no one in the flat and no sign of anything being cooked for his dinner. Where the hell is she? he wondered. She'd no right being out at this time. She knew he'd be coming in starving. Finally he was forced to peel a potato, which was all he could find in the vegetable rack, along with the tin of beans on a shelf.

He was opening it when Jim, his older son, came into the kitchenette and asked him with a bemused look on his face what he was doing.

'Opening a bloody tin of beans,' said Harry, 'and if you think that's funny, I'll tell you something funnier, your mother has gone.'

'Gone?'

'Yes, gone, beat it, scarpered.'

'You mean for good?'

'I wouldn't be surprised.'

Depression seeped all over Jim. If this was true it meant he would have to make his own food and do his own washing. Even at this moment he noticed the denims he'd been going to put on later were still up on the pulley.

'This is terrible,' he said. 'Didn't she leave a letter or something?'

'Not even a bloody postcard, but that's your mother all over, selfish to the core.'

'How do you know she's gone? She might just be out somewhere. Maybe still at the bingo.'

'I don't think so,' said Harry. 'She's been saying she was going for a long time. I never thought she would do it, though.'

'Oh,' said Jim, becoming more dejected with every word his father spoke.

'Where's Peter?' he asked listlessly. 'Does he know?'

'I don't know and I don't care,' said Harry. 'He's likely out somewhere smoking himself to death and she'll be away with another man. All these nights at the bingo didn't fool me.'

'You think so?' said Jim, trying to picture his mother with another man, and failing since he couldn't see her being attractive enough.

'To think all these years I knocked my pan in working for her,' said Harry, 'and this is the thanks I get. If she does come back I'm not letting her in, and I don't want you letting her in either.'

Jim had stopped listening. All he could think of was that he'd have to cough up money for a fish supper if he wanted to eat, which meant he would have hardly any money left for a night out with his mates.

'Christ,' he groaned, hating his mother for leaving.

Whoever she'd been thinking of certainly wasn't him.

6

'I t's you,' said Shanky when he opened the door.

'Sorry to disappoint you,' said Tom. 'Were you expecting someone else?'

'None of your business,' said Shanky, turning and walking up the lobby while Tom followed wanting to sit down. His feet were killing him.

'Right,' he began when they were inside the living room. 'I know you're not prepared to leave but let me point out it's quite possible this building is going to collapse any day, and it seems to me persisting in staying on is just another way of committing suicide.'

'Nothing's going to collapse,' said Shanky. As if to prove his point he punched the wall.

'Another thing,' said Tom. 'There are rats everywhere. They're going to get into your food if you're not careful, that is if they haven't got in already. Maybe you don't care about that but being poisoned by rat droppings is one of the worst ways to go.'

'I've never seen rats no more than usual,' said Shanky. 'And if there are it's because of these damned tinkers throwing rubbish everywhere. Get on to them. They're the ones who should be put out.'

'Maybe,' said Tom. 'But they don't come under my authority. However, if it's any consolation to you they should be going away soon.'

'Meanwhile they can break into my house and steal everything I've got?' said Shanky pettishly.

'I can only suggest you get a strong lock on your door,' said Tom.

'I heard tinkers can break strong locks,' said Shanky.

'Then leave,' said Tom. 'I've told you a thousand times the council is prepared to give you a new flat, with a cooker, a bath, and central heating that can be turned on by a switch. What more could you ask for?'

'I like my own house better,' said Shanky.

'But your own house is going to be pulled down,' said Tom. 'Can't you get it into your head?'

Past caring what Shanky thought, he sat down and lit up a cigarette.

Shanky stared hard at it then said, 'Since you're so worried about me being poisoned by rats you should be worried about yourself smoking. I've heard it can kill you as well and I keep telling the young fellow that, but he doesn't listen.'

'What young fellow?' said Tom.

A wary looked passed over Shanky's face. 'He's nobody in particular. Just somebody I know.'

'Do you see this young fellow often?'

'Only when he passes by my window,' said Shanky. Then he added impatiently, 'Look, I can't stand here talking all day. I've got my work to go to.'

Tom could barely conceal his surprise. 'What kind of work?'

'I'm a night-watchman at the sawmill.'

'That's very good,' Tom said, glad to hear the man was doing something useful.

Before he left, he reminded Shanky to think about the new flat since he might not get another chance and could finish up in a seedy lodging house or something similar.

'I'll think about it,' said Shanky, in a weak sort of voice as though he had no intention.

'I may be home late this evening,' said the councillor. 'It's one of those meetings that can go on for hours.'

His wife said she didn't know why he was bothering to tell her this, as he didn't usually.

'I'm sure I always do,' said the councillor, gazing at her long-suffering face and wishing he didn't dislike her so much.

On his way out he stopped in the hallway to look at himself in the mirror and was reassured by what he saw, a man with heavy and powerful features something like Marlon Brando in *The Godfather* but not nearly as gross.

Rita was waiting by the railings outside the county buildings when he drew up in his car.

'Sorry if I'm late,' he said. 'The meeting took longer than I anticipated.'

'That's all right. I've just got here.'

He drove to the outskirts of the town where they got out and entered a posh-looking hotel. Inside it was just as posh with its plush seats and pink lampshades. When they were seated in a secluded spot picked out by the councillor a waitress came over and asked what they wanted.

'Nothing really,' said Rita, wishing she hadn't come.

The councillor frowned. 'You must have something, it looks odd otherwise.'

'All right, a beer.'

'Are you sure?' he said. 'Only a beer?'

In the end they both ordered gin and tonics. When the waitress had gone he put his hand over hers saying he was glad she managed to come.

'I came because of the flat,' said Rita stiffly.

'Ah yes, the flat,' said the councillor. 'Unfortunately the housing meeting has been postponed for a fortnight, so I won't be seeing the housing manager until then.'

Rita looked dismayed. 'But I can't wait that long. I have left my husband and am staying with my sister. Already she's making it plain she doesn't want me. If she tells me to get out I've nowhere to go.'

The councillor said nothing for the moment, then declared, 'I'm afraid you'll just have to try and hang on with her as long as possible. I'm sure if you explain the situation she'll be reasonable.'

'Do you think so?' said Rita gloomily.

When the waitress arrived with the order Rita drank the contents of her glass in a gulp, then felt exceedingly hot.

'You look pretty when you blush,' he said.

'I'm not blushing,' she said. 'It's the drink.'

'Then I'll have to get you another,' he said, and before she could refuse he was on his way up to the bar.

When he returned she told him he shouldn't have bothered. She was going as her sister wouldn't like her staying out late and drinking.

'But we've hardly been in the place,' he said. 'And you can't call this late.'

'I know, but I'd better go,' said Rita firmly.

He shrugged his shoulders and said if that's what she wanted he would drive her back.

'So long as you don't stop too near my sister's house.'

As they left the hotel he took her arm in a friendly way, which surprised her and encouraged her to ask if he was still going to see about the flat in a fortnight's time.

'Of course,' he said soothingly, 'so don't worry your pretty little head about it.'

The words reassured her. She decided she had misjudged him and said she was really sorry she had to leave so soon but she felt it was for the best.

'I understand,' he said, but when they got into the car he made no move to drive off.

'Have you ran out of petrol?' she asked.

He turned to her with a smile. 'No, my dear, but I really don't think we should go back so soon.'

'This isn't good enough,' said her sister, coming to the door in her dressing gown.

'You should have gave me a door key then if you didn't want disturbed.'

'And have you coming in drunk at all hours.'

'I only had a couple of drinks with a friend.'

'That is if you're speaking the truth,' said her sister. 'But I'm not going to stand here all night arguing.'

Rita watched her go with dismay. She wouldn't be surprised if she was asked to leave, and despite what had happened in the car she was no nearer to getting what she wanted.

'See what you can do with this,' he'd said, thrusting his penis into her hand, which she almost let go, that is until it occurred to her this could be the price she'd have to pay in return for the flat. Oh well, she thought, if that was all he wanted she was quite willing. Masturbation was likely all he could manage anyway.

Afterwards she asked him if everything had been all right.

'Fine,' he said, pulling up his zip. 'What about you?'

'Oh, I'm all right,' she said. 'Actually I've got my period, so –'

'That settles it,' he said. 'Better luck next time. I'll be in touch.'

Although his tone was brusque she was glad there was going to be a next time, which would allow her to bring up the subject of the flat, otherwise she might be forced back to Harry, a prospect she couldn't face. But as she was climbing in between her sister's cold sheets she remembered he'd said nothing about how he would be in touch.

7

'I tell ye I've never seen hide nor hair o' her.'

The speaker was a ravaged-faced woman in her late forties with short bleached hair. She wore clothes that were skimpy and tight-fitting but in comparison to her sister Flora, whom she was addressing, she looked smart.

Flora said to her husband, 'Listen tae that, George. She's never been near Maggie's. Whit'll we dae?'

'How should I know,' said George, sinking into a chair and rolling himself a cigarette from the tobacco tin on the table.

When Flora began to cry weakly Maggie told her to pull herself together.

'She canny be faur away,' she said. 'Folk don't jist disappear. It'll be a matter o' lookin' for her mair thoroughly.'

'We've looked thoroughly,' said George. 'Whit else can we dae?'

Maggie stared round the miserable room with hardly any furniture then at the fire in the grate, which appeared to be out.

'Nae wonder she left,' she said. 'This place is no' fit for animals. Whitever happened tae that nice caravan ye had?'

'We selt it,' said Flora. 'There wis a' these fines.' She looked at her husband as she spoke, whose gaze immediately became fixed elsewhere.

Maggie pushed down the child, who'd been trying to climb on her lap ever since she'd arrived.

'Take him away,' said Maggie. 'He's dirtyin' ma new skirt, and put some shoes on his feet. They must be frozen.'

'He'll only kick them aff,' said Flora, lifting him up and holding him close as if he was very precious.

Maggie shook her head at the sight of them, then told George to go and get her a bottle of something that would put her in a good mood, for she was damned if she could do it herself in this place.

'Anythin' else while you're at it?' he asked.

'Fags, which no doubt you'll be smokin' as well as me.'

Once he was out the door she said to Flora, 'I don't know how you can stick him, pregnant or no'. You should get away frae here afore it's too late.'

Flora said, 'If it wisny for Greta disappearin' I wid, but I'm aye thinkin' she'll be back, and if I'm no' here she'll no' know where to get me.'

'Don't make that the excuse. Ye jist huvny the guts,' said Maggie.

They dropped the subject when George came in with a big black bottle and a packet of fags, both of which he put on the table.

'I suppose ye'll hae been talkin' aboot me as usual?' he said with a toothless grin.

'We've better things tae talk aboot,' said Maggie. 'For instance where the hell can Greta be?'

'We've been talkin' aboot that oorselves for the past week,' said George. 'And we're nae further forward.'

He then put the bottle to his mouth before Maggie could grab it off him.

'Act civilized for once,' she said, pouring out the liquor into three cracked cups.

'Whit I canny understaun',' she added, after taking a sip then smacking her lips appreciatively, 'is how ye never telt the cops. Ye'd hae thought that wid have been the first thing tae dae.'

'Because,' said George, 'as soon as we gi'ed them this address they wid have put us oot. We're no' supposed to be here.'

'That's nae excuse,' said Maggie. 'It's yer daughter that's disappeared, no' some dug.'

'Stepdaughter,' George corrected.

'Right, stepdaughter,' said Maggie in a dry tone.

When the child tried to climb up her knee again she said to nobody in particular, 'Tell him tae get aff me.'

'It's well seen you've never had ony weans,' said Flora huffily, dragging the child over to the sink and wiping him with a wet grey cloth, then adding after a pause, 'I bet George never telt ye aboot the man who stays the other side o' the landin'.'

'Naw, whit aboot him?'

'He wis seen talkin' tae Greta a while back and I'm sure he knows somethin' aboot her disappearance.'

'Don't listen tae her,' said George. 'Because he spoke tae her doesny mean onythin'.'

'I don't care,' said Flora. 'I still think he knows mair than whit he lets on.'

'Maybe he does,' said Maggie. 'So how did ye no' ask him whit they wir talkin' aboot?'

'George says if we ask him onythin' it'll only put him on his guard.'

'Well, I'm gaun tae have a word wi' him first thing in the mornin',' said Maggie, 'and we'll see whit he says then.'

'Dae whit ye like,' said George, 'but watch ye don't end up in the jail insteid o' him.'

'Naw, but whit George really wants is tae breck intae the guy's hoose while he's away,' said Flora. 'That's his main concern, no' Greta.'

'He can dae that wance we've found oot where she is,' said Maggie, 'but no' before.'

'Aye, a'right then,' said George, 'but it never entered ma mind.'

Shanky's heart sank when he saw the woman waiting for him at the bottom of the stairs. He tried to sidle past her but she blocked his path, her arms folded across her chest.

'I want a word wi' you,' she said. 'It's aboot ma niece who seems to have disappeared off the face o' this earth, and since you wir the wan who wis seen speakin' tae her, we were wonderin' jist how much ye know.'

'I know nothing,' said Shanky, trying to avoid her piercing stare.

Maggie began to lose her temper. 'You're nothin' but a lyin' bastard,' she said. 'Ye wir seen takin' her intae yer hoose. And don't deny it. There's witnesses.'

He looked around for means of escape, but seeing none he attempted to push her aside, but she scarcely flinched, her body being so strong and sinewy. Realising he wasn't going to get past her easily he told her that on second thoughts he did remember telling a young girl of maybe around thirteen or so to stop chalking on the stairs. She could have been her niece for all he knew.

'So, ye done her in because she wis chalkin' on your stairs,' said Maggie with a grim smile.

'I tell you I never laid a finger on her,' said Shanky. 'Why don't you believe me?'

'Because you've the face o' a liar and it's no' up tae me whether tae believe ye or no'. It's up tae him.' She pointed in the direction of a window where the tinker could be seen looking stonily down at them.

'I can only tell him the same thing as I'm telling you,' said Shanky, wiping the sweat from his forehead. 'Anyway how do you know something's happened to her. She could have gone off without telling anybody.'

'Maybe,' said Maggie, giving him a dark sardonic glance, 'but if ye want tae convince me ye've never laid a finger on her let me come intae yer hoose and I'll know if Greta's been inside by the smell. She's got that special kind o' smell that only a young lassie has that's still a virgin. If there's nae smell I'll know yer tellin' the truth.'

Shanky was horrified. 'I can't let you in. My mother would turn in her grave.'

'Oh, wid she?' said Maggie, tossing her head. 'Well, if ye don't let me in I'll tell ma brither-in-law you've been acting as guilty as hell and he'll soon sort ye oot.'

Shanky closed his eyes in order to blot out her sharp sneering face, remembering how his mother had warned him never to lash out when angered or provoked since he didn't know his own strength.

'Come in,' he said with a sinking heart.

Maggie stared around the living room with its dull furniture and faded linoleum and said she wouldn't mind having a place like this but with more colour to it as she'd never seen anything so drab. Her gaze fell on the photograph of his mother.

'Who's this?' she asked.

'My mother.'

'The one who's aboot to turn in her grave?'

He gave a nod so brief he might as well have not bothered. Then he asked her if she could smell anything reminding her of her niece.

'It's hard to say when the place is that bloody stinkin',' she said, walking off into the room that used to be his mother's with Shanky following. She then opened the wardrobe door and sniffed inside. 'There's a smell of something rotten in here.'

'That's mothballs. My mother always put mothballs in her coat to keep it good.'

'Well, I just hope you're right,' she said, and went on to remark that there was plenty of clothes here that a poor body would be glad of, especially her sister who'd hardly a stitch to her back.

'Leave my mother's clothes,' said Shanky. 'I won't have you touching them.'

'I widny touch them wi' a bargepole,' she said.

Out on the doorstep he asked her if she was satisfied that there was no smell of her niece in his house and she said she wasn't completely satisfied since there were places she hadn't looked into, for instance under the floorboards. Tomorrow she would get her brother-in-law to come and lift them up just to make sure.

8

Mrs Webb opened her door in time to see Harry Dawson go up the stairs to his flat. She was inclined to think he must be drunk, though it was hard to tell from the back. Actually she'd lost interest in him after his wife had gone away, discovering there's nothing so boring as spying on a drunk man. She was about to go inside when the banging started. He must be locked out, she thought. The last time that happened he'd banged on his door for ages, driving her crazy. She wasn't going to put up with that again.

After rushing upstairs to his landing she went over and shouted in his ear, 'Stop that, there's nobody in. Can't you tell?'

'Shove off,' he said, without looking round.

'I won't shove off until you stop that noise,' she said. 'No wonder your wife left you.'

This time he did look round. 'She didn't leave me, I put her out.'

'That's not what I heard.'

He stared at her in the fixed manner of a drunk, then lifted a cigarette from behind his ear and asked her for a match.

'I haven't got any,' she said indignantly, then went on to say that he should leave a spare key with someone in the close and save all this bother.

'You mean I should leave a spare key with you?'

'Heaven forbid,' she said. 'Leave it with the old man upstairs. He's always in.'

'He wouldn't hear me if I went to his door. He's stone deaf.'

'Suit yourself,' she said impatiently. 'It's your problem.'

He put the cigarette back behind his ear and told her in a burst of confidence that actually his wife left him for another man.

'Really,' said Mrs Webb, trying to sound casual. 'Who?'

'Councillor fucking Healy.'

Two red dots of excitement appeared on the old woman's cheeks. 'Fancy that.'

'Yes, fancy.'

It was then she asked him if he'd like to wait in her flat until somebody arrived with a key, since he could stand out here for long enough.

'I might as well,' he said, following her downstairs.

Once inside she handed him a box of matches then asked if he was really sure his wife was having an affair with Councillor Healy since it seemed unlikely.

'They were seen together,' he said. 'What more do you want?'

'Being seen together might not mean much,' said Mrs Webb, wanting to be certain of her facts before she told Frances.

'In the back of a car?'

'That's different,' she said.

After that the conversation petered out and Mrs Webb became bored.

She pointed up at the ceiling. 'I thought I heard somebody come in.'

'It must be one of my sons,' he said, then apologised to her for any trouble he'd caused.

'That's all right,' she said. 'If you ever need anything let me know.'

'I doubt it,' he said, turning to go.

'That's all right then,' she said again, closing the door behind him and hoping Frances would be in since she could hardly wait to put her in the picture.

★

'So how's things?' asked Peter, making himself at home in Shanky's chair by the fire, which Shanky didn't seem to mind.

'Couldn't be worse,' he said. 'One of them damned tinker women pushed her way in here then said she was going to get her brother-in-law to lift up the floorboards.'

Peter's mouth fell open. 'What for?'

'She thinks I killed her niece.'

'Didn't you once say you'd caught her chalking on your stairs?'

'Yeah, but I didn't know who she was at the time.'

Then he asked Peter if he could smell anything like perfume or sweat or anything like that.

'I can only smell you.'

'It's not me I'm talking about,' said Shanky. 'It's her niece. That damned tinker woman said she could tell if her niece had been in this house by the smell, and that's why her brother-in-law is coming to lift up the floorboards.'

'I don't get it,' said Peter. 'What's floorboards got to do with perfume or sweat?'

'You're not listening,' said Shanky. 'I've already told you, but anyway this tinker woman must be crazy to think I'd harm her niece. As if I'd harm anybody, come to that.'

'You might if they made you mad enough.'

'I'd never be that mad,' said Shanky. 'Though I must admit I wanted to kill her when she was looking at my mother's clothes.'

'And I wouldn't have blamed you,' said Peter. 'But if you ask me I'd say she wanted the floorboards lifted so she could find out if that's where you keep your money.'

Shanky flew into a rage. 'I don't have any money and I don't know where some folk get their ideas from.'

'Me neither,' said Peter.

He considered Shanky must have plenty of money when he was so touchy about it. Then he got an idea on how to find this out for a fact.

'Why don't you buy yourself a gun?' he said. 'I know some-body who'll sell you one for twenty pounds.'

'Where would I get twenty pounds?' said Shanky. 'And anyway what would I do with a gun?'

'With a gun you could protect yourself against these tinkers who're coming to lift your floorboards. You'd just have to point it at them and they'd soon leave you alone.'

Shanky frowned as though considering this point, then he said, 'But what would my mother say? She was always against guns. She wouldn't let me have one when I was a kid.'

'How could she know if she's dead?'

'She'd still know,' said Shanky. 'Anyway I won't get any money until Friday.'

'Friday's too late.'

'Then let's forget it.'

'That's OK,' said Peter, 'but I don't want to hear any more complaints about tinkers.'

'All right, you won't.'

'Especially when I was only trying to do you a good turn.'

'I know,' said Shanky. Then he added, 'Apart from that I don't know how to handle a gun. I might shoot somebody accidentally, even myself.'

'You might,' said Peter. He'd lost interest now that the scheme had fallen flat. 'I've got to go now,' he added, then recollecting his mother wouldn't be in.

'But it's nowhere near four,' said Shanky, looking at the clock on the mantelpiece. 'If it's because you're hungry I could make you a sandwich.'

'I'm not hungry,' said Peter. 'But I could do with some money for fags.'

'I told you I've got no money,' said Shanky, putting his hands into his pockets and showing Peter the lining. Then suddenly his face brightened. 'Wait there a minute, I've just remembered something.'

He dashed out the room, which made Peter think he might be getting some money after all.

A minute later he dashed in again holding aloft an iron bar.

'I just remembered. I had this in the coal cellar. Don't you think this is as good a weapon as any?'

9

'Is it because your mother has left home that you're bunking school?'

Tom was addressing Peter in the small room of the social work department set aside for his clients, while Peter stared blankly ahead.

'I know it can't be great for you with your mother away,' Tom added, 'but that doesn't give you the right to bunk school. You're only making it worse for yourself.'

'I don't care,' said Peter, suddenly breaking his silence. 'In any case my ma's going to send for me when she gets a new flat.'

'Who told you?'

'She did. She sent me a letter.'

Tom wondered on this, but whether true or not it made no difference. He picked up the sheet of paper on his desk and said, 'According to this you haven't been at school for a while but I won't bother reading it all. The gist of it is that if you don't go to school you'll be sent to an approved school, one where you'll be kept in all the time, including weekends. What do you say to that?'

'They can't keep me in for ever. They'll have to let me out sometime.'

'I wouldn't bank on it,' Tom said. 'And if they do let you out who's going to give you a job with your record?'

'I don't want a job.'

'What do you want?'

'To be left alone.'

Tom shook his head. It was impossible to get through to this boy, but he'd have to keep trying.

'Another thing,' he said. 'The school I mentioned is very hot on discipline, especially for those who break the rules.' He thought he'd lay it on a bit and added, 'I believe they have corporal punishment for the really hard cases and you could be one of them. So why don't you go to school? It can't be any worse than that.'

When Peter remained silent Tom decided that it was time to finish the interview.

'All right,' he said. 'Come back next week. Perhaps by then you'll have something to say.'

Peter walked out the room stony-faced leaving Tom to stare at the letter on his desk. Eventually he picked it up and threw it into the waste-paper basket, then put on his coat and left the room. Outside it was still raining.

Maggie sat close to the fire reading a newspaper, while her sister Flora swirled clothes round a sinkful of freezing water.

'Look at ma haunds,' she said, lifting them up. 'They've turned blue. Whit does that mean?'

'Nothing,' said Maggie, without looking up. 'They'll be fine once ye dry them.'

'Listen tae this,' she added. 'It says here that the terrace is comin' doon in a month. Did ye ken that?'

'Naw I didny,' said Flora, her eyes wide. 'If that's the truth where wull we go?'

'I can always go tae ma cousin's,' said Maggie. 'It's a pity I never went sooner.'

Then seeing the look of dismay on her sister's face she added, 'You and the wean can come wi' me if ye like, but' – she gestured towards the room where George lay sleeping – 'I'm no' takin' him.'

'Whit aboot Greta?' said Flora. 'Supposin' she comes back and we're away? She'll no' know where tae find us.'

'If yer gaun tae wait for her,' said Maggie, 'ye'll wait for ever.'

'Don't say that,' said Flora, bursting into tears, while the child on the floor began to wail in sympathy.

'See whit ye've done,' said Maggie. 'Ye've set him aff and noo he'll be wantin' up on ma knee. I don't know how many times I've had tae wash this skirt.'

'Never mind yer skirt,' said Flora, drying her eyes on the sleeve of her jumper. 'Jist watch the wean while I finish aff this washin', if it's no' too much tae ask for.'

'Maybe no',' said Maggie. 'But whit aboot his faither? How no' ask him tae keep an eye on the wean? He does bugger all else.'

'Because I don't want him wakened,' said Flora, in an impassioned tone of voice. 'It's the only time I get ony peace. Mind you,' she added bitterly, 'I think the only real peace I'll get is when I'm deid.'

'Don't say that,' said Maggie. 'The wean needs ye, as well as the one that's comin', and Greta tae when she gets back.'

'I thought she wisny comin' back?'

'Well, no' back here, but somewhere else,' said Maggie. She added, 'Tell ye whit, leave the washin', and we'll get a bottle tae cheer us. It's rainin' onyway.'

'OK,' said Flora with a grudging smile. 'But we'll have tae be quiet about it. I don't want him wakenin' up and guzzlin' the bloody lot.'

'Yer right,' said Maggie. 'For that's whit he'd dae. He's a greedy bugger as well as a lazy one. Why don't you get shot o' him afore it's too late?'

'It's the money. I couldny manage on wan giro.'

Maggie sighed. 'Aye, it's always the money, and if it's no' that it's some other bloody thing.'

She put on her coat and told Flora she wouldn't be long.

Rita and the councillor were in the same lounge as before. She'd ordered vodka and he a pint of lager.

'I thought you didn't like vodka,' he said.

'It depends on how I feel.'

'And how d'you feel?'

'Terrible. I almost didn't phone in case your wife answered.'

'I'm glad you did, but she wouldn't have cared. We go our separate ways.'

Rita thought if that was true bang went another notion of blackmailing him for a flat, which had crossed her mind once or twice.

'By the way, have you heard anything?' she asked him, trying to sound casual as if she wasn't caring.

'Heard anything about what?'

She wished she hadn't opened her mouth. It evidently wasn't the right time to ask such questions.

'I mean about the flat,' she said. 'Did you manage to see the housing manager?'

He looked at her for a minute and then said, 'You'll have to be patient, after all Rome wasn't built in a day.'

'I know,' she said, 'but you see it's my sister. She doesn't want me −'

He cut across her words. 'Look, I'll get us another drink and we can discuss it later on in the car.'

Ah yes, the car, she thought dismally. She could scarcely bear the thought of it.

'All right,' she said, deciding that she would leave the minute his back was turned.

Just when she thought she was safe to go she almost collided with a man coming towards her, then she realised it was Harry her husband looking remarkably smart in his good suit he only wore to special occasions and his hair slicked back like an advert for Brylcreem.

'What are you doing in here?' she asked him faintly.

'I could ask you the same thing.' He looked around the tables. 'So where's the boyfriend?'

'What boyfriend?'

'The one who calls himself a councillor.'

It was at that moment the councillor chose to return with two small glasses which he put on the table. Then he stared at Harry. 'Who's this?' he asked Rita.

Before she could answer Harry said loudly, 'Only the husband of the woman you've been shagging for the past fortnight.'

There was a hush all over the room, then someone began to titter, then more people tittered.

The councillor's face was a deep dark red as he told Harry to get out or he would have him thrown out.

'Is that so?' said Harry, taking a step forward and punching the councillor on the mouth and causing him to fall back down on the carpet, where he lay staring at the ceiling in a dazed manner until someone from the next table helped him to his feet.

'You'll pay for this,' he shouted, touching his nose, which was very tender and beginning to swell.

By this time Harry was heading for the exit and pulling Rita along with him to where a taxi was waiting outside.

'You're coming home,' he said. 'So don't bother to argue.'

'I won't,' she said, relieved at not having to make a decision for once.

Shanky put his key in the lock and was mystified to see his door swing open before he could turn it. Once inside he discovered the reason. The tinker woman was bending over the dining-room table, dishing sausages out on to a plate.

He was so flabbergasted it took him a second or two to find his voice.

'What the hell are you doing?' he roared.

'Gettin' you somethin' tae eat,' she said, as though it was perfectly normal. 'Sit doon and take it afore it gets cauld.'

Stunned by the sight of his mother's good dishes on the table, he sat in a dazed manner and began to eat the sausages with his fingers.

'See,' she said, 'I kent ye'd be hungry.'

When he'd finished eating, though scarcely aware of it, he asked her how she managed to get into his house without a key.

She said, 'I wis just passin' when I noticed yer door was lyin' open, so I thought I'd come in and wait till ye got back, in case that young fella that's aye hingin' aboot got in first and stole somethin'. Then I thought again I might as well make ye somethin' tae eat while I wis in since ye wir bound to be hungry.'

'Are ye tellin' me my door wasn't locked?' he asked her in a voice quivering with rage.

'That's right, ye must have forgot.'

He looked at the nail where a key should be hanging.

'You've stole the spare key the last time you were here and that's how you got in,' he said, but when she held his gaze so fiercely he was forced to drop his eyes and mutter, 'I want you out of my house, and I don't care what your brother does.'

'Brother-in-law,' she corrected. 'Which reminds me, he's willin' to let bygones be bygones if ye let us stay in yer hoose until the rain goes aff. Between the roof leakin' and oor clathes bein' soaked the wean's liable to get pneumonia. I'm sure ye widny like that on yer conscience, especially when you've plenty of room.'

Shanky's face burned with anger. 'I wouldn't let any of you in even if it killed me. You must be mad to think I would.'

'Because if ye don't,' she added, as though he hadn't spoken, 'he's liable tae set yer hoose on fire when you're away. But onyway,' she added in a more conciliatory manner, 'it widny be for that long considerin' the place is comin' doon.'

At that Shanky gave a great howl of anger, then he went in search of the iron bar he'd shown Peter. But by the time he came back with it she'd gone. The only sign that she'd ever

been was the end of her cigarette stubbed out on his mother's
good plate.

10

The councillor got out of bed and went over to the mirror, dreading what he'd see. It turned out he had good reason. His nose was swollen to double its size and his eyes were like two slits within flesh the colour of purple. He could always say he'd tripped over a kerb if anyone asked him, but that might imply he'd been drunk, and anyway the chances of anyone asking were remote. His acquaintances were more likely to go out of their way to avoid him, which was worse than having the chance to explain.

Once dressed he forced himself to go downstairs and enter the dining room hoping his wife wouldn't look at him, which was quite possible, since she seldom looked at him nowadays, being too busy with her bridge meetings and other trivial pursuits. If she did say anything he'd simply say he'd bumped into a lamp post.

He sat down at the table surprised to see his bowl of grape-nuts wasn't out, and neither was the toast and marmalade and pot of tea. He was about to go and look for her when she came in with her coat on, carrying a suitcase, which she dumped on the floor.

'Where on earth are you going?' he asked, forgetting about his damaged face, which she didn't seem to notice anyway.

'I'm going to my lawyer to see about getting a divorce,' she said coolly as though she was speaking about going shopping.

At first he thought she was joking, but something about the steely way she gazed at him said otherwise.

'Good God,' he said, 'what do you want a divorce for?'

'You're having an affair,' she said. 'That's good enough for me.'

'Yes, but —'

He'd been about to say he'd had affairs before and they hadn't seemed to bother her. As though reading his thoughts she said that though he'd had affairs before this one was the last straw, since it was with a much younger woman and a common-looking one at that.

'I don't know who's been telling you this,' he said, 'but it's definitely not true. Besides, you can't just walk out on me after thirty years. Why don't you sit down and we'll talk it over?'

'I'll be talking it over with my lawyer. I should have done it sooner.'

The councillor tried hard to think of something to say to prevent her leaving. He had no great love for her, or even liking, but a divorce might damage his chances of being re-elected.

'How will you manage?' he said. 'You've no money of your own.'

'That's what you think. Between the allowance you'll be required to give me and the job I'm getting as a bookkeeper I won't do so badly, and there's always Bill.'

'Bill?' he said, tugging at his hair, a habit he had when perturbed.

'He's a man whom I met at one of your boring conferences. Don't worry, there's been no affair. He's a decent and considerate man, unlike yourself, and he's willing to wait.'

'You mean you're going to marry him?'

'I might,' she said coyly, then, lifting up her suitcase, 'anyway you'll be hearing from me through my lawyer.'

After she'd gone he began to wonder who on earth would take up with a woman like his wife, who, as far as he was concerned, had as much sex appeal as a jellyfish. But then hadn't he taken up with her himself a long time ago. He began to wonder if it was more than a coincidence that he'd been abandoned by the two women in his life. Was it something to do with his sex drive, which he had to admit had gone down a lot lately, not that his wife would have noticed or cared, but the Dawson woman might have been comparing him to that brute of a husband of hers. She'd gone back to him quickly enough when he showed up. In any event, he told himself bitterly, he'd make sure her name would never appear on any housing list, and for his wife she'd be lucky if she got a penny out of him. Feeling a fraction better for those vengeful thoughts he went into the kitchenette to look for the grape-nuts but couldn't find them anywhere. It was the last straw. He broke down and wept.

Rita sat up in bed staring at the ceiling while Harry lay beside her, smoking his cigarette in short angry puffs.

'Imagine letting an old poof like that touch you,' he said.

Rita sighed. She might have known he'd be like this once he got her home and had what he wanted.

It was hard to believe she was back in the same old trap, listening to the same old rubbish.

'He's not an old poof and he didn't touch me.'

'You must think I'm a fool if I believe that.'

'All right, he touched me if that's what you want to hear.'

'So you had sex with him, is that it?'

'Not exactly.'

'What do you mean, not exactly?' His voice rose and Rita wished she'd got up sooner.

'It means that we never got around to it. I only went out with him hoping he'd use his influence to get me a flat so that I could escape from you.'

'Liar,' said Harry.

She wondered if he meant that she was lying about not having sex or wanting to escape from him. If only he'd go to sleep, she thought, but with one hand behind his head it was doubtful.

Tentatively she put a leg out the bed and he said, 'Where do you think you're going?'

'Nowhere,' she said. 'I've got things to do.'

'Like what?'

'Like making breakfast.'

'Breakfast can wait,' he said, forcing her hand between his legs. 'This can't.'

She closed her eyes, thinking how true it was that men were all alike except for the social worker who seemed different, but one never really knew.

Afterwards she said as she was putting her clothes on, 'I wish you'd consider what I want for a change.'

'What do you mean?'

'How about taking me out to some nice lounge where we could talk to each other in a civilised manner?'

'Like the councillor did? Is that what you mean?'

'Can't you forget the councillor for five minutes? Besides, he wasn't civilized either.'

'Like he wanted sex.'

'Which he didn't get,' said Rita.

'Oh yeah,' said Harry. 'But he must have done you some good, though. You're a lot better in bed than you were before.'

'If you're going to be like this I should never have come back.'

'I was only joking,' said Harry. 'So where's the nice lounge you were talking about?'

'You mean it?' she said.

'Of course I mean it.'

She stared at him intently. It was hard to tell with Harry. He could mean what he said one minute then take it back the next.

'I'll have to think of one first.'

From her kitchenette window Mrs Webb gazed at her washing thinking there was no better sight than sparkling clean clothes blowing on the line, unlike that drab lot further back sagging in the middle and not even properly wrung out. Still, what could one expect from a woman who left her husband and family one week and then was back within the next two or three as if nothing had happened. She was surprised Harry Dawson had taken her back. Underneath all that bluster he must be a right wimp. But what had really annoyed her was that the night before when she'd taken a plate of home-made scones up to them as a gesture of goodwill, though mainly to find out how the land lay, Rita Dawson had come to the door and said she didn't care for her home-made baking, then slammed it in her face. She'd never felt so humiliated. Even thinking about it made her cringe. She'd vowed that from now on there were going to be no more friendly gestures. If it was war they wanted it was war they'd get.

Noticing that the clouds were gathering, she decided to take the washing in. On her way out to the back green she encountered Frances who gave her a strained smile. It was Mrs Webb who spoke first.

'Terrible weather,' she said distantly, in case she got a cool reply or none at all.

'Isn't it?' said Frances, flushing as usual. She asked Mrs Webb how she was keeping.

'Fine,' said Mrs Webb, 'not that anybody gives a damn.'

'I would have enquired sooner,' said Frances, 'but I wasn't sure if we were speaking or not.' She added lamely, 'You know how it is.'

'Of course we're speaking,' said Mrs Webb. 'I'm not one to hold grudges.' She leaned forward and lowered her voice. 'What do you think of that Dawson woman? Back after all her carry-on.'

'I never knew she was away.'

Mrs Webb clicked her tongue. 'Fancy not knowing that. They say she'd gone off with another man. And you'll never guess who.'

'I couldn't even hazard a guess.'

'Councillor Healy,' said Mrs Webb.

Frances's face went from white to red then back to white.

Mrs Webb asked her if she was feeling all right.

'I don't believe it,' said Frances fiercely. 'It'll just be one of these nasty rumours. The people who start them should be put in jail.'

'You're so right,' said Mrs Webb. 'But apparently they've been seen together and it's funny how the councillor's wife has left him.'

Frances flushed again. Mrs Webb thought her face could be compared to a neon sign, the way it kept changing colour.

'If she has it'll likely be her fault,' said Frances. 'She always was a selfish type of woman and not fit to be the wife of a councillor.'

'That's what I've often thought myself,' said Mrs Webb. 'But as you know I'm not too keen on him either. The way he goes on about tinkers being entitled to council houses makes you wonder if he isn't one himself.'

'And even if they've been having an affair,' said Frances in a distraught manner, 'it must be over by now when she's back home.'

'He could still be meeting her on the sly,' Mrs Webb pointed out.

'I shouldn't think so,' said Frances, her tone now becoming lofty. 'You must remember even though he is a councillor he'll be tempted like any other man, just like that priest was in *The Thorn Birds*.'

Mrs Webb's eyes widened. What did this fool know about men being tempted, apart from what she read in rubbishy love stories. It was common knowledge the councillor was a womaniser.

'I still think he should resign,' she said. 'You can't depend on a man who's unfaithful to his wife. It's a sure sign of weakness.'

'I bet there's no real proof he was,' said Frances. 'Besides, it's not his private life that counts. It's what he does for others.'

Mrs Webb sighed. At times she didn't know how she managed to put up with this gullible woman. She supposed it was because she was the only person near at hand who'd listen.

'Better come in for a cup of tea,' she said in her sweetest tone. 'I don't think we should fall out over the councillor's affairs, if you will excuse the pun.'

12

Puddles lay everywhere. In some parts of the terrace lane they were like miniature ponds. Anyone walking along would have to keep close in to the side of the building in order to avoid their shoes being immersed in three inches of water. An occasional tile, slackened by the rain, would smash on to the cobblestones. One just missed Tom Ashton on his way to visit Shanky Devine. Despite everything Tom was reasonably cheerful. The rain was easing off, there was a hint of blue in the sky, and he didn't anticipate too much trouble from Shanky. It was up to the authorities to get him to shift. When he climbed Shanky's stairs he noticed the tinker and his wife watching him from across the landing.

'A better day,' he called over to them and they looked away as if insulted.

When he knocked on Shanky's door he got no answer. This wasn't surprising. On previous occasions he'd had to knock five or six times before Shanky answered. It was when he noticed the door lying open he began to worry. It wasn't like Shanky to leave it open, not unless he'd gone out in a hurry, or simply forgotten to lock it. Either way he'd better make sure.

Tentatively he stepped into the hallway and that's when he saw a woman's high-heeled shoe lying on the hall carpet. He took another few steps and almost tripped over a body lying face-downward with one arm stretched out as if trying to reach for the shoe. More awful than that was the blood that surrounded the head.

'Are you all right?' he said, aware the question was foolish when this person had all the appearance of being dead.

He knelt down beside her, unwilling to abandon her yet at the same time wanting to get away as far as possible. She must be one of the tinkers on the other side of the landing and it looked as though Shanky had killed her since he'd never made any secret of hating them.

When he heard someone coming up from behind he looked round fearfully then said, 'Thank goodness it's only you. For a moment I thought –'

Whatever he thought was never made known since his words were cut off by a blow from a heavy metal bar that immediately crushed his skull causing him to fall on top of the woman making them look like grotesque lovers. The assailant hung over him long enough to go through his pockets without appearing to find anything, then with an angry grunt turned and fled.

Once the news got out people weren't long in saying Shanky was the killer. After all they'd taken place in his house and hadn't he disappeared like a guilty person would?

Harry Dawson said to his wife, 'That'll teach these social workers to barge in where they're not wanted.'

Then he advised Peter to steer clear of the terrace in case he was hauled in for questioning.

Rita was indignant. She told Harry that she didn't know why anyone would have to be hauled in other than Shanky when it was plain as the nose on one's face that he was guilty. 'And I'm not surprised,' she added. 'He always did give me the creeps.'

Harry retorted that there was more than Shanky who gave him the creeps. For instance that councillor boyfriend of hers gave everybody the creeps.

Angered by the remark she rose up from her chair like a startled bird saying if he was going to bring that up again she was off.

'Where do you think you're going?' said Harry, when Peter stood up as if ready to follow.

'Nowhere in particular,' said Peter.

'Well, before you go I want you to know that when your mother left us it was for that fat swine, Councillor Healy. So what do you say to that?'

'Not much.'

'Not much?' said Harry. 'Is that all you can say when the only reason she's come back to us is because he's ditched her? Doesn't that bother you?'

'Nothing bothers me,' said Peter as he walked out the room. 'Not even you.'

Harry called out after him, 'You know what your trouble is, you've got no feelings for anybody but yourself.'

Back inside his study the councillor sat brooding over the minutes of the recent council meeting during which he'd been told to resign.

'Why should I?' he'd asked the members of the committee who were refusing to meet his eye.

'Because,' said the member who'd put forward the proposal, 'you were seen in the back of a stationary car with a woman who wasn't your wife.'

'There is no crime in that,' said the councillor. 'It could have been my niece, or a friend of my wife's or any number of people.'

'Having sex?' said the member.

'Sex?' said the councillor, frowning as though he'd never heard of the word. Then he asked the member if the person who'd made the statement was willing to come forward and testify.

'I would have to enquire about that,' said the member, 'but it's not the first time there have been similar stories.'

'Oh I see,' said the councillor with a sneer. 'I'm expected to resign on the basis of a story that cannot be confirmed, backed up by other stories that cannot be proven. Is that it?'

No one answered. The atmosphere became very tense and not lessened by the councillor standing up and saying, 'All right, I'll make it easy for you all. Those who think I should resign put up their hand.'

Nobody put their hand up except the member who'd made the proposal.

'That settles it,' said the chairman, who had been irritated by the proceedings all along.

'Perhaps we can now move on to more appropriate matters.'

When the meeting broke up two hours later nobody said a word to the councillor, not even goodbye, and he had the feeling he wasn't off the hook yet.

Now as he sat sloshing back the whisky he began to wonder how long it would take Rita Dawson to blab out the details of their affair, that is if it could be called an affair. But no doubt she'd exaggerate everything to such an extent he wouldn't be surprised if it reached the press. He could see the headline 'COUNCILLOR DEMANDS SEX IN RETURN FOR COUNCIL FLAT' or 'COUNCILLOR DECEIVES WIFE WITH ANOTHER WOMAN'. He toyed with the notion of ringing the local newspaper to say he'd been approached by a woman who threatened that if he didn't get her a council flat she would say he'd raped her. On second thoughts he decided against it in case some readers might think it was true, especially those on the housing committee. Disconsolately he took another drink anticipating one more evening of drunken loneliness when the doorbell rang.

At first he hardly recognised the woman on the doorstep, her face being so thick with powder. Then it dawned on him she was the one who'd been pestering him recently about her plumbing.

'Come in,' he said, relieved that it wasn't a reporter, and beckoned her to follow him.

'It's my overflow pipe,' she began, once they were inside the study.

'The water's been gushing for two days and the plumber won't answer the phone.'

'How dreadful,' he said, offering her some whisky straight from the bottle.

'I don't drink,' she said, blinking with confusion.

'Just a teensy weensy one.'

'All right, but with lots of water.'

When his hand brushed her shoulder as he stood up to get the glass she couldn't help blushing, at the same time thinking he must be in a bad way when he was drinking on his own, but then if his wife had left him that would explain everything.

Peter was attending school, much to his mother's relief. The school board hadn't been near the door for a fortnight now, and though her fags were still being pinched she thought it was a small price to pay.

'It's not natural staying in all the time at your age,' she said. 'And why have you no friends?'

'Because they'd only bore me,' he said, staring at her dully as if she also bored him.

'Is there something bothering you?' she asked. 'If there is you can tell me. I won't tell your da.'

'Why should anything be bothering me?' he replied, looking beyond her to the television.

'I thought what happened to poor Mr Ashton would have bothered you,' said Rita.

'Why should it? I never liked him.'

Rita was shocked. 'What a dreadful thing to say. I hardly knew him myself but he struck me as being a decent enough man. I thought you got on well with him.'

'Because he was murdered doesn't mean to say I had to like him. He was always interfering in other people's business.'

Rita became furious. 'It was his job to interfere.'

Then it occurred to her perhaps Peter was adopting this callous attitude in order to cover up his real feelings in the matter. Some boys were like that, reluctant to show emotion in case people would laugh at them, and Peter never had been one for showing it on most occasions. Even when his dog was put down he hadn't said much.

'I'm sorry,' she said. 'I didn't mean to nag. It's just that I remember him saying something like that you'd be all right with a little patience and understanding.'

'And when did I ever get it?' said Peter with a harsh laugh.

Rita shook her head. She could get nowhere with this boy, but she wasn't going to let it get to her. She'd enough on her plate with Harry. She asked him if he'd like to go to the pictures with her. There was a good one on at the Plaza with Clint Eastwood. He replied saying who'd want to be seen at the pictures with their mother.

Rita was hurt but she tried not to show it. 'That's all right,' she said. 'Actually I'd rather go to the bingo.'

Then she remembered Harry wouldn't allow her to go. At one time he wouldn't have been able to stop her, but that was before the affair with the councillor. Nowadays she felt so guilty about everything she'd lost the will to stand up to him. Coming back hadn't improved a thing.

'Do what you want,' she said. 'It appears there's no pleasing anybody in this house.'

'That's because you went off with the councillor.'

She looked at him dismayed. 'Who told you that?'

'Da says you did.'

'Well, I don't know why he said that when he's a drunkard and a liar and nothing to be proud of himself. I was staying with your aunt and the only reason I came back was to take care of you.'

Peter didn't know whether to believe her or not. But at least though his da was bad enough at times he hadn't gone off and left him, and as for not being proud of him, well, he wasn't all that proud of her either, especially if she'd gone away with another man, and he was inclined to believe that she had.

'Since I'm not going to the pictures can I have a couple of bob instead?' he asked.

'All right, but don't buy fags,' she said. 'They're not good for you.'

'I won't,' he said.

13

The tinker and his wife sat huddled over a low fire. They'd hardly spoken a word all day and Flora had done nothing but cry.

Now George was saying, 'I'm surprised they huvny taken us in for questionin'.'

'Why should they when we've done nothin'?'

'Because, when it comes tae murder, relatives are always the first they suspect.'

'And so are ye tryin' tae tell me ye murdered them?' said Flora with a wry smile.

'Don't be daft. I telt ye already that when I went intae the hoose that mornin' tae see whit wis keepin' Maggie, I found her already deid, and the social worker as well. The big guy must have killed them baith before I got in. It's a wonder he didny kill me.'

'Aye, so it is,' said Flora absently, then lifting Maggie's white jumper off the table and holding it up against her chest.

'Tae think she wis gaun tae put it on that very mornin',' she said in a woeful tone, then stood up adding, 'I'm gaun oot tae get masel a drink if ye don't mind.'

'I thought ye'd nae money?' said George.

'There wis three quid left in her purse, which I'm entitled tae.'

'Show me the purse,' demanded George.

Reluctantly Flora brought out a purse from inside her blouse and threw it on the table. 'See for yersel',' she said.

George undid the clip. He took out the three notes and put them in his pocket.

'Gimme them back,' said Flora. 'It wis ma sister's money. I'm entitled tae it.'

'Don't worry,' said George. 'I'm only gaun tae go and get us baith a drink while you and the wean get ready. We'll have tae leave soon. It's no' safe here.'

After he'd gone she put Maggie's jumper on top of her blouse. It was too tight for her but she felt better with it on. Then she pulled the struggling child over to the sink.

'Stay at peace,' she said, wiping his face and hands with the grey wet cloth. 'Ye need to look clean for the new place.'

'Whit place?' he lisped.

'I don't know. Likely some place worse than this,' she said gloomily.

When George returned carrying the bottle inside his jacket he was breathing hard.

'Whit's wrang?' she asked. 'You look as if ye'd seen a ghost.'

'Worse than that,' he said. 'The barman was gi'en me some funny looks and so wir the customers.'

'Don't be daft,' said Flora. 'Everybody knows it wis him next door that done the murders. It's jist that he husny been caught yit.'

'Then the sooner he's caught the better,' said George as he opened the bottle and poured the liquor into two cracked cups, while the child on the floor watched him intently.

George noticed this and said, 'Tell him tae stop lookin' at me. He's been daein' it a' mornin'.'

'He doesny mean onythin',' said Flora. 'He's only a wean.'

They'd almost finished the bottle when Flora said, 'Dae ye know whit I wis thinkin'?'

'Naw, whit?'

'If we'd reported Greta amissing at first then maybe Maggie widny hae got killed.'

George stared at her exasperated. 'Ye mean yer blamin' me for that?'

'Naw, but I wis jist thinkin' maybe we should hae reported it.'

'Well, don't bother thinkin' onythin',' said George. 'Jist get yersel' and the wean ready while I get a bit o' shut eye, for I'll need a' ma energy for later on.'

'We are ready,' said Flora, but by this time he'd taken off his jacket and disappeared into the back room.

When he was gone, Flora went through his pockets to see if there was change from Maggie's three pound. She reckoned there should be, but there wasn't any, it seemed, though her hand had fastened on something solid which, when she brought it out, turned out to be a small wad of notes. Her first impulse was to go and ask George where he'd got it from. Then she hesitated knowing he was liable to lash out if awakened suddenly. She could only think he'd stolen it off somebody in the pub and that's why he was in a hurry to leave. She returned the wad to his pocket, more dejected than before, and fell asleep with her head on top of her arms folded on the table. When she awoke she discovered he'd gone.

14

Mrs Webb could find nothing to complain about as far as the Dawsons were concerned. They were all as quiet as mice and just about as dull. That was the way it should be, she told herself, but as fate would have it when one problem's solved another takes its place, the one in question being the empty bottom flat in the next close. She could have sworn she'd heard noises coming from it in the early hours of the morning. She decided she would tell Frances about it even though she didn't expect to get much joy from her, since Frances never seemed to hear or see anything nowadays.

Frances answered the door in her nightdress.

'I thought you would've been up by this time,' said Mrs Webb. 'It's half-past nine.'

'Is it?' said Frances, astonished. 'I couldn't have heard the alarm go off. I'm so tired this weather, I could sleep all day.'

'It's not a crime,' said Mrs Webb, making it sound as though it was.

Frances then asked Mrs Webb if there was anything wrong when she was at her door so early.

'As a matter of fact there is,' said Mrs Webb.

Frances's eyes grew big. 'You'd better come in,' she said, then dashing off into a bedroom to put on some clothes.

When she returned Mrs Webb explained how she'd heard noises through the night coming from the empty flat in the next close.

'You did?' said Frances. 'Maybe it was a cat or some other kind of animal.'

'A cat that walks up and down with shoes on?'

'Maybe it was –' Frances had begun to say when she broke off, biting her lip.

'I suppose you were going to say maybe it was Shanky Devine,' said Mrs Webb.

'Actually I was going to say maybe it was one of those homeless people you were always on about.'

'You think so?' said Mrs Webb, becoming outraged at the very idea.

Angrily she went on, 'We can't have people like that squatting in perfectly good council flats. It's not as if they pay any rates. In any case I'll be reporting it.'

'Report it to Councillor Healy then,' said Frances. 'He's the one who deals with the homeless.'

'I shouldn't think so, not when he's all for them,' said Mrs Webb. 'Which reminds me,' she added looking close into her neighbour's face, 'did you get any satisfaction that last time you saw him? You know how you're always round at his door for something or other.'

Frances became indignant. 'I'm not always round at his door. I was forced to go to him about my cistern. The caretaker doesn't do a thing for anybody nowadays.'

'You can say that again,' said Mrs Webb. 'But I thought it was your overflow pipe that needed fixed?'

'That was the time before. It so happens everything is falling apart in my place. Those flats have been up too long.'

'You're so right,' said Mrs Webb, then in the same breath, 'Is his wife still away?'

'Whose wife?'

'The councillor's. Who else?'

'I never asked him.'

Mrs Webb sighed and shook her head. It looked as though she wasn't going to be offered tea. Definitely Frances wasn't as friendly as she used to be.

'Anyway,' she said. 'I'd watch out if I were you.'

'Watch out for what?'

'Watch out that what happened to Rita Dawson doesn't happen to you.'

'What's that?'

'That you become another one of his playthings.'

Frances drew back as if she'd been scalded. 'I don't know what you mean.'

'For God's sake,' said Mrs Webb. 'Do I have to spell it out? What I'm saying is the next time you go round to his house be on your guard in case he tries to take advantage. He'll be desperate for a woman, not having had one recently now his wife has gone and Rita Dawson is back with her husband. The man's a charlatan.'

The colour drained from Frances's face. She stood up and held on to the chair for support. 'That's a terrible thing to say about anyone, and you couldn't be more wrong. The councillor's one of the kindest and sweetest men I've ever met.'

'Balls,' said Mrs Webb, walking out and slamming the door to convey contempt at her neighbour's refusal to see anything but good in the man.

And to think all she'd wanted to do was talk about the noise coming from the empty flat. Instead of that she gets cut off for absolutely nothing.

Flora was always the first to sit up in bed when the tea trolley was being brought into the ward, which was roughly ten minutes before visiting time. Not that she expected any visitors. It was a relief that she got no one. Being served with tea and a scone was good enough for her. She'd never been so comfortable in all her life. She only wished she didn't have to worry about what would happen when she got out. Her older child was already in care and if she didn't have a decent place to go to she would lose the other one as well. At times she wanted to howl with anxiety but she always managed to smile and look composed when the nurses came round.

One of them came over and told her a gentleman was waiting to see her in the reception room. Flora panicked thinking it might be George, or worse still somebody from the fraud squad enquiring about the child benefit book. She'd been cashing the same amount for weeks without letting them know Greta was no longer with her.

She asked the nurse if she could finish her tea first.

'Hurry up then,' said the nurse. 'He doesn't look the type you'd want to keep waiting.'

Flora gulped down her tea then hid the scone under the pillow for later on. The man waiting in the reception, smooth-faced and well-dressed, introduced himself as Councillor Healy, then told her to sit down. He'd some good news for her.

'Oh,' said Flora, wondering if that meant they'd found George, for anything connected with him was seldom good news.

'It's like this,' he began. 'The housing committee has seen fit to allocate you one of the high-rise flats, complete with all the modern fittings, and a splendid view of the town. What do you say to that?'

She didn't know what to say, scarcely being able to take it in. Finally she said, 'That sounds great.'

'Yes, doesn't it?' he said, with a beaming smile, than added, 'You see we thought it right you should be the first travelling person within the area to get one. If everything goes well, and there is no reason why it shouldn't, then we can go ahead with others. How does that suit you?'

'Fine,' she said cautiously, wondering if this was a trap to get her to say where George was, not that she knew, but this man wouldn't know that.

'So you will be our first experiment,' he said.

'That's nice,' she said, her eyes sore with squinting up at him.

He then went on to tell her she could be allowed a grant for a cooker, a bed, and some second-hand furniture, including a carpet and anything else she would need. Realising that all this couldn't have anything to do with George or the child benefit book she began to relax.

'That'll be great,' she said, then she asked the question upper-most in her mind, which was could she have her two kids to stay with her.

'Certainly,' he said. 'Your husband and your children are allowed to stay with you, but no lodgers or pets. We can't emphasise this enough.'

At that point Flora thought it best to say nothing about her husband.

'And will I still get ma giro?' she asked. 'They might no' know where to send it if I'm at a different address.'

'Don't worry,' he said, 'everything will be taken care of.'

He was buttoning his coat and ready to leave when she said, 'And whit aboot Greta?'

'Greta?' he asked sharply. 'Who's Greta?'

'I forgot to tell ye. She's ma eldest daughter and nearly fifteen. She disappeared a while ago but I'm sure she'll be back soon, and when she does, can she stay wi' me as well?'

The councillor frowned. He didn't like the sound of this somehow. It could be a matter for the police and it would do him no good if he was involved with people who'd committed a major crime.

'Have you reported this to anyone?' he asked. 'I mean officially?'

Flora wasn't sure what he meant by officially but she thought it best to say, 'Naw, because we expected her back ony day. Actually it's no' the first time.'

The councillor considered this for a minute then he said, 'I expect it will be all right,' and hurried away before any more awkward questions could arise.

'I'm much obliged to ye, mister,' Flora called after him, glad to see him go, for she'd never trusted do-gooders with their posh accents and put-on smiles who expected you to be grateful to them for ruining your life. At least if a cop took you in for ques-tioning they sometimes gied ye a fag.

★

Rita stretched out her arm to turn off the alarm. As always she was reluctant to get up and face making the breakfast. It wasn't so much the making of it that bothered her, it was the strained silence at the table when no one said a word except Harry, and that was mainly to lay down the law.

She'd once read in an article that breakfast meals should be a time of peace and tranquillity when families met and discussed their problems after saying good morning. Once when she'd tried it they'd stared at her as if she was mad. Now Harry was nudging her and saying she'd better get up since he didn't want to be late for his work. Rita longed to tell him to get up and make it himself but she couldn't face the row it would cause.

'All right, I'm going,' she said.

In the kitchenette she stood over the cooker smoking a cigarette. The first one of the day was always the best, especially when there was no one around like Harry. If only he would die, she'd often thought, and she and Peter could go a holiday with the insurance money. Mind you, she wasn't sure Peter would want to go judging by the way he'd been acting recently. But at the very least she'd be free to go to the bingo.

'I thought you'd given these up,' said Harry, coming in and lifting the cigarette out of her fingers and throwing it in the sink.

'It's my only pleasure,' she said, moving as far away from him as she could.

'Surely not your only one?' he said, pressing himself up against her with his arms round her waist.

'Get dressed,' she said. 'The boys will be coming in any minute and it doesn't look right you going about half naked.'

'I bet if it was the councillor you wouldn't be saying that.'

'For God's sake, can't you leave the subject alone?' she said angrily.

'You're lucky I still take an interest in you,' he said, stamping off in his bare feet then returning a minute later to ask if she knew that Peter wasn't in his room and his bed hadn't been slept in, judging by the covers.

'I thought he was still asleep,' she said stupidly.

'If you thought a little less and acted a little more you would have known he wasn't. You're so lackadaisical you don't know what you're doing half the time.'

'Maybe he made his bed then went out for a walk,' she said, knowing this was unlikely.

'Without his breakfast?'

'He doesn't need to cook anything. He takes Coco Pops.'

'Then where's his plate?' said Harry. 'And don't tell me he washed it. I wouldn't believe that.'

Rita lit up a cigarette, toying with the idea of taking an overdose then remembering there were no pills in the house. After her last attempt Harry had thrown them all out.

'I'll phone the school when it opens,' she said. 'Maybe he's gone there to play football.'

'Maybe you should phone the loony bin and get yourself signed in while you're at it,' said Harry.

'Maybe I should,' she said, running out of the kitchenette with tears in her eyes.

'What's the matter with her?' asked Jim, who'd passed her on the way in.

'You may well ask,' said Harry. 'All I know is because of her damn mood swings I'll have to make my own breakfast.'

'Oh,' said Jim, reaching for the Coco Pops. He was about to ask why Peter wasn't up yet, then thought better of it since the mention of his brother's name might cause another row.

At this very moment, unknown to anyone, Peter was lying bound and gagged in the bedroom of the empty flat, and had been like that since the previous evening. What led up to it was that when he was coming home from school and passing this same flat, he'd thought he'd seen a face at the window. This he dismissed as being a hallucination. He'd been prone to having them since the time of the murders. Later on it occurred to him that the face at the window could have been Shanky's. After all, what better place to hide out in than an empty flat if he was on the run.

He waited until his parents were in bed then slipped out the front door, and round the back then over the fence, taking a torch with him. When he climbed in a bottom window Shanky stepped forward shielding his eyes from the glare of the torch.

'I thought you'd never show up,' he said.

'I didn't want to,' said Peter. 'I'm in trouble if I'm seen talking to you.'

'Yes,' said Shanky heavily. 'But I'm innocent. I never killed anybody.'

'Then give yourself up. They might believe you.'

'I'm not so sure of that,' said Shanky. 'My idea was to hide out until they got the real killer.'

'And who would that be?'

'The tinker, who else? If I'd been in the house that morning he'd likely have killed me too, though it might have been better if he had. I don't know how much longer I can keep going like this.'

'If you give yourself up you'll get a chance to explain,' said Peter. 'But if you stay in this flat you're bound to get caught. Every day people come to look at it, and for all we know they could be coming first thing tomorrow morning.'

'I guess you're right,' said Shanky. 'If you get me some food and a blanket I'll leave before it gets light.'

'All right,' said Peter. 'But you'll have to be extra quiet if you don't want to waken the old bitch through the wall.'

He climbed back out the window taking the torch with him. Then half an hour later he returned with some bread and cheese and a blanket.

'Sorry to be so long,' he said. 'But my brother came in and I had to wait until he'd gone to bed.'

'That's OK,' said Shanky, taking the food and then the blanket, which to Peter's amazement he began to tear into strips.

'Hey,' said Peter, trying to take back what was left of it. 'Have you gone mad?'

Shanky's answer was to let it go causing Peter to totter backwards as the big man caught hold of him and began to tie strips round his mouth, telling Peter not to struggle or he would be forced to choke him. Once he had Peter well and truly bound and gagged and sat up against a wall, he explained that he had guessed the reason Peter took so long in coming back was because he'd been phoning for the cops. Peter shook his head frantically at this and Shanky added that he didn't expect him to admit it as nearly everybody he spoke to nowadays was a liar, except his mother. He then climbed back out the window taking the food and the torch with him, leaving Peter to struggle in the dark.

'You mean to say he hasn't come home yet?' said Harry, after coming into the living room and throwing his jacket over the armchair, then sinking into it himself.

Rita nodded, her face white and strained. She'd expected her son to be in before his father. Now it looked as though he might never be in.

'And so you didn't check with the school?'

'I didn't think to check. I thought he was at it.'

'I don't understand you,' he said. 'Any normal person would have checked. What's the matter with you?'

'There's nothing the matter with me,' she said. 'Maybe we should get the police in.'

'I don't believe this,' said Harry. 'You had all day to get the police in, yet you wait until I come home. Why didn't you get them in sooner?'

'I really don't know,' she said wearily.

Harry went on, 'And I'll bet anything he'll be skulking around in that old terrace smoking your fags.'

She looked over at him sharply. She hadn't thought of the terrace but obviously that's where he would have gone. Her main impulse was to go there straight away, but then she figured it would be a better idea to sneak out after dinner when Harry was asleep by the fire. If he saw her leaving now he'd accuse her of going to meet the councillor.

'I'll put out the dinner,' she said. 'It might get cold.'

'I should think so,' he retorted. 'There's no point in not eating just because he hasn't came home, but I'll say this much, if he's going to continue the way he's doing he'll have to get out. I'm not having this kind of carry-on every time I get back from work.'

Rita nodded as if agreeing but really thinking if she hurried with the meal she might reach the terrace before it became dark.

But for the moon being out in full the lane would have been in total blackness. Rita thought it was going to be difficult to find Shanky's house, until she remembered that every year his mother had painted the stairs white on each edge and she was the only one who'd done that. On reaching Shanky's house it occurred to her Shanky might not be at home if he'd been on the run since the time of the murders, despite the fact that he had the alibi of being in the woodyard at the time. So it was something of a shock when he opened the door to her, his face the colour of wax in the moonlight.

'I've come for my son,' she said, before he could speak.

'Your son?' he said, in a hollow tone of voice.

'Yes, my son Peter. I believe he's been staying in your house instead of going to school. So if you don't send him out I'll have you charged with kidnapping at the very least.'

'I don't know anything about your son,' Shanky growled. 'Go away.'

She thought he could possibly be telling the truth. There was no proof Peter was in his house, that is until she noticed the scratch marks on his face.

'Your face is bleeding,' she said. 'Did Peter do that?'

'Mind your own business,' he said, attempting to close the door, which she pushed back in sheer desperation.

'What have you done with him?' she said, as her hand fastened round the nail file she always had in her pocket. In a flash she had it out and pressed it against his neck. 'If you don't tell me where he is I'll stick this right in.'

When she pressed it in harder he let out a small scream.

'All right,' he said, 'he's tied up in the empty flat next to where you stay. He'll still be there for I tied him up real tight.'

'Why did you tie him up?'

'He was going to get the cops on to me and I've done nothing.'

'And how long has he been tied?'

'Since last night. I wouldn't have done it if he hadn't —'

'So he's been tied up for nearly twenty-four hours.'

'Something like that, but I didn't mean him no harm. I just wanted to teach him a lesson. I thought he was my friend.'

But Rita wasn't listening. She was running down the stairs two at a time then along the lane as fast as she could without tripping over the cobblestones and twisting her ankle in case she was too late.

15

The councillor poured himself out a generous measure of whisky in order to celebrate the afternoon's meeting during which the committee had officially accepted the new housing bill that allowed travelling people to be considered homeless and given a chance to occupy council houses if they so wished. The bill had became law anyway, which could have had a lot to do with it, but he preferred to think it was his persistence that had won the day. By the time he was on to his second glass he began to consider he might be in a good position to stand for parliament. There were signs that certain left-wing members of the community were looking upon him favourably, which was a good start if one wished to go far, and, if he had made some enemies in the past, such as the members of the committee, then this was no bad thing either as they'd never been popular with the voters anyway.

He was meditating along these encouraging lines when the doorbell rang. Tutting he went to answer it and his heart sank when he saw it was the same woman who'd recently been pestering him about her plumbing.

'Yes,' he said a trifle coolly, then to his consternation she burst into tears.

'Please come in,' he said, mainly in order to get her off his doorstep. Who knows what people might think if they saw her like that.

Inside his study she explained she'd been accused of shoplifting by the manager of the local supermarket and she hadn't done anything other than accidentally put a tin of pilchards into her shopping bag.

'I had no intention of stealing it,' she said. 'It was purely by accident, but when I tried to explain that he said he was going to have me charged.' She then went into a fit of wild sobbing.

'Do sit down and compose yourself,' he said. 'Miss er –'

'Brown. Frances Brown.'

'Ah yes, I remember, Miss Brown.'

He began to wonder if she was the type who went around making a nuisance of themselves to certain important people in order to gain their attention. Oh well, if that was the case he'd better get used to it if he wanted to become an MP.

'I'd go home and forget it if I was you,' he said. 'Some shop managers are too officious for their own good. I expect he'll have forgotten it by tomorrow.'

'And what if he hasn't?'

'Then I'll have a talk with him and let him know where he stands.'

'Oh, thank you,' she said. 'You've restored my faith in human nature.'

'It's nice of you to say so,' he said, and then he asked her if at any time she'd been a member of a church, recalling hazily her hands fluttering over pots of jam at the church bazaar.

'I was,' she said, blushing, 'but that was a long time ago.'

'No matter,' he said. 'We all have our lapses, but as I've always said, once a churchgoer, always a churchgoer. If that manager gives you any trouble I'll let him know that you are a practising Christian and he won't have a leg to stand on.'

'Thank you again,' she said, gazing at him with such eyes of worship he thought she might kiss him.

Quickly he stood up and saw her to the door.

Once back in the study he brought out the bottle and the glass then remembered he'd forgotten to ask her the name of the supermarket.

Still, what did it matter, he'd no intention of going there in the first place. Dismissing the matter from his mind he poured himself out a big glassful in order to recapture his former good mood, but the spell was broken, depression set in and he began to consider he should be out enjoying himself with some beautiful woman instead of drinking alone. No doubt his wife would be out enjoying herself with that guy Bill.

It was at that point something came into his head which he hadn't thought about for ages. Opening the drawer in his writing bureau he brought out the article he'd purchased from an antique shop in the days when he and his wife had gone on holidays together. She had purchased a blouse of a Tyrolean design which didn't suit her at all, but he'd said nothing about it since it gave him the opportunity to buy what he wanted.

'You're not going to buy that awful thing,' she'd said. 'It's not anything you'd want to display anywhere.'

'That's because you know nothing about art,' he'd replied, pointing to the intricately carved handle on the whip. 'But if you feel that way I'll hang it in the spare room.'

In those days the study was the spare room until he got it furnished to his taste. It turned out his wife never wore the blouse, and the whip was eventually kept in a drawer, and only taken out occasionally to let the slippery thong slide through his fingers. He rather liked the sensation.

There was the other occasion when his wife had gone on holiday by herself and he'd brought a woman to the house, then on an impulse showed her the whip.

'Very good,' she'd said. 'What am I supposed to do with it?'

After a lot of persuasion she agreed to use it on him, and though the experience had been painful he'd never had such a huge erection before. The woman had said she wouldn't have believed it if she hadn't seen it for her own eyes. Before she left she asked if she could take the whip and try it on her husband as he was poorly endowed in that area. When he told her he wouldn't dream of letting it out of the house she'd gone off in a huff. Since then the time and opportunity for using it had never arisen again. There was no one he knew to ask. Strangely enough the name Frances Brown popped into his mind before he dozed off.

Frances was over the moon when she received a letter from the manager of the supermarket apologising for any distress he'd caused her. He now fully accepted that she'd put the pilchards into her bag by error, and despite the misunderstanding he hoped she would continue to do business with him, signing himself, 'Your obedient servant'.

'I knew the councillor would help me,' she told Mrs Webb, after getting her out of bed early.

'You got me up to tell me that?' said the old woman, sounding quite bad-tempered.

'I thought you would have been pleased,' said Frances.

'Oh, I am,' said her neighbour sarcastically, then adding, 'You might as well come in now that you're here.'

Over a cup of tea which Mrs Webb grudged making, except she was dying for one herself, Frances read out the letter and at the end of it said, 'You can see that the councillor's got a lot of influence over people.'

'Too much if you ask me,' said Mrs Webb. 'Anyway how do you know he influenced anybody? That manager could have had a change of heart. It was only a measly tin of pilchards, after all.'

'I think he'd be worried the councillor might get him the sack if he didn't apologise.'

'I'm damned sure he wouldn't have worried me,' said Mrs Webb, 'nor anybody else that's got half a brain. He's all bluff, the councillor, and that business of him sticking up for the tinkers is because he wants to get his name in the papers. And there's one thing I'd never do,' she added, 'and that's trust a womaniser, which is just what he is.'

Frances banged down her cup, her face scarlet. 'I really must go,' she said. 'I'm sure I've left the teapot on the gas.'

'Again?' said Mrs Webb. 'You're always doing that and here's me about to tell you something that's a lot better than your letter.'

'What?' said Frances, curiosity getting the better of her.

'A police van drew up outside the close last night and I saw a policeman go inside. I wouldn't be surprised if it had something to do with the murders.'

'You think so,' said Frances, tired of hearing about the murders. As a topic with Mrs Webb it had taken precedence over the Dawsons.

'Maybe it was kids vandalising the place,' she suggested.

'At that time in the morning, I shouldn't think so,' said Mrs Webb. 'It's more likely they were looking for Shanky Devine. I hope they catch him soon before we all get murdered in our beds.'

'I heard he was innocent,' said Frances. 'So it could have been somebody else.'

'Like who?'

'I don't know exactly.'

'Then you shouldn't open your mouth. That's how rumours start.'

Frances was speechless. How could she start a rumour if she didn't know anything? She said, 'Yes, it makes you wonder who started the rumour about Mrs Dawson and the councillor that went on for ages.'

'That wasn't a rumour. That was a fact,' said Mrs Webb. 'Still, thank goodness we don't have to worry about such rumours at our age.'

What did she mean, at our age? thought Frances indignantly, when she was only fifty-two.

'I definitely must go,' she said, flouncing off before Mrs Webb could say another word.

Inside her own flat she studied herself in the mirror and was less pleased than usual at what she saw: nondescript features, frizzy hair and a lacklustre skin. Perhaps if she got a more modern haircut, and applied some lipstick and eye shadow and face cream, she might look a lot younger. The trouble was she didn't know what colours would suit her – it had been so long since she'd tried anything.

16

It was like living on top of a mountain, Flora thought, as she looked out her window. Normally she never looked out if she could help it – the height made her sick and dizzy. But she'd been drawn to it by a seagull banging itself against the pane. When the seagull fell like a stone she was panic-stricken, thinking it could have been her child that had fallen. She could still hear the bird screaming, then she discovered it was the baby in the pram who was screaming. She ran over and stuck a dummy in his mouth, which he spat out. Then she tried giving him the milk left over in a bottle from his last feed. This pacified him for the moment, but she knew it wouldn't last. Soon he'd be crying with the wind that came after every feed and then he'd bring it all up.

Looking at him now she thought he was much too pale. Likely he wasn't too healthy with hardly ever getting out and the central heating always on. The problem with the heating was that she didn't know how to switch it off. She was never sure whether to turn the knob to the right or to the left. But whichever way she turned it there was always constant heat. Then again they hardly ever went out because she was afraid to use the lift in case she pressed the wrong button and they all hurtled to the bottom. The last time she'd waited outside the lift for someone else to press the button it took ages. She didn't think she could be bothered facing that again. But when the baby continued to scream she decided she had to get out or she was liable to kill him.

'Wullie,' she called to her older child, drawing on a colouring-in book on the floor, 'get your coat on.'

She was struggling with his coat, too tight for him under the arms, when the doorbell rang.

'It's that bluidy district nurse,' she muttered under her breath, exasperated at the idea of having to undress the baby for an examination, which they always insisted on. She suspected they were looking for bruises, as if she was the type to hit her kids.

The female on the doorstep was nothing like the district nurse, being young and pretty with blonde-streaked hair.

'Are you frae the housin'?' asked Flora, expecting it to be about her not washing the stairs on the landing.

She was all ready to explain she didn't wash them because she couldn't leave the baby alone for five minutes in case it took a seizure when the young woman said, 'For God's sake, Ma. Don't ye know yer ain daughter?'

Flora reeled back, a hand to her mouth. 'It's you, Greta?' she gasped out. 'Where hae ye been? I've been worried sick.'

'Let me in and I'll tell ye.'

Inside the white-emulsioned living room Greta looked about and said that this was a lot better than she'd expected and was it all right for her and her boyfriend to stay here until they got a place to go to. 'He's waitin' ootside,' she added.

'Your boyfriend?' said Flora, tugging at her lower lip anxiously.

'Aye. We're engaged, look!'

When she showed her mother the big ruby ring on her finger Flora said immediately, 'Tell him tae come in. I'll be gled o' the company.'

17

The bulldozer moved forward ripping through bricks and mortar. A piece of masonry enscribed 'Built in 1887' shattered on to the lane.

'How long will it take to finish this?' said the councillor to the foreman in charge of the operation.

'Couldn't say,' said the foreman. He beckoned on the driver to come out for a break.

The councillor asked him if they really needed a break considering the job was supposed to be finished in a day.

'That's impossible,' said the foreman, a glance of derision passing between him and the driver.

'I don't see why not,' said the councillor. 'It's not a block of office flats, just one small row of terraces.' He added in a pompous tone, 'I hope you know this area has to be cleared as soon as possible in order to go ahead with the plans for a new school.'

He'd been mentioning plans for a new school to everyone he met that morning.

'First I've heard of it,' said the foreman, who had been reflecting on the days when he used to visit his granny who had lived in the terrace at that time. Then it had seemed like a place of magic with its cobblestone lane, steep stone stairs, and old wash houses that looked as though they might conceal dark secrets, or so his favoured imagination had supposed.

And now it was his job to pull it down, he felt bad.

'They don't need another school,' he said. 'It would have been better to restore the place to what it was. You don't get good red sandstone like that any more.'

'That's because they don't use it any more,' said the councillor.

Unthinkingly, he stepped towards the rubble and a slate that had been hanging loose on part of the building still standing fell off, narrowly missing his head.

'That could have killed me,' he said, white and shaken.

'You were warned to keep back,' said the foreman. 'Anyway you shouldn't be here telling us what to do. This is none of your business.'

'Is that so?' said the councillor. 'Well, I'll tell you something that is my business – I'm going to report you for negligence. You should have known that slate was going to fall. That's what you're paid for.'

The foreman became angry. 'I don't know who you are, but do yourself a favour and get out of here before I run you off by the scruff of the neck.'

The councillor, whose face was now a blotchy red, said, 'You'll soon find out who I am when I get you fired.'

After the councillor had gone the foreman said to the driver, 'Honest to God, I don't know where he gets the idea they're going to build a school when I know for a fact this is going to be a rubbish tip.

'He's a councillor,' said the driver. 'Bit of a lad with the women, I've heard.'

Meanwhile further along the lane Shanky sat crouched on the floor waiting for the bulldozer. Already plaster had fallen off his ceiling and two of his windows were cracked. He closed his eyes and clasped his hands in front of him since it seemed like an occasion for praying, though he couldn't think of anything to pray for, unless it was a sudden and painless end. When he opened his eyes he was shocked to see a man in the doorway. For a moment he wondered if this was Jesus Christ in the guise of a workman, coming to save his soul.

'Get out,' said the foreman. 'This building is being demolished. Can't you hear the noise? Are you deaf?'

'I'm not leaving,' said Shanky. 'This is my home.'

'Look here,' said the foreman. 'I've got my orders and nobody's going to stop me from carrying them out.'

'I'm staying here and you can't shift me.'

The foreman took off his helmet and wiped his sweating forehead.

'Right,' he said. 'I'm going for the cops and you can explain all that to them.'

Then from the direction of the rafters Shanky heard a voice telling him to get out before it was too late.

'Is that you, Mother?' he said, becoming agitated. He hadn't heard from her for ages, nor did he want to.

'Yes, it's me,' the voice said. 'Do as I say and stop behaving like a fool.'

'All right,' he said. 'But from now on I don't want you giving me any more advice. Just leave me alone.'

The foreman hesitated. The guy had said something. Did that mean he was leaving?

'I'll give you one last chance,' he'd begun, when Shanky bolted past him, down the stairs, then round the corner and out into the main street where a group of people were coming towards him carrying banners which read 'PRESERVE OUR OLD BUILDINGS AND SAVE OUR HERITAGE'.

A middle-aged woman holding out her hand came from the group to say to Shanky, 'I'm proud to meet you, sir. You're a credit to our cause.'

'What cause?'

'Don't be so modest. Your efforts in trying to keep the old terrace intact have not gone unnoticed. And even though the battle for it has been lost, there are other battles which we hope to win. You are very welcome to join us in the struggle.'

Shanky thought about this for a minute then said, 'I may as well. I've nowhere else to go.'

'Don't worry,' said the woman. 'There are plenty of other apartments lying empty in old buildings that they want to demolish. But this time we won't let them. We shall put up barricades.'

When Shanky hesitated she added, 'Only twenty pounds a week, including laundry.'

'Are they very high up?' he asked anxiously.

'Not if you don't want them to be. There's plenty of them low down.'

'That should do me fine,' he said. Then having a sudden vision of the social worker's disapproving face watching him he added, 'I never fancied the new council flat they offered me because it was too high up and I can't stand heights.'

'It's a deal then,' said the woman.

She shook his hand and together they marched up the street to the beat of a solitary drum.

Postscript

Peter was taking a long time in recovering from his ordeal, or so it seemed to Rita who had to bring meals into his room while he lay in bed. Despite this he was adamant that Shanky should not be charged for attempting to murder him, since he didn't want the cops asking any questions.

'Why not?' said Rita.

'Because I don't want them to connect me with him in any way. If he's not a suspect then they might think it's me who's the murderer, especially if they find out I used to hang around the terrace.'

Rita sighed. She was always hoping to have a sensible talk with her son, but it never happened. 'Why should they suspect you?' she said. 'You're not even an adult. Besides, you wouldn't have the guts to kill anybody.'

Then she became serious. 'You really should have had him charged. You could have died in that flat.'

'Well, I never,' said Peter. He began to yawn. He was always yawning. He thought it was because he didn't sleep well.

'Anyway,' he added. 'I don't want to be known as a grass.'

He turned away, hoping that would be the end of it. With the questions she asked he was beginning to hate her as much as he did his da.

'Your father says if you don't get up you'll never get better.'

'I am better,' said Peter. 'I just don't want to see his ugly mush.'

'If you're better why don't you go to school?'

'There's no point in going when I'm leaving in a fortnight.'

'All the same you should,' said Rita. 'It's not right leaving before the time. They'll hold it against you.'

'Who'll hold it against me?'

'The employers. You might not get a job.'

'I don't want a job. I wish you'd shut up. You're just like that social worker.'

'I won't shut up. Somebody's got to try and make you see sense.'

However, she drew back when he raised himself on one elbow, to say, 'Piss off. It's you who's making me ill.'

She was about to give an angry retort but the look on his face stopped her.

'Stay in bed for ever for all I care,' she said, tossing her head as she walked out the room.

After she'd gone he waited for a good while in case she came back, before going down on his knees to drag out the iron bar from under the bed. The bloodstains and hairs were still plain to see, but that wouldn't matter. Once the coast was clear he'd walk outside with it under his jacket then toss it in the deepest part of the river, which already had been dredged for the murder weapon. He didn't think they'd dredge it again.

JEN'S PARTY

Maude Boulting banged the plate of scrambled egg down on the table and looked around at her thirteen-year-old daughter Jen who was cleaning her nails with a kirby grip.

'Take this through to your Aunt Belle,' she said. 'She'll still be in bed.'

'Don't want to,' said Jen.

Maude stared at her incredulously then moved towards her. 'What do you mean you don't want to?'

Jen picked up the plate, left the room and returned two minutes later. 'She's not there. I left the plate on the dresser.'

'Not there?' said Maude, her face sagging. 'Well, that's the bloody limit.'

She marched into her sister's room where the unmade bed met her eye, but with no Belle lying upon it. She opened the wardrobe as if expecting to find her inside, but it only held Belle's clothes.

'Jen,' she roared. 'Go and find your Aunt Belle at once, and tell her the food's out and this is not a bloody hotel.'

But Jen had gone outside to avoid further involvement and was crouching under the hedge.

'What are you doing?' hissed a voice from the other side of the hedge.

It was Betty Woods from next door. Betty was supposed to be a friend, but at times she seemed like an enemy.

'I'm supposed to be looking for my aunt, but I don't know where to begin. Why weren't you at school yesterday?'

'I wasn't well. I've got my period.'

Jen struggled up, inwardly cringing. It seemed to her that all the girls in her class had got their period, except herself. She suspected there was something wrong with her.

'I don't suppose you saw my aunt,' she asked weakly.

'I didn't and I don't want to see her. If you ask me she's as crazy as a bat.'

'She's not crazy,' said Jen. 'She's eccentric. There is a difference.'

'Well, I wouldn't like to have her in my house,' said Betty. 'My mother says –'

'Who's caring what your stupid mother says?' said Jen, running back into the kitchen where Maude was scraping black off the toast.

'Did you find her?' she asked.

'Betty Woods said she saw her going along the street,' Jen lied, hoping that would get her off the hook.

'Did she have her coat on?'

Jen's voice rose. 'I don't know and I don't care and I'm fed up with people saying she's crazy. Why does she have to live with us?'

'Because she's my sister.'

'I don't care if she's your sister. She should live somewhere else.'

'Shut up and eat your scrambled egg,' said Maude. 'We don't get food for nothing, you know.'

Jen turned and ran out the kitchen leaving her plate untouched.

Maude went over to the window and drank her tea wondering where it would all end.

Everything had seemed so cheerful when Belle arrived on the doorstep like a plump gaudy fairy bestowing gifts such as cheap perfume and hand cream. It had been like Christmas for weeks on end with wine on the table as regular as sauce bottles and Jen listening to them both as they reminisced, mainly the laughable bits for the past hadn't been wonderful. She preferred not to think of scenes in the months that followed, particularly the one with the policeman standing in the kitchen and accusing Belle of shoplifting. It was even better to forget how Belle had managed to pay the fines that were always cropping up. Maude visualised her going round the supermarket and filling her bag straight from the shelves. So far she'd got away with that, which wasn't so bad, and the tins of salmon came in handy, but it still wasn't right. Even now she could be arguing with the manager in broken French which she usually assumed to get out of a hole. Then like an apparition she was suddenly present, jarring Maude's senses with her orange hair and purple eye shadow.

'Sorry to be so long,' she said, in an Irish brogue which she sometimes adopted when squiffy.

'Where the hell have you been?' said Maude, wanting to slap that bold painted face.

'Sure I was only in the toilet dyeing my hair. D'ye like it?'

'You're like an old-aged hippy,' said Maude, positive the bathroom had been open and vacant when she passed it ten minutes ago.

'Well, we can't all be having the same styles,' said Belle, giving Maude an insinuating stare.

'Your scrambled egg is on the dresser,' said Maude, trying to remember where she'd put the aspirins, for the sight of her sister gave her a sore head.

'Scrambled egg again, is it?' said Belle. She sashayed out of the kitchen, returning a minute later with the plate saying she couldn't face eating this, delicious though it may be, then swept the contents into the bin adding, 'I'll just run down to the chippy's and get some chips if you don't mind.'

'She's lucky,' said Jen, coming in as Belle was leaving. 'Can I get money for chips?'

'You bloody well can't,' said Maude. 'I'm not making food for it to be slung out. If Belle wants to waste money on chips that's up to her.'

'She always gets what she wants anyway,' said Jen, her face pinched with resentment.

'Do you think so?' said Maude (a sharp pain stabbing the back of her head, despite having swallowed the aspirins, which she found in her bag).

'Well, don't forget, if it wasn't for your Aunt Belle handing in some money now and again we wouldn't even be having scrambled egg.'

'I don't care,' said Jen, beating her fist on the table.

Wearily Maude took out some money from her purse. 'Here,' she said, 'go and get them and give me peace.'

Triumphantly Jen shot out the door. 'Wait for me, Aunt Belle,' she called.

When they came out of the chippy shoving hot soggy chips into their mouths Jen confided to her aunt that it was her birthday soon and she wished she could have a party.

'Have one then,' said Belle.

'You know what Ma's like – can't afford it is what she'll say,' moaned Jen.

'I'll talk to her about it,' said Belle, bestowing a dazzling smile on old man Spence who was being pulled along the road by his black mongrel. When she bent down and spoke to the dog Jen marched on hating those demonstrations of affection which Belle could produce at a moment's notice.

'I think a birthday party would be just the thing to cheer us up,' screeched Belle when she caught up.

'Don't let the world know about it,' said Jen sulkily.

'I could make fairy cakes and a dumpling,' said Belle.

'It wouldn't be that kind of party,' muttered Jen. 'It would be more like a disco. You know, with records and Coke.'

'I'll buy the Coke then.'

'Anyway the record player's broken,' said Jen, wishing she'd never mentioned a party.

'I can always borrow one from old Sandy Girvan.' She nudged Jen adding, 'He'd do anything for me.' She let out a high-pitched squeal of laughter, which attracted the attention of two men standing outside Jackson's pub.

'Coming inside?' one of them called over.

'Later,' said Belle.

Then she gripped Jen's arm hard. 'As I was saying, we could make it a great party, the best in the street.'

Jen nodded glumly saying, 'She won't allow it.'

'We'll see,' said Belle, throwing her empty chip poke on to the ground. She prattled on relentlessly, the party already established in her head as a reality with at least twenty invitations.

'Ten of them must be boys,' she said, 'otherwise it'll be a flop.'

She promised to do something with Jen's hair and spoke of buying a blouse from Potter's drapery, which was bound to fit her a treat. Meanwhile Jen tried to blot out the fear that took hold of her at everything Belle suggested.

'The answer is no,' said Maude later, and retreated into the toilet.

'But there's really no reason why she shouldn't have a party,' said Belle from her side of the door. 'I already said I would get the Coke and the record player. That just leaves you with the crisps. And anyway she's plenty of friends who will be glad to come.'

She swivelled round and winked at Jen standing slackly behind her.

'No, I haven't,' said Jen, but Belle wasn't listening.

'If you can't afford the crisps I'll buy them myself,' she shouted.

Maude finally pulled the plug and emerged from the toilet, but halted cowering as Belle blocked her path.

'Surely the child can have a party for her fourteenth birthday?' she said.

'Apart from anything else I couldn't stand the noise,' whined Maude.

'Go out then. Go to the cinema or the bingo. I'll do the organising. Remember how I organised your wedding and everyone said that they enjoyed themselves.'

Everyone but me, thought Maude, recalling how she'd caught

Belle in the pantry with the bridegroom, but it was scarcely worth mentioning now.

'I couldn't face the mess afterwards,' she said.

'Mother of God,' stormed Belle. 'I'll clean up afterwards and –'

Maude interrupted. 'Another thing. These parties can go on for hours. I wouldn't want the neighbours complaining.'

'That's all I ever hear,' said Jen, lost in a haze of detestation for them both. 'What will the neighbours say?'

'That child is being stifled because of the neighbours,' said Belle. 'She's being sacrificed to their petty-bourgeois ideas.'

Maude made a dash for the kitchen. 'Don't start all that. I feel ill.'

Belle followed, her face a mask of concern. She took out a dark bottle from a cupboard, pushed Maude into a chair and before she could say anything handed her a substantial glass of Hooker's best sherry.

'Did you pay for that?' she said, struck by a fresh anxiety.

'Your nerves are definitely bad,' said Belle. 'Drink it over, don't sip, swallow and you'll feel better.'

Maude did as she was told.

'Now,' said Belle, pulsating with energy. 'We'll make out a list and then get the invitations off, twenty of them.'

Jen, who'd followed them into the kitchen said, 'I don't know twenty people.'

'Names, that's all I want,' said Belle. 'Dig up twenty names and we'll set the wheels in motion.'

'But I only know Betty Woods and she's not speaking to me.'

'C'mon, you can do better than that,' said Belle. 'Get me a pencil and paper.'

Trance-like, Maude rose up and rustled through a drawer in the table.

'I don't want a party,' wailed Jen. 'I've changed my mind.'

'Don't be so dreary about everything,' said Belle. 'A party will do you the world of good. This house needs a bit of fun.'

She snatched the pencil and jotter Maude had produced, sat down and wrote Betty Woods' name in big capital letters. 'There's the butcher's boy and the milk boy. What are their names?'

Jen was horrified. 'I don't know and anyway they're far too old and they wouldn't even know who I am.'

'They can't be that old,' said Belle. 'And even if they don't know you I bet they'd love a party. I'll soon find out their names.'

Once started there was no end to the people Belle suggested, though Jen knew very few of them. As the list grew longer she became quite desperate trying to think of anybody to invite.

Finally she said, 'You can put down Ollie Paterson.'

Belle beamed. 'Certainly.'

Maude was aroused from her torpor. 'Not him,' she said.

'Why, what's wrong with him?' asked Belle.

'He was expelled from school for setting fire to the dining room,' said Maude. 'We can't have types like that in the house.'

'Setting fire to schools doesn't count for much nowadays,' said Belle. 'It happens all the time.' She asked Jen if apart from that was he quite nice.

'He's all right,' said Jen hoarsely, her heart pounding. Already she could see Betty Woods' face screwed up with jealousy as she, Jen, danced around the room with Ollie. The idea of it made her feel as dizzy as though she were standing on the edge of a diving board.

Belle peered into her face. 'Why, you look better already. There's colour in your face!'

Jen's eyes swivelled away. 'Don't forget the blouse then.'

'Of course not. We'll go to Potter's drapery first thing after school.'

Maude watched their two heads touching as they pored over the list. It was just like the old days, she thought, when Belle made all the plans and she went along with them blindly.

'Don't forget I'm taking nothing to do with this,' she said.

Belle replied with a blank face. 'We don't expect you to. Do we, Jen?'

'No we don't,' said Jen, with some hostility.

'Help yourself to some more Hooker's,' said Belle.

Maude did. She hoped it would quell her uneasiness about the blouse Belle was supposed to be buying.

'Just look at that Ollie Paterson sitting on the railings,' Betty Woods said to Jen as they headed out of the school gate.

Jen's face automatically burned at the mention of his name. In the past two years he'd changed from a gangling schoolboy to a sturdy young fellow, always in trouble and with a different girl-friend every week. Jen was never one of them, being too plain and shy for him to notice, so she bent down to tie her shoelace, giving herself time to cool off. Though she needn't have bothered. He was staring ahead, kicking his heels against the school railings, impervious to them both.

'He's got some nerve coming here,' said Betty when they'd gone a few yards.

'I suppose he can come here if he wants to,' said Jen, hoping his eyes would alight on the back of her legs, which she considered much more shapely than Betty's muscular ones.

'You'd think he wouldn't want to expose himself so near the school after what he's done,' said Betty.

'Expose?' said Jen, tittering at the word, but inwardly alarmed.

The birthday party loomed before her like a nightmare. She'd scarcely slept a wink the previous night for thinking of nineteen guests completely ignoring her, or having none at all. It was unthinkable that a person of Ollie's stature would want to come in the first place, and apart from that she hadn't even invited Betty, anticipating a point-blank refusal.

When she'd tried to convey this to Belle, she'd said in her usual high-handed manner, 'Don't bother to tell anyone about it. Once they get the invitations they'll be glad to come.' She'd even used the word 'irresistible' to describe their reaction, which Jen thought was ridiculous.

She stole a glance at Betty's chubby profile then said, 'By the way, I'm thinking of having a party on my birthday, well, not so much a party but more of a disco, and I wondered if you'd come.'

But Betty wasn't listening. A crowd of youths on the other side of the road were calling over to them. One of them said he fancied Betty Woods and would she go out with him. Betty shouted back no way then called him a dick. Jen was overwhelmed by this. No one had ever asked her out or said that he fancied her. The nearest she'd got to it was when a boy shoved her against a wall and put his hand up her skirt. She hadn't told anyone.

'So what was it you were telling me?' said Betty.

'I said I was thinking of having a birthday party,' Jen mumbled, which caused Betty to stop dead in her tracks.

'You're joking,' she said, then asked if Jen's aunt would be at the party.

Jen was surprised and dismayed at the question. She hadn't considered this before.

'Only to give a hand,' she said.

'Hmm,' said Betty. 'So when is it?'

'Saturday.'

Betty's eyes narrowed. 'So who else is coming?'

'Ten boys and ten girls counting you and me,' said Jen, appalled at her foolhardiness, but there was no turning back now.

The party would have to take place or she'd be the laughing stock of the school. Betty would see to that. Perhaps she could feign illness when the day came.

'I was thinking of asking Ollie Paterson,' she said, as if her tongue couldn't help saying things that would make the situation worse.

Betty's eyes bulged. 'I don't believe it. So why didn't you say anything to him when we passed?'

'Because my Aunt Belle has asked him and he said he'd come.'

Betty's forehead puckered in puzzlement. 'Does your Aunt Belle know about him?'

'My Aunt Belle knows about everything,' said Jen.

'No doubt she does,' said Betty sarcastically.

'Actually my Aunt Belle knows lots of people and is not as crazy as some folk might think,' said Jen.

That shut Betty up for a while and Jen thought she might have scored a point over her.

As they neared Potter's drapery Jen said she'd have to go now.

'Where to?' said Betty, looking around almost anxiously.

'To Potter's, for a blouse,' said Jen with a sense of triumph, which vanished when she peered in at the various blouses in the window, all flounces and frills.

Then she noticed a green blouse with a plain collar, the only one suitable for someone her age, but then again she knew the colour wouldn't go with her sallow complexion. She couldn't visualise any style or colour capable of transforming her thin anxious reflection in the window into anything that Ollie Paterson might fancy, even if he did deign to come.

Suddenly Belle appeared at her side. 'What are you doing standing there like some refugee from outer Mongolia?'

Belle still lived in the times when the average refugee came from outer Mongolia. She pulled Jen into the draper's shop and informed the owner Mrs Potter that she'd like to see the green blouse in the window. Jen was about to say she didn't like it and didn't want to try it when Belle gave her such a dig in the ribs it took her breath away.

'Is it for her?' asked Mrs Potter, inclining her head towards Jen, then adding, 'If it is I doubt it will fit.'

'Bring it out anyway, seel voos play,' Belle cooed.

Mrs Potter's thin face hardened. 'What did you say?'

'I said bring out the green blouse if you don't mind,' said Belle, waving her arms around as if she was liable to buy the whole shop.

'I don't like that blouse,' hissed Jen when Mrs Potter was delving into the back of the window.

'Who said it was for you?' said Belle, mouthing the words as if she was a dummy. Then she instructed Jen to take off her coat to allow Mrs Potter to hold up the blouse against her shoulders.

'You can see it's much too big,' said Mrs Potter.

'You may be right,' said Belle.

'Now I'll have to put it back in the window and I had a lot of bother fitting it in in the first place.'

'I'm sorry to put you to all this trouble,' said Belle with a curl to her lips, 'but how were we to know it was going to be too big? Perhaps if you take her measurements we might get somewhere.'

Grim-faced, Mrs Potter threw the blouse on to the counter, took out a measuring tape from a drawer and placed it around Jen's skimpy chest. Then she began to open drawers and bring out different kinds of blouses, which she dumped down with an air of challenge. One by one Belle picked them to place them against Jen who stood as lifeless as a tailor's dummy, too mortified to notice anything from the time her aunt whipped the green blouse into her shopping bag when Mrs Potter's back was turned.

Finally Belle said, 'You don't seem to have anything that's suitable, do you?'

Mrs Potter returned the blouses to the drawers, her lips clamped together like a martyr's at the stake, while Jen dashed outside in order to put as much distance as she could between herself and the shop.

When Belle caught up with her she said, 'You stole that blouse, didn't you?'

'Yes,' said Belle. 'Wasn't it a scream?'

'A scream?' said Jen. 'Well, you're bound to get found out when she goes to put it back in the window, then the police will be round at our house again. And,' she added, as though this was the unkindest cut of all, 'you never got me anything.'

She wiped her nose on the back of her hand which had

begun to run with being upset and Belle handed her a crumpled handkerchief from her pocket.

'Don't carry on so much,' she said as the tears dripped off Jen's chin. 'Everyone's looking at you.'

Jen stared about and could only see a dog urinating against a lamp post.

'Listen,' said Belle fiercely. 'She won't miss it for a good while. She'll think she's put it away with the other blouses, then when it does dawn on her she won't be able to do anything about it.' She added, patting Jen's cheek, 'She's a mean old bag anyway.'

Jen pushed her hand away. 'I don't care what she is. I hate you.'

'No you don't,' said Belle. 'I'll tell you what, we'll go to the café and have a nice cuppa along with one of those iced doughnuts with cream in the centre.'

Despite herself, Jen was attracted. But she couldn't help retorting, 'Then you'll leave without paying.'

'No I won't,' said Belle. 'I've had my fun for the day. Besides,' she added slyly, 'I did get you something – look!'

Jen looked to see Belle draw out a bit of cloth from her shopping bag. She gasped when she realised it was the embroidered collar of the only blouse she'd fancied.

Belle laughed at the look on Jen's face, and Jen couldn't help laughing too.

'In for a penny in for a pound,' said Belle.

'All I can say is I just hope she's paid for that,' said Maude later on as Jen was parading up and down the kitchen as dainty as a doll with the embroidered blouse on and her hair pinned up.

'Of course,' said Jen, darting a meaningful look at Belle. 'What do you think?'

'Don't ask me to think about anything nowadays,' said Maude. Then she addressed Belle. 'I suppose it's no use me asking how you managed to buy a blouse off your dole money?'

'I always have a bit put by for emergencies,' Belle said haughtily.

'I still don't know how you do it —' Maude began, when Belle interrupted.

'Any of that sherry left? I could do with a pick-me-up of some kind.'

Maude looked guilty. 'As a matter of fact I finished it off. I thought you wouldn't mind.'

Belle shrugged. 'It doesn't matter. I can always buy more.'

'What about some dinner,' said Maude placatingly. 'I've got some nice pork links.'

'Don't bother. I'm going out,' said Belle. She winked at Jen. 'I've got things to arrange.'

'What things?' asked Maude.

'The party, or should I say the disco. It's only four days away, if you remember.'

'So it is,' said Maude without enthusiasm.

'Don't tell me you've forgotten,' said Jen.

'Never mind if she has,' said Belle. 'Your mother's going out that day.'

Maude looked at her helplessly. 'I haven't thought about where to go.'

'What about the bingo?' said Jen.

'I suppose I could,' said Maude. 'Though I haven't been at it for ages.'

'That's a great idea,' said Belle. 'Then afterwards you could go to the lounge upstairs and get yourself a drink. There's always a good band playing.'

'That'll cost plenty,' said Maude, then immediately regretted it, thinking it was mean of her to complain about money when Belle was arranging the party and had bought Jen a blouse into the bargain.

'All right, I'll go,' she added quickly.

'What are you going to arrange?' Jen asked Belle curiously. 'I mean about the party?'

Belle tapped her nose. 'Don't ask questions. Just trust me.'

Maude said uncertainly to Belle, 'I must say it's very good of you to go to all this bother. Are you sure you don't want me to stay in and give you a hand?'

Belle was firm. 'You go to the bingo. Who knows, you might enjoy yourself for once.'

'I told Betty Woods about it,' said Jen, with an air of importance inspired by the new blouse, which she felt made her fashionably slim.

'Is she coming?' asked Maude.

'I think so.'

'I never liked that girl. She's too old for her age.'

'Come off it, Maude,' said Belle. 'It's you that's too old for your age.'

Maude thought that Belle looked ridiculous for her age, but she refrained from making any comment. She was content to avoid any involvement in their plans.

'Funny about these matches on the doorstep,' she remarked later on to Jen, who was combing her hair in front of the mirror. 'I hope it wasn't you.'

'What are you talking about?' said Jen, preoccupied by blackheads that had appeared overnight on each side of her nose.

'You'll have to give me money for cleansing cream,' she added. 'Look at those blackheads. They're getting worse.'

Maude was incredulous. 'Cleansing cream? What you need is soap and water. And about those matches. Was it you that dropped them, smoking on the doorstep?'

Jen looked at her mother as if she'd gone crazy. 'Smoking? Where would I get the money?'

'So, if you'd money, you'd smoke?'

'No I wouldn't,' said Jen. 'If I had the money I'd buy cleansing cream.'

'You get fifty pence a week. What's wrong with that?'

'What can I do with fifty pence? Betty Woods gets two pounds.'

'Betty Woods' father has a good job.'

'If you hadn't divorced my father we'd have been a lot better off.'

'That's what you think,' said Maude.

'Anyway, why did you divorce him?'

Maude was at a loss as to what to say. It didn't seem right to tell her daughter he had been carrying on with other women, including her own sister, and that was before he went to jail for housebreaking.

Besides, it was a humiliating admission.

'You should have thought of me instead of yourself,' Jen went on. 'It's not good for girls to be brought up without a father.'

Maude felt like saying it hadn't done her much good either.

'You don't know what you're talking about,' she said. 'I'm sure I've done my best.'

At that point Belle shuffled into the room looking like one of Macbeth's witches, her eyes smudged black with mascara, her dressing gown trailing on the floor behind her.

'What's going on now?' she asked listlessly.

'It's her,' said Maude. 'Starting trouble as usual.'

'No I'm not,' said Jen. 'She won't give me money for cleansing cream.'

'Leave me out of it,' said Belle. 'I'm completely exhausted. I only came in for a drink of water.'

'Been working hard, have you?' said Maude.

Ignoring the irony in Maude's tone, Belle drifted past her towards the tap while Jen asked her if she'd managed to arrange anything yet.

Belle choked on the water. 'What do you mean, arrange?'

'I mean for the party,' said Jen. 'You know, the Coke and crisps and that –'

She broke off when Belle looked at her blankly, as though she didn't know what she was talking about.

'So you've forgot about the party already?' sneered Maude.

Belle lost her placidity. 'Who said I forgot? If you want to know, twenty bottles of Coke are being delivered by my friend Lenny who works in the pub.'

'Only twenty?' said Jen. She'd been anticipating several cases.

Belle became annoyed. 'What do you mean, only twenty?'

'See what I mean,' said Maude. 'Nothing is good enough for her.'

'Don't start,' said Jen. 'Just because I asked for money for cleansing cream.'

'I wish I'd never got up if this is what I've to listen to,' said Belle. 'I might as well go back to bed.'

Pausing in the doorway, she told Jen to look in the bathroom cabinet. She was positive there was a jar of cleansing cream in there somewhere.

Jen's face brightened. 'Thanks, Aunt Belle,' she said gratefully.

Maude thought how easy it was for Belle to manipulate her daughter and yet she, her mother, could scarcely get a civil word out of her.

When Belle had gone Maude said to Jen in a confidential manner, 'I bet it was her that left the matches on the doorstep when she was standing around with one of her pick-ups.'

Jen looked at her mother disapprovingly. 'Surely she's allowed to have a boyfriend at her age?'

'Oh so you've fairly changed your tune,' said Maude. 'It wasn't that long since you were saying she was crazy and wanted rid of her.'

'I wish I could get rid of myself,' said Jen. 'It's nothing but arguments all the time in this house.' She lifted her jacket off the peg behind the kitchen door and ran outside.

Maude wanted to call her back but there was nothing she could say to her daughter nowadays. She tried to see it as a stage she was going through.

'I've been waiting on you for ages,' said Betty Woods, standing outside the school gates at four in the afternoon.

'Have you been crying?' she added, giving Jen a suspicious glance.

'I've got a cold,' said Jen.

'Oh,' said Betty. Then after a pause she added, 'I've been thinking about the party you were having and I might just come if it's all right with you.'

'Of course,' said Jen, struggling to pay attention. She'd been thinking about her father, which she sometimes did when things were at their blackest, visualising him as being moderately well off and married to a plump motherly woman who would welcome Jen with open arms if she ever went to see them.

'What time should I come round at?' said Betty impatiently.

'Come round whenever you like,' said Jen. 'It should start about seven.'

'I suppose you're still having one?' said Betty, peering close into Jen's pale drawn face.

'Of course,' said Jen, her voice faltering.

'Is Ollie Paterson still coming?' Betty asked.

'I suppose so,' said Jen, wishing Betty would simply vanish.

'Well, I'm going to ask him to make sure that he is,' said Betty defiantly.

Jen was jolted out of her apathy. 'Bloody keep your nose out of things,' she shouted. 'It's not your party and if you breathe a word to Ollie Paterson about it before I do, I'll – I'll give you two black eyes.'

Betty's eyes widened at the sight of Jen's fist held a mere two inches away from her face. It was unbelievable and horrific that a person of Jen's inferior stature would dare threaten her in this way.

'If you lay a finger on me I'll tell the teacher,' she said.

'Tell the teacher, I don't care,' said Jen, punching Betty on the nose and pulling her hair, out of sheer nerves. A handful of hair came away in her hand.

When Betty began to yell for help at the top of her voice Jen ran down the street in the direction of her home. When she arrived her legs were shaking like jelly.

'Somebody at the door,' Belle called out from the bathroom.

Maude stopped making the bed, thinking her sister should at least have the decency to answer it instead of spending half the morning doing her face up. On opening the door she was startled to see Mrs Woods standing on the doorstep, a woman she'd always tried to avoid at all costs. She could only think she was selling raffle tickets for the hospital, which she did every so often.

Maude was all ready to say she didn't want to buy one when the woman said, 'It's about your daughter. She belted my Betty outside the school gates today and the poor child was so upset when she came home I had to put her to bed with an aspirin.'

'My Jen did that?' said Maude, recollecting how Betty's chunky body looked as resilient as a punchbag.

'Vicious, that's what she is,' said Mrs Woods. 'You'll have to do something about her before she gets any worse.'

'But that's not like our Jen,' said Maude, having difficulty ungluing her eyes from Mrs Wood's bulging ones.

'What's that woman wanting?' said Belle, arriving on the scene to look over Maude's shoulder. She had been driven out of the bathroom by the voices.

'It's our Jen,' said Maude. 'She's apparently been fighting with Betty Woods, and I don't understand it. You know how timid she is.'

Mrs Woods shoved her face close into Maude's saying, 'Whether you understand it or not you can tell her from me that my daughter won't be going to her party. I wouldn't allow it after such a display of temper.'

'Is that so,' said Belle, pushing her sister aside. 'If our Jen hit your Betty then she must have had a good reason. She's quiet and well-behaved, not like that stuck-up daughter of yours, so don't come round here shooting your mouth off when you don't know the facts. Another thing,' she went on before Mrs Woods, whose face had turned puce, could interrupt, 'we wouldn't have your daughter in our house at any price. She's a sly piece if there ever was one and I wouldn't trust her an inch if there were any boys around. She'd only get us a bad name.'

Mrs Woods breathed deep as if trying to ward off a stroke. Blotchy red patches stood out on her neck. Ignoring Belle as if she wasn't there she said to Maude, 'Is it possible that I'm hearing right, my daughter's name being bandied about by a person of such a low character as your sister, the talk of the town in fact –'

'Get going, you old bag,' said Belle, slamming the door shut before Mrs Woods could say any more.

Maude wrung her hands in agitation as she watched Mrs Woods stamp down the garden path and bang the gate shut as if trying to take it off by the hinges.

'I don't know what Jen's been up to,' she moaned, 'but that woman has certainly got it in for us.'

'Forget it,' said Belle. 'She's just a load of old rubbish.'

Maude continued to look worried. 'And I don't know what's got into Jen nowadays. You can't talk to her about anything, and now this. Maybe I should take her to see a doctor.'

Belle sniffed. 'Take yourself to see a doctor is more like it. You know what I think,' she went on without waiting for an answer, 'I think you're letting everything get you down. Look at you, it's as if you've got all the cares in the world.'

'Well, I feel as if I've got all the cares in the world,' said Maude defiantly, 'between this party and not knowing who's coming to the door, and I'm not complaining about Jen either.'

Belle bridled. 'What do you mean?'

'For instance, I don't know what you're going to be up to next, and that's a fact.'

Belle became angry. 'I've never heard the like in all my life. I can't think where you get these ideas from. I suppose it's a case of a honee swa kee malee pongs.' Then she added in a hurt tone, 'To think how I've always tried to keep up my spirits in the face of adversity, which includes your everlasting dreary outlook towards the least little thing, like handing in gifts now and then and arranging a birthday party for your daughter, since you couldn't be bothered arranging one yourself. And now because somebody comes to the door complaining about her attitude, to put it mildly, you're trying to put the blame on me.'

'Talking of spirits,' said Maude, 'how do you manage to get those bottles of sherry so regular? It's not as if they cost nothing. In fact there's a lot of things I don't know how you manage to get, including that blouse for Jen. It's getting to the stage I'm frightened to go into shops in case the assistants tell me you've been pinching things.'

Belle collapsed on to a chair. 'This I don't believe. My own sister accusing me of pinching things when all I've tried to do is bring a little happiness to both your miserable lives.'

As she spoke her face crumpled like a paper bag and a tear slid out the corner of her eye. Maude wasn't impressed but she thought she might have gone too far.

'What else can I think when you're always so flush?' she said.

'I think I'd better pack my bags,' said Belle, rising shakily. 'There's nothing else for it.'

Maude felt a pang of guilt. 'I didn't say you should leave, did I?'

'I couldn't stay,' said Belle. 'Not after being accused of being a thief – it would be quite impossible.'

'Where will you go?' said Maude, feeling suddenly hopeful.

Belle wiped her wet cheek. 'Don't worry about me,' she said. 'I'll find some place.' Then she left the room with her chin in the air.

After she'd gone Maude began to wonder where Belle would find a decent bag to put her clothes in, since she'd arrived with all her possessions in plastic ones. Then she decided it was stupid of her to consider this, since Belle would have no intention of leaving.

★

Maude panicked when a neighbour informed her that a man had been at the door when she was out. She told Belle about it when she tottered in carrying two plastic bags filled with Coke bottles.

'What of it?' said Belle, collapsing in a chair.

'It could be trouble,' said Maude, flinging her arms around.

'Why should it be?'

'It would be too much to expect anything else,' said Maude.

'Why can't you look on the bright side for a change?' said Belle. 'It could have been anyone.'

'Like a cop or a detective,' said Maude. 'I wouldn't be surprised if we're all bunged out in the street the way things are going.'

Belle raised her eyebrows. 'I've no idea what you're talking about.'

At that point Jen, who'd been listening at the door, walked in and said, 'Maybe it was my da.'

Maude let out a shriek. 'Don't say that, for God's sake.'

Belle smiled. 'It's nice to know there are worse things than a cop at the door.' Then she proceeded to take the bottles of Coke out of the bags and place them on the table.

'How about these?' she said to Jen. 'Aren't you pleased?'

Jen looked at them both as though she was going to burst out crying, then she ran out.

'What's she talking about her da for?' said Maude. 'It's not like her to mention his name.'

'I'm sure I don't know,' said Belle. 'But you'll have to tell her about him sometime. She seems to be under the impression he's a wonderful guy with plenty of money to burn, which is far from the truth as you and I well know.'

'It's not so much him not having plenty of money that bothers me,' said Maude. 'It's the fact that he's in and out of jail all the time. How can I tell her that?'

'She's bound to find out sometime,' said Belle. 'And she'll blame you for not telling her sooner.'

'Maybe you're right,' said Maude. 'But I'm not going to tell her right now. Let's get this bloody birthday party over first.'

'It's up to you,' said Belle, then adding, 'Here, help me put these bottles away before they get opened before the time.'

After they'd done this Maude asked her how much they cost.

'Not a penny,' said Belle. 'Lenny slipped them to me out of the pub.'

When Maude asked who Lenny was Belle said he was a young man who served behind the bar. 'A really nice guy,' she added. 'If he gets the time off he said he would come to the party, if that's all right with you.'

'That's OK,' said Maude vaguely.

'By the way,' said Belle, taking a five-pound note out of her purse, 'I meant to give you this.'

'I couldn't take it,' said Maude. 'I might not even go to the bingo.'

'Of course you'll go. Bingo costs a lot but there should be enough for a drink afterwards.'

'Thanks,' said Maude, grasping the note with the tip of her fingers. 'I might not need it, but I'll take it just in case.'

Belle assured her she would need it, adding with a laugh, 'And don't say I'm not good to you.'

Burdened down by a feeling of guilt, Maude said she would buy the crisps for the party. Belle said not to worry. It was all taken care of. Then she kicked off her shoes and sat down teetering back on the kitchen chair.

'What a day I've had,' she said, shaking her head.

'In what way?' said Maude.

'You may well ask,' said Belle, then she went quiet for a while before adding, 'You might not think it but things can get me down at times too, even though I always try to look on the bright side.'

Maude wondered what the things were. She said, 'You should settle down, Belle. You don't seem to have a hold on anything, if you know what I mean.'

'I know what you mean,' said Belle. 'The fact is I've never had anything much to hold on to.'

Maude wondered if she'd been drinking. It was hard to tell at times.

'Anyway, I could never settle from the day Mother died,' Belle added. 'It broke my heart when she left us.'

'Ah yes, Mother,' said Maude. 'We were all upset.'

Belle's face went slack with grief. 'She did everything she could for us, if you remember.'

'Yes,' said Maude, recalling the black rages that possessed her mother for the slightest thing.

'On the day of the funeral I cracked,' said Belle.

'So you did,' said Maude, recollecting how Belle had been roaring drunk and singing 'For she's a jolly good fellow' as the coffin was being carried outside.

Belle sighed. 'I think that's why I never got married really.'

'Because of Mother?'

'Partially.'

'That's why I did get married,' said Maude. 'To get away.'

'But then you never got on with her, did you?'

'The truth was nobody did, apart from yourself,' said Maude, thinking that despite the fiver she'd be damned if she was going to keep up the pretence about Mother being a wonderful person.

'The least thing we did drove her into a rage,' she added, 'except at the end. She was peaceful enough then.'

'She was strict, I know,' Belle conceded. 'But it was good for us.'

'Was it?' said Maude. 'She pushed me into marrying someone that was no use, and as for you —'

'What about me?' said Belle belligerently.

'You didn't marry because Mother bullied you into giving up any boyfriend you ever had.'

'Well, I had boyfriends after she died,' said Belle. 'And I still didn't marry.'

Maude kept silent. There was no point in arguing with Belle's inbuilt image of a devoted mother.

'I wish Mother was here right now,' said Belle. 'She'd understand what I'm going through.'

Maude considered that was one prospect she could do without.

Belle closed her eyes, leaning back in her chair as if this talk about Mother had been too much for her. Maude thought she looked like a ruin with her fat legs spreadeagled and showing off heavily veined thighs. She was a parody of the bold beautiful Belle who had drawn the male eye like a magnet leaving Maude feeling shy and inadequate and plain. Yet despite all the years since then they both remained unattached with no man around, the difference being Jen had taken the place of Mother. The thought gave her a creepy feeling as if someone had walked over her grave. She picked up one of Belle's magazines to divert her thoughts.

Jen lay on her stomach on top of the bed brooding about the party, which was bound to be a flop now that her association with Betty Woods was finished. She'd been severely reprimanded by her teacher over the fight, and her mother had nagged on for ages about Mrs Woods coming to the door. Even Belle hadn't much to say to her. Every time Jen came into the room she would start humming 'The Mull of Kintyre' under her breath as if to avoid any talk on the subject.

Becoming cold and stiff with lying in the one position, Jen left the bed and looked out the window. With increasing despair she saw Ollie Paterson astride a bicycle, talking to Betty Woods. They were both laughing and Jen figured they'd be laughing at her. She darted back from the window wishing she was dead, then heard her mother calling, 'Jen, there's somebody at the door. Go and answer it.' She received the words with indifference. It wouldn't be anything worthwhile. She continued staring at the faded pattern on the wallpaper.

'Are you deaf?' her mother called again.

'I'm coming,' said Jen in a ragged tone, rubbing the gooseflesh on her arms as she went towards the door. Ollie Paterson stood on the doorstep, his pimply face swimming before her eyes.

'Er – I came about the party,' he said.

'The party?' she repeated dully.

'So,' he said. 'What time does it start?'

She managed to answer through shaky lips, 'Half-past seven.'

'Well er – tell your Aunt Belle I'll be round about then.' He jumped off the step, mounted his bike and rode off.

Jen stared after him with dismay. What did he mean, tell your Aunt Belle? Didn't he realise it was her party? Not a grown-up one with booze and sing-songs. She ran into the kitchen, found her aunt asleep in a chair and shook her hard.

Belle sat up straight. 'What is it? What's happening?'

'Ollie Paterson was at our door,' said Jen, her voice heavy with accusation.

'So, what am I supposed to do about that?'

'He thinks it's your party, not mine.'

Belle reached for her cigarettes. 'Is that what you wakened me up for?'

Jen's lip quivered. 'Well, did you tell him it was your party?'

'I don't think so. But what the hell difference does it make whose party it is?'

'It makes a big difference to me.'

'Well, all I can say,' said Belle, 'is that he must have got it mixed up, for never at any time did I say it was my party.'

'You must have given him that impression or he wouldn't have mentioned your name,' said Jen.

Belle said to Maude, who had been listening to all this with a sneer on her face, 'That daughter of yours has certainly got the jags. Can't you do something about it?'

'It's not me that's doing all the arranging,' said Maude smugly.

Belle glared at her and said, 'There won't be any arranging if she doesn't stop her continual moaning. I'm fed up with it all.'

As if she hadn't heard this Jen said, 'And I suppose everyone else thinks it's your party?'

'Who's everyone else?'

'The ones you sent the invitations to.'

There was a pause during which Belle blew smoke into the air and then said, 'As a matter of fact I haven't sent them yet.'

Jen's eyes went as wide as they could go. She said on a high-pitched hysterical note, 'If they haven't gone out by this time it'll be too late. Then no one will come and I'll be the laughing stock of the school.' After that she slumped, sobbing, on to the chair opposite Belle's.

'There, there,' said Maude, stroking her daughter's hair. 'It's not the end of the world.' But secretly she was glad. If the party was cancelled it would save her having to go to the bingo.

'There's plenty of time,' said Belle. 'This is only Thursday. We have two days left.'

'It's too late,' shrieked Jen. 'And even if it's not no one will come anyway.' She began to sob again.

Maude said to Belle with anger, 'This is all your fault. You promised to arrange a party, and now look what's happened. As I've always said it's far better never to promise anything unless you're sure you can carry it out. That's why I never make promises.'

'Shit,' said Belle. 'You never make anything.'

Then she stood up, afire with determination. 'Listen,' she went on, 'I said Jen was going to have a party and if it's the last thing I do she bloody well will. Look how I got her the blouse and the Coke and now I'll get her the guests. Wait and see.'

'You can't,' snivelled Jen. 'I've fell out with Betty Woods and she's the only person in school I speak to. If you must know I'm the most unpopular person in the class.'

Maude was taken aback. Any considerations about Jen's popularity had never entered her head. The fact that her daughter was always mulling around the house with a discontented expression she took as normal.

'What's wrong with you?' she asked.

'I'm thin, plain and have no personality.'

Maude was indignant. 'Who said that?'

Jen sighed. 'I can't remember, but I know somebody did.'

'I've never heard the like,' said Maude, viewing Jen's statement as an attack on herself. 'I'm sure I've done my best —'

'Shut up,' said Belle. 'It's not your problem. Come to think of it, you weren't so popular yourself at her age. In fact you still aren't. How many friends have you got?'

'I don't want friends,' said Maude. 'I believe in keeping myself to myself.'

'Is that why you go on like the ghost of Christmas past?' Belle jeered. Then she said to Jen, 'Get a grip of yourself or you'll end up like your mother.'

'It's more like you'll end up like your aunt,' said Maude. 'And we all know how popular she is.'

'There you both go,' groaned Jen. 'Everything ends up with you two arguing. What about me, and what about the invitations?'

Belle sat down and screwed up her eyes as if in pain. 'Let me think,' she muttered, and remained spellbound for a time, while Maude held her breath and Jen looked on cynically.

After five minutes of this Belle slapped her thigh and announced, 'I've got it.'

No one answered. They both stared at her goggle-eyed.

Then Belle said, 'I know what I'll do. I'll pay Mrs Woods a visit.'

Maude gasped. 'You can't go near her. Not after what you said.'

'Of course I can,' said Belle. 'I'll apologise, of course, then I'll get round her by some way or other. I can always get round people if I put my mind to it. After that I'll get her to help me with the invitations since by then she'll be eating out my hand. And as for that fight between Jen and Betty I'll simply tell her that Jen wasn't feeling well that day, all nervy and that, because of her age.' (She means periods, thought Jen.) 'Then I'll ask her casual-like if Betty would deliver the invitations, since Jen's been under the weather ever since it happened.'

'We haven't got any cards,' said Maude quickly.

'I'll just write the names on a bit of paper. That should be good enough.'

'You're not right in the head,' said Maude.

'Just wait and see,' said Belle, glowing with optimism, while Jen sat puzzling out the plan.

Later on that same evening Maude was heard to grumble it was all one what she did in this house – it always came to nothing.

'What's up now?' asked Belle, as she studied a list of names she'd written on a page torn out of Jen's school jotter.

'This wringer's not working properly and look at all the clothes I've still got to wring out.'

'Buy a washing machine then,' said Belle.

'You know I can't afford it.'

'Everybody has a washing machine, whether they can afford it or not,' said Belle. 'By the way,' she added, 'Lenny says he'll be able to come to the party.'

Maude didn't answer, being too busy trying to release a jumper from the rollers.

'Didn't you hear what I said?' declared Belle.

'I heard, but can't you see I'm busy?'

'It seems to me you're getting impossible to talk to nowadays,' said Belle. 'I don't understand you.'

Maude flung the jumper into a basin and said, 'Instead of trying to understand me it would fit you better if you gave me a hand with this washing and stopped going on and on about this damned party. And if it isn't that it's gadding off to the pub while I do all the work. I really can't take any more,' she added, her face white and strained.

Belle shook her head sadly and said, 'You should have told me things were getting on top of you. Sit down, and I'll do the rest.'

She began to put all the other clothes through the wringer with what seemed like comparative ease.

'You always make everything look so easy,' said Maude wistfully. 'I wonder how that is.'

'Because I'm smarter than you,' said Belle with a laugh.

Maude gave her a bleak smile. 'Maybe.'

Belle returned to the subject of the party. 'As I was saying, I'm so glad Lenny's coming. He's such a nice young fellow and it was good of him to give us the Coke for nothing. Apart from that don't you think Jen could be doing with a boyfriend at her age?'

Maude bit her lip. She didn't care to think of Jen being kissed and fondled and maybe worse.

'I know what you're thinking,' said Belle. 'You're thinking that with a boyfriend she could get pregnant.'

Maude was startled. Her thoughts hadn't got that far.

'But you'll just have to face the fact that she has to get used to the company of boys, otherwise she's more liable to get pregnant through sheer ignorance. That's why I'm arranging this party, before the rot sets in.'

'What rot?'

'If we allow her to carry on moping around the house she'll do something desperate. Mark my words.'

Maude was flabbergasted to discover events had got to this stage. Yet she had to admit Jen's surly behaviour was too apparent to overlook. On the other hand Belle's glib assessment of this situation only irritated her.

'You seem to think this party is the solution to everything,' she said.

'Why not?' said Belle. 'Besides, you can't shut her away forever.'

'I don't want her shut away. In fact it's the opposite. She simply won't go anywhere. What am I to do?'

'Let events take their course, that's all you can do,' said Belle.

Then she began to sing as she hung the clothes over the pulley with all the serenity of a peasant woman in a field. After a time she stopped to say, 'In case I forget, remind me to call on the Woods woman tomorrow morning so I can talk her into letting Betty come to the party.'

Maude could only nod her head hoping nothing ominous would come of this.

Betty Woods drew aside the curtain to see what was going on in the street then dropped it quickly when she saw Belle enter their garden path.

'Mum,' she shouted. 'That crazy aunt of Jen Boulting's is coming to the door.'

'What?' shrieked Mrs Woods, almost letting the cup in her hand fall to the floor.

Desperately she looked around for a weapon, since she was about to be confronted by a person of potential violence, but when the doorbell rang she rushed towards the door without thinking then scarcely recognised Belle standing on the doorstep wearing a black coat and a black veiled hat.

'What do you want?' she asked in a very hostile voice.

'I wondered if I could have a word with you,' said Belle in a tone of husky refinement.

'About what?'

Belle gave a breathy noise that might have been a sob or a gasp. 'It's difficult to talk here. I wonder –' Then she looked behind her as though people could be listening.

'Come in then,' said Mrs Woods, curiosity getting the better of her. Besides, Belle's appearance exuded humbleness rather than violence.

She marched up the hallway with Belle following and lifting her veil every so often to get a better look at the tapestry wall-paper. When Belle entered the oak-panelled living room she was asked to sit down. Sinking into the plush velvet sofa she took off her hat allowing Mrs Woods to note that without make-up Belle's face was as pale as a lump of dough.

'What is it you want to say?' she asked in the clear modulated tone she usually reserved for the better class of person.

Belle hesitated then said, 'It's about Jen's father.'

Mrs Woods' eyes widened. She'd always been curious about Jen's father, suspecting he hadn't existed in a legitimate way, though when it came to letting anything slip she'd discovered the Boulting woman was as close as a dumb canary.

'What about him?' she asked.

'He's dead,' said Belle, taking out a paper handkerchief from her coat pocket and dabbing the top of her cheek.

Mrs Woods made a sympathetic noise, though really wanted to say, 'Is that all?'

'As you probably know,' Belle went on, 'my sister was divorced a long time ago.'

Mrs Woods nodded. She wasn't going to waste time in saying that she didn't know.

Belle continued. 'You see, before you came to the door yesterday I had just newly heard about his death, so naturally when you complained about our Jen fighting with Betty and being so upset about this I simply lost my head.' She leaned forward and touched the back of Mrs Woods' hand. 'I hope you'll forgive me.'

'Yes, of course,' said Mrs Woods, disliking the way Belle had settled herself comfortably on the couch.

Belle added, 'Jen doesn't know.'

'Doesn't know what?'

'That her father's dead and I don't know how to break it to her.'

'I would have thought it was up to the mother to break it to her,' said Mrs Woods.

Belle replied with emotion. 'You don't know our Maude. She's a very bitter person, even if she is my sister. She never talks to Jen about anything concerning her father. It's always been up to me to keep his memory alive, perhaps thinking one day she would meet him in the flesh, and now it's finished,' she added, as she covered her face with her hands.

'I know what you mean about your sister,' said Mrs Woods. 'She never struck me as being a friendly type.' Then she broke off, thinking she'd better not say too much under the circumstances. Abruptly she asked, 'So when's the funeral?'

'It was this morning,' said Belle, making another sound like a sob. 'Such a sad affair too.'

'Did your sister go?'

Belle shook her head. 'I was the only one there to represent the family.' Then she stared so hard at the teapot that Mrs Woods felt obliged to offer her some tea.

'I wouldn't mind,' said Belle.

In a somewhat dour fashion Mrs Woods brought out a cup from the wall unit, and told Belle to help herself.

'You are so kind,' said Belle, taking three spoonfuls of sugar.

Mrs Woods began to fidget. Why was she entertaining this vulgar woman instead of throwing her out? The death of Jen's father wasn't all that interesting when she thought about it.

'What I was going to ask you,' Belle began, 'is if you could see your way to excuse my dreadful outburst yesterday and allow your Betty to come to the party, or should I say disco. Jen's really fond of Betty, despite their little fracas, which is bound to happen between friends now and again.'

'I don't think so,' snapped Mrs Woods. 'I feel Betty has been deeply humiliated and I doubt if she will ever forgive your niece.'

Belle nodded, as if she couldn't expect anything else. 'I understand,' she said, 'but since I'll have to break the news to her about her father's death at some point it would have been nice if she had at least one happy birthday beforehand. And it would have made a big difference to her enjoyment if your daughter came.'

Mrs Woods' face remained frosty.

Belle went on as though she hadn't noticed. 'In fact I wouldn't have said anything about her father's death, but she'll have to find out on account of the money involved.'

'Money?' said Mrs Woods.

'According to what the lawyer said at the funeral she'll inherit a fair amount. I hardly dare mention it to Maude, she's so proud about everything, but after all if the father wished to leave everything to his daughter, it's only fair that she gets it, whether her mother refuses it or not. What would you think?'

'I should say so,' said Mrs Woods, rearing up at the idea of anyone refusing money. 'That child goes about like a tramp.'

'I'm sure Maude does her best,' said Belle distantly.

Hurriedly Mrs Woods said, 'I didn't mean to cast any reflection on anyone, but I'm sure like everyone else your niece could do with a new set of clothes now and again.'

Belle nodded. 'Still, it's a good job my sister didn't hear you say that. It'll take me all my time to persuade her to let Jen accept the money.'

Offhandedly, Mrs Woods asked her if it was a lot.

'I couldn't say for sure,' said Belle, 'but it's my guess it will be quite a bit. He did have a business, you know.'

Mrs Woods refilled Belle's cup. 'What kind of business?'

'Actually it's a grocery shop.'

They both pondered on this for a bit then Belle said, 'But as far as I'm concerned the money is of little importance compared to the grief Jen is bound to feel. What I'm mainly concerned about is that her party should be a success, so that she'll have something pleasant to remember before she is plunged into mourning.'

'If you ask me,' said Mrs Woods, 'that mother of hers should be the one that's concerned and not yourself.'

'That may be,' said Belle gravely, 'but as I am exceedingly fond of my niece, having no children myself, I'd go to any length to make her happy. That's why I'm sitting here throwing myself on your mercy, so to speak.'

Before Mrs Woods could open her mouth Belle went on,

'Who knows, later on Jen might go abroad to get some decent education. The lawyer said there was some stipulation about it in the will, but I can't see our Jen going on her own. Maybe if she took a friend – but forgive me for rambling on. Right now I just want her to have a good party so perhaps –'

Mrs Woods interrupted to say, a red spot showing on each cheek, that, although she had been very upset when Jen had attacked her daughter, she could understand that incidents like this can happen between friends.

'I'll speak to Betty,' she added, 'but it's up to her.'

'Thanks ever so much,' said Belle. 'But don't breathe a word about Jen's father. We'd rather tell her ourselves when the time is ripe.'

'I wouldn't dream of it,' said Mrs Woods. 'I'm not the one for repeating confidences.'

On her way out Belle shook hands with the woman and thanked her for being so understanding.

'Not at all,' she said. 'I'd do the same for anybody.'

Once Belle had gone she shouted on her daughter, 'Betty, I want a word with you.'

Much later that evening Belle was standing outside the pub in the company of two men, one of whom was giving an atrocious rendering of 'Danny Boy' while the other listened to him with tears in his eyes.

'Do you have to keep singing that?' said Belle. 'You're beginning to give me a sore head.'

The one with the tears said, 'All the same, you've got to admit he has a lovely voice.'

Belle said, 'I don't think so, but anyway it's been nice knowing you. Thanks for the loan.'

'If you come round the back,' said the other one, who had stopped singing, 'I'll give you a loan as well.'

'No fear,' said Belle. 'I'm not wasting time with a chancer like yourself.' Then she walked away with a slight stagger.

On opening the kitchen door it was something of a dampener to be met with Maude's reproving stare.

'So,' said Belle. 'What are you looking at?'

'I suppose you've been drinking,' said Maude.

'I had a drink,' Belle admitted.

'Only one?'

'Maybe two or three. I hope you don't mind.'

'It's all one what I mind,' said Maude. 'But you'll have to let me know what the arrangements are for Jen's party. I mean I can't just ignore the whole bloody thing, can I? And there are those invitations. Have you sent them yet?'

When Belle remained silent Maude added, 'Did you hear what I said?'

Belle took her coat off and threw it in the direction of a chair, where it missed its mark and fell on the floor.

'Don't worry,' she said. 'Everything is under control, and as well as that I've got the Woods woman eating out of my hand. She is sending her daughter to the party. So everything seems to be going swimmingly.' Then she collapsed on to the couch, and closed her eyes. Within a few minutes she was snoring.

Maude bit her lip to keep from going into a rage and attacking her sister. She vowed that after the party was over she'd definitely take steps to get Belle out the house.

Jen tossed and turned in her bed, trying to ignore the urge to go to the toilet and face the fact that this was the dawn of her birthday. Groaning, she pulled the sheet over her head to blot out the rays from the sun that were penetrating through a gap in the curtains. She could foresee with a certainty that this day was going to be bloody awful, just like the time she'd joined the youth club and had stood alone, stiff with embarrassment, while everybody else jerked around to the sound of the records. She threw the blankets off. It was no use. She was bursting.

In the next room Maude was thrashing about with a rapist and just as her breath was about to expire she woke up with the slamming of a door. Perspiring, she stared at the ceiling wondering why she was always having dreams about being raped even though it never actually happened. When she told Belle about it she said it was a sign of insecurity, and what she needed was a man. Maude had said that while she might be right about the insecurity the last thing she needed was a man.

'Your subconscious knows better,' said Belle at the time.

Her relief at being awakened subsided into the dreary realisation that this was the day she would have to go to the bingo in order to avoid the party, which didn't seem right somehow considering she was Jen's mother. It was all Belle's fault for putting her in this position, she thought bitterly. Besides, she wasn't sure she could handle bingo. Her heart always pounded like a hammer if she came anywhere near to winning. It was definitely bad for her nerves, she decided, as she got up and put her clothes on, against all her inclinations.

Meanwhile Jen had gone back to bed, lying with her eyes shut in order to avoid hearing her mother shuffle down the stairs in her worn-out slippers. Some day she could trip over them and fall, possibly breaking her neck. Though that might not be such a bad thing if her father and his homely wife took her in and gave her everything she wanted, she thought. This notion lulled her into a suffocating sleep.

In the kitchen Maude clattered dirty dishes in the sink and swore under her breath.

'Talking to yourself again?' said Belle, coming in silently and giving Maude such a fright that she dropped a plate on the floor. It broke in two.

'Look what you made me do,' she groaned.

'It's only a plate,' said Belle. 'You want to watch it, though. Your nerves must be bad.'

'No bloody wonder,' said Maude, 'coming in without as much

as a warning, especially when you don't usually get up before eleven.'

'Today's different,' said Belle. 'There's a lot to do, so we might as well make an early start.'

'Who's we?' said Maude.

'Sorry, I forgot. You don't need to lift a finger. The party's my responsibility.'

'I'll give you a hand with the sandwiches,' said Maude in a grudging tone.

'We're not having sandwiches,' said Belle.

'Not having sandwiches?'

'Crisps and Coke. That's all you need for a disco. Though I might take a glass of sherry myself.'

'Are you sure people will come?' said Maude. 'I mean I wouldn't want Jen to be disappointed.'

'Of course they'll come,' said Belle, pouring herself out a cup of black stewed tea and putting in three teaspoonfuls of sugar.

'What about Betty Woods?' said Maude. 'Is she really coming?'

'I told you she was. Her mother more or less said she would talk her into it.'

'What did you do? Hold a gun to her head?'

Belle winked. 'There are more ways than one of killing the cat.'

'So what did you say then?'

Belle stirred her tea saying, 'I merely told her the truth.'

'The truth.'

'I simply said it would break Jen's heart if her daughter didn't come to the party, then I reminded her about the Minister's sermon last Sunday when he preached that we should forgive and forget those who trespass against us.'

'Don't tell me you were at church?' said Maude.

'Indeed I was. I slipped in for a bit of kip before Maloney's opened and I distinctly remember him saying those words before I dropped off.'

A spasm of rage shot through Maude. To think she'd always felt too dowdy to join the church, though she'd have dearly loved to, and here was Belle blatantly using it to pass the time! She forced a laugh. 'I don't believe you.'

Belle sipped her tea then said, 'Believe me I did, and Mrs Woods isn't the type to risk offending the Minister.'

Scarcely knowing what she was doing Maude took out a small box from her apron pocket.

'I got something for Jen's birthday,' she said, displaying a tiny silver cross and chain.

'Is it real silver?' said Belle, looking impressed.

'Yes, maybe not the dearest, but not the cheapest either.'

Belle studied it between her fat fingers. 'I like that. It's very –'

'I hope you're not going to say Catholic,' said Maude.

'Of course I wasn't, though I don't know what you've got against the Catholics. I was merely going to say it's very tasteful, even if everyone has them.'

'Do they?' said Maude uneasily. 'But I suppose it's something she'll always have.'

'True,' said Belle. 'Though it's such a fragile piece, so easily mislaid, but I'm sure she'll take care of it.'

Maude snatched it back and put it in the box. 'I'd better get Jen up,' she said.

Belle watched her go, smiling to herself, as she heard Maude's threatening cry from the hallway: 'Time to get up and see what I got for your birthday.'

'I think it's going to be a lovely day outside,' said Belle when Maude came back.

'You'd think it was a garden party the way you're going on,' snapped Maude.

'You don't have to be so crabbit about everything,' said Belle. 'Isn't it better to have a birthday on a nice day?'

Maude tightened the wrap-over apron she had on.

'Don't ask me. It's not my birthday,' she said, just as Jen entered with a scowl on her face.

'Wait and see what your mother's got you,' said Belle, her voice heavy with suspense, while Maude handed her daughter the present.

'Do you like it?' Maude said, when Jen opened the box.

'Beautiful, isn't it?' said Belle in a hushed tone.

Jen dangled the chain listlessly. She would have preferred a locket so that she could put inside it a photo of Ollie Paterson in a football team that she'd cut out from the local newspaper.

'Well, do you like it?' asked Maude, her voice rising.

'Of course I do,' said Jen, putting it down on the table. 'By the way,' she added to Maude, 'you'll have to get me sanitary towels. I've got my period,' before her mother could say anything.

For the rest of the morning Maude polished the furniture and cleaned the windows while Belle washed and dried her hair in the bathroom, taking so long that neither Jen nor Maude could use the toilet unless they pounded on the door.

'You shouldn't bother with all that cleaning,' she said to Maude when she finally came out. 'Nobody will notice anyway.'

'Maybe it's not a fancy house,' said Maude. 'But I won't have it looking like a pigsty, whether folk notice or not.'

'If folk are enjoying themselves, that is the main thing,' said Belle, putting her tin of hair lacquer down on the polished table.

Maude stepped back to get a better view of the windows. 'Do you think I should go over them again? They look a bit smeary.'

'Please yourself,' said Belle.

Jen came in at that point and looked up at her mother wiping a window pane. 'I didn't know the Queen was coming,' she said.

Maude turned round and caught Belle rolling her eyes around her head. 'That's it,' she said. 'I'm damned if I'm going to bother any more,' then charged out, slamming the door.

Belle said to Jen, 'I don't know what she's so upset about, considering nobody asked her to do a hand's turn, but anyway,' she added in a more excited tone, 'there's another guy I know apart from Lenny. He's much better looking than Ollie Paterson. He said he'd love to come to the party.'

Jen's eyes went cold. 'You don't say.'

'He looks a lot like Robert Redford.'

'There's nobody here looks like Robert Redford, and even if there was he wouldn't be interested in me.'

'Why not?'

'You know why. I'm skinny and plain-looking and I suppose he thinks it's your party.'

'What gives you that idea?'

'Ollie Paterson thinks it's your party. He said so.' She added, 'So you can cancel everything for I won't be there.'

Belle opened her mouth to say something then closed it again, and flopped down on a chair. She lifted up her cigarette packet then put it down again. Finally she said, 'I don't understand you, Jen, really I don't. I'm simply shattered at what you're saying. In fact I feel a migraine coming on. Do you think you could get me an aspirin from somewhere?'

'We don't have any left. Mum eats them like sweeties.'

'Well, a small sherry then. There's a bottle at the back of the cupboard.'

Jen located the bottle then handed it to Belle along with a glass.

Belle poured out the sherry then took a sip and said, 'That's better,' while Jen stood slack and pinched-faced. Then Belle began to speak slowly and seriously. 'Do you know that you've got something that I would have given my eye teeth for when I was your age?'

'No, what?' said Jen, her face determinedly sullen.

'Elfin charm, that's what. When I was your age I was fat and coarse like Betty Woods and sick with envy of all the girls that had your kind of elfin charm. Though in those days I didn't know it was called that. I only knew that's what I wanted to have, and you are bursting with it and all you can call yourself is skinny and plain. I think you're very stupid, Jen, even if you are attractive. It's your main bad point, stupidity.'

Jen blushed then she thrust a hand under Belle's nose. 'You can't say these warts have elfin charm.'

Belle looked at the hand. 'They're easily cured.'

'Who by, witches?'

'Funny you should say that. Your mother thinks I'm a witch.'

Jen sniggered. 'So cure my warts then.'

'I might at that,' said Belle thoughtfully. 'We'll try the chemist first.'

Maude put on the tweed coat and furry hat she'd inherited from her mother, willing herself to look on the bright side. She'd received five pounds from Belle to pay for the bingo, which was good of her, when she thought it over. There was no point in worrying about the party. She wouldn't be there to see what was happening, so she should forget about it and enjoy herself for once. Rubbing her mouth with a lipstick called Passionel, a gift from Belle, half used when she got it, she stared in the mirror and noticed it gave her face a boldness which she rather liked.

'Have you got a membership card?' said the female in the ticket office. 'We can't let you in without it.'

'I haven't, but I'm willing to pay for one,' said Maude.

'I'm afraid you won't get it here,' said the female. 'See the manager.'

'Where will I find him?' Maude asked, but before she could get an answer she was shoved aside by a surge of bodies from behind, though none of them looked like a manager. Nerves shattered, she fought her way outside and in a dazed manner entered a café next to the bingo hall where a waitress came over and asked her what she wanted before she could draw her breath.

'Tea and a bun,' said Maude.

Despite quick service the tea was cold and the bun hard. Maude decided to go home. There was no point in traipsing round the town in shoes that were too tight. She wouldn't be welcome, but that was too bad. It was her house after all. It took her two hours to get home because the bus broke down.

In a state of trepidation Maude entered the living room then became immediately relieved to see that people had come to the party, most of them about Jen's age, except for a man who sat at the back of the room, thin and haggard-faced, wearing a shabby dark suit. She thought he looked familiar, but before she could think any more about it Belle rushed up with a glass in her hand.

'Drink this,' she said. 'You'll need it.' She then added, pointing to the man, 'Don't you know who he is?'

'My God, it's Alex,' said Maude, the colour draining from her face. 'How did he get in here?'

'He barged in before I could stop him,' said Belle. 'Then he told me he'd come for Jen's birthday. So what could I say?'

Maude tossed the drink over in a single gulp. 'So has she met him yet?'

'Not yet. I don't think she's even noticed him.'

'I don't want her to meet him,' said Maude. 'She's going to feel terrible. She thinks her father's well off. Can you imagine?'

'What made her think that?'

'She once asked me if he was and I just said yes to keep her happy –' She broke off then added, 'Oh my God, here he comes.'

'How are you, my dear?' he asked when he came close up.

'I was fine until I saw you,' she said, surprised to see how much he'd aged with his sallow complexion and closely cropped hair. Yet at one time he'd been good-looking, she remembered with a pang.

'You may as well know I don't want you in this house, or anywhere near it,' she said.

'Just the same old Maude,' he said with a tired smile. 'But I haven't came to see you. I've came to see my daughter, though I don't suppose I'd recognise her now she's grown up.'

'You're not going to recognise her if I can help it,' said Maude. 'You gave up any rights you had when you stopped sending the money.'

'I'm sorry about that,' he said. 'But in the end I never had any money to send. I lost my job and various other things happened. Then I gradually went downhill, I suppose, but I'm not so badly off now that I'm working again.'

'So you think you can come back here and worm your way in with us,' said Maude bitterly. 'Well, you can't.'

'All I want to see is my daughter,' he said. 'It's not as if I'm going to do her any harm. She's as much my flesh and blood as she is yours.'

His statement touched a spark of acknowledgement within her, but she remained adamant. 'It makes no difference,' she said. 'I want you to go.'

She turned and entered the kitchen where food was laid out on a table in the form of crisps, peanuts and bottles of Coke.

'What can I do to get rid of him?' she asked Belle who'd followed her in.

'I'm damned if I know, other than getting the police. And that might be more upsetting than if you'd told her who he is.'

'Are you saying I should tell her?'

'I'm not saying anything,' said Belle. 'But it does seem a pity to spoil things for her when she's enjoying herself for once.'

'That's what I mean,' said Maude.

Some youths came in and finished off the crisps, then they passed round a bottle of vodka between them and began to talk in loud raucous tones.

'Look at them,' said Maude. 'They shouldn't be allowed in if they're going to drink spirits.'

Belle shrugged. 'It's what they all do at parties nowadays.'

'I hope our Jen's not doing it,' said Maude, but Belle wasn't listening.

She was beckoning on a young man who stood in the doorway. When he came over she introduced him as Lenny, the nice young man who gave us the Coke for nothing.

'It was very good of you,' said Maude, taking a dislike to his pencil-thin moustache, which made him look like a foreigner. She'd never ever felt comfortable in the company of foreigners.

'It was a pleasure,' said Lenny, flashing her a wide smile.

When Jen and Betty Woods came in to see what was going on Belle immediately introduced them to Lenny, who shook their hands in a formal sort of way, which made them to go into such fits of laughter that Maude began to wonder if they'd been drinking vodka too. She was about to mention this to Belle, but saw her attention was totally taken by Lenny. Feeling like an intruder she returned to the living room, and discovered Alex sitting where she'd first seen him, and to make it worse her head began to pound.

'I thought you'd gone,' she said.

'I was thinking about it,' he said. 'But maybe you should tell these drunken louts to go as well.'

She looked across the room to where some youths were shouting abuse at each other. 'I'm sure they're quite harmless,' she said. 'At least they were invited.'

'Please yourself,' he said. 'But I'd watch out for Jen. She strikes me as being a sensitive sort of girl.'

His sanctimonious tone irritated her. Who did he think he was, giving orders? 'I thought you didn't know who she was.'

'Well, I know now,' he said.

'And so did you tell her you were her father?' she asked him cautiously.

'Not yet. But I think I should. She's bound to find out anyway.'

A feeling of helplessness swept over her. Years of secrecy would go for nothing, if her ex-husband spoiled Jen's dream of having a father who was reasonably well off. The truth was enough to give her a complex for the rest of her life, and she was bad enough as it was.

'I suppose you'll do what you want to,' she said, walking out into the hallway only to find Jen being closely embraced by Ollie Paterson. They didn't see her until she tapped him on the back and asked what did he think he was doing.

'We're not doing anything,' said Jen, as they quickly sprang apart. 'It's just your suspicious mind that thinks we are.'

For two pins Maude would have slapped Jen's sharp angry face, especially now that she could see the resemblance to Alex. But what she said instead was, 'There's a man in the living room who's got something to tell you.'

'You mean that old man who looks like a tramp?' said Jen. 'I thought he was one of Belle's boyfriends.'

'Alas no,' said Maude. 'But you'd better listen to what he's got to say, and I'll wait here until you come back. As for you,' she said to Ollie, 'I don't want you putting a hand on my daughter ever again.'

'I won't,' he said hoarsely.

A moment later Jen charged back. 'Who is this guy who says he's my father? Is he some kind of nut?'

'He is your father,' said Maude, dimly aware of Ollie standing behind her.

'He can't be my father,' Jen said. 'He's nothing but an old tramp.'

'Pardon me, but it's you that's the tramp,' said Maude, boiling over with anger. 'Kissing and cuddling a boy who's too drunk to know what he's doing. I wouldn't be surprised if you finish up pregnant.'

'You're telling me you get pregnant by kissing?' said Jen. 'Well, I don't think so, but I'd rather be pregnant than have him for a father and anyway he can't be my father. Didn't you say my father was well off?'

'So I am when I'm robbing banks,' said Alex at her back, in a jocular attempt to take some heat out of the situation.

'Is that what you do, rob banks?' said Ollie admiringly.

'Not really,' said Alex, 'but if it makes you any happier I was once caught stealing a bottle of whisky plus two tenners out of a licensed grocer's. But what I really got that impressed me was six months in the jail.'

'Is that right?' said Ollie, in a tone no less admiring. 'Well, I burnt some of the school down and was sent to a special one. I've chucked doing things like that now, and I'm not going back to that school if I can help it.'

'Good for you, lad,' said Alex, 'but that doesn't mean you can take liberties with my daughter.'

'I'm not your daughter,' said Jen furiously, stamping off down the hallway then out the front door, slamming it hard.

'See what you've done,' Maude said to Alex. 'The way she feels about you she's liable to throw herself under a bus.'

'I'll get her back,' said Alex, starting to run after her with Ollie trailing behind.

At that point Betty Woods came out from the living room to tell Maude that a perfectly awful-looking man had came up to Jen and said he was her father.

'That's right,' said Maude. 'He is.'

'But he can't be,' said Betty. 'Your sister told my mother that Jen's father had died and left her a lot of money and she would be going abroad to get a better education, and I was supposed to go with her for company.'

'My sister's not right in the head,' said Maude.

Betty looked at her as though she'd been struck dumb. Then she said Belle wasn't the only one not right in the head. The whole family wasn't right in the head, and she might have known that before coming to the party.

Alone in the kitchen Maude was making herself a cup of tea in order to wash down the hundred aspirins she intended to take. Then she decided it might be easier to swallow fifty and if these didn't work she'd try a second fifty. While waiting for the kettle to boil she heard the sound of something smash in the living room. Maybe a window or the television she was still paying up. Not that it mattered, for she wouldn't be around to pay for anything. Then she could hear voices raised in anger, the sound of feet running down the hall, then the outside door banging.

She waited for a minute, poured out the tea, counted out the aspirins and was about to swallow them, when Alex entered breathlessly and said, 'Ollie and I soon got rid of that lot who were smashing up the place. Don't worry, I'll pay for the damage.'

'I thought you were poor,' she said.

'I'm not all that poor,' he told her with a wink.

'That's very kind of you,' she said, surreptitiously putting the aspirins in her cardigan pocket. 'Would you like a cup of tea?'

'I wouldn't mind,' he said.

'Did you find Jen? I nearly forgot to ask,' she added.

'I did. She's in the living room talking to Ollie and the good news is she's quite reconciled to me being her father.'

'She is?' said Maude. 'Just like that?'

'Maybe because I gave her a tenner for her birthday,' said Alex.

'She always was a mercenary little bitch,' said Maude.

'Then she takes after her father,' he said with a wry smile.

He looked more like the Alex she had married, she thought, but it wasn't going to change anything.

'Where are you staying?' she asked, to get the subject away from Jen.

'At a working-man's hostel, which is really another name for a place for down-and-outs. But it's only temporary. I intend to get something better.'

Then to her surprise she found herself saying, as if she'd no will of her own, 'You can stay here until you get settled if you want to.'

'That's good of you, Maude,' he said, leaning over and touching her hand.

'Of course it's only temporary,' she said.

'Of course.'

As she went looking for Belle to tell her about the new arrangement she began to wonder where they'd all sleep. She came to
the conclusion that Belle would have to sleep with Jen and neither
of them would be pleased about that, but it couldn't be helped.
She wondered if she'd been too hasty in allowing Alex to stay.
She'd taken Belle in and never got rid of her. But then again,
would she want rid of him? What if they started living together
as husband and wife? She could feel her cheeks going hot at the
idea. In a confused state of mind she opened Belle's bedroom door
and saw her sister stark naked astride Lenny on the bed, her head
flung back either in agony or ecstasy. Quietly Maude closed the
door, thankful they hadn't seen her. It would have been too embarrassing to even contemplate. But tomorrow she'd tell Belle to leave.
She couldn't have her house being used more or less as a brothel,
and apart from that she had Jen's feelings to consider.

Thinking along these lines made her wonder how far Jen had
gone with Ollie, but she wasn't going to go into that right now.
Things were bound to be different from now on with Alex in
the house. Then a picture came into her head of Belle crying over
her mother, drunk of course, but in a genuine way, which made
Maude consider that Belle had always been a soft-hearted woman,
though her own worst enemy. Look at those useless gifts she was
always bringing home, stolen yes, but she meant well. And they
both enjoyed the sherry she brought back at the weekends. There
was a lot she had to admit liking about Belle, one of them being
that she cared for Jen, maybe even more than she did herself. Belle
was always trying to please Jen and make her laugh.

On deep reflection she discovered she didn't want Belle to go.
She was her sister and her soulmate and no doubt this fling with
Lenny was a one-off, and the chances were it wouldn't happen
again. She'd make sure it didn't. And as for Alex she'd just have

to tell him she'd changed her mind when she suddenly realised there was no room for him in the house, but maybe in the future, who knows? Firmly she returned to the kitchen and threw the aspirins in the bin, vowing never to take a single one again. In the same determined mood she set out to find Alex in order to tell him the bad news. And if he thought she must be a right idiot to change her mind in such a short space of time then all the better. He might even consider he'd had a lucky escape.

A Note on the Author

Agnes Owens was born in 1926 and has worked in a factory, as a typist and as a school cleaner among other things. She has been married twice and has seven children. She lives in Balloch.

Agnes is the author of *Gentlemen of the West*, *Lean Tales* (with Alasdair Gray and James Kelman), *Like Birds in the Wilderness*, *A Working Mother*, *For the Love of Willie*, *Bad Attitudes*, *Jen's Party* and *People Like That*.